Five Weeks in a Balloon

Five Weeks in a Balloon

Jules Verne

MINT EDITIONS

Five Weeks in a Balloon was first published in 1863.

This edition published by Mint Editions 2021.

ISBN 9781513266336 | E-ISBN 9781513266770

Published by Mint Editions®

 MINT
EDITIONS
minteditionbooks.com

Publishing Director: Jennifer Newens
Project Manager: Gabrielle Maudiere
Design & Production: Rachel Lopez Metzger
Typesetting: Westchester Publishing Services

Contents

Chapter 1

There was a large audience assembled on the 14th of January, 1862, at the session of the Royal Geographical Society, No. 3 Waterloo Place, London. The president, Sir Francis M——, made an important communication to his colleagues, in an address that was frequently interrupted by applause.

This rare specimen of eloquence terminated with the following sonorous phrases bubbling over with patriotism:

"England has always marched at the head of nations" (for, the reader will observe, the nations always march at the head of each other), "by the intrepidity of her explorers in the line of geographical discovery." (General assent). "Dr. Samuel Ferguson, one of her most glorious sons, will not reflect discredit on his origin." ("No, indeed!" from all parts of the hall.)

"This attempt, should it succeed" ("It will succeed!"), "will complete and link together the notions, as yet disjointed, which the world entertains of African cartology" (vehement applause); "and, should it fail, it will, at least, remain on record as one of the most daring conceptions of human genius!" (Tremendous cheering.)

"Huzza! huzza!" shouted the immense audience, completely electrified by these inspiring words.

"Huzza for the intrepid Ferguson!" cried one of the most excitable of the enthusiastic crowd.

The wildest cheering resounded on all sides; the name of Ferguson was in every mouth, and we may safely believe that it lost nothing in passing through English throats. Indeed, the hall fairly shook with it.

And there were present, also, those fearless travellers and explorers whose energetic temperaments had borne them through every quarter of the globe, many of them grown old and worn out in the service of science. All had, in some degree, physically or morally, undergone the sorest trials. They had escaped shipwreck; conflagration; Indian tomahawks and war-clubs; the fagot and the stake; nay, even the cannibal maws of the South Sea Islanders. But still their hearts beat high during Sir Francis M——'s address, which certainly was the finest oratorical success that the Royal Geographical Society of London had yet achieved.

But, in England, enthusiasm does not stop short with mere words. It strikes off money faster than the dies of the Royal Mint itself. So a subscription to encourage Dr. Ferguson was voted there and then, and it at once attained the handsome amount of two thousand five hundred pounds. The sum was made commensurate with the importance of the enterprise.

A member of the Society then inquired of the president whether Dr. Ferguson was not to be officially introduced.

"The doctor is at the disposition of the meeting," replied Sir Francis.

"Let him come in, then! Bring him in!" shouted the audience. "We'd like to see a man of such extraordinary daring, face to face!"

"Perhaps this incredible proposition of his is only intended to mystify us," growled an apoplectic old admiral.

"Suppose that there should turn out to be no such person as Dr. Ferguson?" exclaimed another voice, with a malicious twang.

"Why, then, we'd have to invent one!" replied a facetious member of this grave Society.

"Ask Dr. Ferguson to come in," was the quiet remark of Sir Francis M——.

And come in the doctor did, and stood there, quite unmoved by the thunders of applause that greeted his appearance.

He was a man of about forty years of age, of medium height and physique. His sanguine temperament was disclosed in the deep color of his cheeks. His countenance was coldly expressive, with regular features, and a large nose—one of those noses that resemble the prow of a ship, and stamp the faces of men predestined to accomplish great discoveries. His eyes, which were gentle and intelligent, rather than bold, lent a peculiar charm to his physiognomy. His arms were long, and his feet were planted with that solidity which indicates a great pedestrian.

A calm gravity seemed to surround the doctor's entire person, and no one would dream that he could become the agent of any mystification, however harmless.

Hence, the applause that greeted him at the outset continued until he, with a friendly gesture, claimed silence on his own behalf. He stepped toward the seat that had been prepared for him on his presentation, and then, standing erect and motionless, he, with a determined glance, pointed his right forefinger upward, and pronounced aloud the single word—

"Excelsior!"

Never had one of Bright's or Cobden's sudden onslaughts, never had one of Palmerston's abrupt demands for funds to plate the rocks of the English coast with iron, made such a sensation. Sir Francis M——'s address was completely overshadowed. The doctor had shown himself moderate, sublime, and self-contained, in one; he had uttered the word of the situation—

"Excelsior!"

The gouty old admiral who had been finding fault, was completely won over by the singular man before him, and immediately moved the insertion of Dr. Ferguson's speech in "The Proceedings of the Royal Geographical Society of London."

Who, then, was this person, and what was the enterprise that he proposed?

Ferguson's father, a brave and worthy captain in the English Navy, had associated his son with him, from the young man's earliest years, in the perils and adventures of his profession. The fine little fellow, who seemed to have never known the meaning of fear, early revealed a keen and active mind, an investigating intelligence, and a remarkable turn for scientific study; moreover, he disclosed uncommon address in extricating himself from difficulty; he was never perplexed, not even in handling his fork for the first time—an exercise in which children generally have so little success.

His fancy kindled early at the recitals he read of daring enterprise and maritime adventure, and he followed with enthusiasm the discoveries that signalized the first part of the nineteenth century. He mused over the glory of the Mungo Parks, the Bruces, the Caillies, the Levaillants, and to some extent, I verily believe, of Selkirk (Robinson Crusoe), whom he considered in no wise inferior to the rest. How many a well-employed hour he passed with that hero on his isle of Juan Fernandez! Often he criticised the ideas of the shipwrecked sailor, and sometimes discussed his plans and projects. He would have done differently, in such and such a case, or quite as well at least—of that he felt assured. But of one thing he was satisfied, that he never should have left that pleasant island, where he was as happy as a king without subjects—no, not if the inducement held out had been promotion to the first lordship in the admiralty!

It may readily be conjectured whether these tendencies were developed during a youth of adventure, spent in every nook and corner of the Globe. Moreover, his father, who was a man of thorough instruction, omitted no opportunity to consolidate this keen intelligence by serious studies in hydrography, physics, and mechanics, along with a slight tincture of botany, medicine, and astronomy.

Upon the death of the estimable captain, Samuel Ferguson, then twenty-two years of age, had already made his voyage around the world. He had enlisted in the Bengalese Corps of Engineers, and distinguished himself in several affairs; but this soldier's life had not exactly suited him; caring but little for command, he had not been fond of obeying. He, therefore, sent in his resignation, and half botanizing, half playing the hunter, he made his way toward the north of the Indian Peninsula, and crossed it from Calcutta to Surat—a mere amateur trip for him.

From Surat we see him going over to Australia, and in 1845 participating in Captain Sturt's expedition, which had been sent out to explore the new Caspian Sea, supposed to exist in the centre of New Holland.

Samuel Ferguson returned to England about 1850, and, more than ever possessed by the demon of discovery, he spent the intervening time, until 1853, in accompanying Captain McClure on the expedition that went around the American Continent from Behring's Straits to Cape Farewell.

Notwithstanding fatigues of every description, and in all climates, Ferguson's constitution continued marvellously sound. He felt at ease in the midst of the most complete privations; in fine, he was the very type of the thoroughly accomplished explorer whose stomach expands or contracts at will; whose limbs grow longer or shorter according to the resting-place that each stage of a journey may bring; who can fall asleep at any hour of the day or awake at any hour of the night.

Nothing, then, was less surprising, after that, than to find our traveller, in the period from 1855 to 1857, visiting the whole region west of the Thibet, in company with the brothers Schlagintweit, and bringing back some curious ethnographic observations from that expedition.

During these different journeys, Ferguson had been the most active and interesting correspondent of the Daily Telegraph, the penny newspaper whose circulation amounts to 140,000 copies, and yet scarcely suffices for its many legions of readers. Thus, the doctor had become well known to the public, although he could not claim membership in either of the Royal Geographical Societies of London, Paris, Berlin, Vienna, or St. Petersburg, or yet with the Travellers' Club, or even the Royal Polytechnic Institute, where his friend the statistician Cockburn ruled in state.

The latter savant had, one day, gone so far as to propose to him the following problem: Given the number of miles travelled by the doctor in making the circuit of the Globe, how many more had his head described than his feet, by reason of the different lengths of the radii?—or, the number of miles traversed by the doctor's head and feet respectively being given, required the exact height of that gentleman?

This was done with the idea of complimenting him, but the doctor had held himself aloof from all the learned bodies—belonging, as he did, to the church militant and not to the church polemical. He found his time better employed in seeking than in discussing, in discovering rather than discoursing.

There is a story told of an Englishman who came one day to Geneva, intending to visit the lake. He was placed in one of those odd vehicles in which the passengers sit side by side, as they do in an omnibus. Well, it so happened that the Englishman got a seat that left him with his back turned toward the lake. The vehicle completed its circular trip without his thinking to turn around once, and he went back to London delighted with the Lake of Geneva.

Doctor Ferguson, however, had turned around to look about him on his journeyings, and turned to such good purpose that he had seen a great deal. In doing so, he had simply obeyed the laws of his nature, and we have good reason to believe that he was, to some extent, a fatalist, but of an orthodox school of fatalism withal, that led him to rely upon himself and even upon Providence. He claimed that he was impelled, rather than drawn by his own volition, to journey as he did, and that he traversed the world like the locomotive, which does not direct itself, but is guided and directed by the track it runs on.

"I do not follow my route;" he often said, "it is my route that follows me."

The reader will not be surprised, then, at the calmness with which the doctor received the applause that welcomed him in the Royal Society. He was above all such trifles, having no pride, and less vanity. He looked upon the proposition addressed to him by Sir Francis M——as the simplest thing in the world, and scarcely noticed the immense effect that it produced.

When the session closed, the doctor was escorted to the rooms of the Travellers' Club, in Pall Mall. A superb entertainment had been prepared there in his honor. The dimensions of the dishes served were made to correspond with the importance of the personage entertained, and the boiled sturgeon that figured at this magnificent repast was not an inch shorter than Dr. Ferguson himself.

Numerous toasts were offered and quaffed, in the wines of France, to the celebrated travellers who had made their names illustrious by their explorations of African territory. The guests drank to their health or to their memory, in alphabetical order, a good old English way of doing the thing. Among those remembered thus, were: Abbadie, Adams, Adamson, Anderson, Arnaud, Baikie, Baldwin, Barth, Batouda, Beke, Beltram, Du Berba, Bimbachi, Bolognesi, Bolwik, Belzoni, Bonnemain, Brisson, Browne, Bruce, Brun-Rollet, Burchell, Burckhardt, Burton, Cailland, Caillie, Campbell, Chapman, Clapperton, Clot-Bey, Colomieu, Courval, Cumming, Cuny, Debono, Decken, Denham, Desavanchers, Dicksen, Dickson, Dochard, Du Chaillu, Duncan, Durand, Duroule, Duveyrier, D'Escayrac, De Lauture, Erhardt, Ferret, Fresnel, Galinier, Galton, Geoffroy, Golberry, Hahn, Halm, Harnier, Hecquart, Heuglin, Hornemann, Houghton, Imbert, Kauffmann, Knoblecher, Krapf, Kummer, Lafargue, Laing, Lafaille, Lambert, Lamiral, Lampriere, John Lander, Richard Lander, Lefebvre, Lejean, Levaillant, Livingstone, MacCarthy, Maggiar, Maizan, Malzac, Moffat, Mollien, Monteiro, Morrison, Mungo Park, Neimans, Overweg, Panet, Partarrieau, Pascal, Pearse, Peddie, Penney, Petherick, Poncet, Prax, Raffenel, Rabh, Rebmann, Richardson, Riley, Ritchey, Rochet d'Hericourt, Rongawi, Roscher, Ruppel, Saugnier, Speke, Steidner, Thibaud, Thompson, Thornton, Toole, Tousny, Trotter, Tuckey, Tyrwhitt, Vaudey, Veyssiere, Vincent, Vinco, Vogel, Wahlberg, Warrington, Washington, Werne, Wild, and last, but not least, Dr. Ferguson, who, by his incredible attempt, was to link together the achievements of all these explorers, and complete the series of African discovery.

Chapter 2

THE ARTICLE IN THE DAILY TELEGRAPH.—WAR BETWEEN THE
SCIENTIFIC JOURNALS.—MR. PETERMANN BACKS HIS FRIEND
DR. FERGUSON.—REPLY OF THE SAVANT KONER.—BETS MADE.—
SUNDRY PROPOSITIONS OFFERED TO THE DOCTOR.

On the next day, in its number of January 15th, the Daily Telegraph published an article couched in the following terms:

"Africa is, at length, about to surrender the secret of her vast solitudes; a modern OEdipus is to give us the key to that enigma which the learned men of sixty centuries have not been able to decipher. In other days, to seek the sources of the Nile—fontes Nili quoerere—was regarded as a mad endeavor, a chimera that could not be realized.

"Dr. Barth, in following out to Soudan the track traced by Denham and Clapperton; Dr. Livingstone, in multiplying his fearless explorations from the Cape of Good Hope to the basin of the Zambesi; Captains Burton and Speke, in the discovery of the great interior lakes, have opened three highways to modern civilization. *Their point of intersection*, which no traveller has yet been able to reach, is the very heart of Africa, and it is thither that all efforts should now be directed.

"The labors of these hardy pioneers of science are now about to be knit together by the daring project of Dr. Samuel Ferguson, whose fine explorations our readers have frequently had the opportunity of appreciating.

"This intrepid discoverer proposes to traverse all Africa from east to west *in a balloon*. If we are well informed, the point of departure for this surprising journey is to be the island of Zanzibar, upon the eastern coast. As for the point of arrival, it is reserved for Providence alone to designate.

"The proposal for this scientific undertaking was officially made, yesterday, at the rooms of the Royal Geographical Society, and the sum of twenty-five hundred pounds was voted to defray the expenses of the enterprise.

"We shall keep our readers informed as to the progress of this enterprise, which has no precedent in the annals of exploration."

As may be supposed, the foregoing article had an enormous echo among scientific people. At first, it stirred up a storm of incredulity;

Dr. Ferguson passed for a purely chimerical personage of the Barnum stamp, who, after having gone through the United States, proposed to "do" the British Isles.

A humorous reply appeared in the February number of the Bulletins de la Societe Geographique of Geneva, which very wittily showed up the Royal Society of London and their phenomenal sturgeon.

But Herr Petermann, in his Mittheilungen, published at Gotha, reduced the Geneva journal to the most absolute silence. Herr Petermann knew Dr. Ferguson personally, and guaranteed the intrepidity of his dauntless friend.

Besides, all manner of doubt was quickly put out of the question: preparations for the trip were set on foot at London; the factories of Lyons received a heavy order for the silk required for the body of the balloon; and, finally, the British Government placed the transport-ship Resolute, Captain Bennett, at the disposal of the expedition.

At once, upon word of all this, a thousand encouragements were offered, and felicitations came pouring in from all quarters. The details of the undertaking were published in full in the bulletins of the Geographical Society of Paris; a remarkable article appeared in the Nouvelles Annales des Voyages, de la Geographie, de l'Histoire, et de l'Archaeologie de M. V. A. Malte-Brun ("New Annals of Travels, Geography, History, and Archaeology, by M. V. A. Malte-Brun"); and a searching essay in the Zeitschrift fur Allgemeine Erdkunde, by Dr. W. Koner, triumphantly demonstrated the feasibility of the journey, its chances of success, the nature of the obstacles existing, the immense advantages of the aerial mode of locomotion, and found fault with nothing but the selected point of departure, which it contended should be Massowah, a small port in Abyssinia, whence James Bruce, in 1768, started upon his explorations in search of the sources of the Nile. Apart from that, it mentioned, in terms of unreserved admiration, the energetic character of Dr. Ferguson, and the heart, thrice panoplied in bronze, that could conceive and undertake such an enterprise.

The North American Review could not, without some displeasure, contemplate so much glory monopolized by England. It therefore rather ridiculed the doctor's scheme, and urged him, by all means, to push his explorations as far as America, while he was about it.

In a word, without going over all the journals in the world, there was not a scientific publication, from the Journal of Evangelical Missions to the Revue Algerienne et Coloniale, from the Annales de la

Propagation de la Foi to the Church Missionary Intelligencer, that had not something to say about the affair in all its phases.

Many large bets were made at London and throughout England generally, first, as to the real or supposititious existence of Dr. Ferguson; secondly, as to the trip itself, which, some contended, would not be undertaken at all, and which was really contemplated, according to others; thirdly, upon the success or failure of the enterprise; and fourthly, upon the probabilities of Dr. Ferguson's return. The betting-books were covered with entries of immense sums, as though the Epsom races were at stake.

Thus, believers and unbelievers, the learned and the ignorant, alike had their eyes fixed on the doctor, and he became the lion of the day, without knowing that he carried such a mane. On his part, he willingly gave the most accurate information touching his project. He was very easily approached, being naturally the most affable man in the world. More than one bold adventurer presented himself, offering to share the dangers as well as the glory of the undertaking; but he refused them all, without giving his reasons for rejecting them.

Numerous inventors of mechanism applicable to the guidance of balloons came to propose their systems, but he would accept none; and, when he was asked whether he had discovered something of his own for that purpose, he constantly refused to give any explanation, and merely busied himself more actively than ever with the preparations for his journey.

Chapter 3

The Doctor's Friend.—The Origin of their Friendship.—
Dick Kennedy at London.—An Unexpected but Not Very
Consoling Proposal.—A Proverb by No Means Cheering.—
A Few Names from the African Martyrology.—
The Advantages of a Balloon.—Dr. Ferguson's Secret.

D r. Ferguson had a friend—not another self, indeed, an alter ego, for friendship could not exist between two beings exactly alike.

But, if they possessed different qualities, aptitudes, and temperaments, Dick Kennedy and Samuel Ferguson lived with one and the same heart, and that gave them no great trouble. In fact, quite the reverse.

Dick Kennedy was a Scotchman, in the full acceptation of the word—open, resolute, and headstrong. He lived in the town of Leith, which is near Edinburgh, and, in truth, is a mere suburb of Auld Reekie. Sometimes he was a fisherman, but he was always and everywhere a determined hunter, and that was nothing remarkable for a son of Caledonia, who had known some little climbing among the Highland mountains. He was cited as a wonderful shot with the rifle, since not only could he split a bullet on a knife-blade, but he could divide it into two such equal parts that, upon weighing them, scarcely any difference would be perceptible.

Kennedy's countenance strikingly recalled that of Herbert Glendinning, as Sir Walter Scott has depicted it in "The Monastery"; his stature was above six feet; full of grace and easy movement, he yet seemed gifted with herculean strength; a face embrowned by the sun; eyes keen and black; a natural air of daring courage; in fine, something sound, solid, and reliable in his entire person, spoke, at first glance, in favor of the bonny Scot.

The acquaintanceship of these two friends had been formed in India, when they belonged to the same regiment. While Dick would be out in pursuit of the tiger and the elephant, Samuel would be in search of plants and insects. Each could call himself expert in his own province, and more than one rare botanical specimen, that to science was as great a victory won as the conquest of a pair of ivory tusks, became the doctor's booty.

These two young men, moreover, never had occasion to save each other's lives, or to render any reciprocal service. Hence, an unalterable friendship. Destiny sometimes bore them apart, but sympathy always united them again.

Since their return to England they had been frequently separated by the doctor's distant expeditions; but, on his return, the latter never failed to go, not to *ask* for hospitality, but to bestow some weeks of his presence at the home of his crony Dick.

The Scot talked of the past; the doctor busily prepared for the future. The one looked back, the other forward. Hence, a restless spirit personified in Ferguson; perfect calmness typified in Kennedy—such was the contrast.

After his journey to the Thibet, the doctor had remained nearly two years without hinting at new explorations; and Dick, supposing that his friend's instinct for travel and thirst for adventure had at length died out, was perfectly enchanted. They would have ended badly, some day or other, he thought to himself; no matter what experience one has with men, one does not travel always with impunity among cannibals and wild beasts. So, Kennedy besought the doctor to tie up his bark for life, having done enough for science, and too much for the gratitude of men.

The doctor contented himself with making no reply to this. He remained absorbed in his own reflections, giving himself up to secret calculations, passing his nights among heaps of figures, and making experiments with the strangest-looking machinery, inexplicable to everybody but himself. It could readily be guessed, though, that some great thought was fermenting in his brain.

"What can he have been planning?" wondered Kennedy, when, in the month of January, his friend quitted him to return to London.

He found out one morning when he looked into the Daily Telegraph.

"Merciful Heaven!" he exclaimed, "the lunatic! the madman! Cross Africa in a balloon! Nothing but that was wanted to cap the climax! That's what he's been bothering his wits about these two years past!"

Now, reader, substitute for all these exclamation points, as many ringing thumps with a brawny fist upon the table, and you have some idea of the manual exercise that Dick went through while he thus spoke.

When his confidential maid-of-all-work, the aged Elspeth, tried to insinuate that the whole thing might be a hoax—

"Not a bit of it!" said he. "Don't I know my man? Isn't it just like him? Travel through the air! There, now, he's jealous of the eagles, next! No! I warrant you, he'll not do it! I'll find a way to stop him! He! why if they'd let him alone, he'd start some day for the moon!"

On that very evening Kennedy, half alarmed, and half exasperated, took the train for London, where he arrived next morning.

Three-quarters of an hour later a cab deposited him at the door of the doctor's modest dwelling, in Soho Square, Greek Street. Forthwith he bounded up the steps and announced his arrival with five good, hearty, sounding raps at the door.

Ferguson opened, in person.

"Dick! you here?" he exclaimed, but with no great expression of surprise, after all.

"Dick himself!" was the response.

"What, my dear boy, you at London, and this the mid-season of the winter shooting?"

"Yes! here I am, at London!"

"And what have you come to town for?"

"To prevent the greatest piece of folly that ever was conceived."

"Folly!" said the doctor.

"Is what this paper says, the truth?" rejoined Kennedy, holding out the copy of the Daily Telegraph, mentioned above.

"Ah! that's what you mean, is it? These newspapers are great tattlers! But, sit down, my dear Dick."

"No, I won't sit down!—Then, you really intend to attempt this journey?"

"Most certainly! all my preparations are getting along finely, and I—"

"Where are your traps? Let me have a chance at them! I'll make them fly! I'll put your preparations in fine order." And so saying, the gallant Scot gave way to a genuine explosion of wrath.

"Come, be calm, my dear Dick!" resumed the doctor. "You're angry at me because I did not acquaint you with my new project."

"He calls this his new project!"

"I have been very busy," the doctor went on, without heeding the interruption; "I have had so much to look after! But rest assured that I should not have started without writing to you."

"Oh, indeed! I'm highly honored."

"Because it is my intention to take you with me."

Upon this, the Scotchman gave a leap that a wild goat would not have been ashamed of among his native crags.

"Ah! really, then, you want them to send us both to Bedlam!"

"I have counted positively upon you, my dear Dick, and I have picked you out from all the rest."

Kennedy stood speechless with amazement.

"After listening to me for ten minutes," said the doctor, "you will thank me!"

"Are you speaking seriously?"

"Very seriously."

"And suppose that I refuse to go with you?"

"But you won't refuse."

"But, suppose that I were to refuse?"

"Well, I'd go alone."

"Let us sit down," said Kennedy, "and talk without excitement. The moment you give up jesting about it, we can discuss the thing."

"Let us discuss it, then, at breakfast, if you have no objections, my dear Dick."

The two friends took their seats opposite to each other, at a little table with a plate of toast and a huge tea-urn before them.

"My dear Samuel," said the sportsman, "your project is insane! it is impossible! it has no resemblance to anything reasonable or practicable!"

"That's for us to find out when we shall have tried it!"

"But trying it is exactly what you ought not to attempt."

"Why so, if you please?"

"Well, the risks, the difficulty of the thing."

"As for difficulties," replied Ferguson, in a serious tone, "they were made to be overcome; as for risks and dangers, who can flatter himself that he is to escape them? Every thing in life involves danger; it may even be dangerous to sit down at one's own table, or to put one's hat on one's own head. Moreover, we must look upon what is to occur as having already occurred, and see nothing but the present in the future, for the future is but the present a little farther on."

"There it is!" exclaimed Kennedy, with a shrug. "As great a fatalist as ever!"

"Yes! but in the good sense of the word. Let us not trouble ourselves, then, about what fate has in store for us, and let us not forget our good old English proverb: 'The man who was born to be hung will never be drowned!'"

There was no reply to make, but that did not prevent Kennedy from resuming a series of arguments which may be readily conjectured, but which were too long for us to repeat.

"Well, then," he said, after an hour's discussion, "if you are absolutely determined to make this trip across the African continent—if it is necessary for your happiness, why not pursue the ordinary routes?"

"Why?" exclaimed the doctor, growing animated. "Because, all attempts to do so, up to this time, have utterly failed. Because, from Mungo Park, assassinated on the Niger, to Vogel, who disappeared in the Wadai country; from Oudney, who died at Murmur, and Clapperton, lost at Sackatou, to the Frenchman Maizan, who was cut to pieces; from Major Laing, killed by the Touaregs, to Roscher, from Hamburg, massacred in the beginning of 1860, the names of victim after victim have been inscribed on the lists of African martyrdom! Because, to contend successfully against the elements; against hunger, and thirst, and fever; against savage beasts, and still more savage men, is impossible! Because, what cannot be done in one way, should be tried in another. In fine, because what one cannot pass through directly in the middle, must be passed by going to one side or overhead!"

"If passing over it were the only question!" interposed Kennedy; "but passing high up in the air, doctor, there's the rub!"

"Come, then," said the doctor, "what have I to fear? You will admit that I have taken my precautions in such manner as to be certain that my balloon will not fall; but, should it disappoint me, I should find myself on the ground in the normal conditions imposed upon other explorers. But, my balloon will not deceive me, and we need make no such calculations."

"Yes, but you must take them into view."

"No, Dick. I intend not to be separated from the balloon until I reach the western coast of Africa. With it, every thing is possible; without it, I fall back into the dangers and difficulties as well as the natural obstacles that ordinarily attend such an expedition: with it, neither heat, nor torrents, nor tempests, nor the simoom, nor unhealthy climates, nor wild animals, nor savage men, are to be feared! If I feel too hot, I can ascend; if too cold, I can come down. Should there be a mountain, I can pass over it; a precipice, I can sweep across it; a river, I can sail beyond it; a storm, I can rise away above it; a torrent, I can skim it like a bird! I can advance without fatigue, I can halt without need of repose! I can soar above the nascent cities! I can speed onward with the rapidity of a tornado, sometimes at the loftiest heights, sometimes only a hundred feet above the soil, while the map of Africa unrolls itself beneath my gaze in the great atlas of the world."

Even the stubborn Kennedy began to feel moved, and yet the spectacle thus conjured up before him gave him the vertigo. He riveted his eyes upon the doctor with wonder and admiration, and yet with fear, for he already felt himself swinging aloft in space.

"Come, come," said he, at last. "Let us see, Samuel. Then you have discovered the means of guiding a balloon?"

"Not by any means. That is a Utopian idea."

"Then, you will go—"

"Whithersoever Providence wills; but, at all events, from east to west."

"Why so?"

"Because I expect to avail myself of the trade-winds, the direction of which is always the same."

"Ah! yes, indeed!" said Kennedy, reflecting; "the trade-winds—yes—truly—one might—there's something in that!"

"Something in it—yes, my excellent friend—there's *every thing* in it. The English Government has placed a transport at my disposal, and three or four vessels are to cruise off the western coast of Africa, about the presumed period of my arrival. In three months, at most, I shall be at Zanzibar, where I will inflate my balloon, and from that point we shall launch ourselves."

"We!" said Dick.

"Have you still a shadow of an objection to offer? Speak, friend Kennedy."

"An objection! I have a thousand; but among other things, tell me, if you expect to see the country. If you expect to mount and descend at pleasure, you cannot do so, without losing your gas. Up to this time no other means have been devised, and it is this that has always prevented long journeys in the air."

"My dear Dick, I have only one word to answer—I shall not lose one particle of gas."

"And yet you can descend when you please?"

"I shall descend when I please."

"And how will you do that?"

"Ah, ha! therein lies my secret, friend Dick. Have faith, and let my device be yours—'Excelsior!'"

"'Excelsior' be it then," said the sportsman, who did not understand a word of Latin.

But he made up his mind to oppose his friend's departure by all means in his power, and so pretended to give in, at the same time keeping on the watch. As for the doctor, he went on diligently with his preparations.

Chapter 4

African Explorations.—Barth, Richardson, Overweg, Werne, Brun-Rollet, Penney, Andrea, Debono, Miani, Guillaume Lejean, Bruce, Krapf and Rebmann, Maizan, Roscher, Burton and Speke.

The aerial line which Dr. Ferguson counted upon following had not been chosen at random; his point of departure had been carefully studied, and it was not without good cause that he had resolved to ascend at the island of Zanzibar. This island, lying near to the eastern coast of Africa, is in the sixth degree of south latitude, that is to say, four hundred and thirty geographical miles below the equator.

From this island the latest expedition, sent by way of the great lakes to explore the sources of the Nile, had just set out.

But it would be well to indicate what explorations Dr. Ferguson hoped to link together. The two principal ones were those of Dr. Barth in 1849, and of Lieutenants Burton and Speke in 1858.

Dr. Barth is a Hamburger, who obtained permission for himself and for his countryman Overweg to join the expedition of the Englishman Richardson. The latter was charged with a mission in the Soudan.

This vast region is situated between the fifteenth and tenth degrees of north latitude; that is to say, that, in order to approach it, the explorer must penetrate fifteen hundred miles into the interior of Africa.

Until then, the country in question had been known only through the journeys of Denham, of Clapperton, and of Oudney, made from 1822 to 1824. Richardson, Barth, and Overweg, jealously anxious to push their investigations farther, arrived at Tunis and Tripoli, like their predecessors, and got as far as Mourzouk, the capital of Fezzan.

They then abandoned the perpendicular line, and made a sharp turn westward toward Ghat, guided, with difficulty, by the Touaregs. After a thousand scenes of pillage, of vexation, and attacks by armed forces, their caravan arrived, in October, at the vast oasis of Asben. Dr. Barth separated from his companions, made an excursion to the town of Aghades, and rejoined the expedition, which resumed its march on the 12th of December. At length it reached the province of Damerghou; there the three travellers parted, and Barth took the road to Kano, where he arrived by dint of perseverance, and after paying considerable tribute.

In spite of an intense fever, he quitted that place on the 7th of March, accompanied by a single servant. The principal aim of his journey was to reconnoitre Lake Tchad, from which he was still three hundred and fifty miles distant. He therefore advanced toward the east, and reached the town of Zouricolo, in the Bornou country, which is the core of the great central empire of Africa. There he heard of the death of Richardson, who had succumbed to fatigue and privation. He next arrived at Kouka, the capital of Bornou, on the borders of the lake. Finally, at the end of three weeks, on the 14th of April, twelve months after having quitted Tripoli, he reached the town of Ngornou.

We find him again setting forth on the 29th of March, 1851, with Overweg, to visit the kingdom of Adamaoua, to the south of the lake, and from there he pushed on as far as the town of Yola, a little below nine degrees north latitude. This was the extreme southern limit reached by that daring traveller.

He returned in the month of August to Kouka; from there he successively traversed the Mandara, Barghimi, and Klanem countries, and reached his extreme limit in the east, the town of Masena, situated at seventeen degrees twenty minutes west longitude.

On the 25th of November, 1852, after the death of Overweg, his last companion, he plunged into the west, visited Sockoto, crossed the Niger, and finally reached Timbuctoo, where he had to languish, during eight long months, under vexations inflicted upon him by the sheik, and all kinds of ill-treatment and wretchedness. But the presence of a Christian in the city could not long be tolerated, and the Foullans threatened to besiege it. The doctor, therefore, left it on the 17th of March, 1854, and fled to the frontier, where he remained for thirty-three days in the most abject destitution. He then managed to get back to Kano in November, thence to Kouka, where he resumed Denham's route after four months' delay. He regained Tripoli toward the close of August, 1855, and arrived in London on the 6th of September, the only survivor of his party.

Such was the venturesome journey of Dr. Barth.

Dr. Ferguson carefully noted the fact, that he had stopped at four degrees north latitude and seventeen degrees west longitude.

Now let us see what Lieutenants Burton and Speke accomplished in Eastern Africa.

The various expeditions that had ascended the Nile could never manage to reach the mysterious source of that river. According to the narrative of the German doctor, Ferdinand Werne, the expedition attempted in 1840, under the auspices of Mehemet Ali, stopped at Gondokoro, between the fourth and fifth parallels of north latitude.

In 1855, Brun-Rollet, a native of Savoy, appointed consul for Sardinia in Eastern Soudan, to take the place of Vaudey, who had just died, set out from Karthoum, and, under the name of Yacoub the merchant, trading in gums and ivory, got as far as Belenia, beyond the fourth degree, but had to return in ill-health to Karthoum, where he died in 1857.

Neither Dr. Penney—the head of the Egyptian medical service, who, in a small steamer, penetrated one degree beyond Gondokoro, and then came back to die of exhaustion at Karthoum—nor Miani, the Venetian, who, turning the cataracts below Gondokoro, reached the second parallel—nor the Maltese trader, Andrea Debono, who pushed his journey up the Nile still farther—could work their way beyond the apparently impassable limit.

In 1859, M. Guillaume Lejean, intrusted with a mission by the French Government, reached Karthoum by way of the Red Sea, and embarked upon the Nile with a retinue of twenty-one hired men and twenty soldiers, but he could not get past Gondokoro, and ran extreme risk of his life among the negro tribes, who were in full revolt. The expedition directed by M. d'Escayrac de Lauture made an equally unsuccessful attempt to reach the famous sources of the Nile.

This fatal limit invariably brought every traveller to a halt. In ancient times, the ambassadors of Nero reached the ninth degree of latitude, but in eighteen centuries only from five to six degrees, or from three hundred to three hundred and sixty geographical miles, were gained.

Many travellers endeavored to reach the sources of the Nile by taking their point of departure on the eastern coast of Africa.

Between 1768 and 1772 the Scotch traveller, Bruce, set out from Massowah, a port of Abyssinia, traversed the Tigre, visited the ruins of Axum, saw the sources of the Nile where they did not exist, and obtained no serious result.

In 1844, Dr. Krapf, an Anglican missionary, founded an establishment at Monbaz, on the coast of Zanguebar, and, in company with the Rev. Dr. Rebmann, discovered two mountain-ranges three hundred miles from the coast. These were the mountains of Kilimandjaro and Kenia, which Messrs. de Heuglin and Thornton have partly scaled so recently.

In 1845, Maizan, the French explorer, disembarked, alone, at Bagamayo, directly opposite to Zanzibar, and got as far as Deje-la-Mhora, where the chief caused him to be put to death in the most cruel torment.

In 1859, in the month of August, the young traveller, Roscher, from Hamburg, set out with a caravan of Arab merchants, reached Lake Nyassa, and was there assassinated while he slept.

Finally, in 1857, Lieutenants Burton and Speke, both officers in the Bengal army, were sent by the London Geographical Society to explore the great African lakes, and on the 17th of June they quitted Zanzibar, and plunged directly into the west.

After four months of incredible suffering, their baggage having been pillaged, and their attendants beaten and slain, they arrived at Kazeh, a sort of central rendezvous for traders and caravans. They were in the midst of the country of the Moon, and there they collected some precious documents concerning the manners, government, religion, fauna, and flora of the region. They next made for the first of the great lakes, the one named Tanganayika, situated between the third and eighth degrees of south latitude. They reached it on the 14th of February, 1858, and visited the various tribes residing on its banks, the most of whom are cannibals.

They departed again on the 26th of May, and reentered Kazeh on the 20th of June. There Burton, who was completely worn out, lay ill for several months, during which time Speke made a push to the northward of more than three hundred miles, going as far as Lake Okeracua, which he came in sight of on the 3d of August; but he could descry only the opening of it at latitude two degrees thirty minutes.

He reached Kazeh, on his return, on the 25th of August, and, in company with Burton, again took up the route to Zanzibar, where they arrived in the month of March in the following year. These two daring explorers then reembarked for England; and the Geographical Society of Paris decreed them its annual prize medal.

Dr. Ferguson carefully remarked that they had not gone beyond the second degree of south latitude, nor the twenty-ninth of east longitude.

The problem, therefore, was how to link the explorations of Burton and Speke with those of Dr. Barth, since to do so was to undertake to traverse an extent of more than twelve degrees of territory.

Chapter 5

Dr. Ferguson energetically pushed the preparations for his departure, and in person superintended the construction of his balloon, with certain modifications; in regard to which he observed the most absolute silence. For a long time past he had been applying himself to the study of the Arab language and the various Mandingoe idioms, and, thanks to his talents as a polyglot, he had made rapid progress.

In the mean while his friend, the sportsman, never let him out of his sight—afraid, no doubt, that the doctor might take his departure, without saying a word to anybody. On this subject, he regaled him with the most persuasive arguments, which, however, did *not* persuade Samuel Ferguson, and wasted his breath in pathetic entreaties, by which the latter seemed to be but slightly moved. In fine, Dick felt that the doctor was slipping through his fingers.

The poor Scot was really to be pitied. He could not look upon the azure vault without a sombre terror: when asleep, he felt oscillations that made his head reel; and every night he had visions of being swung aloft at immeasurable heights.

We must add that, during these fearful nightmares, he once or twice fell out of bed. His first care then was to show Ferguson a severe contusion that he had received on the cranium. "And yet," he would add, with warmth, "that was at the height of only three feet—not an inch more—and such a bump as this! Only think, then!"

This insinuation, full of sad meaning as it was, did not seem to touch the doctor's heart.

"We'll not fall," was his invariable reply.

"But, still, suppose that we *were* to fall!"

"We will *not* fall!"

This was decisive, and Kennedy had nothing more to say.

What particularly exasperated Dick was, that the doctor seemed completely to lose sight of his personality—of his—Kennedy's—and to look upon him as irrevocably destined to become his aerial companion. Not even the shadow of a doubt was ever suggested; and Samuel made an intolerable misuse of the first person plural:

"'We' are getting along; 'we' shall be ready on the——; 'we' shall start on the——," etc., etc.

And then there was the singular possessive adjective:

"'Our' balloon; 'our' car; 'our' expedition."

And the same in the plural, too:

"'Our' preparations; 'our' discoveries; 'our' ascensions."

Dick shuddered at them, although he was determined not to go; but he did not want to annoy his friend. Let us also disclose the fact that, without knowing exactly why himself, he had sent to Edinburgh for a certain selection of heavy clothing, and his best hunting-gear and fire-arms.

One day, after having admitted that, with an overwhelming run of good-luck, there *might* be one chance of success in a thousand, he pretended to yield entirely to the doctor's wishes; but, in order to still put off the journey, he opened the most varied series of subterfuges. He threw himself back upon questioning the utility of the expedition— its opportuneness, etc. This discovery of the sources of the Nile, was it likely to be of any use?—Would one have really labored for the welfare of humanity?—When, after all, the African tribes should have been civilized, would they be any happier?—Were folks certain that civilization had not its chosen abode there rather than in Europe?— Perhaps!—And then, couldn't one wait a little longer?—The trip across Africa would certainly be accomplished some day, and in a less hazardous manner.—In another month, or in six months before the year was over, some explorer would undoubtedly come in—etc., etc.

These hints produced an effect exactly opposite to what was desired or intended, and the doctor trembled with impatience.

"Are you willing, then, wretched Dick—are you willing, false friend— that this glory should belong to another? Must I then be untrue to my past history; recoil before obstacles that are not serious; requite with cowardly hesitation what both the English Government and the Royal Society of London have done for me?"

"But," resumed Kennedy, who made great use of that conjunction.

"But," said the doctor, "are you not aware that my journey is to compete with the success of the expeditions now on foot? Don't you know that fresh explorers are advancing toward the centre of Africa?"

"Still—"

"Listen to me, Dick, and cast your eyes over that map."

Dick glanced over it, with resignation.

"Now, ascend the course of the Nile."

"I have ascended it," replied the Scotchman, with docility.

"Stop at Gondokoro."

"I am there."

And Kennedy thought to himself how easy such a trip was—on the map!

"Now, take one of the points of these dividers and let it rest upon that place beyond which the most daring explorers have scarcely gone."

"I have done so."

"And now look along the coast for the island of Zanzibar, in latitude six degrees south."

"I have it."

"Now, follow the same parallel and arrive at Kazeh."

"I have done so."

"Run up again along the thirty-third degree of longitude to the opening of Lake Oukereoue, at the point where Lieutenant Speke had to halt."

"I am there; a little more, and I should have tumbled into the lake."

"Very good! Now, do you know what we have the right to suppose, according to the information given by the tribes that live along its shores?"

"I haven't the least idea."

"Why, that this lake, the lower extremity of which is in two degrees and thirty minutes, must extend also two degrees and a half above the equator."

"Really!"

"Well from this northern extremity there flows a stream which must necessarily join the Nile, if it be not the Nile itself."

"That is, indeed, curious."

"Then, let the other point of your dividers rest upon that extremity of Lake Oukereoue."

"It is done, friend Ferguson."

"Now, how many degrees can you count between the two points?"

"Scarcely two."

"And do you know what that means, Dick?"

"Not the least in the world."

"Why, that makes scarcely one hundred and twenty miles—in other words, a nothing."

"Almost nothing, Samuel."

"Well, do you know what is taking place at this moment?"

"No, upon my honor, I do not."

"Very well, then, I'll tell you. The Geographical Society regard as very important the exploration of this lake of which Speke caught a glimpse. Under their auspices, Lieutenant (now Captain) Speke has associated with him Captain Grant, of the army in India; they have put themselves at the head of a numerous and well-equipped expedition; their mission is to ascend the lake and return to Gondokoro; they have received a subsidy of more than five thousand pounds, and the Governor of the Cape of Good Hope has placed Hottentot soldiers at their disposal; they set out from Zanzibar at the close of October, 1860. In the mean while John Petherick, the English consul at the city of Karthoum, has received about seven hundred pounds from the foreign office; he is to equip a steamer at Karthoum, stock it with sufficient provisions, and make his way to Gondokoro; there, he will await Captain Speke's caravan, and be able to replenish its supplies to some extent."

"Well planned," said Kennedy.

"You can easily see, then, that time presses if we are to take part in these exploring labors. And that is not all, since, while some are thus advancing with sure steps to the discovery of the sources of the Nile, others are penetrating to the very heart of Africa."

"On foot?" said Kennedy.

"Yes, on foot," rejoined the doctor, without noticing the insinuation. "Doctor Krapf proposes to push forward, in the west, by way of the Djob, a river lying under the equator. Baron de Decken has already set out from Monbaz, has reconnoitred the mountains of Kenaia and Kilimandjaro, and is now plunging in toward the centre."

"But all this time on foot?"

"On foot or on mules."

"Exactly the same, so far as I am concerned," exclaimed Kennedy.

"Lastly," resumed the doctor, "M. de Heuglin, the Austrian vice-consul at Karthoum, has just organized a very important expedition, the first aim of which is to search for the traveller Vogel, who, in 1853, was sent into the Soudan to associate himself with the labors of Dr. Barth. In 1856, he quitted Bornou, and determined to explore the unknown country that lies between Lake Tchad and Darfur. Nothing has been seen of him since that time. Letters that were received in Alexandria, in 1860, said that he was killed at the order of the King of Wadai; but other letters, addressed by Dr. Hartmann to the traveller's father, relate that, according to the recital of a felatah of Bornou, Vogel was merely held as a prisoner at Wara. All hope is not then lost. Hence, a committee has been organized under the presidency of the Regent of Saxe-Cogurg-Gotha; my friend Petermann is its secretary; a national subscription has provided for the expense of the expedition, whose strength has been increased by the voluntary accession of several learned men, and M. de Heuglin set out from Massowah, in the month of June. While engaged in looking for Vogel, he is also to explore all the country between the Nile and Lake Tchad, that is to say, to knit together the operations of Captain Speke and those of Dr. Barth, and then Africa will have been traversed from east to west."*

"Well," said the canny Scot, "since every thing is getting on so well, what's the use of our going down there?"

Dr. Ferguson made no reply, but contented himself with a significant shrug of the shoulders.

---

* After the departure of Dr. Ferguson, it was ascertained that M. de Heuglin, owing to some disagreement, took a route different from the one assigned to his expedition, the command of the latter having been transferred to Mr. Muntzinger.

Chapter 6

A Servant—Match Him!—He Can See the Satellites of Jupiter.—Dick and Joe Hard at It.—Doubt and Faith.— The Weighing Ceremony.—Joe and Wellington.— He Gets a Half-Crown.

D r. Ferguson had a servant who answered with alacrity to the name of Joe. He was an excellent fellow, who testified the most absolute confidence in his master, and the most unlimited devotion to his interests, even anticipating his wishes and orders, which were always intelligently executed. In fine, he was a Caleb without the growling, and a perfect pattern of constant good-humor. Had he been made on purpose for the place, it could not have been better done. Ferguson put himself entirely in his hands, so far as the ordinary details of existence were concerned, and he did well. Incomparable, whole-souled Joe! a servant who orders your dinner; who likes what you like; who packs your trunk, without forgetting your socks or your linen; who has charge of your keys and your secrets, and takes no advantage of all this!

But then, what a man the doctor was in the eyes of this worthy Joe! With what respect and what confidence the latter received all his decisions! When Ferguson had spoken, he would be a fool who should attempt to question the matter. Every thing he thought was exactly right; every thing he said, the perfection of wisdom; every thing he ordered to be done, quite feasible; all that he undertook, practicable; all that he accomplished, admirable. You might have cut Joe to pieces—not an agreeable operation, to be sure—and yet he would not have altered his opinion of his master.

So, when the doctor conceived the project of crossing Africa through the air, for Joe the thing was already done; obstacles no longer existed; from the moment when the doctor had made up his mind to start, he had arrived—along with his faithful attendant, too, for the noble fellow knew, without a word uttered about it, that he would be one of the party.

Moreover, he was just the man to render the greatest service by his intelligence and his wonderful agility. Had the occasion arisen to name a professor of gymnastics for the monkeys in the Zoological Garden (who are smart enough, by-the-way!), Joe would certainly have received the appointment. Leaping, climbing, almost flying—these were all sport to him.

If Ferguson was the head and Kennedy the arm, Joe was to be the right hand of the expedition. He had, already, accompanied his master on several journeys, and had a smattering of science appropriate to his condition and style of mind, but he was especially remarkable for a sort of mild philosophy, a charming turn of optimism. In his sight every thing was easy, logical, natural, and, consequently, he could see no use in complaining or grumbling.

Among other gifts, he possessed a strength and range of vision that were perfectly surprising. He enjoyed, in common with Moestlin, Kepler's professor, the rare faculty of distinguishing the satellites of Jupiter with the naked eye, and of counting fourteen of the stars in the group of Pleiades, the remotest of them being only of the ninth magnitude. He presumed none the more for that; on the contrary, he made his bow to you, at a distance, and when occasion arose he bravely knew how to use his eyes.

With such profound faith as Joe felt in the doctor, it is not to be wondered at that incessant discussions sprang up between him and Kennedy, without any lack of respect to the latter, however.

One doubted, the other believed; one had a prudent foresight, the other blind confidence. The doctor, however, vibrated between doubt and confidence; that is to say, he troubled his head with neither one nor the other.

"Well, Mr. Kennedy," Joe would say.

"Well, my boy?"

"The moment's at hand. It seems that we are to sail for the moon."

"You mean the Mountains of the Moon, which are not quite so far off. But, never mind, one trip is just as dangerous as the other!"

"Dangerous! What! with a man like Dr. Ferguson?"

"I don't want to spoil your illusions, my good Joe; but this undertaking of his is nothing more nor less than the act of a madman. He won't go, though!"

"He won't go, eh? Then you haven't seen his balloon at Mitchell's factory in the Borough?"

"I'll take precious good care to keep away from it!"

"Well, you'll lose a fine sight, sir. What a splendid thing it is! What a pretty shape! What a nice car! How snug we'll feel in it!"

"Then you really think of going with your master?"

"I?" answered Joe, with an accent of profound conviction. "Why, I'd go with him wherever he pleases! Who ever heard of such a thing? Leave him to go off alone, after we've been all over the world together! Who would help him, when he was tired? Who would give him a hand in climbing over the rocks? Who would attend him when he was sick? No, Mr. Kennedy, Joe will always stick to the doctor!"

"You're a fine fellow, Joe!"

"But, then, you're coming with us!"

"Oh! certainly," said Kennedy; "that is to say, I will go with you up to the last moment, to prevent Samuel even then from being guilty of such an act of folly! I will follow him as far as Zanzibar, so as to stop him there, if possible."

"You'll stop nothing at all, Mr. Kennedy, with all respect to you, sir. My master is no hare-brained person; he takes a long time to think over what he means to do, and then, when he once gets started, the Evil One himself couldn't make him give it up."

"Well, we'll see about that."

"Don't flatter yourself, sir—but then, the main thing is, to have you with us. For a hunter like you, sir, Africa's a great country. So, either way, you won't be sorry for the trip."

"No, that's a fact, I shan't be sorry for it, if I can get this crazy man to give up his scheme."

"By-the-way," said Joe, "you know that the weighing comes off to-day."

"The weighing—what weighing?"

"Why, my master, and you, and I, are all to be weighed to-day!"

"What! like horse-jockeys?"

"Yes, like jockeys. Only, never fear, you won't be expected to make yourself lean, if you're found to be heavy. You'll go as you are."

"Well, I can tell you, I am not going to let myself be weighed," said Kennedy, firmly.

"But, sir, it seems that the doctor's machine requires it."

"Well, his machine will have to do without it."

"Humph! and suppose that it couldn't go up, then?"

"Egad! that's all I want!"

"Come! come, Mr. Kennedy! My master will be sending for us directly."

"I shan't go."

"Oh! now, you won't vex the doctor in that way!"

"Aye! that I will."

"Well!" said Joe with a laugh, "you say that because he's not here; but when he says to your face, 'Dick!' (with all respect to you, sir,) 'Dick, I want to know exactly how much you weigh,' you'll go, I warrant it."

"No, I will *not* go!"

At this moment the doctor entered his study, where this discussion had been taking place; and, as he came in, cast a glance at Kennedy, who did not feel altogether at his ease.

"Dick," said the doctor, "come with Joe; I want to know how much you both weigh."

"But—"

"You may keep your hat on. Come!" And Kennedy went.

They repaired in company to the workshop of the Messrs. Mitchell, where one of those so-called "Roman" scales was in readiness. It was necessary, by the way, for the doctor to know the weight of his companions, so as to fix the equilibrium of his balloon; so he made Dick get up on the platform of the scales. The latter, without making any resistance, said, in an undertone:

"Oh! well, that doesn't bind me to any thing."

"One hundred and fifty-three pounds," said the doctor, noting it down on his tablets.

"Am I too heavy?"

"Why, no, Mr. Kennedy!" said Joe; "and then, you know, I am light to make up for it."

So saying, Joe, with enthusiasm, took his place on the scales, and very nearly upset them in his ready haste. He struck the attitude of Wellington where he is made to ape Achilles, at Hyde-Park entrance, and was superb in it, without the shield.

"One hundred and twenty pounds," wrote the doctor.

"Ah! ha!" said Joe, with a smile of satisfaction And why did he smile? He never could tell himself.

"It's my turn now," said Ferguson—and he put down one hundred and thirty-five pounds to his own account.

"All three of us," said he, "do not weigh much more than four hundred pounds."

"But, sir," said Joe, "if it was necessary for your expedition, I could make myself thinner by twenty pounds, by not eating so much."

"Useless, my boy!" replied the doctor. "You may eat as much as you like, and here's half-a-crown to buy you the ballast."

Chapter 7

Geometrical Details.—Calculation of the Capacity of the Balloon.—The Double Receptacle.—The Covering.—The Car.—The Mysterious Apparatus.—The Provisions and Stores.—The Final Summing Up.

D r. Ferguson had long been engaged upon the details of his expedition. It is easy to comprehend that the balloon—that marvellous vehicle which was to convey him through the air—was the constant object of his solicitude.

At the outset, in order not to give the balloon too ponderous dimensions, he had decided to fill it with hydrogen gas, which is fourteen and a half times lighter than common air. The production of this gas is easy, and it has given the greatest satisfaction hitherto in aerostatic experiments.

The doctor, according to very accurate calculations, found that, including the articles indispensable to his journey and his apparatus, he should have to carry a weight of 4,000 pounds; therefore he had to find out what would be the ascensional force of a balloon capable of raising such a weight, and, consequently, what would be its capacity.

A weight of four thousand pounds is represented by a displacement of the air amounting to forty-four thousand eight hundred and forty-seven cubic feet; or, in other words, forty-four thousand eight hundred and forty-seven cubic feet of air weigh about four thousand pounds.

By giving the balloon these cubic dimensions, and filling it with hydrogen gas, instead of common air—the former being fourteen and a half times lighter and weighing therefore only two hundred and seventy-six pounds—a difference of three thousand seven hundred and twenty-four pounds in equilibrium is produced; and it is this difference between the weight of the gas contained in the balloon and the weight of the surrounding atmosphere that constitutes the ascensional force of the former.

However, were the forty-four thousand eight hundred and forty-seven cubic feet of gas of which we speak, all introduced into the balloon, it would be entirely filled; but that would not do, because, as the balloon continued to mount into the more rarefied layers of the atmosphere, the gas within would dilate, and soon burst the cover containing it. Balloons, then, are usually only two-thirds filled.

But the doctor, in carrying out a project known only to himself, resolved to fill his balloon only one-half; and, since he had to carry forty-four thousand eight hundred and forty-seven cubic feet of gas, to give his balloon nearly double capacity he arranged it in that elongated, oval shape which has come to be preferred. The horizontal diameter was fifty feet, and the vertical diameter seventy-five feet. He thus obtained a spheroid, the capacity of which amounted, in round numbers, to ninety thousand cubic feet.

Could Dr. Ferguson have used two balloons, his chances of success would have been increased; for, should one burst in the air, he could, by throwing out ballast, keep himself up with the other. But the management of two balloons would, necessarily, be very difficult, in view of the problem how to keep them both at an equal ascensional force.

After having pondered the matter carefully, Dr. Ferguson, by an ingenious arrangement, combined the advantages of two balloons, without incurring their inconveniences. He constructed two of different sizes, and inclosed the smaller in the larger one. His external balloon, which had the dimensions given above, contained a less one of the same shape, which was only forty-five feet in horizontal, and sixty-eight feet in vertical diameter. The capacity of this interior balloon was only sixty-seven thousand cubic feet: it was to float in the fluid surrounding it. A valve opened from one balloon into the other, and thus enabled the aeronaut to communicate with both.

This arrangement offered the advantage, that if gas had to be let off, so as to descend, that which was in the outer balloon would go first; and, were it completely emptied, the smaller one would still remain intact. The outer envelope might then be cast off as a useless encumbrance; and the second balloon, left free to itself, would not offer the same hold to the currents of air as a half-inflated one must needs present.

Moreover, in case of an accident happening to the outside balloon, such as getting torn, for instance, the other would remain intact.

The balloons were made of a strong but light Lyons silk, coated with gutta percha. This gummy, resinous substance is absolutely water-proof, and also resists acids and gas perfectly. The silk was doubled, at the upper extremity of the oval, where most of the strain would come.

Such an envelope as this could retain the inflating fluid for any length of time. It weighed half a pound per nine square feet. Hence the surface of the outside balloon being about eleven thousand six hundred square feet, its envelope weighed six hundred and fifty pounds. The envelope of the second or inner balloon, having nine thousand two hundred square feet of surface, weighed only about five hundred and ten pounds, or say eleven hundred and sixty pounds for both.

The network that supported the car was made of very strong hempen cord, and the two valves were the object of the most minute and careful attention, as the rudder of a ship would be.

The car, which was of a circular form and fifteen feet in diameter, was made of wicker-work, strengthened with a slight covering of iron, and protected below by a system of elastic springs, to deaden the shock of collision. Its weight, along with that of the network, did not exceed two hundred and fifty pounds.

In addition to the above, the doctor caused to be constructed two sheet-iron chests two lines in thickness. These were connected by means of pipes furnished with stopcocks. He joined to these a spiral, two inches in diameter, which terminated in two branch pieces of unequal length, the longer of which, however, was twenty-five feet in height and the shorter only fifteen feet.

These sheet-iron chests were embedded in the car in such a way as to take up the least possible amount of space. The spiral, which was not to be adjusted until some future moment, was packed up, separately, along with a very strong Buntzen electric battery. This apparatus had been so ingeniously combined that it did not weigh more than seven hundred pounds, even including twenty-five gallons of water in another receptacle.

The instruments provided for the journey consisted of two barometers, two thermometers, two compasses, a sextant, two chronometers, an artificial horizon, and an altazimuth, to throw out the height of distant and inaccessible objects.

The Greenwich Observatory had placed itself at the doctor's disposal. The latter, however, did not intend to make experiments in physics; he merely wanted to be able to know in what direction he was passing, and to determine the position of the principal rivers, mountains, and towns.

He also provided himself with three thoroughly tested iron anchors, and a light but strong silk ladder fifty feet in length.

He at the same time carefully weighed his stores of provision, which consisted of tea, coffee, biscuit, salted meat, and pemmican, a preparation which comprises many nutritive elements in a small space.

Besides a sufficient stock of pure brandy, he arranged two water-tanks, each of which contained twenty-two gallons.

The consumption of these articles would necessarily, little by little, diminish the weight to be sustained, for it must be remembered that the equilibrium of a balloon floating in the atmosphere is extremely sensitive. The loss of an almost insignificant weight suffices to produce a very noticeable displacement.

Nor did the doctor forget an awning to shelter the car, nor the coverings and blankets that were to be the bedding of the journey, nor some fowling pieces and rifles, with their requisite supply of powder and ball.

Here is the summing up of his various items, and their weight, as he computed it:

Ferguson	135 pounds.
Kennedy	153 ”
Joe	120 ”
Weight of the outside balloon	650 ”
Weight of the second balloon	510 ”
Car and network	280 ”
Anchors, instruments, awnings, and sundry utensils, guns, coverings, etc.	190 ”
Meat, pemmican, biscuits, tea, coffee, brandy	386 ”
Water	400 ”
Apparatus	700 ”
Weight of the hydrogen	276 ”
Ballast	200 ”
	4,000 pounds.

Such were the items of the four thousand pounds that Dr. Ferguson proposed to carry up with him. He took only two hundred pounds of ballast for "unforeseen emergencies," as he remarked, since otherwise he did not expect to use any, thanks to the peculiarity of his apparatus.

Chapter 8

About the 10th of February, the preparations were pretty well completed; and the balloons, firmly secured, one within the other, were altogether finished. They had been subjected to a powerful pneumatic pressure in all parts, and the test gave excellent evidence of their solidity and of the care applied in their construction.

Joe hardly knew what he was about, with delight. He trotted incessantly to and fro between his home in Greek Street, and the Mitchell establishment, always full of business, but always in the highest spirits, giving details of the affair to people who did not even ask him, so proud was he, above all things, of being permitted to accompany his master. I have even a shrewd suspicion that what with showing the balloon, explaining the plans and views of the doctor, giving folks a glimpse of the latter, through a half-opened window, or pointing him out as he passed along the streets, the clever scamp earned a few half-crowns, but we must not find fault with him for that. He had as much right as anybody else to speculate upon the admiration and curiosity of his contemporaries.

On the 16th of February, the Resolute cast anchor near Greenwich. She was a screw propeller of eight hundred tons, a fast sailer, and the very vessel that had been sent out to the polar regions, to revictual the last expedition of Sir James Ross. Her commander, Captain Bennet, had the name of being a very amiable person, and he took a particular interest in the doctor's expedition, having been one of that gentleman's admirers for a long time. Bennet was rather a man of science than a man of war, which did not, however, prevent his vessel from carrying four carronades, that had never hurt any body, to be sure, but had performed the most pacific duty in the world.

The hold of the Resolute was so arranged as to find a stowing-place for the balloon. The latter was shipped with the greatest precaution on the 18th of February, and was then carefully deposited at the bottom of the vessel in such a way as to prevent accident. The car and its accessories, the anchors, the cords, the supplies, the water-tanks, which were to be filled on arriving, all were embarked and put away under Ferguson's own eyes.

Ten tons of sulphuric acid and ten tons of iron filings, were put on board for the future production of the hydrogen gas. The quantity was more than enough, but it was well to be provided against accident. The apparatus to be employed in manufacturing the gas, including some thirty empty casks, was also stowed away in the hold.

These various preparations were terminated on the 18th of February, in the evening. Two state-rooms, comfortably fitted up, were ready for the reception of Dr. Ferguson and his friend Kennedy. The latter, all the while swearing that he would not go, went on board with a regular arsenal of hunting weapons, among which were two double-barrelled breech-loading fowling-pieces, and a rifle that had withstood every test, of the make of Purdey, Moore & Dickson, at Edinburgh. With such a weapon a marksman would find no difficulty in lodging a bullet in the eye of a chamois at the distance of two thousand paces. Along with these implements, he had two of Colt's six-shooters, for unforeseen emergencies. His powder-case, his cartridge-pouch, his lead, and his bullets, did not exceed a certain weight prescribed by the doctor.

The three travellers got themselves to rights on board during the working-hours of February 19th. They were received with much distinction by the captain and his officers, the doctor continuing as reserved as ever, and thinking of nothing but his expedition. Dick seemed a good deal moved, but was unwilling to betray it; while Joe was fairly dancing and breaking out in laughable remarks. The worthy fellow soon became the jester and merry-andrew of the boatswain's mess, where a berth had been kept for him.

On the 20th, a grand farewell dinner was given to Dr. Ferguson and Kennedy by the Royal Geographical Society. Commander Bennet and his officers were present at the entertainment, which was signalized by copious libations and numerous toasts. Healths were drunk, in sufficient abundance to guarantee all the guests a lifetime of centuries. Sir Francis M—— presided, with restrained but dignified feeling.

To his own supreme confusion, Dick Kennedy came in for a large share in the jovial felicitations of the night. After having drunk to the "intrepid Ferguson, the glory of England," they had to drink to "the no less courageous Kennedy, his daring companion."

Dick blushed a good deal, and that passed for modesty; whereupon the applause redoubled, and Dick blushed again.

A message from the Queen arrived while they were at dessert. Her Majesty offered her compliments to the two travellers, and expressed her wishes for their safe and successful journey. This, of course, rendered imperative fresh toasts to "Her most gracious Majesty."

At midnight, after touching farewells and warm shaking of hands, the guests separated.

The boats of the Resolute were in waiting at the stairs of Westminster Bridge. The captain leaped in, accompanied by his officers and passengers, and the rapid current of the Thames, aiding the strong arms of the rowers, bore them swiftly to Greenwich. In an hour's time all were asleep on board.

The next morning, February 21st, at three o'clock, the furnaces began to roar; at five, the anchors were weighed, and the Resolute, powerfully driven by her screw, began to plough the water toward the mouth of the Thames.

It is needless to say that the topic of conversation with every one on board was Dr. Ferguson's enterprise. Seeing and hearing the doctor soon inspired everybody with such confidence that, in a very short time, there was no one, excepting the incredulous Scotchman, on the steamer who had the least doubt of the perfect feasibility and success of the expedition.

During the long, unoccupied hours of the voyage, the doctor held regular sittings, with lectures on geographical science, in the officers' mess-room. These young men felt an intense interest in the discoveries made during the last forty years in Africa; and the doctor related to them the explorations of Barth, Burton, Speke, and Grant, and depicted the wonders of this vast, mysterious country, now thrown open on all sides to the investigations of science. On the north, the young Duveyrier was exploring Sahara, and bringing the chiefs of the Touaregs to Paris. Under the inspiration of the French Government, two expeditions were preparing, which, descending from the north, and coming from the west, would cross each other at Timbuctoo. In the south, the indefatigable Livingstone was still advancing toward the equator; and, since March, 1862, he had, in company with Mackenzie, ascended the river Rovoonia. The nineteenth century would, assuredly, not pass, contended the doctor, without Africa having been compelled to surrender the secrets she has kept locked up in her bosom for six thousand years.

But the interest of Dr. Ferguson's hearers was excited to the highest pitch when he made known to them, in detail, the preparations for his own journey. They took pleasure in verifying his calculations; they discussed them; and the doctor frankly took part in the discussion.

As a general thing, they were surprised at the limited quantity of provision that he took with him; and one day one of the officers questioned him on that subject.

"That peculiar point astonishes you, does it?" said Ferguson.

"It does, indeed."

"But how long do you think my trip is going to last? Whole months? If so, you are greatly mistaken. Were it to be a long one, we should be lost; we should never get back. But you must know that the distance from Zanzibar to the coast of Senegal is only thirty-five hundred— say four thousand miles. Well, at the rate of two hundred and forty miles every twelve hours, which does not come near the rapidity of our railroad trains, by travelling day and night, it would take only seven days to cross Africa!"

"But then you could see nothing, make no geographical observations, or reconnoitre the face of the country."

"Ah!" replied the doctor, "if I am master of my balloon—if I can ascend and descend at will, I shall stop when I please, especially when too violent currents of air threaten to carry me out of my way with them."

"And you will encounter such," said Captain Bennet. "There are tornadoes that sweep at the rate of more than two hundred and forty miles per hour."

"You see, then, that with such speed as that, we could cross Africa in twelve hours. One would rise at Zanzibar, and go to bed at St. Louis!"

"But," rejoined the officer, "could any balloon withstand the wear and tear of such velocity?"

"It has happened before," replied Ferguson.

"And the balloon withstood it?"

"Perfectly well. It was at the time of the coronation of Napoleon, in 1804. The aeronaut, Gernerin, sent up a balloon at Paris, about eleven o'clock in the evening. It bore the following inscription, in letters of gold: 'Paris, 25 Frimaire; year XIII; Coronation of the Emperor Napoleon by his Holiness, Pius VII.' On the next morning, the inhabitants of Rome saw the same balloon soaring above the Vatican, whence it crossed the Campagna, and finally fluttered down into the lake of Bracciano. So you see, gentlemen, that a balloon can resist such velocities."

"A balloon—that might be; but a man?" insinuated Kennedy.

"Yes, a man, too!—for the balloon is always motionless with reference to the air that surrounds it. What moves is the mass of the atmosphere itself: for instance, one may light a taper in the car, and the flame will not even waver. An aeronaut in Garnerin's balloon would not have suffered in the least from the speed. But then I have no occasion to attempt such velocity; and if I can anchor to some tree, or some favorable inequality of the ground, at night, I shall not fail to do so. Besides, we take provision for two months with us, after all; and there is nothing to prevent our skilful huntsman here from furnishing game in abundance when we come to alight."

"Ah! Mr. Kennedy," said a young midshipman, with envious eyes, "what splendid shots you'll have!"

"Without counting," said another, "that you'll have the glory as well as the sport!"

"Gentlemen," replied the hunter, stammering with confusion, "I greatly—appreciate—your compliments—but they—don't—belong to me."

"You!" exclaimed every body, "don't you intend to go?"

"I am not going!"

"You won't accompany Dr. Ferguson?"

"Not only shall I not accompany him, but I am here so as to be present at the last moment to prevent his going."

Every eye was now turned to the doctor.

"Never mind him!" said the latter, calmly. "This is a matter that we can't argue with him. At heart he knows perfectly well that he *is* going."

"By Saint Andrew!" said Kennedy, "I swear—"

"Swear to nothing, friend Dick; you have been ganged and weighed— you and your powder, your guns, and your bullets; so don't let us say anything more about it."

And, in fact, from that day until the arrival at Zanzibar, Dick never opened his mouth. He talked neither about that nor about anything else. He kept absolutely silent.

Chapter 9

They Double the Cape.—The Forecastle.—A Course of
Cosmography by Professor Joe.—Concerning the Method
of Guiding Balloons.—How to Seek Out Atmospheric
Currents.—Eureka.

The Resolute plunged along rapidly toward the Cape of Good
Hope, the weather continuing fine, although the sea ran
heavier.

On the 30th of March, twenty-seven days after the departure from
London, the Table Mountain loomed up on the horizon. Cape City
lying at the foot of an amphitheatre of hills, could be distinguished
through the ship's glasses, and soon the Resolute cast anchor in the
port. But the captain touched there only to replenish his coal bunkers,
and that was but a day's job. On the morrow, he steered away to the
south'ard, so as to double the southernmost point of Africa, and enter
the Mozambique Channel.

This was not Joe's first sea-voyage, and so, for his part, he soon found
himself at home on board; every body liked him for his frankness and
good-humor. A considerable share of his master's renown was reflected
upon him. He was listened to as an oracle, and he made no more
mistakes than the next one.

So, while the doctor was pursuing his descriptive course of lecturing
in the officers' mess, Joe reigned supreme on the forecastle, holding
forth in his own peculiar manner, and making history to suit himself—a
style of procedure pursued, by the way, by the greatest historians of all
ages and nations.

The topic of discourse was, naturally, the aerial voyage. Joe had
experienced some trouble in getting the rebellious spirits to believe in it;
but, once accepted by them, nothing connected with it was any longer
an impossibility to the imaginations of the seamen stimulated by Joe's
harangues.

Our dazzling narrator persuaded his hearers that, after this trip,
many others still more wonderful would be undertaken. In fact, it was
to be but the first of a long series of superhuman expeditions.

"You see, my friends, when a man has had a taste of that kind of
travelling, he can't get along afterward with any other; so, on our next

expedition, instead of going off to one side, we'll go right ahead, going up, too, all the time."

"Humph! then you'll go to the moon!" said one of the crowd, with a stare of amazement.

"To the moon!" exclaimed Joe, "To the moon! pooh! that's too common. Every body might go to the moon, that way. Besides, there's no water there, and you have to carry such a lot of it along with you. Then you have to take air along in bottles, so as to breathe."

"Ay! ay! that's all right! But can a man get a drop of the real stuff there?" said a sailor who liked his toddy.

"Not a drop!" was Joe's answer. "No! old fellow, not in the moon. But we're going to skip round among those little twinklers up there—the stars—and the splendid planets that my old man so often talks about. For instance, we'll commence with Saturn—"

"That one with the ring?" asked the boatswain.

"Yes! the wedding-ring—only no one knows what's become of his wife!"

"What? will you go so high up as that?" said one of the ship-boys, gaping with wonder. "Why, your master must be Old Nick himself."

"Oh! no, he's too good for that."

"But, after Saturn—what then?" was the next inquiry of his impatient audience.

"After Saturn? Well, we'll visit Jupiter. A funny place that is, too, where the days are only nine hours and a half long—a good thing for the lazy fellows—and the years, would you believe it—last twelve of ours, which is fine for folks who have only six months to live. They get off a little longer by that."

"Twelve years!" exclaimed the boy.

"Yes, my youngster; so that in that country you'd be toddling after your mammy yet, and that old chap yonder, who looks about fifty, would only be a little shaver of four and a half."

"Blazes! that's a good 'un!" shouted the whole forecastle together.

"Solemn truth!" said Joe, stoutly.

"But what can you expect? When people will stay in this world, they learn nothing and keep as ignorant as bears. But just come along to Jupiter and you'll see. But they have to look out up there, for he's got satellites that are not just the easiest things to pass."

All the men laughed, but they more than half believed him. Then he went on to talk about Neptune, where seafaring men get a jovial reception, and Mars, where the military get the best of the sidewalk to such an extent that folks can hardly stand it. Finally, he drew them a heavenly picture of the delights of Venus.

"And when we get back from that expedition," said the indefatigable narrator, "they'll decorate us with the Southern Cross that shines up there in the Creator's button-hole."

"Ay, and you'd have well earned it!" said the sailors.

Thus passed the long evenings on the forecastle in merry chat, and during the same time the doctor went on with his instructive discourses.

One day the conversation turned upon the means of directing balloons, and the doctor was asked his opinion about it.

"I don't think," said he, "that we shall succeed in finding out a system of directing them. I am familiar with all the plans attempted and proposed, and not one has succeeded, not one is practicable. You may readily understand that I have occupied my mind with this subject, which was, necessarily, so interesting to me, but I have not been able to solve the problem with the appliances now known to mechanical science. We would have to discover a motive power of extraordinary force, and almost impossible lightness of machinery. And, even then, we could not resist atmospheric currents of any considerable strength. Until now, the effort has been rather to direct the car than the balloon, and that has been one great error."

"Still there are many points of resemblance between a balloon and a ship which is directed at will."

"Not at all," retorted the doctor, "there is little or no similarity between the two cases. Air is infinitely less dense than water, in which the ship is only half submerged, while the whole bulk of a balloon is plunged in the atmosphere, and remains motionless with reference to the element that surrounds it."

"You think, then, that aerostatic science has said its last word?"

"Not at all! not at all! But we must look for another point in the case, and if we cannot manage to guide our balloon, we must, at least, try to keep it in favorable aerial currents. In proportion as we ascend, the latter become much more uniform and flow more constantly in one direction. They are no longer disturbed by the mountains and valleys that traverse the surface of the globe, and these, you know, are the chief cause of the variations of the wind and the inequality of their force. Therefore, these zones having been once determined, the balloon will merely have to be placed in the currents best adapted to its destination."

"But then," continued Captain Bennet, "in order to reach them, you must keep constantly ascending or descending. That is the real difficulty, doctor."

"And why, my dear captain?"

"Let us understand one another. It would be a difficulty and an obstacle only for long journeys, and not for short aerial excursions."

"And why so, if you please?"

"Because you can ascend only by throwing out ballast; you can descend only after letting off gas, and by these processes your ballast and your gas are soon exhausted."

"My dear sir, that's the whole question. There is the only difficulty that science need now seek to overcome. The problem is not how to guide the balloon, but how to take it up and down without expending the gas which is its strength, its life-blood, its soul, if I may use the expression."

"You are right, my dear doctor; but this problem is not yet solved; this means has not yet been discovered."

"I beg your pardon, it *has* been discovered."

"By whom?"

"By me!"

"By you?"

"You may readily believe that otherwise I should not have risked this expedition across Africa in a balloon. In twenty-four hours I should have been without gas!"

"But you said nothing about that in England?"

"No! I did not want to have myself overhauled in public. I saw no use in that. I made my preparatory experiments in secret and was satisfied. I have no occasion, then, to learn any thing more from them."

"Well! doctor, would it be proper to ask what is your secret?"

"Here it is, gentlemen—the simplest thing in the world!"

The attention of his auditory was now directed to the doctor in the utmost degree as he quietly proceeded with his explanation.

Chapter 10

The attempt has often been made, gentlemen," said the doctor, "to rise and descend at will, without losing ballast or gas from the balloon. A French aeronaut, M. Meunier, tried to accomplish this by compressing air in an inner receptacle. A Belgian, Dr. Van Hecke, by means of wings and paddles, obtained a vertical power that would have sufficed in most cases, but the practical results secured from these experiments have been insignificant.

"I therefore resolved to go about the thing more directly; so, at the start, I dispensed with ballast altogether, excepting as a provision for cases of special emergency, such as the breakage of my apparatus, or the necessity of ascending very suddenly, so as to avoid unforeseen obstacles.

"My means of ascent and descent consist simply in dilating or contracting the gas that is in the balloon by the application of different temperatures, and here is the method of obtaining that result.

"You saw me bring on board with the car several cases or receptacles, the use of which you may not have understood. They are five in number.

"The first contains about twenty-five gallons of water, to which I add a few drops of sulphuric acid, so as to augment its capacity as a conductor of electricity, and then I decompose it by means of a powerful Buntzen battery. Water, as you know, consists of two parts of hydrogen to one of oxygen gas.

"The latter, through the action of the battery, passes at its positive pole into the second receptacle. A third receptacle, placed above the second one, and of double its capacity, receives the hydrogen passing into it by the negative pole.

"Stopcocks, of which one has an orifice twice the size of the other, communicate between these receptacles and a fourth one, which is called the mixture reservoir, since in it the two gases obtained by the decomposition of the water do really commingle. The capacity of this fourth tank is about forty-one cubic feet.

"On the upper part of this tank is a platinum tube provided with a stopcock.

"You will now readily understand, gentlemen, the apparatus that I have described to you is really a gas cylinder and blow-pipe for oxygen and hydrogen, the heat of which exceeds that of a forge fire.

"This much established, I proceed to the second part of my apparatus. From the lowest part of my balloon, which is hermetically closed, issue two tubes a little distance apart. The one starts among the upper layers of the hydrogen gas, the other amid the lower layers.

"These two pipes are provided at intervals with strong jointings of india-rubber, which enable them to move in harmony with the oscillations of the balloon.

"Both of them run down as far as the car, and lose themselves in an iron receptacle of cylindrical form, which is called the heat-tank. The latter is closed at its two ends by two strong plates of the same metal.

"The pipe running from the lower part of the balloon runs into this cylindrical receptacle through the lower plate; it penetrates the latter and then takes the form of a helicoidal or screw-shaped spiral, the rings of which, rising one over the other, occupy nearly the whole of the height of the tank. Before again issuing from it, this spiral runs into a small cone with a concave base, that is turned downward in the shape of a spherical cap.

"It is from the top of this cone that the second pipe issues, and it runs, as I have said, into the upper beds of the balloon.

"The spherical cap of the small cone is of platinum, so as not to melt by the action of the cylinder and blow-pipe, for the latter are placed upon the bottom of the iron tank in the midst of the helicoidal spiral, and the extremity of their flame will slightly touch the cap in question.

"You all know, gentlemen, what a calorifere, to heat apartments, is. You know how it acts. The air of the apartments is forced to pass through its pipes, and is then released with a heightened temperature. Well, what I have just described to you is nothing more nor less than a calorifere.

"In fact, what is it that takes place? The cylinder once lighted, the hydrogen in the spiral and in the concave cone becomes heated, and rapidly ascends through the pipe that leads to the upper part of the balloon. A vacuum is created below, and it attracts the gas in the lower parts; this becomes heated in its turn, and is continually replaced; thus, an extremely rapid current of gas is established in the pipes and in the spiral, which issues from the balloon and then returns to it, and is heated over again, incessantly.

"Now, the cases increase 1/480 of their volume for each degree of heat applied. If, then, I force the temperature 18 degrees, the hydrogen of the balloon will dilate 18/480 or 1614 cubic feet, and will, therefore, displace 1614 more cubic feet of air, which will increase its ascensional power by 160 pounds. This is equivalent to throwing out that weight of ballast. If I augment the temperature by 180 degrees, the gas will dilate 180/480 and will displace 16,740 cubic feet more, and its ascensional force will be augmented by 1,600 pounds.

"Thus, you see, gentlemen, that I can easily effect very considerable changes of equilibrium. The volume of the balloon has been calculated in such manner that, when half inflated, it displaces a weight of air exactly equal to that of the envelope containing the hydrogen gas, and of the car occupied by the passengers, and all its apparatus and accessories. At this point of inflation, it is in exact equilibrium with the air, and neither mounts nor descends.

"In order, then, to effect an ascent, I give the gas a temperature superior to the temperature of the surrounding air by means of my cylinder. By this excess of heat it obtains a larger distention, and inflates the balloon more. The latter, then, ascends in proportion as I heat the hydrogen.

"The descent, of course, is effected by lowering the heat of the cylinder, and letting the temperature abate. The ascent would be, usually, more rapid than the descent; but that is a fortunate circumstance, since it is of no importance to me to descend rapidly, while, on the other hand, it is by a very rapid ascent that I avoid obstacles. The real danger lurks below, and not above.

"Besides, as I have said, I have a certain quantity of ballast, which will enable me to ascend more rapidly still, when necessary. My valve, at the top of the balloon, is nothing more nor less than a safety-valve. The balloon always retains the same quantity of hydrogen, and the variations of temperature that I produce in the midst of this shut-up gas are, of themselves, sufficient to provide for all these ascending and descending movements.

"Now, gentlemen, as a practical detail, let me add this:

"The combustion of the hydrogen and of the oxygen at the point of the cylinder produces solely the vapor or steam of water. I have, therefore, provided the lower part of the cylindrical iron box with a scape-pipe, with a valve operating by means of a pressure of two atmospheres; consequently, so soon as this amount of pressure is attained, the steam escapes of itself.

"Here are the exact figures: 25 gallons of water, separated into its constituent elements, yield 200 pounds of oxygen and 25 pounds of hydrogen. This represents, at atmospheric tension, 1,800 cubic feet of the former and 3,780 cubic feet of the latter, or 5,670 cubic feet, in all, of the mixture. Hence, the stopcock of my cylinder, when fully open, expends 27 cubic feet per hour, with a flame at least six times as strong as that of the large lamps used for lighting streets. On an average, then, and in order to keep myself at a very moderate elevation, I should not burn more than nine cubic feet per hour, so that my twenty-five gallons of water represent six hundred and thirty-six hours of aerial navigation, or a little more than twenty-six days.

"Well, as I can descend when I please, to replenish my stock of water on the way, my trip might be indefinitely prolonged.

"Such, gentlemen, is my secret. It is simple, and, like most simple things, it cannot fail to succeed. The dilation and contraction of the gas in the balloon is my means of locomotion, which calls for neither cumbersome wings, nor any other mechanical motor. A calorifere to produce the changes of temperature, and a cylinder to generate the heat, are neither inconvenient nor heavy. I think, therefore, that I have combined all the elements of success."

Dr. Ferguson here terminated his discourse, and was most heartily applauded. There was not an objection to make to it; all had been foreseen and decided.

"However," said the captain, "the thing may prove dangerous."

"What matters that," replied the doctor, "provided that it be practicable?"

Chapter 11

THE ARRIVAL AT ZANZIBAR.—THE ENGLISH CONSUL.—ILL-WILL
OF THE INHABITANTS.—THE ISLAND OF KOUMBENI.—THE
RAIN-MAKERS.—INFLATION OF THE BALLOON.—DEPARTURE ON
THE 18TH OF APRIL.—THE LAST GOOD-BY.—THE VICTORIA.

An invariably favorable wind had accelerated the progress of the
Resolute toward the place of her destination. The navigation
of the Mozambique Channel was especially calm and pleasant. The
agreeable character of the trip by sea was regarded as a good omen
of the probable issue of the trip through the air. Every one looked
forward to the hour of arrival, and sought to give the last touch to the
doctor's preparations.

At length the vessel hove in sight of the town of Zanzibar, upon the
island of the same name, and, on the 15th of April, at 11 o'clock in the
morning, she anchored in the port.

The island of Zanzibar belongs to the Imaum of Muscat, an ally of
France and England, and is, undoubtedly, his finest settlement. The port
is frequented by a great many vessels from the neighboring countries.

The island is separated from the African coast only by a channel, the
greatest width of which is but thirty miles.

It has a large trade in gums, ivory, and, above all, in "ebony," for
Zanzibar is the great slave-market. Thither converges all the booty
captured in the battles which the chiefs of the interior are continually
fighting. This traffic extends along the whole eastern coast, and as far as
the Nile latitudes. Mr. G. Lejean even reports that he has seen it carried
on, openly, under the French flag.

Upon the arrival of the Resolute, the English consul at Zanzibar
came on board to offer his services to the doctor, of whose projects the
European newspapers had made him aware for a month past. But, up
to that moment, he had remained with the numerous phalanx of the
incredulous.

"I doubted," said he, holding out his hand to Dr. Ferguson, "but now
I doubt no longer."

He invited the doctor, Kennedy, and the faithful Joe, of course, to
his own dwelling. Through his courtesy, the doctor was enabled to have
knowledge of the various letters that he had received from Captain

Speke. The captain and his companions had suffered dreadfully from hunger and bad weather before reaching the Ugogo country. They could advance only with extreme difficulty, and did not expect to be able to communicate again for a long time.

"Those are perils and privations which we shall manage to avoid," said the doctor.

The baggage of the three travellers was conveyed to the consul's residence. Arrangements were made for disembarking the balloon upon the beach at Zanzibar. There was a convenient spot, near the signal-mast, close by an immense building, that would serve to shelter it from the east winds. This huge tower, resembling a tun standing on one end, beside which the famous Heidelberg tun would have seemed but a very ordinary barrel, served as a fortification, and on its platform were stationed Belootchees, armed with lances. These Belootchees are a kind of brawling, good-for-nothing Janizaries.

But, when about to land the balloon, the consul was informed that the population of the island would oppose their doing so by force. Nothing is so blind as fanatical passion. The news of the arrival of a Christian, who was to ascend into the air, was received with rage. The negroes, more exasperated than the Arabs, saw in this project an attack upon their religion. They took it into their heads that some mischief was meant to the sun and the moon. Now, these two luminaries are objects of veneration to the African tribes, and they determined to oppose so sacrilegious an enterprise.

The consul, informed of their intentions, conferred with Dr. Ferguson and Captain Bennet on the subject. The latter was unwilling to yield to threats, but his friend dissuaded him from any idea of violent retaliation.

"We shall certainly come out winners," he said. "Even the imaum's soldiers will lend us a hand, if we need it. But, my dear captain, an accident may happen in a moment, and it would require but one unlucky blow to do the balloon an irreparable injury, so that the trip would be totally defeated; therefore we must act with the greatest caution."

"But what are we to do? If we land on the coast of Africa, we shall encounter the same difficulties. What are we to do?"

"Nothing is more simple," replied the consul. "You observe those small islands outside of the port; land your balloon on one of them; surround it with a guard of sailors, and you will have no risk to run."

"Just the thing!" said the doctor, "and we shall be entirely at our ease in completing our preparations."

The captain yielded to these suggestions, and the Resolute was headed for the island of Koumbeni. During the morning of the 16th April, the balloon was placed in safety in the middle of a clearing in the great woods, with which the soil is studded.

Two masts, eighty feet in height, were raised at the same distance from each other. Blocks and tackle, placed at their extremities, afforded the means of elevating the balloon, by the aid of a transverse rope. It was then entirely uninflated. The interior balloon was fastened to the exterior one, in such manner as to be lifted up in the same way. To the lower end of each balloon were fixed the pipes that served to introduce the hydrogen gas.

The whole day, on the 17th, was spent in arranging the apparatus destined to produce the gas; it consisted of some thirty casks, in which the decomposition of water was effected by means of iron-filings and sulphuric acid placed together in a large quantity of the first-named fluid. The hydrogen passed into a huge central cask, after having been washed on the way, and thence into each balloon by the conduit-pipes. In this manner each of them received a certain accurately-ascertained quantity of gas. For this purpose, there had to be employed eighteen hundred and sixty-six pounds of sulphuric acid, sixteen thousand and fifty pounds of iron, and nine thousand one hundred and sixty-six gallons of water. This operation commenced on the following night, about three A.M., and lasted nearly eight hours. The next day, the balloon, covered with its network, undulated gracefully above its car, which was held to the ground by numerous sacks of earth. The inflating apparatus was put together with extreme care, and the pipes issuing from the balloon were securely fitted to the cylindrical case.

The anchors, the cordage, the instruments, the travelling-wraps, the awning, the provisions, and the arms, were put in the place assigned to them in the car. The supply of water was procured at Zanzibar. The two hundred pounds of ballast were distributed in fifty bags placed at the bottom of the car, but within arm's-reach.

These preparations were concluded about five o'clock in the evening, while sentinels kept close watch around the island, and the boats of the Resolute patrolled the channel.

The blacks continued to show their displeasure by grimaces and contortions. Their obi-men, or wizards, went up and down among the angry throngs, pouring fuel on the flame of their fanaticism; and some of the excited wretches, more furious and daring than the rest, attempted to get to the island by swimming, but they were easily driven off.

Thereupon the sorceries and incantations commenced; the "rain-makers," who pretend to have control over the clouds, invoked the storms and the "stone-showers," as the blacks call hail, to their aid. To compel them to do so, they plucked leaves of all the different trees that grow in that country, and boiled them over a slow fire, while, at the same time, a sheep was killed by thrusting a long needle into its heart. But, in spite of all their ceremonies, the sky remained clear and beautiful, and they profited nothing by their slaughtered sheep and their ugly grimaces.

The blacks then abandoned themselves to the most furious orgies, and got fearfully drunk on "tembo," a kind of ardent spirits drawn from the cocoa-nut tree, and an extremely heady sort of beer called "togwa." Their chants, which were destitute of all melody, but were sung in excellent time, continued until far into the night.

About six o'clock in the evening, the captain assembled the travellers and the officers of the ship at a farewell repast in his cabin. Kennedy, whom nobody ventured to question now, sat with his eyes riveted on Dr. Ferguson, murmuring indistinguishable words. In other respects, the dinner was a gloomy one. The approach of the final moment filled everybody with the most serious reflections. What had fate in store for these daring adventurers? Should they ever again find themselves in the midst of their friends, or seated at the domestic hearth? Were their travelling apparatus to fail, what would become of them, among those ferocious savage tribes, in regions that had never been explored, and in the midst of boundless deserts?

Such thoughts as these, which had been dim and vague until then, or but slightly regarded when they came up, returned upon their excited fancies with intense force at this parting moment. Dr. Ferguson, still cold and impassible, talked of this, that, and the other; but he strove in vain to overcome this infectious gloominess. He utterly failed.

As some demonstration against the personal safety of the doctor and his companions was feared, all three slept that night on board the Resolute. At six o'clock in the morning they left their cabin, and landed on the island of Koumbeni.

The balloon was swaying gently to and fro in the morning breeze; the sand-bags that had held it down were now replaced by some twenty strong-armed sailors, and Captain Bennet and his officers were present to witness the solemn departure of their friends.

At this moment Kennedy went right up to the doctor, grasped his hand, and said:

"Samuel, have you absolutely determined to go?"

"Solemnly determined, my dear Dick."

"I have done every thing that I could to prevent this expedition, have I not?"

"Every thing!"

"Well, then, my conscience is clear on that score, and I will go with you."

"I was sure you would!" said the doctor, betraying in his features swift traces of emotion.

At last the moment of final leave-taking arrived. The captain and his officers embraced their dauntless friends with great feeling, not excepting even Joe, who, worthy fellow, was as proud and happy as a prince. Every one in the party insisted upon having a final shake of the doctor's hand.

At nine o'clock the three travellers got into their car. The doctor lit the combustible in his cylinder and turned the flame so as to produce a rapid heat, and the balloon, which had rested on the ground in perfect equipoise, began to rise in a few minutes, so that the seamen had to slacken the ropes they held it by. The car then rose about twenty feet above their heads.

"My friends!" exclaimed the doctor, standing up between his two companions, and taking off his hat, "let us give our aerial ship a name that will bring her good luck! let us christen her Victoria!"

This speech was answered with stentorian cheers of "Huzza for the Queen! Huzza for Old England!"

At this moment the ascensional force of the balloon increased prodigiously, and Ferguson, Kennedy, and Joe, waved a last good-by to their friends.

"Let go all!" shouted the doctor, and at the word the Victoria shot rapidly up into the sky, while the four carronades on board the Resolute thundered forth a parting salute in her honor.

Chapter 12

CROSSING THE STRAIT.—THE MRIMA.—DICK'S REMARK AND JOE'S PROPOSITION.—A RECIPE FOR COFFEE-MAKING.—THE UZARAMO.—THE UNFORTUNATE MAIZAN.—MOUNT DATHUMI.—THE DOCTOR'S CARDS.—NIGHT UNDER A NOPAL.

The air was pure, the wind moderate, and the balloon ascended almost perpendicularly to a height of fifteen hundred feet, as indicated by a depression of two inches in the barometric column.

At this height a more decided current carried the balloon toward the southwest. What a magnificent spectacle was then outspread beneath the gaze of the travellers! The island of Zanzibar could be seen in its entire extent, marked out by its deeper color upon a vast planisphere; the fields had the appearance of patterns of different colors, and thick clumps of green indicated the groves and thickets.

The inhabitants of the island looked no larger than insects. The huzzaing and shouting were little by little lost in the distance, and only the discharge of the ship's guns could be heard in the concavity beneath the balloon, as the latter sped on its flight.

"How fine that is!" said Joe, breaking silence for the first time.

He got no reply. The doctor was busy observing the variations of the barometer and noting down the details of his ascent.

Kennedy looked on, and had not eyes enough to take in all that he saw.

The rays of the sun coming to the aid of the heating cylinder, the tension of the gas increased, and the Victoria attained the height of twenty-five hundred feet.

The Resolute looked like a mere cockle-shell, and the African coast could be distinctly seen in the west marked out by a fringe of foam.

"You don't talk?" said Joe, again.

"We are looking!" said the doctor, directing his spy-glass toward the mainland.

"For my part, I must talk!"

"As much as you please, Joe; talk as much as you like!"

And Joe went on alone with a tremendous volley of exclamations. The "ohs!" and the "ahs!" exploded one after the other, incessantly, from his lips.

During his passage over the sea the doctor deemed it best to keep at his present elevation. He could thus reconnoitre a greater stretch of the coast. The thermometer and the barometer, hanging up inside of the half-opened awning, were always within sight, and a second barometer suspended outside was to serve during the night watches.

At the end of about two hours the Victoria, driven along at a speed of a little more than eight miles, very visibly neared the coast of the mainland. The doctor, thereupon, determined to descend a little nearer to the ground. So he moderated the flame of his cylinder, and the balloon, in a few moments, had descended to an altitude only three hundred feet above the soil.

It was then found to be passing just over the Mrima country, the name of this part of the eastern coast of Africa. Dense borders of mango-trees protected its margin, and the ebb-tide disclosed to view their thick roots, chafed and gnawed by the teeth of the Indian Ocean. The sands which, at an earlier period, formed the coast-line, rounded away along the distant horizon, and Mount Nguru reared aloft its sharp summit in the northwest.

The Victoria passed near to a village which the doctor found marked upon his chart as Kaole. Its entire population had assembled in crowds, and were yelling with anger and fear, at the same time vainly directing their arrows against this monster of the air that swept along so majestically away above all their powerless fury.

The wind was setting to the southward, but the doctor felt no concern on that score, since it enabled him the better to follow the route traced by Captains Burton and Speke.

Kennedy had, at length, become as talkative as Joe, and the two kept up a continual interchange of admiring interjections and exclamations.

"Out upon stage-coaches!" said one.

"Steamers indeed!" said the other.

"Railroads! eh? rubbish!" put in Kennedy, "that you travel on, without seeing the country!"

"Balloons! they're the sort for me!" Joe would add. "Why, you don't feel yourself going, and Nature takes the trouble to spread herself out before one's eyes!"

"What a splendid sight! What a spectacle! What a delight! a dream in a hammock!"

"Suppose we take our breakfast?" was Joe's unpoetical change of tune, at last, for the keen, open air had mightily sharpened his appetite.

"Good idea, my boy!"

"Oh! it won't take us long to do the cooking—biscuit and potted meat?"

"And as much coffee as you like," said the doctor. "I give you leave to borrow a little heat from my cylinder. There's enough and to spare, for that matter, and so we shall avoid the risk of a conflagration."

"That would be a dreadful misfortune!" exclaimed Kennedy. "It's the same as a powder-magazine suspended over our heads."

"Not precisely," said Ferguson, "but still if the gas were to take fire it would burn up gradually, and we should settle down on the ground, which would be disagreeable; but never fear—our balloon is hermetically sealed."

"Let us eat a bite, then," replied Kennedy.

"Now, gentlemen," put in Joe, "while doing the same as you, I'm going to get you up a cup of coffee that I think you'll have something to say about."

"The fact is," added the doctor, "that Joe, along with a thousand other virtues, has a remarkable talent for the preparation of that delicious beverage: he compounds it of a mixture of various origin, but he never would reveal to me the ingredients."

"Well, master, since we are so far above-ground, I can tell you the secret. It is just to mix equal quantities of Mocha, of Bourbon coffee, and of Rio Nunez."

A few moments later, three steaming cups of coffee were served, and topped off a substantial breakfast, which was additionally seasoned by the jokes and repartees of the guests. Each one then resumed his post of observation.

The country over which they were passing was remarkable for its fertility. Narrow, winding paths plunged in beneath the overarching verdure. They swept along above cultivated fields of tobacco, maize, and barley, at full maturity, and here and there immense rice-fields, full of straight stalks and purple blossoms. They could distinguish sheep and goats too, confined in large cages, set up on piles to keep them out of reach of the leopards' fangs. Luxuriant vegetation spread in wild profuseness over this prodigal soil.

Village after village rang with yells of terror and astonishment at the sight of the Victoria, and Dr. Ferguson prudently kept her above the reach of the barbarian arrows. The savages below, thus baffled, ran together from their huddle of huts and followed the travellers with their vain imprecations while they remained in sight.

At noon, the doctor, upon consulting his map, calculated that they were passing over the Uzaramo* country. The soil was thickly studded with cocoa-nut, papaw, and cotton-wood trees, above which the balloon seemed to disport itself like a bird. Joe found this splendid vegetation a matter of course, seeing that they were in Africa. Kennedy descried some hares and quails that asked nothing better than to get a good shot from his fowling-piece, but it would have been powder wasted, since there was no time to pick up the game.

The aeronauts swept on with the speed of twelve miles per hour, and soon were passing in thirty-eight degrees twenty minutes east longitude, over the village of Tounda.

"It was there," said the doctor, "that Burton and Speke were seized with violent fevers, and for a moment thought their expedition ruined. And yet they were only a short distance from the coast, but fatigue and privation were beginning to tell upon them severely."

In fact, there is a perpetual malaria reigning throughout the country in question. Even the doctor could hope to escape its effects only by rising above the range of the miasma that exhales from this damp region whence the blazing rays of the sun pump up its poisonous vapors. Once in a while they could descry a caravan resting in a "kraal," awaiting the freshness and cool of the evening to resume its route. These kraals are wide patches of cleared land, surrounded by hedges and jungles, where traders take shelter against not only the wild beasts, but also the robber tribes of the country. They could see the natives running and scattering in all directions at the sight of the Victoria. Kennedy was keen to get a closer look at them, but the doctor invariably held out against the idea.

"The chiefs are armed with muskets," he said, "and our balloon would be too conspicuous a mark for their bullets."

"Would a bullet-hole bring us down?" asked Joe.

"Not immediately; but such a hole would soon become a large torn orifice through which our gas would escape."

"Then, let us keep at a respectful distance from yon miscreants. What must they think as they see us sailing in the air? I'm sure they must feel like worshipping us!"

"Let them worship away, then," replied the doctor, "but at a distance. There is no harm done in getting as far away from them as possible. See! the country is already changing its aspect: the villages are fewer and farther

---

* U and Ou signify country in the language of that region.

between; the mango-trees have disappeared, for their growth ceases at this latitude. The soil is becoming hilly and portends mountains not far off."

"Yes," said Kennedy, "it seems to me that I can see some high land on this side."

"In the west—those are the nearest ranges of the Ourizara—Mount Duthumi, no doubt, behind which I hope to find shelter for the night. I'll stir up the heat in the cylinder a little, for we must keep at an elevation of five or six hundred feet."

"That was a grant idea of yours, sir," said Joe. "It's mighty easy to manage it; you turn a cock, and the thing's done."

"Ah! here we are more at our ease," said the sportsman, as the balloon ascended; "the reflection of the sun on those red sands was getting to be insupportable."

"What splendid trees!" cried Joe. "They're quite natural, but they are very fine! Why a dozen of them would make a forest!"

"Those are baobabs," replied Dr. Ferguson. "See, there's one with a trunk fully one hundred feet in circumference. It was, perhaps, at the foot of that very tree that Maizan, the French traveller, expired in 1845, for we are over the village of Deje-la-Mhora, to which he pushed on alone. He was seized by the chief of this region, fastened to the foot of a baobab, and the ferocious black then severed all his joints while the war-song of his tribe was chanted; he then made a gash in the prisoner's neck, stopped to sharpen his knife, and fairly tore away the poor wretch's head before it had been cut from the body. The unfortunate Frenchman was but twenty-six years of age."

"And France has never avenged so hideous a crime?" said Kennedy.

"France did demand satisfaction, and the Said of Zanzibar did all in his power to capture the murderer, but in vain."

"I move that we don't stop here!" urged Joe; "let us go up, master, let us go up higher by all means."

"All the more willingly, Joe, that there is Mount Duthumi right ahead of us. If my calculations be right we shall have passed it before seven o'clock in the evening."

"Shall we not travel at night?" asked the Scotchman.

"No, as little as possible. With care and vigilance we might do so safely, but it is not enough to sweep across Africa. We want to see it."

"Up to this time we have nothing to complain of, master. The best cultivated and most fertile country in the world instead of a desert! Believe the geographers after that!"

"Let us wait, Joe! we shall see by-and-by."

About half-past six in the evening the Victoria was directly opposite Mount Duthumi; in order to pass, it had to ascend to a height of more than three thousand feet, and to accomplish that the doctor had only to raise the temperature of his gas eighteen degrees. It might have been correctly said that he held his balloon in his hand. Kennedy had only to indicate to him the obstacles to be surmounted, and the Victoria sped through the air, skimming the summits of the range.

At eight o'clock it descended the farther slope, the acclivity of which was much less abrupt. The anchors were thrown out from the car and one of them, coming in contact with the branches of an enormous nopal, caught on it firmly. Joe at once let himself slide down the rope and secured it. The silk ladder was then lowered to him and he remounted to the car with agility. The balloon now remained perfectly at rest sheltered from the eastern winds.

The evening meal was got ready, and the aeronauts, excited by their day's journey, made a heavy onslaught upon the provisions.

"What distance have we traversed to-day?" asked Kennedy, disposing of some alarming mouthfuls.

The doctor took his bearings, by means of lunar observations, and consulted the excellent map that he had with him for his guidance. It belonged to the Atlas of "Der Neuester Endeckungen in Afrika" ("The Latest Discoveries in Africa"), published at Gotha by his learned friend Dr. Petermann, and by that savant sent to him. This Atlas was to serve the doctor on his whole journey; for it contained the itinerary of Burton and Speke to the great lakes; the Soudan, according to Dr. Barth; the Lower Senegal, according to Guillaume Lejean; and the Delta of the Niger, by Dr. Blaikie.

Ferguson had also provided himself with a work which combined in one compilation all the notions already acquired concerning the Nile. It was entitled "The Sources of the Nile; being a General Survey of the Basin of that River and of its Head-Stream, with the History of the Nilotic Discovery, by Charles Beke, D.D."

He also had the excellent charts published in the "Bulletins of the Geographical Society of London;" and not a single point of the countries already discovered could, therefore, escape his notice.

Upon tracing on his maps, he found that his latitudinal route had been two degrees, or one hundred and twenty miles, to the westward.

Kennedy remarked that the route tended toward the south; but this direction was satisfactory to the doctor, who desired to reconnoitre the tracks of his predecessors as much as possible. It was agreed that the night should be divided into three watches, so that each of the party should take his turn in watching over the safety of the rest. The doctor took the watch commencing at nine o'clock; Kennedy, the one commencing at midnight; and Joe, the three o'clock morning watch.

So Kennedy and Joe, well wrapped in their blankets, stretched themselves at full length under the awning, and slept quietly; while Dr. Ferguson kept on the lookout.

Chapter 13

CHANGE OF WEATHER.—KENNEDY HAS THE FEVER.—THE DOCTOR'S
MEDICINE.—TRAVELS ON LAND.—THE BASIN OF IMENGE.—MOUNT
RUBEHO.—SIX THOUSAND FEET ELEVATION.—
A HALT IN THE DAYTIME.

The night was calm. However, on Saturday morning, Kennedy, as he awoke, complained of lassitude and feverish chills. The weather was changing. The sky, covered with clouds, seemed to be laying in supplies for a fresh deluge. A gloomy region is that Zungomoro country, where it rains continually, excepting, perhaps, for a couple of weeks in the month of January.

A violent shower was not long in drenching our travellers. Below them, the roads, intersected by "nullahs," a sort of instantaneous torrent, were soon rendered impracticable, entangled as they were, besides, with thorny thickets and gigantic lianas, or creeping vines. The sulphuretted hydrogen emanations, which Captain Burton mentions, could be distinctly smelt.

"According to his statement, and I think he's right," said the doctor, "one could readily believe that there is a corpse hidden behind every thicket."

"An ugly country this!" sighed Joe; "and it seems to me that Mr. Kennedy is none the better for having passed the night in it."

"To tell the truth, I have quite a high fever," said the sportsman.

"There's nothing remarkable about that, my dear Dick, for we are in one of the most unhealthy regions in Africa; but we shall not remain here long; so let's be off."

Thanks to a skilful manoeuvre achieved by Joe, the anchor was disengaged, and Joe reascended to the car by means of the ladder. The doctor vigorously dilated the gas, and the Victoria resumed her flight, driven along by a spanking breeze.

Only a few scattered huts could be seen through the pestilential mists; but the appearance of the country soon changed, for it often happens in Africa that some of the unhealthiest districts lie close beside others that are perfectly salubrious.

Kennedy was visibly suffering, and the fever was mastering his vigorous constitution.

"It won't do to fall ill, though," he grumbled; and so saying, he wrapped himself in a blanket, and lay down under the awning.

"A little patience, Dick, and you'll soon get over this," said the doctor.

"Get over it! Egad, Samuel, if you've any drug in your travelling-chest that will set me on my feet again, bring it without delay. I'll swallow it with my eyes shut!"

"Oh, I can do better than that, friend Dick; for I can give you a febrifuge that won't cost any thing."

"And how will you do that?"

"Very easily. I am simply going to take you up above these clouds that are now deluging us, and remove you from this pestilential atmosphere. I ask for only ten minutes, in order to dilate the hydrogen."

The ten minutes had scarcely elapsed ere the travellers were beyond the rainy belt of country.

"Wait a little, now, Dick, and you'll begin to feel the effect of pure air and sunshine."

"There's a cure for you!" said Joe; "why, it's wonderful!"

"No, it's merely natural."

"Oh! natural; yes, no doubt of that!"

"I bring Dick into good air, as the doctors do, every day, in Europe, or, as I would send a patient at Martinique to the Pitons, a lofty mountain on that island, to get clear of the yellow fever."

"Ah! by Jove, this balloon is a paradise!" exclaimed Kennedy, feeling much better already.

"It leads to it, anyhow!" replied Joe, quite gravely.

It was a curious spectacle—that mass of clouds piled up, at the moment, away below them! The vapors rolled over each other, and mingled together in confused masses of superb brilliance, as they reflected the rays of the sun. The Victoria had attained an altitude of four thousand feet, and the thermometer indicated a certain diminution of temperature. The land below could no longer be seen. Fifty miles away to the westward, Mount Rubeho raised its sparkling crest, marking the limit of the Ugogo country in east longitude thirty-six degrees twenty minutes. The wind was blowing at the rate of twenty miles an hour, but the aeronauts felt nothing of this increased speed. They observed no jar, and had scarcely any sense of motion at all.

Three hours later, the doctor's prediction was fully verified. Kennedy no longer felt a single shiver of the fever, but partook of some breakfast with an excellent appetite.

"That beats sulphate of quinine!" said the energetic Scot, with hearty emphasis and much satisfaction.

"Positively," said Joe, "this is where I'll have to retire to when I get old!"

About ten o'clock in the morning the atmosphere cleared up, the clouds parted, and the country beneath could again be seen, the Victoria meanwhile rapidly descending. Dr. Ferguson was in search of a current that would carry him more to the northeast, and he found it about six hundred feet from the ground. The country was becoming more broken, and even mountainous. The Zungomoro district was fading out of sight in the east with the last cocoa-nut-trees of that latitude.

Ere long, the crests of a mountain-range assumed a more decided prominence. A few peaks rose here and there, and it became necessary to keep a sharp lookout for the pointed cones that seemed to spring up every moment.

"We're right among the breakers!" said Kennedy.

"Keep cool, Dick. We shan't touch them," was the doctor's quiet answer.

"It's a jolly way to travel, anyhow!" said Joe, with his usual flow of spirits.

In fact, the doctor managed his balloon with wondrous dexterity.

"Now, if we had been compelled to go afoot over that drenched soil," said he, "we should still be dragging along in a pestilential mire. Since our departure from Zanzibar, half our beasts of burden would have died with fatigue. We should be looking like ghosts ourselves, and despair would be seizing on our hearts. We should be in continual squabbles with our guides and porters, and completely exposed to their unbridled brutality. During the daytime, a damp, penetrating, unendurable humidity! At night, a cold frequently intolerable, and the stings of a kind of fly whose bite pierces the thickest cloth, and drives the victim crazy! All this, too, without saying any thing about wild beasts and ferocious native tribes!"

"I move that we don't try it!" said Joe, in his droll way.

"I exaggerate nothing," continued Ferguson, "for, upon reading the narratives of such travellers as have had the hardihood to venture into these regions, your eyes would fill with tears."

About eleven o'clock they were passing over the basin of Imenge, and the tribes scattered over the adjacent hills were impotently menacing the Victoria with their weapons. Finally, she sped along as far as the last undulations of the country which precede Rubeho. These form the last and loftiest chain of the mountains of Usagara.

The aeronauts took careful and complete note of the orographic conformation of the country. The three ramifications mentioned, of which the Duthumi forms the first link, are separated by immense longitudinal plains. These elevated summits consist of rounded cones, between which the soil is bestrewn with erratic blocks of stone and gravelly bowlders. The most abrupt declivity of these mountains confronts the Zanzibar coast, but the western slopes are merely inclined planes. The depressions in the soil are covered with a black, rich loam, on which there is a vigorous vegetation. Various water-courses filter through, toward the east, and work their way onward to flow into the Kingani, in the midst of gigantic clumps of sycamore, tamarind, calabash, and palmyra trees.

"Attention!" said Dr. Ferguson. "We are approaching Rubeho, the name of which signifies, in the language of the country, the 'Passage of the Winds,' and we would do well to double its jagged pinnacles at a certain height. If my chart be exact, we are going to ascend to an elevation of five thousand feet."

"Shall we often have occasion to reach those far upper belts of the atmosphere?"

"Very seldom: the height of the African mountains appears to be quite moderate compared with that of the European and Asiatic ranges; but, in any case, our good Victoria will find no difficulty in passing over them."

In a very little while, the gas expanded under the action of the heat, and the balloon took a very decided ascensional movement. Besides, the dilation of the hydrogen involved no danger, and only three-fourths of the vast capacity of the balloon was filled when the barometer, by a depression of eight inches, announced an elevation of six thousand feet.

"Shall we go this high very long?" asked Joe.

"The atmosphere of the earth has a height of six thousand fathoms," said the doctor; "and, with a very large balloon, one might go far. That is what Messrs. Brioschi and Gay-Lussac did; but then the blood burst from their mouths and ears. Respirable air was wanting. Some years ago, two fearless Frenchmen, Messrs. Barral and Bixio, also ventured into the very lofty regions; but their balloon burst—"

"And they fell?" asked Kennedy, abruptly.

"Certainly they did; but as learned men should always fall—namely, without hurting themselves."

"Well, gentlemen," said Joe, "you may try their fall over again, if you like; but, as for me, who am but a dolt, I prefer keeping at the medium height—neither too far up, nor too low down. It won't do to be too ambitious."

At the height of six thousand feet, the density of the atmosphere has already greatly diminished; sound is conveyed with difficulty, and the voice is not so easily heard. The view of objects becomes confused; the gaze no longer takes in any but large, quite ill-distinguishable masses; men and animals on the surface become absolutely invisible; the roads and rivers get to look like threads, and the lakes dwindle to ponds.

The doctor and his friends felt themselves in a very anomalous condition; an atmospheric current of extreme velocity was bearing them away beyond arid mountains, upon whose summits vast fields of snow surprised the gaze; while their convulsed appearance told of Titanic travail in the earliest epoch of the world's existence.

The sun shone at the zenith, and his rays fell perpendicularly upon those lonely summits. The doctor took an accurate design of these mountains, which form four distinct ridges almost in a straight line, the northernmost being the longest.

The Victoria soon descended the slope opposite to the Rubeho, skirting an acclivity covered with woods, and dotted with trees of very deep-green foliage. Then came crests and ravines, in a sort of desert which preceded the Ugogo country; and lower down were yellow plains, parched and fissured by the intense heat, and, here and there, bestrewn with saline plants and brambly thickets.

Some underbrush, which, farther on, became forests, embellished the horizon. The doctor went nearer to the ground; the anchors were thrown out, and one of them soon caught in the boughs of a huge sycamore.

Joe, slipping nimbly down the tree, carefully attached the anchor, and the doctor left his cylinder at work to a certain degree in order to retain sufficient ascensional force in the balloon to keep it in the air. Meanwhile the wind had suddenly died away.

"Now," said Ferguson, "take two guns, friend Dick—one for yourself and one for Joe—and both of you try to bring back some nice cuts of antelope-meat; they will make us a good dinner."

"Off to the hunt!" exclaimed Kennedy, joyously.

He climbed briskly out of the car and descended. Joe had swung himself down from branch to branch, and was waiting for him below, stretching his limbs in the mean time.

"Don't fly away without us, doctor!" shouted Joe.

"Never fear, my boy!—I am securely lashed. I'll spend the time getting my notes into shape. A good hunt to you! but be careful. Besides, from my post here, I can observe the face of the country, and, at the least suspicious thing I notice, I'll fire a signal-shot, and with that you must rally home."

"Agreed!" said Kennedy; and off they went.

Chapter 14

The country, dry and parched as it was, consisting of a clayey soil that cracked open with the heat, seemed, indeed, a desert: here and there were a few traces of caravans; the bones of men and animals, that had been half-gnawed away, mouldering together in the same dust.

After half an hour's walking, Dick and Joe plunged into a forest of gum-trees, their eyes alert on all sides, and their fingers on the trigger. There was no foreseeing what they might encounter. Without being a rifleman, Joe could handle fire-arms with no trifling dexterity.

"A walk does one good, Mr. Kennedy, but this isn't the easiest ground in the world," he said, kicking aside some fragments of quartz with which the soil was bestrewn.

Kennedy motioned to his companion to be silent and to halt. The present case compelled them to dispense with hunting-dogs, and, no matter what Joe's agility might be, he could not be expected to have the scent of a setter or a greyhound.

A herd of a dozen antelopes were quenching their thirst in the bed of a torrent where some pools of water had lodged. The graceful creatures, snuffing danger in the breeze, seemed to be disturbed and uneasy. Their beautiful heads could be seen between every draught, raised in the air with quick and sudden motion as they sniffed the wind in the direction of our two hunters, with their flexible nostrils.

Kennedy stole around behind some clumps of shrubbery, while Joe remained motionless where he was. The former, at length, got within gunshot and fired.

The herd disappeared in the twinkling of an eye; one male antelope only, that was hit just behind the shoulder-joint, fell headlong to the ground, and Kennedy leaped toward his booty.

It was a blauwbok, a superb animal of a pale-bluish color shading upon the gray, but with the belly and the inside of the legs as white as the driven snow.

"A splendid shot!" exclaimed the hunter. "It's a very rare species of the antelope, and I hope to be able to prepare his skin in such a way as to keep it."

"Indeed!" said Joe, "do you think of doing that, Mr. Kennedy?"

"Why, certainly I do! Just see what a fine hide it is!"

"But Dr. Ferguson will never allow us to take such an extra weight!"

"You're right, Joe. Still it is a pity to have to leave such a noble animal."

"The whole of it? Oh, we won't do that, sir; we'll take all the good eatable parts of it, and, if you'll let me, I'll cut him up just as well as the chairman of the honorable corporation of butchers of the city of London could do."

"As you please, my boy! But you know that in my hunter's way I can just as easily skin and cut up a piece of game as kill it."

"I'm sure of that, Mr. Kennedy. Well, then, you can build a fireplace with a few stones; there's plenty of dry dead-wood, and I can make the hot coals tell in a few minutes."

"Oh! that won't take long," said Kennedy, going to work on the fireplace, where he had a brisk flame crackling and sparkling in a minute or two.

Joe had cut some of the nicest steaks and the best parts of the tenderloin from the carcass of the antelope, and these were quickly transformed to the most savory of broils.

"There, those will tickle the doctor!" said Kennedy.

"Do you know what I was thinking about?" said Joe.

"Why, about the steaks you're broiling, to be sure!" replied Dick.

"Not the least in the world. I was thinking what a figure we'd cut if we couldn't find the balloon again."

"By George, what an idea! Why, do you think the doctor would desert us?"

"No; but suppose his anchor were to slip!"

"Impossible! and, besides, the doctor would find no difficulty in coming down again with his balloon; he handles it at his ease."

"But suppose the wind were to sweep it off, so that he couldn't come back toward us?"

"Come, come, Joe! a truce to your suppositions; they're any thing but pleasant."

"Ah! sir, every thing that happens in this world is natural, of course; but, then, any thing may happen, and we ought to look out beforehand."

At this moment the report of a gun rang out upon the air.

"What's that?" exclaimed Joe.

"It's my rifle, I know the ring of her!" said Kennedy.

"A signal!"

"Yes; danger for us!"

"For him, too, perhaps."

"Let's be off!"

And the hunters, having gathered up the product of their expedition, rapidly made their way back along the path that they had marked by breaking boughs and bushes when they came. The density of the underbrush prevented their seeing the balloon, although they could not be far from it.

A second shot was heard.

"We must hurry!" said Joe.

"There! a third report!"

"Why, it sounds to me as if he was defending himself against something."

"Let us make haste!"

They now began to run at the top of their speed. When they reached the outskirts of the forest, they, at first glance, saw the balloon in its place and the doctor in the car.

"What's the matter?" shouted Kennedy.

"Good God!" suddenly exclaimed Joe.

"What do you see?"

"Down there! look! a crowd of blacks surrounding the balloon!"

And, in fact, there, two miles from where they were, they saw some thirty wild natives close together, yelling, gesticulating, and cutting all kinds of antics at the foot of the sycamore. Some, climbing into the tree itself, were making their way to the topmost branches. The danger seemed pressing.

"My master is lost!" cried Joe.

"Come! a little more coolness, Joe, and let us see how we stand. We hold the lives of four of those villains in our hands. Forward, then!"

They had made a mile with headlong speed, when another report was heard from the car. The shot had, evidently, told upon a huge black demon, who had been hoisting himself up by the anchor-rope. A lifeless body fell from bough to bough, and hung about twenty feet from the ground, its arms and legs swaying to and fro in the air.

"Ha!" said Joe, halting, "what does that fellow hold by?"

"No matter what!" said Kennedy; "let us run! let us run!"

"Ah! Mr. Kennedy," said Joe, again, in a roar of laughter, "by his tail! by his tail! it's an ape! They're all apes!"

"Well, they're worse than men!" said Kennedy, as he dashed into the midst of the howling crowd.

It was, indeed, a troop of very formidable baboons of the dog-faced species. These creatures are brutal, ferocious, and horrible to look upon, with their dog-like muzzles and savage expression. However, a few shots scattered them, and the chattering horde scampered off, leaving several of their number on the ground.

In a moment Kennedy was on the ladder, and Joe, clambering up the branches, detached the anchor; the car then dipped to where he was, and he got into it without difficulty. A few minutes later, the Victoria slowly ascended and soared away to the eastward, wafted by a moderate wind.

"That was an attack for you!" said Joe.

"We thought you were surrounded by natives."

"Well, fortunately, they were only apes," said the doctor.

"At a distance there's no great difference," remarked Kennedy.

"Nor close at hand, either," added Joe.

"Well, however that may be," resumed Ferguson, "this attack of apes might have had the most serious consequences. Had the anchor yielded to their repeated efforts, who knows whither the wind would have carried me?"

"What did I tell you, Mr. Kennedy?"

"You were right, Joe; but, even right as you may have been, you were, at that moment, preparing some antelope-steaks, the very sight of which gave me a monstrous appetite."

"I believe you!" said the doctor; "the flesh of the antelope is exquisite."

"You may judge of that yourself, now, sir, for supper's ready."

"Upon my word as a sportsman, those venison-steaks have a gamy flavor that's not to be sneezed at, I tell you."

"Good!" said Joe, with his mouth full, "I could live on antelope all the days of my life; and all the better with a glass of grog to wash it down."

So saying, the good fellow went to work to prepare a jorum of that fragrant beverage, and all hands tasted it with satisfaction.

"Every thing has gone well thus far," said he.

"Very well indeed!" assented Kennedy.

"Come, now, Mr. Kennedy, are you sorry that you came with us?"

"I'd like to see anybody prevent my coming!"

It was now four o'clock in the afternoon. The Victoria had struck a more rapid current. The face of the country was gradually rising, and, ere long, the barometer indicated a height of fifteen hundred feet above the level of the sea. The doctor was, therefore, obliged to keep his balloon up by a quite considerable dilation of gas, and the cylinder was hard at work all the time.

Toward seven o'clock, the balloon was sailing over the basin of Kanyeme. The doctor immediately recognized that immense clearing, ten miles in extent, with its villages buried in the midst of baobab and calabash trees. It is the residence of one of the sultans of the Ugogo country, where civilization is, perhaps, the least backward. The natives there are less addicted to selling members of their own families, but still, men and animals all live together in round huts, without frames, that look like haystacks.

Beyond Kanyeme the soil becomes arid and stony, but in an hour's journey, in a fertile dip of the soil, vegetation had resumed all its vigor at some distance from Mdaburu. The wind fell with the close of the day, and the atmosphere seemed to sleep. The doctor vainly sought for a current of air at different heights, and, at last, seeing this calm of all nature, he resolved to pass the night afloat, and, for greater safety, rose to the height of one thousand feet, where the balloon remained motionless. The night was magnificent, the heavens glittering with stars, and profoundly silent in the upper air.

Dick and Joe stretched themselves on their peaceful couch, and were soon sound asleep, the doctor keeping the first watch. At twelve o'clock the latter was relieved by Kennedy.

"Should the slightest accident happen, waken me," said Ferguson, "and, above all things, don't lose sight of the barometer. To us it is the compass!"

The night was cold. There were twenty-seven degrees of difference between its temperature and that of the daytime. With nightfall had begun the nocturnal concert of animals driven from their hiding-places by hunger and thirst. The frogs struck in their guttural soprano, redoubled by the yelping of the jackals, while the imposing bass of the African lion sustained the accords of this living orchestra.

Upon resuming his post, in the morning, the doctor consulted his compass, and found that the wind had changed during the night. The balloon had been bearing about thirty miles to the northwest during the last two hours. It was then passing over Mabunguru, a stony country, strewn with blocks of syenite of a fine polish, and knobbed with huge bowlders and angular ridges of rock; conic masses, like the rocks of Karnak, studded the soil like so many Druidic dolmens; the bones of buffaloes and elephants whitened it here and there; but few trees could be seen, excepting in the east, where there were dense woods, among which a few villages lay half concealed.

Toward seven o'clock they saw a huge round rock nearly two miles in extent, like an immense tortoise.

"We are on the right track," said Dr. Ferguson. "There's Jihoue-la-Mkoa, where we must halt for a few minutes. I am going to renew the supply of water necessary for my cylinder, and so let us try to anchor somewhere."

"There are very few trees," replied the hunter.

"Never mind, let us try. Joe, throw out the anchors!"

The balloon, gradually losing its ascensional force, approached the ground; the anchors ran along until, at last, one of them caught in the fissure of a rock, and the balloon remained motionless.

It must not be supposed that the doctor could entirely extinguish his cylinder, during these halts. The equilibrium of the balloon had been calculated at the level of the sea; and, as the country was continually ascending, and had reached an elevation of from six to seven hundred feet, the balloon would have had a tendency to go lower than the surface of the soil itself. It was, therefore, necessary to sustain it by a certain dilation of the gas. But, in case the doctor, in the absence of all wind, had let the car rest upon the ground, the balloon, thus relieved of a considerable weight, would have kept up of itself, without the aid of the cylinder.

The maps indicated extensive ponds on the western slope of the Jihoue-la-Mkoa. Joe went thither alone with a cask that would hold about ten gallons. He found the place pointed out to him, without difficulty, near to a deserted village; got his stock of water, and returned in less than three-quarters of an hour. He had seen nothing particular excepting some immense elephant-pits. In fact, he came very near falling into one of them, at the bottom of which lay a half-eaten carcass.

He brought back with him a sort of clover which the apes eat with avidity. The doctor recognized the fruit of the "mbenbu"—tree which grows in profusion, on the western part of Jihoue-la-Mkoa. Ferguson waited for Joe with a certain feeling of impatience, for even a short halt in this inhospitable region always inspires a degree of fear.

The water was got aboard without trouble, as the car was nearly resting on the ground. Joe then found it easy to loosen the anchor and leaped lightly to his place beside the doctor. The latter then replenished the flame in the cylinder, and the balloon majestically soared into the air.

It was then about one hundred miles from Kazeh, an important establishment in the interior of Africa, where, thanks to a south-southeasterly current, the travellers might hope to arrive on that same day. They were moving at the rate of fourteen miles per hour, and the guidance of the balloon was becoming difficult, as they dared not rise very high without extreme dilation of the gas, the country itself being at an average height of three thousand feet. Hence, the doctor preferred not to force the dilation, and so adroitly followed the sinuosities of a pretty sharply-inclined plane, and swept very close to the villages of Thembo and Tura-Wels. The latter forms part of the Unyamwezy, a magnificent country, where the trees attain enormous dimensions; among them the cactus, which grows to gigantic size.

About two o'clock, in magnificent weather, but under a fiery sun that devoured the least breath of air, the balloon was floating over the town of Kazeh, situated about three hundred and fifty miles from the coast.

"We left Zanzibar at nine o'clock in the morning," said the doctor, consulting his notes, "and, after two days' passage, we have, including our deviations, travelled nearly five hundred geographical miles. Captains Burton and Speke took four months and a half to make the same distance!"

Chapter 15

Kazeh, an important point in Central Africa, is not a city; in truth, there are no cities in the interior. Kazeh is but a collection of six extensive excavations. There are enclosed a few houses and slave-huts, with little courtyards and small gardens, carefully cultivated with onions, potatoes, cucumbers, pumpkins, and mushrooms, of perfect flavor, growing most luxuriantly.

The Unyamwezy is the country of the Moon—above all the rest, the fertile and magnificent garden-spot of Africa. In its centre is the district of Unyanembe—a delicious region, where some families of Omani, who are of very pure Arabic origin, live in luxurious idleness.

They have, for a long period, held the commerce between the interior of Africa and Arabia: they trade in gums, ivory, fine muslin, and slaves. Their caravans traverse these equatorial regions on all sides; and they even make their way to the coast in search of those articles of luxury and enjoyment which the wealthy merchants covet; while the latter, surrounded by their wives and their attendants, lead in this charming country the least disturbed and most horizontal of lives—always stretched at full length, laughing, smoking, or sleeping.

Around these excavations are numerous native dwellings; wide, open spaces for the markets; fields of cannabis and datura; superb trees and depths of freshest shade—such is Kazeh!

There, too, is held the general rendezvous of the caravans—those of the south, with their slaves and their freightage of ivory; and those of the west, which export cotton, glassware, and trinkets, to the tribes of the great lakes.

So in the market-place there reigns perpetual excitement, a nameless hubbub, made up of the cries of mixed-breed porters and carriers, the beating of drums, and the twanging of horns, the neighing of mules, the braying of donkeys, the singing of women, the squalling of children, and the banging of the huge rattan, wielded by the jemadar or leader of the caravans, who beats time to this pastoral symphony.

There, spread forth, without regard to order—indeed, we may say, in charming disorder—are the showy stuffs, the glass beads, the ivory tusks, the rhinoceros'-teeth, the shark's-teeth, the honey, the tobacco, and the cotton of these regions, to be purchased at the strangest of bargains by customers in whose eyes each article has a price only in proportion to the desire it excites to possess it.

All at once this agitation, movement and noise stopped as though by magic. The balloon had just come in sight, far aloft in the sky, where it hovered majestically for a few moments, and then descended slowly, without deviating from its perpendicular. Men, women, children, merchants and slaves, Arabs and negroes, as suddenly disappeared within the "tembes" and the huts.

"My dear doctor," said Kennedy, "if we continue to produce such a sensation as this, we shall find some difficulty in establishing commercial relations with the people hereabouts."

"There's one kind of trade that we might carry on, though, easily enough," said Joe; "and that would be to go down there quietly, and walk off with the best of the goods, without troubling our heads about the merchants; we'd get rich that way!"

"Ah!" said the doctor, "these natives are a little scared at first; but they won't be long in coming back, either through suspicion or through curiosity."

"Do you really think so, doctor?"

"Well, we'll see pretty soon. But it wouldn't be prudent to go too near to them, for the balloon is not iron-clad, and is, therefore, not proof against either an arrow or a bullet."

"Then you expect to hold a parley with these blacks?"

"If we can do so safely, why should we not? There must be some Arab merchants here at Kazeh, who are better informed than the rest, and not so barbarous. I remember that Burton and Speke had nothing but praises to utter concerning the hospitality of these people; so we might, at least, make the venture."

The balloon having, meanwhile, gradually approached the ground, one of the anchors lodged in the top of a tree near the market-place.

By this time the whole population had emerged from their hiding-places stealthily, thrusting their heads out first. Several "waganga," recognizable by their badges of conical shellwork, came boldly forward. They were the sorcerers of the place. They bore in their girdles small gourds, coated with tallow, and several other articles of witchcraft, all of them, by-the-way, most professionally filthy.

Little by little the crowd gathered beside them, the women and children grouped around them, the drums renewed their deafening uproar, hands were violently clapped together, and then raised toward the sky.

"That's their style of praying," said the doctor; "and, if I'm not mistaken, we're going to be called upon to play a great part."

"Well, sir, play it!"

"You, too, my good Joe—perhaps you're to be a god!"

"Well, master, that won't trouble me much. I like a little flattery!"

At this moment, one of the sorcerers, a "myanga," made a sign, and all the clamor died away into the profoundest silence. He then addressed a few words to the strangers, but in an unknown tongue.

Dr. Ferguson, not having understood them, shouted some sentences in Arabic, at a venture, and was immediately answered in that language.

The speaker below then delivered himself of a very copious harangue, which was also very flowery and very gravely listened to by his audience. From it the doctor was not slow in learning that the balloon was mistaken for nothing less than the moon in person, and that the amiable goddess in question had condescended to approach the town with her three sons—an honor that would never be forgotten in this land so greatly loved by the god of day.

The doctor responded, with much dignity, that the moon made her provincial tour every thousand years, feeling the necessity of showing herself nearer at hand to her worshippers. He, therefore, begged them not to be disturbed by her presence, but to take advantage of it to make known all their wants and longings.

The sorcerer, in his turn, replied that the sultan, the "mwani," who had been sick for many years, implored the aid of heaven, and he invited the son of the moon to visit him.

The doctor acquainted his companions with the invitation.

"And you are going to call upon this negro king?" asked Kennedy.

"Undoubtedly so; these people appear well disposed; the air is calm; there is not a breath of wind, and we have nothing to fear for the balloon?"

"But, what will you do?"

"Be quiet on that score, my dear Dick. With a little medicine, I shall work my way through the affair!"

Then, addressing the crowd, he said:

"The moon, taking compassion on the sovereign who is so dear to the children of Unyamwezy, has charged us to restore him to health. Let him prepare to receive us!"

The clamor, the songs and demonstrations of all kinds increased twofold, and the whole immense ants' nest of black heads was again in motion.

"Now, my friends," said Dr. Ferguson, "we must look out for every thing beforehand; we may be forced to leave this at any moment, unexpectedly, and be off with extra speed. Dick had better remain, therefore, in the car, and keep the cylinder warm so as to secure a sufficient ascensional force for the balloon. The anchor is solidly fastened, and there is nothing to fear in that respect. I shall descend, and Joe will go with me, only that he must remain at the foot of the ladder."

"What! are you going alone into that blackamoor's den?"

"How! doctor, am I not to go with you?"

"No! I shall go alone; these good folks imagine that the goddess of the moon has come to see them, and their superstition protects me; so have no fear, and each one remain at the post that I have assigned to him."

"Well, since you wish it," sighed Kennedy.

"Look closely to the dilation of the gas."

"Agreed!"

By this time the shouts of the natives had swelled to double volume as they vehemently implored the aid of the heavenly powers.

"There, there," said Joe, "they're rather rough in their orders to their good moon and her divine sons."

The doctor, equipped with his travelling medicine-chest, descended to the ground, preceded by Joe, who kept a straight countenance and looked as grave and knowing as the circumstances of the case required. He then seated himself at the foot of the ladder in the Arab fashion, with his legs crossed under him, and a portion of the crowd collected around him in a circle, at respectful distances.

In the meanwhile the doctor, escorted to the sound of savage instruments, and with wild religious dances, slowly proceeded toward the royal "tembe," situated a considerable distance outside of the town.

It was about three o'clock, and the sun was shining brilliantly. In fact, what less could it do upon so grand an occasion!

The doctor stepped along with great dignity, the waganga surrounding him and keeping off the crowd. He was soon joined by the natural son of the sultan, a handsomely-built young fellow, who, according to the custom of the country, was the sole heir of the paternal goods, to the exclusion of the old man's legitimate children. He prostrated himself before the son of the moon, but the latter graciously raised him to his feet.

Three-quarters of an hour later, through shady paths, surrounded by all the luxuriance of tropical vegetation, this enthusiastic procession arrived at the sultan's palace, a sort of square edifice called ititenya, and situated on the slope of a hill.

A kind of veranda, formed by the thatched roof, adorned the outside, supported upon wooden pillars, which had some pretensions to being carved. Long lines of dark-red clay decorated the walls in characters that strove to reproduce the forms of men and serpents, the latter better imitated, of course, than the former. The roofing of this abode did not rest directly upon the walls, and the air could, therefore, circulate freely, but windows there were none, and the door hardly deserved the name.

Dr. Ferguson was received with all the honors by the guards and favorites of the sultan; these were men of a fine race, the Wanyamwezi so-called, a pure type of the central African populations, strong, robust, well-made, and in splendid condition. Their hair, divided into a great number of small tresses, fell over their shoulders, and by means of black-and-blue incisions they had tattooed their cheeks from the temples to the mouth. Their ears, frightfully distended, held dangling to them disks of wood and plates of gum copal. They were clad in brilliantly-painted cloths, and the soldiers were armed with the saw-toothed war-club, the bow and arrows barbed and poisoned with the juice of the euphorbium, the cutlass, the "sima," a long sabre (also with saw-like teeth), and some small battle-axes.

The doctor advanced into the palace, and there, notwithstanding the sultan's illness, the din, which was terrific before, redoubled the instant that he arrived. He noticed, at the lintels of the door, some rabbits' tails and zebras' manes, suspended as talismans. He was received by the whole troop of his majesty's wives, to the harmonious accords of the "upatu," a sort of cymbal made of the bottom of a copper kettle, and to the uproar of the "kilindo," a drum five feet high, hollowed out from the trunk of a tree, and hammered by the ponderous, horny fists of two jet-black virtuosi.

Most of the women were rather good-looking, and they laughed and chattered merrily as they smoked their tobacco and "thang" in huge black pipes. They seemed to be well made, too, under the long robes that they wore gracefully flung about their persons, and carried a sort of "kilt" woven from the fibres of calabash fastened around their girdles.

Six of them were not the least merry of the party, although put aside from the rest, and reserved for a cruel fate. On the death of the sultan, they were to be buried alive with him, so as to occupy and divert his mind during the period of eternal solitude.

Dr. Ferguson, taking in the whole scene at a rapid glance, approached the wooden couch on which the sultan lay reclining. There he saw a man of about forty, completely brutalized by orgies of every description, and in a condition that left little or nothing to be done. The sickness that had afflicted him for so many years was simply perpetual drunkenness. The royal sot had nearly lost all consciousness, and all the ammonia in the world would not have set him on his feet again.

His favorites and the women kept on bended knees during this solemn visit. By means of a few drops of powerful cordial, the doctor for a moment reanimated the imbruted carcass that lay before him. The sultan stirred, and, for a dead body that had given no sign whatever of life for several hours previously, this symptom was received with a tremendous repetition of shouts and cries in the doctor's honor.

The latter, who had seen enough of it by this time, by a rapid motion put aside his too demonstrative admirers and went out of the palace, directing his steps immediately toward the balloon, for it was now six o'clock in the evening.

Joe, during his absence, had been quietly waiting at the foot of the ladder, where the crowd paid him their most humble respects. Like a genuine son of the moon, he let them keep on. For a divinity, he had the air of a very clever sort of fellow, by no means proud, nay, even pleasingly familiar with the young negresses, who seemed never to tire of looking at him. Besides, he went so far as to chat agreeably with them.

"Worship me, ladies! worship me!" he said to them. "I'm a clever sort of devil, if I am the son of a goddess."

They brought him propitiatory gifts, such as are usually deposited in the fetich huts or mzimu. These gifts consisted of stalks of barley and of "pombe." Joe considered himself in duty bound to taste the latter species of strong beer, but his palate, although accustomed to gin and whiskey, could not withstand the strength of the new beverage, and he had to make a horrible grimace, which his dusky friends took to be a benevolent smile.

Thereupon, the young damsels, conjoining their voices in a drawling chant, began to dance around him with the utmost gravity.

"Ah! you're dancing, are you?" said he. "Well, I won't be behind you in politeness, and so I'll give you one of my country reels."

So at it he went, in one of the wildest jigs that ever was seen, twisting, turning, and jerking himself in all directions; dancing with his hands, dancing with his body, dancing with his knees, dancing with his feet; describing the most fearful contortions and extravagant evolutions; throwing himself into incredible attitudes; grimacing beyond all belief, and, in fine giving his savage admirers a strange idea of the style of ballet adopted by the deities in the moon.

Then, the whole collection of blacks, naturally as imitative as monkeys, at once reproduced all his airs and graces, his leaps and shakes and contortions; they did not lose a single gesticulation; they did not forget an attitude; and the result was, such a pandemonium of movement, noise, and excitement, as it would be out of the question even feebly to describe. But, in the very midst of the fun, Joe saw the doctor approaching.

The latter was coming at full speed, surrounded by a yelling and disorderly throng. The chiefs and sorcerers seemed to be highly excited. They were close upon the doctor's heels, crowding and threatening him.

Singular reaction! What had happened? Had the sultan unluckily perished in the hands of his celestial physician?

Kennedy, from his post of observation, saw the danger without knowing what had caused it, and the balloon, powerfully urged by the dilation of the gas, strained and tugged at the ropes that held it as though impatient to soar away.

The doctor had got as far as the foot of the ladder. A superstitious fear still held the crowd aloof and hindered them from committing any violence on his person. He rapidly scaled the ladder, and Joe followed him with his usual agility.

"Not a moment to lose!" said the doctor. "Don't attempt to let go the anchor! We'll cut the cord! Follow me!"

"But what's the matter?" asked Joe, clambering into the car.

"What's happened?" questioned Kennedy, rifle in hand.

"Look!" replied the doctor, pointing to the horizon.

"Well?" exclaimed the Scot.

"Well! the moon!"

And, in fact, there was the moon rising red and magnificent, a globe of fire in a field of blue! It was she, indeed—she and the balloon!—both in one sky!

Either there were two moons, then, or these strangers were imposters, designing scamps, false deities!

Such were the very natural reflections of the crowd, and hence the reaction in their feelings.

Joe could not, for the life of him, keep in a roar of laughter; and the population of Kazeh, comprehending that their prey was slipping through their clutches, set up prolonged howlings, aiming, the while, their bows and muskets at the balloon.

But one of the sorcerers made a sign, and all the weapons were lowered. He then began to climb into the tree, intending to seize the rope and bring the machine to the ground.

Joe leaned out with a hatchet ready. "Shall I cut away?" said he.

"No; wait a moment," replied the doctor.

"But this black?"

"We may, perhaps, save our anchor—and I hold a great deal by that. There'll always be time enough to cut loose."

The sorcerer, having climbed to the right place, worked so vigorously that he succeeded in detaching the anchor, and the latter, violently jerked, at that moment, by the start of the balloon, caught the rascal between the limbs, and carried him off astride of it through the air.

The stupefaction of the crowd was indescribable as they saw one of their waganga thus whirled away into space.

"Huzza!" roared Joe, as the balloon—thanks to its ascensional force— shot up higher into the sky, with increased rapidity.

"He holds on well," said Kennedy; "a little trip will do him good."

"Shall we let this darky drop all at once?" inquired Joe.

"Oh no," replied the doctor, "we'll let him down easily; and I warrant me that, after such an adventure, the power of the wizard will be enormously enhanced in the sight of his comrades."

"Why, I wouldn't put it past them to make a god of him!" said Joe, with a laugh.

The Victoria, by this time, had risen to the height of one thousand feet, and the black hung to the rope with desperate energy. He had become completely silent, and his eyes were fixed, for his terror was blended with amazement. A light west wind was sweeping the balloon right over the town, and far beyond it.

Half an hour later, the doctor, seeing the country deserted, moderated the flame of his cylinder, and descended toward the ground. At twenty feet above the turf, the affrighted sorcerer made up his mind in a twinkling: he let himself drop, fell on his feet, and scampered off at a furious pace toward Kazeh; while the balloon, suddenly relieved of his weight, again shot up on her course.

Chapter 16

SYMPTOMS OF A STORM.—THE COUNTRY OF THE MOON.—THE
FUTURE OF THE AFRICAN CONTINENT.—THE LAST MACHINE OF
ALL.—A VIEW OF THE COUNTRY AT SUNSET.—FLORA AND FAUNA.—
THE TEMPEST.—THE ZONE OF FIRE.—THE STARRY HEAVENS.

S ee," said Joe, "what comes of playing the sons of the moon without
her leave! She came near serving us an ugly trick. But say, master,
did you damage your credit as a physician?"

"Yes, indeed," chimed in the sportsman. "What kind of a dignitary
was this Sultan of Kazeh?"

"An old half-dead sot," replied the doctor, "whose loss will not be
very severely felt. But the moral of all this is that honors are fleeting,
and we must not take too great a fancy to them."

"So much the worse!" rejoined Joe. "I liked the thing—to be
worshipped!—Play the god as you like! Why, what would any one ask
more than that? By-the-way, the moon did come up, too, and all red, as
if she was in a rage."

While the three friends went on chatting of this and other things, and
Joe examined the luminary of night from an entirely novel point of view,
the heavens became covered with heavy clouds to the northward, and the
lowering masses assumed a most sinister and threatening look. Quite a
smart breeze, found about three hundred feet from the earth, drove the
balloon toward the north-northeast; and above it the blue vault was clear;
but the atmosphere felt close and dull.

The aeronauts found themselves, at about eight in the evening,
in thirty-two degrees forty minutes east longitude, and four degrees
seventeen minutes latitude. The atmospheric currents, under the
influence of a tempest not far off, were driving them at the rate of from
thirty to thirty-five miles an hour; the undulating and fertile plains
of Mfuto were passing swiftly beneath them. The spectacle was one
worthy of admiration—and admire it they did.

"We are now right in the country of the Moon," said Dr. Ferguson;
"for it has retained the name that antiquity gave it, undoubtedly, because
the moon has been worshipped there in all ages. It is, really, a superb
country."

"It would be hard to find more splendid vegetation."

"If we found the like of it around London it would not be natural, but it would be very pleasant," put in Joe. "Why is it that such savage countries get all these fine things?"

"And who knows," said the doctor, "that this country may not, one day, become the centre of civilization? The races of the future may repair hither, when Europe shall have become exhausted in the effort to feed her inhabitants."

"Do you think so, really?" asked Kennedy.

"Undoubtedly, my dear Dick. Just note the progress of events: consider the migrations of races, and you will arrive at the same conclusion assuredly. Asia was the first nurse of the world, was she not? For about four thousand years she travailed, she grew pregnant, she produced, and then, when stones began to cover the soil where the golden harvests sung by Homer had flourished, her children abandoned her exhausted and barren bosom. You next see them precipitating themselves upon young and vigorous Europe, which has nourished them for the last two thousand years. But already her fertility is beginning to die out; her productive powers are diminishing every day. Those new diseases that annually attack the products of the soil, those defective crops, those insufficient resources, are all signs of a vitality that is rapidly wearing out and of an approaching exhaustion. Thus, we already see the millions rushing to the luxuriant bosom of America, as a source of help, not inexhaustible indeed, but not yet exhausted. In its turn, that new continent will grow old; its virgin forests will fall before the axe of industry, and its soil will become weak through having too fully produced what had been demanded of it. Where two harvests bloomed every year, hardly one will be gathered from a soil completely drained of its strength. Then, Africa will be there to offer to new races the treasures that for centuries have been accumulating in her breast. Those climates now so fatal to strangers will be purified by cultivation and by drainage of the soil, and those scattered water supplies will be gathered into one common bed to form an artery of navigation. Then this country over which we are now passing, more fertile, richer, and fuller of vitality than the rest, will become some grand realm where more astonishing discoveries than steam and electricity will be brought to light."

"Ah! sir," said Joe, "I'd like to see all that."

"You got up too early in the morning, my boy!"

"Besides," said Kennedy, "that may prove to be a very dull period when industry will swallow up every thing for its own profit. By dint of inventing machinery, men will end in being eaten up by it! I have always fancied that the end of the earth will be when some enormous boiler, heated to three thousand millions of atmospheric pressure, shall explode and blow up our Globe!"

"And I add that the Americans," said Joe, "will not have been the last to work at the machine!"

"In fact," assented the doctor, "they are great boiler-makers! But, without allowing ourselves to be carried away by such speculations, let us rest content with enjoying the beauties of this country of the Moon, since we have been permitted to see it."

The sun, darting his last rays beneath the masses of heaped-up cloud, adorned with a crest of gold the slightest inequalities of the ground below; gigantic trees, arborescent bushes, mosses on the even surface—all had their share of this luminous effulgence. The soil, slightly undulating, here and there rose into little conical hills; there were no mountains visible on the horizon; immense brambly palisades, impenetrable hedges of thorny jungle, separated the clearings dotted with numerous villages, and immense euphorbiae surrounded them with natural fortifications, interlacing their trunks with the coral-shaped branches of the shrubbery and undergrowth.

Ere long, the Malagazeri, the chief tributary of Lake Tanganayika, was seen winding between heavy thickets of verdure, offering an asylum to many water-courses that spring from the torrents formed in the season of freshets, or from ponds hollowed in the clayey soil. To observers looking from a height, it was a chain of waterfalls thrown across the whole western face of the country.

Animals with huge humps were feeding in the luxuriant prairies, and were half hidden, sometimes, in the tall grass; spreading forests in bloom redolent of spicy perfumes presented themselves to the gaze like immense bouquets; but, in these bouquets, lions, leopards, hyenas, and tigers, were then crouching for shelter from the last hot rays of the setting sun. From time to time, an elephant made the tall tops of the undergrowth sway to and fro, and you could hear the crackling of huge branches as his ponderous ivory tusks broke them in his way.

"What a sporting country!" exclaimed Dick, unable longer to restrain his enthusiasm; "why, a single ball fired at random into those forests would bring down game worthy of it. Suppose we try it once!"

"No, my dear Dick; the night is close at hand—a threatening night with a tempest in the background—and the storms are awful in this country, where the heated soil is like one vast electric battery."

"You are right, sir," said Joe, "the heat has got to be enough to choke one, and the breeze has died away. One can feel that something's coming."

"The atmosphere is saturated with electricity," replied the doctor; "every living creature is sensible that this state of the air portends a struggle of the elements, and I confess that I never before was so full of the fluid myself."

"Well, then," suggested Dick, "would it not be advisable to alight?"

"On the contrary, Dick, I'd rather go up, only that I am afraid of being carried out of my course by these counter-currents contending in the atmosphere."

"Have you any idea, then, of abandoning the route that we have followed since we left the coast?"

"If I can manage to do so," replied the doctor, "I will turn more directly northward, by from seven to eight degrees; I shall then endeavor to ascend toward the presumed latitudes of the sources of the Nile; perhaps we may discover some traces of Captain Speke's expedition or of M. de Heuglin's caravan. Unless I am mistaken, we are at thirty-two degrees forty minutes east longitude, and I should like to ascend directly north of the equator."

"Look there!" exclaimed Kennedy, suddenly, "see those hippopotami sliding out of the pools—those masses of blood-colored flesh—and those crocodiles snuffing the air aloud!"

"They're choking!" exclaimed Joe. "Ah! what a fine way to travel this is; and how one can snap his fingers at all that vermin!—Doctor! Mr. Kennedy! see those packs of wild animals hurrying along close together. There are fully two hundred. Those are wolves."

"No! Joe, not wolves, but wild dogs; a famous breed that does not hesitate to attack the lion himself. They are the worst customers a traveller could meet, for they would instantly tear him to pieces."

"Well, it isn't Joe that'll undertake to muzzle them!" responded that amiable youth. "After all, though, if that's the nature of the beast, we mustn't be too hard on them for it!"

Silence gradually settled down under the influence of the impending storm: the thickened air actually seemed no longer adapted to the transmission of sound; the atmosphere appeared *muffled*, and, like a room hung with tapestry, lost all its sonorous reverberation. The "rover bird" so-called, the coroneted crane, the red and blue jays, the mocking-bird, the flycatcher, disappeared among the foliage of the immense trees, and all nature revealed symptoms of some approaching catastrophe.

At nine o'clock the Victoria hung motionless over Msene, an extensive group of villages scarcely distinguishable in the gloom. Once in a while, the reflection of a wandering ray of light in the dull water disclosed a succession of ditches regularly arranged, and, by one last gleam, the eye could make out the calm and sombre forms of palm-trees, sycamores, and gigantic euphorbiae.

"I am stifling!" said the Scot, inhaling, with all the power of his lungs, as much as possible of the rarefied air. "We are not moving an inch! Let us descend!"

"But the tempest!" said the doctor, with much uneasiness.

"If you are afraid of being carried away by the wind, it seems to me that there is no other course to pursue."

"Perhaps the storm won't burst to-night," said Joe; "the clouds are very high."

"That is just the thing that makes me hesitate about going beyond them; we should have to rise still higher, lose sight of the earth, and not know all night whether we were moving forward or not, or in what direction we were going."

"Make up your mind, dear doctor, for time presses!"

"It's a pity that the wind has fallen," said Joe, again; "it would have carried us clear of the storm."

"It is, indeed, a pity, my friends," rejoined the doctor. "The clouds are dangerous for us; they contain opposing currents which might catch us in their eddies, and lightnings that might set on fire. Again, those perils avoided, the force of the tempest might hurl us to the ground, were we to cast our anchor in the tree-tops."

"Then what shall we do?"

"Well, we must try to get the balloon into a medium zone of the atmosphere, and there keep her suspended between the perils of the heavens and those of the earth. We have enough water for the cylinder, and our two hundred pounds of ballast are untouched. In case of emergency I can use them."

"We will keep watch with you," said the hunter.

"No, my friends, put the provisions under shelter, and lie down; I will rouse you, if it becomes necessary."

"But, master, wouldn't you do well to take some rest yourself, as there's no danger close on us just now?" insisted poor Joe.

"No, thank you, my good fellow, I prefer to keep awake. We are not moving, and should circumstances not change, we'll find ourselves to-morrow in exactly the same place."

"Good-night, then, sir!"

"Good-night, if you can only find it so!"

Kennedy and Joe stretched themselves out under their blankets, and the doctor remained alone in the immensity of space.

However, the huge dome of clouds visibly descended, and the darkness became profound. The black vault closed in upon the earth as if to crush it in its embrace.

All at once a violent, rapid, incisive flash of lightning pierced the gloom, and the rent it made had not closed ere a frightful clap of thunder shook the celestial depths.

"Up! up! turn out!" shouted Ferguson.

The two sleepers, aroused by the terrible concussion, were at the doctor's orders in a moment.

"Shall we descend?" said Kennedy.

"No! the balloon could not stand it. Let us go up before those clouds dissolve in water, and the wind is let loose!" and, so saying, the doctor actively stirred up the flame of the cylinder, and turned it on the spirals of the serpentine siphon.

The tempests of the tropics develop with a rapidity equalled only by their violence. A second flash of lightning rent the darkness, and was followed by a score of others in quick succession. The sky was crossed and dotted, like the zebra's hide, with electric sparks, which danced and flickered beneath the great drops of rain.

"We have delayed too long," exclaimed the doctor; "we must now pass through a zone of fire, with our balloon filled as it is with inflammable gas!"

"But let us descend, then! let us descend!" urged Kennedy.

"The risk of being struck would be just about even, and we should soon be torn to pieces by the branches of the trees!"

"We are going up, doctor!"

"Quicker, quicker still!"

In this part of Africa, during the equatorial storms, it is not rare to count from thirty to thirty-five flashes of lightning per minute. The sky is literally on fire, and the crashes of thunder are continuous.

The wind burst forth with frightful violence in this burning atmosphere; it twisted the blazing clouds; one might have compared it to the breath of some gigantic bellows, fanning all this conflagration.

Dr. Ferguson kept his cylinder at full heat, and the balloon dilated and went up, while Kennedy, on his knees, held together the curtains of the awning. The balloon whirled round wildly enough to make their heads turn, and the aeronauts got some very alarming jolts, indeed, as their machine swung and swayed in all directions. Huge cavities would form in the silk of the balloon as the wind fiercely bent it in, and the stuff fairly cracked like a pistol as it flew back from the pressure. A sort of hail, preceded by a rumbling noise, hissed through the air and rattled on the covering of the Victoria. The latter, however, continued to ascend, while the lightning described tangents to the convexity of her circumference; but she bore on, right through the midst of the fire.

"God protect us!" said Dr. Ferguson, solemnly, "we are in His hands; He alone can save us—but let us be ready for every event, even for fire—our fall could not be very rapid."

The doctor's voice could scarcely be heard by his companions; but they could see his countenance calm as ever even amid the flashing of the lightnings; he was watching the phenomena of phosphorescence produced by the fires of St. Elmo, that were now skipping to and fro along the network of the balloon.

The latter whirled and swung, but steadily ascended, and, ere the hour was over, it had passed the stormy belt. The electric display was going on below it like a vast crown of artificial fireworks suspended from the car.

Then they enjoyed one of the grandest spectacles that Nature can offer to the gaze of man. Below them, the tempest; above them, the starry firmament, tranquil, mute, impassible, with the moon projecting her peaceful rays over these angry clouds.

Dr. Ferguson consulted the barometer; it announced twelve thousand feet of elevation. It was then eleven o'clock at night.

"Thank Heaven, all danger is past; all we have to do now, is, to keep ourselves at this height," said the doctor.

"It was frightful!" remarked Kennedy.

"Oh!" said Joe, "it gives a little variety to the trip, and I'm not sorry to have seen a storm from a trifling distance up in the air. It's a fine sight!"

Chapter 17

THE MOUNTAINS OF THE MOON.—AN OCEAN OF VERDURE.—THEY
CAST ANCHOR.—THE TOWING ELEPHANT.—A RUNNING FIRE.—
DEATH OF THE MONSTER.—THE FIELD-OVEN.—A MEAL
ON THE GRASS.—A NIGHT ON THE GROUND.

About four in the morning, Monday, the sun reappeared in the
horizon; the clouds had dispersed, and a cheery breeze refreshed
the morning dawn.

The earth, all redolent with fragrant exhalations, reappeared to the
gaze of our travellers. The balloon, whirled about by opposing currents,
had hardly budged from its place, and the doctor, letting the gas
contract, descended so as to get a more northerly direction. For a long
while his quest was fruitless; the wind carried him toward the west until
he came in sight of the famous Mountains of the Moon, which grouped
themselves in a semicircle around the extremity of Lake Tanganayika;
their ridges, but slightly indented, stood out against the bluish horizon,
so that they might have been mistaken for a natural fortification, not to
be passed by the explorers of the centre of Africa. Among them were a
few isolated cones, revealing the mark of the eternal snows.

"Here we are at last," said the doctor, "in an unexplored country!
Captain Burton pushed very far to the westward, but he could not reach
those celebrated mountains; he even denied their existence, strongly as
it was affirmed by Speke, his companion. He pretended that they were
born in the latter's fancy; but for us, my friends, there is no further
doubt possible."

"Shall we cross them?" asked Kennedy.

"Not, if it please God. I am looking for a wind that will take me
back toward the equator. I will even wait for one, if necessary, and will
make the balloon like a ship that casts anchor, until favorable breezes
come up."

But the foresight of the doctor was not long in bringing its reward;
for, after having tried different heights, the Victoria at length began to
sail off to the northeastward with medium speed.

"We are in the right track," said the doctor, consulting his compass,
"and scarcely two hundred feet from the surface; lucky circumstances
for us, enabling us, as they do, to reconnoitre these new regions. When

Captain Speke set out to discover Lake Ukereoue, he ascended more to the eastward in a straight line above Kazeh."

"Shall we keep on long in this way?" inquired the Scot.

"Perhaps. Our object is to push a point in the direction of the sources of the Nile; and we have more than six hundred miles to make before we get to the extreme limit reached by the explorers who came from the north."

"And we shan't set foot on the solid ground?" murmured Joe; "it's enough to cramp a fellow's legs!"

"Oh, yes, indeed, my good Joe," said the doctor, reassuring him; "we have to economize our provisions, you know; and on the way, Dick, you must get us some fresh meat."

"Whenever you like, doctor."

"We shall also have to replenish our stock of water. Who knows but we may be carried to some of the dried-up regions? So we cannot take too many precautions."

At noon the Victoria was at twenty-nine degrees fifteen minutes east longitude, and three degrees fifteen minutes south latitude. She passed the village of Uyofu, the last northern limit of the Unyamwezi, opposite to the Lake Ukereoue, which could still be seen.

The tribes living near to the equator seem to be a little more civilized, and are governed by absolute monarchs, whose control is an unlimited despotism. Their most compact union of power constitutes the province of Karagwah.

It was decided by the aeronauts that they would alight at the first favorable place. They found that they should have to make a prolonged halt, and take a careful inspection of the balloon: so the flame of the cylinder was moderated, and the anchors, flung out from the car, ere long began to sweep the grass of an immense prairie, that, from a certain height, looked like a shaven lawn, but the growth of which, in reality, was from seven to eight feet in height.

The balloon skimmed this tall grass without bending it, like a gigantic butterfly: not an obstacle was in sight; it was an ocean of verdure without a single breaker.

"We might proceed a long time in this style," remarked Kennedy; "I don't see one tree that we could approach, and I'm afraid that our hunt's over."

"Wait, Dick; you could not hunt anyhow in this grass, that grows higher than your head. We'll find a favorable place presently."

In truth, it was a charming excursion that they were making now—a veritable navigation on this green, almost transparent sea, gently undulating in the breath of the wind. The little car seemed to cleave the waves of verdure, and, from time to time, coveys of birds of magnificent plumage would rise fluttering from the tall herbage, and speed away with joyous cries. The anchors plunged into this lake of flowers, and traced a furrow that closed behind them, like the wake of a ship.

All at once a sharp shock was felt—the anchor had caught in the fissure of some rock hidden in the high grass.

"We are fast!" exclaimed Joe.

These words had scarcely been uttered when a shrill cry rang through the air, and the following phrases, mingled with exclamations, escaped from the lips of our travellers:

"What's that?"

"A strange cry!"

"Look! Why, we're moving!"

"The anchor has slipped!"

"No; it holds, and holds fast too!" said Joe, who was tugging at the rope.

"It's the rock, then, that's moving!"

An immense rustling was noticed in the grass, and soon an elongated, winding shape was seen rising above it.

"A serpent!" shouted Joe.

"A serpent!" repeated Kennedy, handling his rifle.

"No," said the doctor, "it's an elephant's trunk!"

"An elephant, Samuel?"

And, as Kennedy said this, he drew his rifle to his shoulder.

"Wait, Dick; wait!"

"That's a fact! The animal's towing us!"

"And in the right direction, Joe—in the right direction."

The elephant was now making some headway, and soon reached a clearing where his whole body could be seen. By his gigantic size, the doctor recognized a male of a superb species. He had two whitish tusks, beautifully curved, and about eight feet in length; and in these the shanks of the anchor had firmly caught. The animal was vainly trying with his trunk to disengage himself from the rope that attached him to the car.

"Get up—go ahead, old fellow!" shouted Joe, with delight, doing his best to urge this rather novel team. "Here is a new style of travelling!—no more horses for me. An elephant, if you please!"

"But where is he taking us to?" said Kennedy, whose rifle itched in his grasp.

"He's taking us exactly to where we want to go, my dear Dick. A little patience!"

"'Wig-a-more! wig-a-more!' as the Scotch country folks say," shouted Joe, in high glee. "Gee-up! gee-up there!"

The huge animal now broke into a very rapid gallop. He flung his trunk from side to side, and his monstrous bounds gave the car several rather heavy thumps. Meanwhile the doctor stood ready, hatchet in hand, to cut the rope, should need arise.

"But," said he, "we shall not give up our anchor until the last moment."

This drive, with an elephant for the team, lasted about an hour and a half; yet the animal did not seem in the least fatigued. These immense creatures can go over a great deal of ground, and, from one day to another, are found at enormous distances from there they were last seen, like the whales, whose mass and speed they rival.

"In fact," said Joe, "it's a whale that we have harpooned; and we're only doing just what whalemen do when out fishing."

But a change in the nature of the ground compelled the doctor to vary his style of locomotion. A dense grove of calmadores was descried on the horizon, about three miles away, on the north of the prairie. So it became necessary to detach the balloon from its draught-animal at last.

Kennedy was intrusted with the job of bringing the elephant to a halt. He drew his rifle to his shoulder, but his position was not favorable to a successful shot; so that the first ball fired flattened itself on the animal's skull, as it would have done against an iron plate. The creature did not seem in the least troubled by it; but, at the sound of the discharge, he had increased his speed, and now was going as fast as a horse at full gallop.

"The deuce!" exclaimed Kennedy.

"What a solid head!" commented Joe.

"We'll try some conical balls behind the shoulder-joint," said Kennedy, reloading his rifle with care. In another moment he fired.

The animal gave a terrible cry, but went on faster than ever.

"Come!" said Joe, taking aim with another gun, "I must help you, or we'll never end it." And now two balls penetrated the creature's side.

The elephant halted, lifted his trunk, and resumed his run toward the wood with all his speed; he shook his huge head, and the blood began to gush from his wounds.

"Let us keep up our fire, Mr. Kennedy."

"And a continuous fire, too," urged the doctor, "for we are close on the woods."

Ten shots more were discharged. The elephant made a fearful bound; the car and balloon cracked as though every thing were going to pieces, and the shock made the doctor drop his hatchet on the ground.

The situation was thus rendered really very alarming; the anchor-rope, which had securely caught, could not be disengaged, nor could it yet be cut by the knives of our aeronauts, and the balloon was rushing headlong toward the wood, when the animal received a ball in the eye just as he lifted his head. On this he halted, faltered, his knees bent under him, and he uncovered his whole flank to the assaults of his enemies in the balloon.

"A bullet in his heart!" said Kennedy, discharging one last rifle-shot.

The elephant uttered a long bellow of terror and agony, then raised himself up for a moment, twirling his trunk in the air, and finally fell with all his weight upon one of his tusks, which he broke off short. He was dead.

"His tusk's broken!" exclaimed Kennedy—"ivory too that in England would bring thirty-five guineas per hundred pounds."

"As much as that?" said Joe, scrambling down to the ground by the anchor-rope.

"What's the use of sighing over it, Dick?" said the doctor. "Are we ivory merchants? Did we come hither to make money?"

Joe examined the anchor and found it solidly attached to the unbroken tusk. The doctor and Dick leaped out on the ground, while the balloon, now half emptied, hovered over the body of the huge animal.

"What a splendid beast!" said Kennedy, "what a mass of flesh! I never saw an elephant of that size in India!"

"There's nothing surprising about that, my dear Dick; the elephants of Central Africa are the finest in the world. The Andersons and the Cummings have hunted so incessantly in the neighborhood of the Cape, that these animals have migrated to the equator, where they are often met with in large herds."

"In the mean while, I hope," added Joe, "that we'll taste a morsel of this fellow. I'll undertake to get you a good dinner at his expense. Mr. Kennedy will go off and hunt for an hour or two; the doctor will make an inspection of the balloon, and, while they're busy in that way, I'll do the cooking."

"A good arrangement!" said the doctor; "so do as you like, Joe."

"As for me," said the hunter, "I shall avail myself of the two hours' recess that Joe has condescended to let me have."

"Go, my friend, but no imprudence! Don't wander too far away."

"Never fear, doctor!" and, so saying, Dick, shouldering his gun, plunged into the woods.

Forthwith Joe went to work at his vocation. At first he made a hole in the ground two feet deep; this he filled with the dry wood that was so abundantly scattered about, where it had been strewn by the elephants, whose tracks could be seen where they had made their way through the forest. This hole filled, he heaped a pile of fagots on it a foot in height, and set fire to it.

Then he went back to the carcass of the elephant, which had fallen only about a hundred feet from the edge of the forest; he next proceeded adroitly to cut off the trunk, which might have been two feet in diameter at the base; of this he selected the most delicate portion, and then took with it one of the animal's spongy feet. In fact, these are the finest morsels, like the hump of the bison, the paws of the bear, and the head of the wild boar.

When the pile of fagots had been thoroughly consumed, inside and outside, the hole, cleared of the cinders and hot coals, retained a very high temperature. The pieces of elephant-meat, surrounded with aromatic leaves, were placed in this extempore oven and covered with hot coals. Then Joe piled up a second heap of sticks over all, and when it had burned out the meat was cooked to a turn.

Then Joe took the viands from the oven, spread the savory mess upon green leaves, and arranged his dinner upon a magnificent patch of greensward. He finally brought out some biscuit, some coffee, and some cognac, and got a can of pure, fresh water from a neighboring streamlet.

The repast thus prepared was a pleasant sight to behold, and Joe, without being too proud, thought that it would also be pleasant to eat.

"A journey without danger or fatigue," he soliloquized; "your meals when you please; a swinging hammock all the time! What more could a man ask? And there was Kennedy, who didn't want to come!"

On his part, Dr. Ferguson was engrossed in a serious and thorough examination of the balloon. The latter did not appear to have suffered from the storm; the silk and the gutta percha had resisted wonderfully, and, upon estimating the exact height of the ground and the ascensional force of the balloon, our aeronaut saw, with satisfaction, that the hydrogen was in exactly the same quantity as before. The covering had remained completely waterproof.

It was now only five days since our travellers had quitted Zanzibar; their pemmican had not yet been touched; their stock of biscuit and potted meat was enough for a long trip, and there was nothing to be replenished but the water.

The pipes and spiral seemed to be in perfect condition, since, thanks to their india-rubber jointings, they had yielded to all the oscillations of the balloon. His examination ended, the doctor betook himself to setting his notes in order. He made a very accurate sketch of the surrounding landscape, with its long prairie stretching away out of sight, the forest of calmadores, and the balloon resting motionless over the body of the dead elephant.

At the end of his two hours, Kennedy returned with a string of fat partridges and the haunch of an oryx, a sort of gemsbok belonging to the most agile species of antelopes. Joe took upon himself to prepare this surplus stock of provisions for a later repast.

"But, dinner's ready!" he shouted in his most musical voice.

And the three travellers had only to sit down on the green turf. The trunk and feet of the elephant were declared to be exquisite. Old England was toasted, as usual, and delicious Havanas perfumed this charming country for the first time.

Kennedy ate, drank, and chatted, like four; he was perfectly delighted with his new life, and seriously proposed to the doctor to settle in this forest, to construct a cabin of boughs and foliage, and, there and then, to lay the foundation of a Robinson Crusoe dynasty in Africa.

The proposition went no further, although Joe had, at once, selected the part of Man Friday for himself.

The country seemed so quiet, so deserted, that the doctor resolved to pass the night on the ground, and Joe arranged a circle of watch-fires as an indispensable barrier against wild animals, for the hyenas, cougars, and jackals, attracted by the smell of the dead elephant, were prowling about in the neighborhood. Kennedy had to fire his rifle several times at these unceremonious visitors, but the night passed without any untoward occurrence.

Chapter 18

The Karagwah.—Lake Ukereoue.—A Night on an Island.—
The Equator.—Crossing the Lake.—The Cascades.—A View
of the Country.—The Sources of the Nile.—The Island
of Benga.—The Signature of Andrea Debono.—The Flag
With the Arms of England.

At five o'clock in the morning, preparations for departure commenced. Joe, with the hatchet which he had fortunately recovered, broke the elephant's tusks. The balloon, restored to liberty, sped away to the northwest with our travellers, at the rate of eighteen miles per hour.

The doctor had carefully taken his position by the altitude of the stars, during the preceding night. He knew that he was in latitude two degrees forty minutes below the equator, or at a distance of one hundred and sixty geographical miles. He swept along over many villages without heeding the cries that the appearance of the balloon excited; he took note of the conformation of places with quick sights; he passed the slopes of the Rubemhe, which are nearly as abrupt as the summits of the Ousagara, and, farther on, at Tenga, encountered the first projections of the Karagwah chains, which, in his opinion, are direct spurs of the Mountains of the Moon. So, the ancient legend which made these mountains the cradle of the Nile, came near to the truth, since they really border upon Lake Ukereoue, the conjectured reservoir of the waters of the great river.

From Kafuro, the main district of the merchants of that country, he descried, at length, on the horizon, the lake so much desired and so long sought for, of which Captain Speke caught a glimpse on the 3d of August, 1858.

Samuel Ferguson felt real emotion: he was almost in contact with one of the principal points of his expedition, and, with his spy-glass constantly raised, he kept every nook and corner of the mysterious region in sight. His gaze wandered over details that might have been thus described:

"Beneath him extended a country generally destitute of cultivation; only here and there some ravines seemed under tillage; the surface, dotted with peaks of medium height, grew flat as it approached the lake; barley-fields took the place of rice-plantations, and there, too, could be seen growing the species of plantain from which the wine of the country is drawn, and mwani, the wild plant which supplies a substitute for coffee. A collection of some fifty or more circular huts, covered with a flowering thatch, constituted the capital of the Karagwah country."

He could easily distinguish the astonished countenances of a rather fine-looking race of natives of yellowish-brown complexion. Women of incredible corpulence were dawdling about through the cultivated grounds, and the doctor greatly surprised his companions by informing them that this rotundity, which is highly esteemed in that region, was obtained by an obligatory diet of curdled milk.

At noon, the Victoria was in one degree forty-five minutes south latitude, and at one o'clock the wind was driving her directly toward the lake.

This sheet of water was christened Uyanza Victoria, or Victoria Lake, by Captain Speke. At the place now mentioned it might measure about ninety miles in breadth, and at its southern extremity the captain found a group of islets, which he named the Archipelago of Bengal. He pushed his survey as far as Muanza, on the eastern coast, where he was received by the sultan. He made a triangulation of this part of the lake, but he could not procure a boat, either to cross it or to visit the great island of Ukereoue which is very populous, is governed by three sultans, and appears to be only a promontory at low tide.

The balloon approached the lake more to the northward, to the doctor's great regret, for it had been his wish to determine its lower outlines. Its shores seemed to be thickly set with brambles and thorny plants, growing together in wild confusion, and were literally hidden, sometimes, from the gaze, by myriads of mosquitoes of a light-brown hue. The country was evidently habitable and inhabited. Troops of hippopotami could be seen disporting themselves in the forests of reeds, or plunging beneath the whitish waters of the lake.

The latter, seen from above, presented, toward the west, so broad an horizon that it might have been called a sea; the distance between the two shores is so great that communication cannot be established, and storms are frequent and violent, for the winds sweep with fury over this elevated and unsheltered basin.

The doctor experienced some difficulty in guiding his course; he was afraid of being carried toward the east, but, fortunately, a current bore him directly toward the north, and at six o'clock in the evening the balloon alighted on a small desert island in thirty minutes south latitude, and thirty-two degrees fifty-two minutes east longitude, about twenty miles from the shore.

The travellers succeeded in making fast to a tree, and, the wind having fallen calm toward evening, they remained quietly at anchor. They dared not dream of taking the ground, since here, as on the shores of the Uyanza, legions of mosquitoes covered the soil in dense clouds. Joe even came back, from securing the anchor in the tree, speckled with bites, but he kept his temper, because he found it quite the natural thing for mosquitoes to treat him as they had done.

Nevertheless, the doctor, who was less of an optimist, let out as much rope as he could, so as to escape these pitiless insects, that began to rise toward him with a threatening hum.

The doctor ascertained the height of the lake above the level of the sea, as it had been determined by Captain Speke, say three thousand seven hundred and fifty feet.

"Here we are, then, on an island!" said Joe, scratching as though he'd tear his nails out.

"We could make the tour of it in a jiffy," added Kennedy, "and, excepting these confounded mosquitoes, there's not a living being to be seen on it."

"The islands with which the lake is dotted," replied the doctor, "are nothing, after all, but the tops of submerged hills; but we are lucky to have found a retreat among them, for the shores of the lake are inhabited by ferocious tribes. Take your sleep, then, since Providence has granted us a tranquil night."

"Won't you do the same, doctor?"

"No, I could not close my eyes. My thoughts would banish sleep. To-morrow, my friends, should the wind prove favorable, we shall go due north, and we shall, perhaps, discover the sources of the Nile, that grand secret which has so long remained impenetrable. Near as we are to the sources of the renowned river, I could not sleep."

Kennedy and Joe, whom scientific speculations failed to disturb to that extent, were not long in falling into sound slumber, while the doctor held his post.

On Wednesday, April 23d, the balloon started at four o'clock in the morning, with a grayish sky overhead; night was slow in quitting the surface of the lake, which was enveloped in a dense fog, but presently a violent breeze scattered all the mists, and, after the balloon had been swung to and fro for a moment, in opposite directions, it at length veered in a straight line toward the north.

Dr. Ferguson fairly clapped his hands for joy.

"We are on the right track!" he exclaimed. "To-day or never we shall see the Nile! Look, my friends, we are crossing the equator! We are entering our own hemisphere!"

"Ah!" said Joe, "do you think, doctor, that the equator passes here?"

"Just here, my boy!"

"Well, then, with all respect to you, sir, it seems to me that this is the very time to moisten it."

"Good!" said the doctor, laughing. "Let us have a glass of punch. You have a way of comprehending cosmography that is any thing but dull."

And thus was the passage of the Victoria over the equator duly celebrated.

The balloon made rapid headway. In the west could be seen a low and but slightly-diversified coast, and, farther away in the background, the elevated plains of the Uganda and the Usoga. At length, the rapidity of the wind became excessive, approaching thirty miles per hour.

The waters of the Nyanza, violently agitated, were foaming like the billows of a sea. By the appearance of certain long swells that followed the sinking of the waves, the doctor was enabled to conclude that the lake must have great depth of water. Only one or two rude boats were seen during this rapid passage.

"This lake is evidently, from its elevated position, the natural reservoir of the rivers in the eastern part of Africa, and the sky gives back to it in rain what it takes in vapor from the streams that flow out of it. I am certain that the Nile must here take its rise."

"Well, we shall see!" said Kennedy.

About nine o'clock they drew nearer to the western coast. It seemed deserted, and covered with woods; the wind freshened a little toward the east, and the other shore of the lake could be seen. It bent around in such a curve as to end in a wide angle toward two degrees forty minutes north latitude. Lofty mountains uplifted their arid peaks at this extremity of Nyanza; but, between them, a deep and winding gorge gave exit to a turbulent and foaming river.

While busy managing the balloon, Dr. Ferguson never ceased reconnoitring the country with eager eyes.

"Look!" he exclaimed, "look, my friends! the statements of the Arabs were correct! They spoke of a river by which Lake Ukereoue discharged its waters toward the north, and this river exists, and we are descending it, and it flows with a speed analogous to our own! And this drop of water now gliding away beneath our feet is, beyond all question, rushing on, to mingle with the Mediterranean! It is the Nile!"

"It is the Nile!" reeechoed Kennedy, carried away by the enthusiasm of his friend.

"Hurrah for the Nile!" shouted Joe, glad, and always ready to cheer for something.

Enormous rocks, here and there, embarrassed the course of this mysterious river. The water foamed as it fell in rapids and cataracts, which confirmed the doctor in his preconceived ideas on the subject. From the environing mountains numerous torrents came plunging and seething down, and the eye could take them in by hundreds. There could be seen, starting from the soil, delicate jets of water scattering in all directions, crossing and recrossing each other, mingling, contending in the swiftness of their progress, and all rushing toward that nascent stream which became a river after having drunk them in.

"Here is, indeed, the Nile!" reiterated the doctor, with the tone of profound conviction. "The origin of its name, like the origin of its waters, has fired the imagination of the learned; they have sought to trace it from the Greek, the Coptic, the Sanscrit; but all that matters little now, since we have made it surrender the secret of its source!"

"But," said the Scotchman, "how are you to make sure of the identity of this river with the one recognized by the travellers from the north?"

"We shall have certain, irrefutable, convincing, and infallible proof," replied Ferguson, "should the wind hold another hour in our favor!"

The mountains drew farther apart, revealing in their place numerous villages, and fields of white Indian corn, doura, and sugar-cane. The tribes inhabiting the region seemed excited and hostile; they manifested more anger than adoration, and evidently saw in the aeronauts only obtrusive strangers, and not condescending deities. It appeared as though, in approaching the sources of the Nile, these men came to rob them of something, and so the Victoria had to keep out of range of their muskets.

"To land here would be a ticklish matter!" said the Scot.

"Well!" said Joe, "so much the worse for these natives. They'll have to do without the pleasure of our conversation."

"Nevertheless, descend I must," said the doctor, "were it only for a quarter of an hour. Without doing so I cannot verify the results of our expedition."

"It is indispensable, then, doctor?"

"Indispensable; and we will descend, even if we have to do so with a volley of musketry."

"The thing suits me," said Kennedy, toying with his pet rifle.

"And I'm ready, master, whenever you say the word!" added Joe, preparing for the fight.

"It would not be the first time," remarked the doctor, "that science has been followed up, sword in hand. The same thing happened to a French savant among the mountains of Spain, when he was measuring the terrestrial meridian."

"Be easy on that score, doctor, and trust to your two body-guards."

"Are we there, master?"

"Not yet. In fact, I shall go up a little, first, in order to get an exact idea of the configuration of the country."

The hydrogen expanded, and in less than ten minutes the balloon was soaring at a height of twenty-five hundred feet above the ground.

From that elevation could be distinguished an inextricable network of smaller streams which the river received into its bosom; others came from the west, from between numerous hills, in the midst of fertile plains.

"We are not ninety miles from Gondokoro," said the doctor, measuring off the distance on his map, "and less than five miles from the point reached by the explorers from the north. Let us descend with great care."

And, upon this, the balloon was lowered about two thousand feet.

"Now, my friends, let us be ready, come what may."

"Ready it is!" said Dick and Joe, with one voice.

"Good!"

In a few moments the balloon was advancing along the bed of the river, and scarcely one hundred feet above the ground. The Nile measured but fifty fathoms in width at this point, and the natives were in great excitement, rushing to and fro, tumultuously, in the villages that lined the banks of the stream. At the second degree it forms a perpendicular cascade of ten feet in height, and consequently impassable by boats.

"Here, then, is the cascade mentioned by Debono!" exclaimed the doctor.

The basin of the river spread out, dotted with numerous islands, which Dr. Ferguson devoured with his eyes. He seemed to be seeking for a point of reference which he had not yet found.

By this time, some blacks, having ventured in a boat just under the balloon, Kennedy saluted them with a shot from his rifle, that made them regain the bank at their utmost speed.

"A good journey to you," bawled Joe, "and if I were in your place, I wouldn't try coming back again. I should be mightily afraid of a monster that can hurl thunderbolts when he pleases."

But, all at once, the doctor snatched up his spy-glass, and directed it toward an island reposing in the middle of the river.

"Four trees!" he exclaimed; "look, down there!" Sure enough, there were four trees standing alone at one end of it.

"It is Bengal Island! It is the very same," repeated the doctor, exultingly.

"And what of that?" asked Dick.

"It is there that we shall alight, if God permits."

"But, it seems to be inhabited, doctor."

"Joe is right; and, unless I'm mistaken, there is a group of about a score of natives on it now."

"We'll make them scatter; there'll be no great trouble in that," responded Ferguson.

"So be it," chimed in the hunter.

The sun was at the zenith as the balloon approached the island.

The blacks, who were members of the Makado tribe, were howling lustily, and one of them waved his bark hat in the air. Kennedy took aim at him, fired, and his hat flew about him in pieces. Thereupon there was a general scamper. The natives plunged headlong into the river, and swam to the opposite bank. Immediately, there came a shower of balls from both banks, along with a perfect cloud of arrows, but without doing the balloon any damage, where it rested with its anchor snugly secured in the fissure of a rock. Joe lost no time in sliding to the ground.

"The ladder!" cried the doctor. "Follow me, Kennedy."

"What do you wish, sir?"

"Let us alight. I want a witness."

"Here I am!"

"Mind your post, Joe, and keep a good lookout."

"Never fear, doctor; I'll answer for all that."

JULES VERNE

"Come, Dick," said the doctor, as he touched the ground.

So saying, he drew his companion along toward a group of rocks that rose upon one point of the island; there, after searching for some time, he began to rummage among the brambles, and, in so doing, scratched his hands until they bled.

Suddenly he grasped Kennedy's arm, exclaiming: "Look! look!"

"Letters!"

Yes; there, indeed, could be descried, with perfect precision of outline, some letters carved on the rock. It was quite easy to make them out:

"A. D."

"A.D.!" repeated Dr. Ferguson. "Andrea Debono—the very signature of the traveller who farthest ascended the current of the Nile."

"No doubt of that, friend Samuel," assented Kennedy.

"Are you now convinced?"

"It is the Nile! We cannot entertain a doubt on that score now," was the reply.

The doctor, for the last time, examined those precious initials, the exact form and size of which he carefully noted.

"And now," said he—"now for the balloon!"

"Quickly, then, for I see some of the natives getting ready to recross the river."

"That matters little to us now. Let the wind but send us northward for a few hours, and we shall reach Gondokoro, and press the hands of some of our countrymen."

Ten minutes more, and the balloon was majestically ascending, while Dr. Ferguson, in token of success, waved the English flag triumphantly from his car.

Chapter 19

THE NILE.—THE TREMBLING MOUNTAIN.—A REMEMBRANCE
OF THE COUNTRY.—THE NARRATIVES OF THE ARABS.—THE
NYAM-NYAMS.—JOE'S SHREWD COGITATIONS.—THE BALLOON
RUNS THE GANTLET.—AEROSTATIC ASCENSIONS.—
MADAME BLANCHARD..

Which way do we head?" asked Kennedy, as he saw his friend consulting the compass.

"North-northeast."

"The deuce! but that's not the north?"

"No, Dick; and I'm afraid that we shall have some trouble in getting to Gondokoro. I am sorry for it; but, at last, we have succeeded in connecting the explorations from the east with those from the north; and we must not complain."

The balloon was now receding gradually from the Nile.

"One last look," said the doctor, "at this impassable latitude, beyond which the most intrepid travellers could not make their way. There are those intractable tribes, of whom Petherick, Arnaud, Miuni, and the young traveller Lejean, to whom we are indebted for the best work on the Upper Nile, have spoken."

"Thus, then," added Kennedy, inquiringly, "our discoveries agree with the speculations of science."

"Absolutely so. The sources of the White Nile, of the Bahr-el-Abiad, are immersed in a lake as large as a sea; it is there that it takes its rise. Poesy, undoubtedly, loses something thereby. People were fond of ascribing a celestial origin to this king of rivers. The ancients gave it the name of an ocean, and were not far from believing that it flowed directly from the sun; but we must come down from these flights from time to time, and accept what science teaches us. There will not always be scientific men, perhaps; but there always will be poets."

"We can still see cataracts," said Joe.

"Those are the cataracts of Makedo, in the third degree of latitude. Nothing could be more accurate. Oh, if we could only have followed the course of the Nile for a few hours!"

"And down yonder, below us, I see the top of a mountain," said the hunter.

"That is Mount Longwek, the Trembling Mountain of the Arabs. This whole country was visited by Debono, who went through it under the name of Latif-Effendi. The tribes living near the Nile are hostile to each other, and are continually waging a war of extermination. You may form some idea, then, of the difficulties he had to encounter."

The wind was carrying the balloon toward the northwest, and, in order to avoid Mount Longwek, it was necessary to seek a more slanting current.

"My friends," said the doctor, "here is where *our* passage of the African Continent really commences; up to this time we have been following the traces of our predecessors. Henceforth we are to launch ourselves upon the unknown. We shall not lack the courage, shall we?"

"Never!" said Dick and Joe together, almost in a shout.

"Onward, then, and may we have the help of Heaven!"

At ten o'clock at night, after passing over ravines, forests, and scattered villages, the aeronauts reached the side of the Trembling Mountain, along whose gentle slopes they went quietly gliding. In that memorable day, the 23d of April, they had, in fifteen hours, impelled by a rapid breeze, traversed a distance of more than three hundred and fifteen miles.

But this latter part of the journey had left them in dull spirits, and complete silence reigned in the car. Was Dr. Ferguson absorbed in the thought of his discoveries? Were his two companions thinking of their trip through those unknown regions? There were, no doubt, mingled with these reflections, the keenest reminiscences of home and distant friends. Joe alone continued to manifest the same careless philosophy, finding it *Quite Natural* that home should not be there, from the moment that he left it; but he respected the silent mood of his friends, the doctor and Kennedy.

About ten the balloon anchored on the side of the Trembling Mountain, so called, because, in Arab tradition, it is said to tremble the instant that a Mussulman sets foot upon it. The travellers then partook of a substantial meal, and all quietly passed the night as usual, keeping the regular watches.

On awaking the next morning, they all had pleasanter feelings. The weather was fine, and the wind was blowing from the right quarter; so that a good breakfast, seasoned with Joe's merry pranks, put them in high good-humor.

The region they were now crossing is very extensive. It borders on the Mountains of the Moon on one side, and those of Darfur on the other—a space about as broad as Europe.

"We are, no doubt, crossing what is supposed to be the kingdom of Usoga. Geographers have pretended that there existed, in the centre of Africa, a vast depression, an immense central lake. We shall see whether there is any truth in that idea," said the doctor.

"But how did they come to think so?" asked Kennedy.

"From the recitals of the Arabs. Those fellows are great narrators—too much so, probably. Some travellers, who had got as far as Kazeh, or the great lakes, saw slaves that had been brought from this region; interrogated them concerning it, and, from their different narratives, made up a jumble of notions, and deduced systems from them. Down at the bottom of it all there is some appearance of truth; and you see that they were right about the sources of the Nile."

"Nothing could be more correct," said Kennedy. "It was by the aid of these documents that some attempts at maps were made, and so I am going to try to follow our route by one of them, rectifying it when need be."

"Is all this region inhabited?" asked Joe.

"Undoubtedly; and disagreeably inhabited, too."

"I thought so."

"These scattered tribes come, one and all, under the title of Nyam-Nyams, and this compound word is only a sort of nickname. It imitates the sound of chewing."

"That's it! Excellent!" said Joe, champing his teeth as though he were eating; "Nyam-Nyam."

"My good Joe, if you were the immediate object of this chewing, you wouldn't find it so excellent."

"Why, what's the reason, sir?"

"These tribes are considered man-eaters."

"Is that really the case?"

"Not a doubt of it! It has also been asserted that these natives had tails, like mere quadrupeds; but it was soon discovered that these appendages belonged to the skins of animals that they wore for clothing."

"More's the pity! a tail's a nice thing to chase away mosquitoes."

"That may be, Joe; but we must consign the story to the domain of fable, like the dogs' heads which the traveller, Brun-Rollet, attributed to other tribes."

"Dogs' heads, eh? Quite convenient for barking, and even for man-eating!"

"But one thing that has been, unfortunately, proven true, is, the ferocity of these tribes, who are really very fond of human flesh, and devour it with avidity."

"I only hope that they won't take such a particular fancy to mine!" said Joe, with comic solemnity.

"See that!" said Kennedy.

"Yes, indeed, sir; if I have to be eaten, in a moment of famine, I want it to be for your benefit and my master's; but the idea of feeding those black fellows—gracious! I'd die of shame!"

"Well, then, Joe," said Kennedy, "that's understood; we count upon you in case of need!"

"At your service, gentlemen!"

"Joe talks in this way so as to make us take good care of him, and fatten him up."

"Maybe so!" said Joe. "Every man for himself."

In the afternoon, the sky became covered with a warm mist, that oozed from the soil; the brownish vapor scarcely allowed the beholder to distinguish objects, and so, fearing collision with some unexpected mountain-peak, the doctor, about five o'clock, gave the signal to halt.

The night passed without accident, but in such profound obscurity, that it was necessary to use redoubled vigilance.

The monsoon blew with extreme violence during all the next morning. The wind buried itself in the lower cavities of the balloon and shook the appendage by which the dilating-pipes entered the main apparatus. They had, at last, to be tied up with cords, Joe acquitting himself very skilfully in performing that operation.

He had occasion to observe, at the same time, that the orifice of the balloon still remained hermetically sealed.

"That is a matter of double importance for us," said the doctor; "in the first place, we avoid the escape of precious gas, and then, again, we do not leave behind us an inflammable train, which we should at last inevitably set fire to, and so be consumed."

"That would be a disagreeable travelling incident!" said Joe.

"Should we be hurled to the ground?" asked Kennedy.

"Hurled! No, not quite that. The gas would burn quietly, and we should descend little by little. A similar accident happened to a French aeronaut, Madame Blanchard. She ignited her balloon while sending off fireworks, but she did not fall, and she would not have been killed, probably, had not her car dashed against a chimney and precipitated her to the ground."

"Let us hope that nothing of the kind may happen to us," said the hunter. "Up to this time our trip has not seemed to me very dangerous, and I can see nothing to prevent us reaching our destination."

"Nor can I either, my dear Dick; accidents are generally caused by the imprudence of the aeronauts, or the defective construction of their apparatus. However, in thousands of aerial ascensions, there have not been twenty fatal accidents. Usually, the danger is in the moment of leaving the ground, or of alighting, and therefore at those junctures we should never omit the utmost precaution."

"It's breakfast-time," said Joe; "we'll have to put up with preserved meat and coffee until Mr. Kennedy has had another chance to get us a good slice of venison."

Chapter 20

The Celestial Bottle.—The Fig-Palms.—The Mammoth Trees.—The Tree of War.—The Winged Team.—Two Native Tribes in Battle.—A Massacre.—An Intervention from Above.

The wind had become violent and irregular; the balloon was running the gantlet through the air. Tossed at one moment toward the north, at another toward the south, it could not find one steady current.

"We are moving very swiftly without advancing much," said Kennedy, remarking the frequent oscillations of the needle of the compass.

"The balloon is rushing at the rate of at least thirty miles an hour. Lean over, and see how the country is gliding away beneath us!" said the doctor.

"See! that forest looks as though it were precipitating itself upon us!"

"The forest has become a clearing!" added the other.

"And the clearing a village!" continued Joe, a moment or two later. "Look at the faces of those astonished darkys!"

"Oh! it's natural enough that they should be astonished," said the doctor. "The French peasants, when they first saw a balloon, fired at it, thinking that it was an aerial monster. A Soudan negro may be excused, then, for opening his eyes *very* wide!"

"Faith!" said Joe, as the Victoria skimmed closely along the ground, at scarcely the elevation of one hundred feet, and immediately over a village, "I'll throw them an empty bottle, with your leave, doctor, and if it reaches them safe and sound, they'll worship it; if it breaks, they'll make talismans of the pieces."

So saying, he flung out a bottle, which, of course, was broken into a thousand fragments, while the negroes scampered into their round huts, uttering shrill cries.

A little farther on, Kennedy called out: "Look at that strange tree! The upper part is of one kind and the lower part of another!"

"Well!" said Joe, "here's a country where the trees grow on top of each other."

"It's simply the trunk of a fig-tree," replied the doctor, "on which there is a little vegetating earth. Some fine day, the wind left the seed of a palm on it, and the seed has taken root and grown as though it were on the plain ground."

"A fine new style of gardening," said Joe, "and I'll import the idea to England. It would be just the thing in the London parks; without counting that it would be another way to increase the number of fruit-trees. We could have gardens up in the air; and the small house-owners would like that!"

At this moment, they had to raise the balloon so as to pass over a forest of trees that were more than three hundred feet in height—a kind of ancient banyan.

"What magnificent trees!" exclaimed Kennedy. "I never saw any thing so fine as the appearance of these venerable forests. Look, doctor!"

"The height of these banyans is really remarkable, my dear Dick; and yet, they would be nothing astonishing in the New World."

"Why, are there still loftier trees in existence?"

"Undoubtedly; among the 'mammoth trees' of California, there is a cedar four hundred and eighty feet in height. It would overtop the Houses of Parliament, and even the Great Pyramid of Egypt. The trunk at the surface of the ground was one hundred and twenty feet in circumference, and the concentric layers of the wood disclosed an age of more than four thousand years."

"But then, sir, there was nothing wonderful in it! When one has lived four thousand years, one ought to be pretty tall!" was Joe's remark.

Meanwhile, during the doctor's recital and Joe's response, the forest had given place to a large collection of huts surrounding an open space. In the middle of this grew a solitary tree, and Joe exclaimed, as he caught sight of it:

"Well! if that tree has produced such flowers as those, for the last four thousand years, I have to offer it my compliments, anyhow," and he pointed to a gigantic sycamore, whose whole trunk was covered with human bones. The flowers of which Joe spoke were heads freshly severed from the bodies, and suspended by daggers thrust into the bark of the tree.

"The war-tree of these cannibals!" said the doctor; "the Indians merely carry off the scalp, but these negroes take the whole head."

"A mere matter of fashion!" said Joe. But, already, the village and the bleeding heads were disappearing on the horizon. Another place offered a still more revolting spectacle—half-devoured corpses; skeletons mouldering to dust; human limbs scattered here and there, and left to feed the jackals and hyenas.

"No doubt, these are the bodies of criminals; according to the custom in Abyssinia, these people have left them a prey to the wild beasts, who kill them with their terrible teeth and claws, and then devour them at their leisure."

"Not a whit more cruel than hanging!" said the Scot; "filthier, that's all!"

"In the southern regions of Africa, they content themselves," resumed the doctor, "with shutting up the criminal in his own hut with his cattle, and sometimes with his family. They then set fire to the hut, and the whole party are burned together. I call that cruel; but, like friend Kennedy, I think that the gallows is quite as cruel, quite as barbarous."

Joe, by the aid of his keen sight, which he did not fail to use continually, noticed some flocks of birds of prey flitting about the horizon.

"They are eagles!" exclaimed Kennedy, after reconnoitring them through the glass, "magnificent birds, whose flight is as rapid as ours."

"Heaven preserve us from their attacks!" said the doctor, "they are more to be feared by us than wild beasts or savage tribes."

"Bah!" said the hunter, "we can drive them off with a few rifle-shots."

"Nevertheless, I would prefer, dear Dick, not having to rely upon your skill, this time, for the silk of our balloon could not resist their sharp beaks; fortunately, the huge birds will, I believe, be more frightened than attracted by our machine."

"Yes! but a new idea, and I have dozens of them," said Joe; "if we could only manage to capture a team of live eagles, we could hitch them to the balloon, and they'd haul us through the air!"

"The thing has been seriously proposed," replied the doctor, "but I think it hardly practicable with creatures naturally so restive."

"Oh! we'd tame them," said Joe. "Instead of driving them with bits, we'd do it with eye-blinkers that would cover their eyes. Half blinded in that way, they'd go to the right or to the left, as we desired; when blinded completely, they would stop."

"Allow me, Joe, to prefer a favorable wind to your team of eagles. It costs less for fodder, and is more reliable."

"Well, you may have your choice, master, but I stick to my idea."

It now was noon. The Victoria had been going at a more moderate speed for some time; the country merely passed below it; it no longer flew.

Suddenly, shouts and whistlings were heard by our aeronauts, and, leaning over the edge of the car, they saw on the open plain below them an exciting spectacle.

Two hostile tribes were fighting furiously, and the air was dotted with volleys of arrows. The combatants were so intent upon their murderous work that they did not notice the arrival of the balloon; there were about three hundred mingled confusedly in the deadly struggle: most of them, red with the blood of the wounded, in which they fairly wallowed, were horrible to behold.

As they at last caught sight of the balloon, there was a momentary pause; but their yells redoubled, and some arrows were shot at the Victoria, one of them coming close enough for Joe to catch it with his hand.

"Let us rise out of range," exclaimed the doctor; "there must be no rashness! We are forbidden any risk."

Meanwhile, the massacre continued on both sides, with battle-axes and war-clubs; as quickly as one of the combatants fell, a hostile warrior ran up to cut off his head, while the women, mingling in the fray, gathered up these bloody trophies, and piled them together at either extremity of the battle-field. Often, too, they even fought for these hideous spoils.

"What a frightful scene!" said Kennedy, with profound disgust.

"They're ugly acquaintances!" added Joe; "but then, if they had uniforms they'd be just like the fighters of all the rest of the world!"

"I have a keen hankering to take a hand in at that fight," said the hunter, brandishing his rifle.

"No! no!" objected the doctor, vehemently; "no, let us not meddle with what don't concern us. Do you know which is right or which is wrong, that you would assume the part of the Almighty? Let us, rather, hurry away from this revolting spectacle. Could the great captains of the world float thus above the scenes of their exploits, they would at last, perhaps, conceive a disgust for blood and conquest."

The chieftain of one of the contending parties was remarkable for his athletic proportions, his great height, and herculean strength. With one hand he plunged his spear into the compact ranks of his enemies, and with the other mowed large spaces in them with his battle-axe. Suddenly he flung away his war-club, red with blood, rushed upon a wounded warrior, and, chopping off his arm at a single stroke, carried the dissevered member to his mouth, and bit it again and again.

"Ah!" exclaimed Kennedy, "the horrible brute! I can hold back no longer," and, as he spoke, the huge savage, struck full in the forehead with a rifle-ball, fell headlong to the ground.

Upon this sudden mishap of their leader, his warriors seemed struck dumb with amazement; his supernatural death awed them, while it reanimated the courage and ardor of their adversaries, and, in a twinkling, the field was abandoned by half the combatants.

"Come, let us look higher up for a current to bear us away. I am sick of this spectacle," said the doctor.

But they could not get away so rapidly as to avoid the sight of the victorious tribe rushing upon the dead and the wounded, scrambling and disputing for the still warm and reeking flesh, and eagerly devouring it.

"Faugh!" uttered Joe, "it's sickening."

The balloon rose as it expanded; the howlings of the brutal horde, in the delirium of their orgy, pursued them for a few minutes; but, at length, borne away toward the south, they were carried out of sight and hearing of this horrible spectacle of cannibalism.

The surface of the country was now greatly varied, with numerous streams of water, bearing toward the east. The latter, undoubtedly, ran into those affluents of Lake Nu, or of the River of the Gazelles, concerning which M. Guillaume Lejean has given such curious details.

At nightfall, the balloon cast anchor in twenty-seven degrees east longitude, and four degrees twenty minutes north latitude, after a day's trip of one hundred and fifty miles.

Chapter 21

The night came on very dark. The doctor had not been able to reconnoitre the country. He had made fast to a very tall tree, from which he could distinguish only a confused mass through the gloom.

As usual, he took the nine-o'clock watch, and at midnight Dick relieved him.

"Keep a sharp lookout, Dick!" was the doctor's good-night injunction.

"Is there any thing new on the carpet?"

"No; but I thought that I heard vague sounds below us, and, as I don't exactly know where the wind has carried us to, even an excess of caution would do no harm."

"You've probably heard the cries of wild beasts."

"No! the sounds seemed to me something altogether different from that; at all events, on the least alarm don't fail to waken us."

"I'll do so, doctor; rest easy."

After listening attentively for a moment or two longer, the doctor, hearing nothing more, threw himself on his blankets and went asleep.

The sky was covered with dense clouds, but not a breath of air was stirring; and the balloon, kept in its place by only a single anchor, experienced not the slightest oscillation.

Kennedy, leaning his elbow on the edge of the car, so as to keep an eye on the cylinder, which was actively at work, gazed out upon the calm obscurity; he eagerly scanned the horizon, and, as often happens to minds that are uneasy or possessed with preconceived notions, he fancied that he sometimes detected vague gleams of light in the distance.

At one moment he even thought that he saw them only two hundred paces away, quite distinctly, but it was a mere flash that was gone as quickly as it came, and he noticed nothing more. It was, no doubt, one of those luminous illusions that sometimes impress the eye in the midst of very profound darkness.

Kennedy was getting over his nervousness and falling into his wandering meditations again, when a sharp whistle pierced his ear.

Was that the cry of an animal or of a night-bird, or did it come from human lips?

Kennedy, perfectly comprehending the gravity of the situation, was on the point of waking his companions, but he reflected that, in any case, men or animals, the creatures that he had heard must be out of reach. So he merely saw that his weapons were all right, and then, with his night-glass, again plunged his gaze into space.

It was not long before he thought he could perceive below him vague forms that seemed to be gliding toward the tree, and then, by the aid of a ray of moonlight that shot like an electric flash between two masses of cloud, he distinctly made out a group of human figures moving in the shadow.

The adventure with the dog-faced baboons returned to his memory, and he placed his hand on the doctor's shoulder.

The latter was awake in a moment.

"Silence!" said Dick. "Let us speak below our breath."

"Has any thing happened?"

"Yes, let us waken Joe."

The instant that Joe was aroused, Kennedy told him what he had seen.

"Those confounded monkeys again!" said Joe.

"Possibly, but we must be on our guard."

"Joe and I," said Kennedy, "will climb down the tree by the ladder."

"And, in the meanwhile," added the doctor, "I will take my measures so that we can ascend rapidly at a moment's warning."

"Agreed!"

"Let us go down, then!" said Joe.

"Don't use your weapons, excepting at the last extremity! It would be a useless risk to make the natives aware of our presence in such a place as this."

Dick and Joe replied with signs of assent, and then letting themselves slide noiselessly toward the tree, took their position in a fork among the strong branches where the anchor had caught.

For some moments they listened minutely and motionlessly among the foliage, and ere long Joe seized Kenedy's hand as he heard a sort of rubbing sound against the bark of the tree.

"Don't you hear that?" he whispered.

"Yes, and it's coming nearer."

"Suppose it should be a serpent? That hissing or whistling that you heard before—"

"No! there was something human in it."

"I'd prefer the savages, for I have a horror of those snakes."

"The noise is increasing," said Kennedy, again, after a lapse of a few moments.

"Yes! something's coming up toward us—climbing."

"Keep watch on this side, and I'll take care of the other."

"Very good!"

There they were, isolated at the top of one of the larger branches shooting out in the midst of one of those miniature forests called baobab-trees. The darkness, heightened by the density of the foliage, was profound; however, Joe, leaning over to Kennedy's ear and pointing down the tree, whispered:

"The blacks! They're climbing toward us."

The two friends could even catch the sound of a few words uttered in the lowest possible tones.

Joe gently brought his rifle to his shoulder as he spoke.

"Wait!" said Kennedy.

Some of the natives had really climbed the baobab, and now they were seen rising on all sides, winding along the boughs like reptiles, and advancing slowly but surely, all the time plainly enough discernible, not merely to the eye but to the nostrils, by the horrible odors of the rancid grease with which they bedaub their bodies.

Ere long, two heads appeared to the gaze of Kennedy and Joe, on a level with the very branch to which they were clinging.

"Attention!" said Kennedy. "Fire!"

The double concussion resounded like a thunderbolt and died away into cries of rage and pain, and in a moment the whole horde had disappeared.

But, in the midst of these yells and howls, a strange, unexpected—nay what seemed an impossible—cry had been heard! A human voice had, distinctly, called aloud in the French language—

"Help! help!"

Kennedy and Joe, dumb with amazement, had regained the car immediately.

"Did you hear that?" the doctor asked them.

"Undoubtedly, that supernatural cry, 'A moi! a moi!' comes from a Frenchman in the hands of these barbarians!"

"A traveller."

"A missionary, perhaps."

"Poor wretch!" said Kennedy, "they're assassinating him—making a martyr of him!"

The doctor then spoke, and it was impossible for him to conceal his emotions.

"There can be no doubt of it," he said; "some unfortunate Frenchman has fallen into the hands of these savages. We must not leave this place without doing all in our power to save him. When he heard the sound of our guns, he recognized an unhoped-for assistance, a providential interposition. We shall not disappoint his last hope. Are such your views?"

"They are, doctor, and we are ready to obey you."

"Let us, then, lay our heads together to devise some plan, and in the morning we'll try to rescue him."

"But how shall we drive off those abominable blacks?" asked Kennedy.

"It's quite clear to me, from the way in which they made off, that they are unacquainted with fire-arms. We must, therefore, profit by their fears; but we shall await daylight before acting, and then we can form our plans of rescue according to circumstances."

"The poor captive cannot be far off," said Joe, "because—"

"Help! help!" repeated the voice, but much more feebly this time.

"The savage wretches!" exclaimed Joe, trembling with indignation. "Suppose they should kill him to-night!"

"Do you hear, doctor," resumed Kennedy, seizing the doctor's hand. "Suppose they should kill him to-night!"

"It is not at all likely, my friends. These savage tribes kill their captives in broad daylight; they must have the sunshine."

"Now, if I were to take advantage of the darkness to slip down to the poor fellow?" said Kennedy.

"And I'll go with you," said Joe, warmly.

"Pause, my friends—pause! The suggestion does honor to your hearts and to your courage; but you would expose us all to great peril, and do still greater harm to the unfortunate man whom you wish to aid."

"Why so?" asked Kennedy. "These savages are frightened and dispersed: they will not return."

"Dick, I implore you, heed what I say. I am acting for the common good; and if by any accident you should be taken by surprise, all would be lost."

"But, think of that poor wretch, hoping for aid, waiting there, praying, calling aloud. Is no one to go to his assistance? He must think that his senses deceived him; that he heard nothing!"

"We can reassure him, on that score," said Dr. Ferguson—and, standing erect, making a speaking-trumpet of his hands, he shouted at the top of his voice, in French: "Whoever you are, be of good cheer! Three friends are watching over you."

A terrific howl from the savages responded to these words—no doubt drowning the prisoner's reply.

"They are murdering him! they are murdering him!" exclaimed Kennedy. "Our interference will have served no other purpose than to hasten the hour of his doom. We must act!"

"But how, Dick? What do you expect to do in the midst of this darkness?"

"Oh, if it was only daylight!" sighed Joe.

"Well, and suppose it were daylight?" said the doctor, in a singular tone.

"Nothing more simple, doctor," said Kennedy. "I'd go down and scatter all these savage villains with powder and ball!"

"And you, Joe, what would you do?"

"I, master? why, I'd act more prudently, maybe, by telling the prisoner to make his escape in a certain direction that we'd agree upon."

"And how would you get him to know that?"

"By means of this arrow that I caught flying the other day. I'd tie a note to it, or I'd just call out to him in a loud voice what you want him to do, because these black fellows don't understand the language that you'd speak in!"

"Your plans are impracticable, my dear friends. The greatest difficulty would be for this poor fellow to escape at all—even admitting that he should manage to elude the vigilance of his captors. As for you, my dear Dick, with determined daring, and profiting by their alarm at our fire-arms, your project might possibly succeed; but, were it to fail, you would be lost, and we should have two persons to save instead of one. No! we must put *all* the chances on *our* side, and go to work differently."

"But let us act at once!" said the hunter.

"Perhaps we may," said the doctor, throwing considerable stress upon the words.

"Why, doctor, can you light up such darkness as this?"

"Who knows, Joe?"

"Ah! if you can do that, you're the greatest learned man in the world!"

The doctor kept silent for a few moments; he was thinking. His two companions looked at him with much emotion, for they were greatly excited by the strangeness of the situation. Ferguson at last resumed:

"Here is my plan: We have two hundred pounds of ballast left, since the bags we brought with us are still untouched. I'll suppose that this prisoner, who is evidently exhausted by suffering, weighs as much as one of us; there will still remain sixty pounds of ballast to throw out, in case we should want to ascend suddenly."

"How do you expect to manage the balloon?" asked Kennedy.

"This is the idea, Dick: you will admit that if I can get to the prisoner, and throw out a quantity of ballast, equal to his weight, I shall have in nowise altered the equilibrium of the balloon. But, then, if I want to get a rapid ascension, so as to escape these savages, I must employ means more energetic than the cylinder. Well, then, in throwing out this overplus of ballast at a given moment, I am certain to rise with great rapidity."

"That's plain enough."

"Yes; but there is one drawback: it consists in the fact that, in order to descend after that, I should have to part with a quantity of gas proportionate to the surplus ballast that I had thrown out. Now, the gas is precious; but we must not haggle over it when the life of a fellow-creature is at stake."

"You are right, sir; we must do every thing in our power to save him."

"Let us work, then, and get these bags all arranged on the rim of the car, so that they may be thrown overboard at one movement."

"But this darkness?"

"It hides our preparations, and will be dispersed only when they are finished. Take care to have all our weapons close at hand. Perhaps we may have to fire; so we have one shot in the rifle; four for the two muskets; twelve in the two revolvers; or seventeen in all, which might be fired in a quarter of a minute. But perhaps we shall not have to resort to all this noisy work. Are you ready?"

"We're ready," responded Joe.

The sacks were placed as requested, and the arms were put in good order.

"Very good!" said the doctor. "Have an eye to every thing. Joe will see to throwing out the ballast, and Dick will carry off the prisoner; but let nothing be done until I give the word. Joe will first detach the anchor, and then quickly make his way back to the car."

Joe let himself slide down by the rope; and, in a few moments, reappeared at his post; while the balloon, thus liberated, hung almost motionless in the air.

In the mean time the doctor assured himself of the presence of a sufficient quantity of gas in the mixing-tank to feed the cylinder, if necessary, without there being any need of resorting for some time to the Buntzen battery. He then took out the two perfectly-isolated conducting-wires, which served for the decomposition of the water, and, searching in his travelling-sack, brought forth two pieces of charcoal, cut down to a sharp point, and fixed one at the end of each wire.

His two friends looked on, without knowing what he was about, but they kept perfectly silent. When the doctor had finished, he stood up erect in the car, and, taking the two pieces of charcoal, one in each hand, drew their points nearly together.

In a twinkling, an intense and dazzling light was produced, with an insupportable glow between the two pointed ends of charcoal, and a huge jet of electric radiance literally broke the darkness of the night.

"Oh!" exclaimed the astonished friends.

"Not a word!" cautioned the doctor.

Chapter 22

The Jet of Light.—The Missionary.—The Rescue in a Ray of Electricity.—A Lazarist Priest.—But Little Hope.—The Doctor's Care.—A Life of Self-Denial.—Passing a Volcano.

D r. Ferguson darted his powerful electric jet toward various points of space, and caused it to rest on a spot from which shouts of terror were heard. His companions fixed their gaze eagerly on the place.

The baobab, over which the balloon was hanging almost motionless, stood in the centre of a clearing, where, between fields of Indian-corn and sugar-cane, were seen some fifty low, conical huts, around which swarmed a numerous tribe.

A hundred feet below the balloon stood a large post, or stake, and at its foot lay a human being—a young man of thirty years or more, with long black hair, half naked, wasted and wan, bleeding, covered with wounds, his head bowed over upon his breast, as Christ's was, when He hung upon the cross.

The hair, cut shorter on the top of his skull, still indicated the place of a half-effaced tonsure.

"A missionary! a priest!" exclaimed Joe.

"Poor, unfortunate man!" said Kennedy.

"We must save him, Dick!" responded the doctor; "we must save him!"

The crowd of blacks, when they saw the balloon over their heads, like a huge comet with a train of dazzling light, were seized with a terror that may be readily imagined. Upon hearing their cries, the prisoner raised his head. His eyes gleamed with sudden hope, and, without too thoroughly comprehending what was taking place, he stretched out his hands to his unexpected deliverers.

"He is alive!" exclaimed Ferguson. "God be praised! The savages have got a fine scare, and we shall save him! Are you ready, friends?"

"Ready, doctor, at the word."

"Joe, shut off the cylinder!"

The doctor's order was executed. An almost imperceptible breath of air impelled the balloon directly over the prisoner, at the same time that it gently lowered with the contraction of the gas. For about ten minutes it remained floating in the midst of luminous waves, for Ferguson continued to flash right down upon the throng his glowing sheaf of rays, which, here and there, marked out swift and vivid sheets of light. The tribe, under the influence of an indescribable terror, disappeared little by little in the huts, and there was complete solitude around the stake. The doctor had, therefore, been right in counting upon the fantastic appearance of the balloon throwing out rays, as vivid as the sun's, through this intense gloom.

The car was approaching the ground; but a few of the savages, more audacious than the rest, guessing that their victim was about to escape from their clutches, came back with loud yells, and Kennedy seized his rifle. The doctor, however, besought him not to fire.

The priest, on his knees, for he had not the strength to stand erect, was not even fastened to the stake, his weakness rendering that precaution superfluous. At the instant when the car was close to the ground, the brawny Scot, laying aside his rifle, and seizing the priest around the waist, lifted him into the car, while, at the same moment, Joe tossed over the two hundred pounds of ballast.

The doctor had expected to ascend rapidly, but, contrary to his calculations, the balloon, after going up some three or four feet, remained there perfectly motionless.

"What holds us?" he asked, with an accent of terror.

Some of the savages were running toward them, uttering ferocious cries.

"Ah, ha!" said Joe, "one of those cursed blacks is hanging to the car!"

"Dick! Dick!" cried the doctor, "the water-tank!"

Kennedy caught his friend's idea on the instant, and, snatching up with desperate strength one of the water-tanks weighing about one hundred pounds, he tossed it overboard. The balloon, thus suddenly lightened, made a leap of three hundred feet into the air, amid the howlings of the tribe whose prisoner thus escaped them in a blaze of dazzling light.

"Hurrah!" shouted the doctor's comrades.

Suddenly, the balloon took a fresh leap, which carried it up to an elevation of a thousand feet.

"What's that?" said Kennedy, who had nearly lost his balance.

"Oh! nothing; only that black villain leaving us!" replied the doctor, tranquilly, and Joe, leaning over, saw the savage that had clung to the car whirling over and over, with his arms outstretched in the air, and presently dashed to pieces on the ground. The doctor then separated his electric wires, and every thing was again buried in profound obscurity. It was now one o'clock in the morning.

The Frenchman, who had swooned away, at length opened his eyes.

"You are saved!" were the doctor's first words.

"Saved!" he with a sad smile replied in English, "saved from a cruel death! My brethren, I thank you, but my days are numbered, nay, even my hours, and I have but little longer to live."

With this, the missionary, again yielding to exhaustion, relapsed into his fainting-fit.

"He is dying!" said Kennedy.

"No," replied the doctor, bending over him, "but he is very weak; so let us lay him under the awning."

And they did gently deposit on their blankets that poor, wasted body, covered with scars and wounds, still bleeding where fire and steel had, in twenty places, left their agonizing marks. The doctor, taking an old handkerchief, quickly prepared a little lint, which he spread over the wounds, after having washed them. These rapid attentions were bestowed with the celerity and skill of a practised surgeon, and, when they were complete, the doctor, taking a cordial from his medicine-chest, poured a few drops upon his patient's lips.

The latter feebly pressed his kind hands, and scarcely had the strength to say, "Thank you! thank you!"

The doctor comprehended that he must be left perfectly quiet; so he closed the folds of the awning and resumed the guidance of the balloon.

The latter, after taking into account the weight of the new passenger, had been lightened of one hundred and eighty pounds, and therefore kept aloft without the aid of the cylinder. At the first dawn of day, a current drove it gently toward the west-northwest. The doctor went in under the awning for a moment or two, to look at his still sleeping patient.

"May Heaven spare the life of our new companion! Have you any hope?" said the Scot.

"Yes, Dick, with care, in this pure, fresh atmosphere."

"How that man has suffered!" said Joe, with feeling. "He did bolder things than we've done, in venturing all alone among those savage tribes!"

"That cannot be questioned," assented the hunter.

During the entire day the doctor would not allow the sleep of his patient to be disturbed. It was really a long stupor, broken only by an occasional murmur of pain that continued to disquiet and agitate the doctor greatly.

Toward evening the balloon remained stationary in the midst of the gloom, and during the night, while Kennedy and Joe relieved each other in carefully tending the sick man, Ferguson kept watch over the safety of all.

By the morning of the next day, the balloon had moved, but very slightly, to the westward. The dawn came up pure and magnificent. The sick man was able to call his friends with a stronger voice. They raised the curtains of the awning, and he inhaled with delight the keen morning air.

"How do you feel to-day?" asked the doctor.

"Better, perhaps," he replied. "But you, my friends, I have not seen you yet, excepting in a dream! I can, indeed, scarcely recall what has occurred. Who are you—that your names may not be forgotten in my dying prayers?"

"We are English travellers," replied Ferguson. "We are trying to cross Africa in a balloon, and, on our way, we have had the good fortune to rescue you."

"Science has its heroes," said the missionary.

"But religion its martyrs!" rejoined the Scot.

"Are you a missionary?" asked the doctor.

"I am a priest of the Lazarist mission. Heaven sent you to me—Heaven be praised! The sacrifice of my life had been accomplished! But you come from Europe; tell me about Europe, about France! I have been without news for the last five years!"

"Five years! alone! and among these savages!" exclaimed Kennedy with amazement.

"They are souls to redeem! ignorant and barbarous brethren, whom religion alone can instruct and civilize."

Dr. Ferguson, yielding to the priest's request, talked to him long and fully about France. He listened eagerly, and his eyes filled with tears. He seized Kennedy's and Joe's hands by turns in his own, which were burning with fever. The doctor prepared him some tea, and he drank it with satisfaction. After that, he had strength enough to raise himself up a little, and smiled with pleasure at seeing himself borne along through so pure a sky.

"You are daring travellers!" he said, "and you will succeed in your bold enterprise. You will again behold your relatives, your friends, your country—you—"

At this moment, the weakness of the young missionary became so extreme that they had to lay him again on the bed, where a prostration, lasting for several hours, held him like a dead man under the eye of Dr. Ferguson. The latter could not suppress his emotion, for he felt that this life now in his charge was ebbing away. Were they then so soon to lose him whom they had snatched from an agonizing death? The doctor again washed and dressed the young martyr's frightful wounds, and had to sacrifice nearly his whole stock of water to refresh his burning limbs. He surrounded him with the tenderest and most intelligent care, until, at length, the sick man revived, little by little, in his arms, and recovered his consciousness if not his strength.

The doctor was able to gather something of his history from his broken murmurs.

"Speak in your native language," he said to the sufferer; "I understand it, and it will fatigue you less."

The missionary was a poor young man from the village of Aradon, in Brittany, in the Morbihan country. His earliest instincts had drawn him toward an ecclesiastical career, but to this life of self-sacrifice he was also desirous of joining a life of danger, by entering the mission of the order of priesthood of which St. Vincent de Paul was the founder, and, at twenty, he quitted his country for the inhospitable shores of Africa. From the sea-coast, overcoming obstacles, little by little, braving all privations, pushing onward, afoot, and praying, he had advanced to the very centre of those tribes that dwell among the tributary streams of the Upper Nile. For two years his faith was spurned, his zeal denied recognition, his charities taken in ill part, and he remained a prisoner to one of the cruelest tribes of the Nyambarra, the object of every species of maltreatment. But still he went on teaching, instructing, and praying. The tribe having been dispersed and he left for dead, in one of those combats which are so frequent between the tribes, instead of retracing his steps, he persisted in his evangelical mission. His most tranquil time was when he was taken for a madman. Meanwhile, he had made himself familiar with the idioms of the country, and he catechised in them. At length, during two more long years, he traversed these barbarous regions, impelled by that superhuman energy that comes from God. For a year past he had been residing with that tribe of the Nyam-Nyams known as the Barafri, one of the wildest and most ferocious of them all. The chief having died a few days before our travellers appeared, his sudden death was attributed to the missionary, and the tribe resolved to immolate him. His sufferings had already continued for the space of forty hours, and, as the doctor had supposed, he was to have perished in the blaze of the noonday sun. When he heard the sound of fire-arms, nature got the best of him, and he had cried out, "Help! help!" He then thought that he must have been dreaming, when a voice, that seemed to come from the sky, had uttered words of consolation.

"I have no regrets," he said, "for the life that is passing away from me; my life belongs to God!"

"Hope still!" said the doctor; "we are near you, and we will save you now, as we saved you from the tortures of the stake."

"I do not ask so much of Heaven," said the priest, with resignation. "Blessed be God for having vouchsafed to me the joy before I die of having pressed your friendly hands, and having heard, once more, the language of my country!"

The missionary here grew weak again, and the whole day went by between hope and fear, Kennedy deeply moved, and Joe drawing his hand over his eyes more than once when he thought that no one saw him.

The balloon made little progress, and the wind seemed as though unwilling to jostle its precious burden.

Toward evening, Joe discovered a great light in the west. Under more elevated latitudes, it might have been mistaken for an immense aurora borealis, for the sky appeared on fire. The doctor very attentively examined the phenomenon.

"It is, perhaps, only a volcano in full activity," said he.

"But the wind is carrying us directly over it," replied Kennedy.

"Very well, we shall cross it then at a safe height!" said the doctor.

Three hours later, the Victoria was right among the mountains. Her exact position was twenty-four degrees fifteen minutes east longitude, and four degrees forty-two minutes north latitude, and four degrees forty-two minutes north latitude. In front of her a volcanic crater was pouring forth torrents of melted lava, and hurling masses of rock to an enormous height. There were jets, too, of liquid fire that fell back in dazzling cascades—a superb but dangerous spectacle, for the wind with unswerving certainty was carrying the balloon directly toward this blazing atmosphere.

This obstacle, which could not be turned, had to be crossed, so the cylinder was put to its utmost power, and the balloon rose to the height of six thousand feet, leaving between it and the volcano a space of more than three hundred fathoms.

From his bed of suffering, the dying missionary could contemplate that fiery crater from which a thousand jets of dazzling flame were that moment escaping.

"How grand it is!" said he, "and how infinite is the power of God even in its most terrible manifestations!"

This overflow of blazing lava wrapped the sides of the mountain with a veritable drapery of flame; the lower half of the balloon glowed redly in the upper night; a torrid heat ascended to the car, and Dr. Ferguson made all possible haste to escape from this perilous situation.

By ten o'clock the volcano could be seen only as a red point on the horizon, and the balloon tranquilly pursued her course in a less elevated zone of the atmosphere.

Chapter 23

A magnificent night overspread the earth, and the missionary lay quietly asleep in utter exhaustion.

"He'll not get over it!" sighed Joe. "Poor young fellow—scarcely thirty years of age!"

"He'll die in our arms. His breathing, which was so feeble before, is growing weaker still, and I can do nothing to save him," said the doctor, despairingly.

"The infamous scoundrels!" exclaimed Joe, grinding his teeth, in one of those fits of rage that came over him at long intervals; "and to think that, in spite of all, this good man could find words only to pity them, to excuse, to pardon them!"

"Heaven has given him a lovely night, Joe—his last on earth, perhaps! He will suffer but little more after this, and his dying will be only a peaceful falling asleep."

The dying man uttered some broken words, and the doctor at once went to him. His breathing became difficult, and he asked for air. The curtains were drawn entirely back, and he inhaled with rapture the light breezes of that clear, beautiful night. The stars sent him their trembling rays, and the moon wrapped him in the white winding-sheet of its effulgence.

"My friends," said he, in an enfeebled voice, "I am going. May God requite you, and bring you to your safe harbor! May he pay for me the debt of gratitude that I owe to you!"

"You must still hope," replied Kennedy. "This is but a passing fit of weakness. You will not die. How could any one die on this beautiful summer night?"

"Death is at hand," replied the missionary, "I know it! Let me look it in the face! Death, the commencement of things eternal, is but the end of earthly cares. Place me upon my knees, my brethren, I beseech you!"

Kennedy lifted him up, and it was distressing to see his weakened limbs bend under him.

"My God! my God!" exclaimed the dying apostle, "have pity on me!"

His countenance shone. Far above that earth on which he had known no joys; in the midst of that night which sent to him its softest radiance; on the way to that heaven toward which he uplifted his spirit, as though in a miraculous assumption, he seemed already to live and breathe in the new existence.

His last gesture was a supreme blessing on his new friends of only one day. Then he fell back into the arms of Kennedy, whose countenance was bathed in hot tears.

"Dead!" said the doctor, bending over him, "dead!" And with one common accord, the three friends knelt together in silent prayer.

"To-morrow," resumed the doctor, "we shall bury him in the African soil which he has besprinkled with his blood."

During the rest of the night the body was watched, turn by turn, by the three travellers, and not a word disturbed the solemn silence. Each of them was weeping.

The next day the wind came from the south, and the balloon moved slowly over a vast plateau of mountains: there, were extinct craters; here, barren ravines; not a drop of water on those parched crests; piles of broken rocks; huge stony masses scattered hither and thither, and, interspersed with whitish marl, all indicated the most complete sterility.

Toward noon, the doctor, for the purpose of burying the body, decided to descend into a ravine, in the midst of some plutonic rocks of primitive formation. The surrounding mountains would shelter him, and enable him to bring his car to the ground, for there was no tree in sight to which he could make it fast.

But, as he had explained to Kennedy, it was now impossible for him to descend, except by releasing a quantity of gas proportionate to his loss of ballast at the time when he had rescued the missionary. He therefore opened the valve of the outside balloon. The hydrogen escaped, and the Victoria quietly descended into the ravine.

As soon as the car touched the ground, the doctor shut the valve. Joe leaped out, holding on the while to the rim of the car with one hand, and with the other gathering up a quantity of stones equal to his own weight. He could then use both hands, and had soon heaped into the car more than five hundred pounds of stones, which enabled both the doctor and Kennedy, in their turn, to get out. Thus the

Victoria found herself balanced, and her ascensional force insufficient to raise her.

Moreover, it was not necessary to gather many of these stones, for the blocks were extremely heavy, so much so, indeed, that the doctor's attention was attracted by the circumstance. The soil, in fact, was bestrewn with quartz and porphyritic rocks.

"This is a singular discovery!" said the doctor, mentally.

In the mean while, Kennedy and Joe had strolled away a few paces, looking up a proper spot for the grave. The heat was extreme in this ravine, shut in as it was like a sort of furnace. The noonday sun poured down its rays perpendicularly into it.

The first thing to be done was to clear the surface of the fragments of rock that encumbered it, and then a quite deep grave had to be dug, so that the wild animals should not be able to disinter the corpse.

The body of the martyred missionary was then solemnly placed in it. The earth was thrown in over his remains, and above it masses of rock were deposited, in rude resemblance to a tomb.

The doctor, however, remained motionless, and lost in his reflections. He did not even heed the call of his companions, nor did he return with them to seek a shelter from the heat of the day.

"What are you thinking about, doctor?" asked Kennedy.

"About a singular freak of Nature, a curious effect of chance. Do you know, now, in what kind of soil that man of self-denial, that poor one in spirit, has just been buried?"

"No! what do you mean, doctor?"

"That priest, who took the oath of perpetual poverty, now reposes in a gold-mine!"

"A gold-mine!" exclaimed Kennedy and Joe in one breath.

"Yes, a gold-mine," said the doctor, quietly. "Those blocks which you are trampling under foot, like worthless stones, contain gold-ore of great purity."

"Impossible! impossible!" repeated Joe.

"You would not have to look long among those fissures of slaty schist without finding peptites of considerable value."

Joe at once rushed like a crazy man among the scattered fragments, and Kennedy was not long in following his example.

"Keep cool, Joe," said his master.

"Why, doctor, you speak of the thing quite at your ease."

"What! a philosopher of your mettle—"

"Ah, master, no philosophy holds good in this case!"

"Come! come! Let us reflect a little. What good would all this wealth do you? We cannot carry any of it away with us."

"We can't take any of it with us, indeed?"

"It's rather too heavy for our car! I even hesitated to tell you any thing about it, for fear of exciting your regret!"

"What!" said Joe, again, "abandon these treasures—a fortune for us!—really for us—our own—leave it behind!"

"Take care, my friend! Would you yield to the thirst for gold? Has not this dead man whom you have just helped to bury, taught you the vanity of human affairs?"

"All that is true," replied Joe, "but gold! Mr. Kennedy, won't you help to gather up a trifle of all these millions?"

"What could we do with them, Joe?" said the hunter, unable to repress a smile. "We did not come hither in search of fortune, and we cannot take one home with us."

"The millions are rather heavy, you know," resumed the doctor, "and cannot very easily be put into one's pocket."

"But, at least," said Joe, driven to his last defences, "couldn't we take some of that ore for ballast, instead of sand?"

"Very good! I consent," said the doctor, "but you must not make too many wry faces when we come to throw some thousands of crowns' worth overboard."

"Thousands of crowns!" echoed Joe; "is it possible that there is so much gold in them, and that all this is the same?"

"Yes, my friend, this is a reservoir in which Nature has been heaping up her wealth for centuries! There is enough here to enrich whole nations! An Australia and a California both together in the midst of the wilderness!"

"And the whole of it is to remain useless!"

"Perhaps! but at all events, here's what I'll do to console you."

"That would be rather difficult to do!" said Joe, with a contrite air.

"Listen! I will take the exact bearings of this spot, and give them to you, so that, upon your return to England, you can tell our countrymen about it, and let them have a share, if you think that so much gold would make them happy."

"Ah! master, I give up; I see that you are right, and that there is nothing else to be done. Let us fill our car with the precious mineral, and what remains at the end of the trip will be so much made."

And Joe went to work. He did so, too, with all his might, and soon had collected more than a thousand pieces of quartz, which contained gold enclosed as though in an extremely hard crystal casket.

The doctor watched him with a smile; and, while Joe went on, he took the bearings, and found that the missionary's grave lay in twenty-two degrees twenty-three minutes east longitude, and four degrees fifty-five minutes north latitude.

Then, casting one glance at the swelling of the soil, beneath which the body of the poor Frenchman reposed, he went back to his car.

He would have erected a plain, rude cross over the tomb, left solitary thus in the midst of the African deserts, but not a tree was to be seen in the environs.

"God will recognize it!" said Kennedy.

An anxiety of another sort now began to steal over the doctor's mind. He would have given much of the gold before him for a little water—for he had to replace what had been thrown overboard when the negro was carried up into the air. But it was impossible to find it in these arid regions; and this reflection gave him great uneasiness. He had to feed his cylinder continually; and he even began to find that he had not enough to quench the thirst of his party. Therefore he determined to lose no opportunity of replenishing his supply.

Upon getting back to the car, he found it burdened with the quartz-blocks that Joe's greed had heaped in it. He got in, however, without saying any thing. Kennedy took his customary place, and Joe followed, but not without casting a covetous glance at the treasures in the ravine.

The doctor rekindled the light in the cylinder; the spiral became heated; the current of hydrogen came in a few minutes, and the gas dilated; but the balloon did not stir an inch.

Joe looked on uneasily, but kept silent.

"Joe!" said the doctor.

Joe made no reply.

"Joe! Don't you hear me?"

Joe made a sign that he heard; but he would not understand.

"Do me the kindness to throw out some of that quartz!"

"But, doctor, you gave me leave—"

"I gave you leave to replace the ballast; that was all!"

"But—"

"Do you want to stay forever in this desert?"

Joe cast a despairing look at Kennedy; but the hunter put on the air of a man who could do nothing in the matter.

"Well, Joe?"

"Then your cylinder don't work," said the obstinate fellow.

"My cylinder? It is lit, as you perceive. But the balloon will not rise until you have thrown off a little ballast."

Joe scratched his ear, picked up a piece of quartz, the smallest in the lot, weighed and reweighed it, and tossed it up and down in his hand. It was a fragment of about three or four pounds. At last he threw it out.

But the balloon did not budge.

"Humph!" said he; "we're not going up yet."

"Not yet," said the doctor. "Keep on throwing."

Kennedy laughed. Joe now threw out some ten pounds, but the balloon stood still.

Joe got very pale.

"Poor fellow!" said the doctor. "Mr. Kennedy, you and I weigh, unless I am mistaken, about four hundred pounds—so that you'll have to get rid of at least that weight, since it was put in here to make up for us."

"Throw away four hundred pounds!" said Joe, piteously.

"And some more with it, or we can't rise. Come, courage, Joe!"

The brave fellow, heaving deep sighs, began at last to lighten the balloon; but, from time to time, he would stop, and ask:

"Are you going up?"

"No, not yet," was the invariable response.

"It moves!" said he, at last.

"Keep on!" replied the doctor.

"It's going up; I'm sure."

"Keep on yet," said Kennedy.

And Joe, picking up one more block, desperately tossed it out of the car. The balloon rose a hundred feet or so, and, aided by the cylinder, soon passed above the surrounding summits.

"Now, Joe," resumed the doctor, "there still remains a handsome fortune for you; and, if we can only keep the rest of this with us until the end of our trip, there you are—rich for the balance of your days!"

Joe made no answer, but stretched himself out luxuriously on his heap of quartz.

"See, my dear Dick!" the doctor went on. "Just see the power of this metal over the cleverest lad in the world! What passions, what greed, what crimes, the knowledge of such a mine as that would cause! It is sad to think of it!"

By evening the balloon had made ninety miles to the westward, and was, in a direct line, fourteen hundred miles from Zanzibar.

Chapter 24

THE WIND DIES AWAY.—THE VICINITY OF THE DESERT.—THE MISTAKE IN THE WATER SUPPLY.—THE NIGHTS OF THE EQUATOR.— DR. FERGUSON'S ANXIETIES.—THE SITUATION FLATLY STATED.— ENERGETIC REPLIES OF KENNEDY AND JOE.—ONE NIGHT MORE.

The balloon, having been made fast to a solitary tree, almost completely dried up by the aridity of the region in which it stood, passed the night in perfect quietness; and the travellers were enabled to enjoy a little of the repose which they so greatly needed. The emotions of the day had left sad impressions on their minds.

Toward morning, the sky had resumed its brilliant purity and its heat. The balloon ascended, and, after several ineffectual attempts, fell into a current that, although not rapid, bore them toward the northwest.

"We are not making progress," said the doctor. "If I am not mistaken, we have accomplished nearly half of our journey in ten days; but, at the rate at which we are going, it would take months to end it; and that is all the more vexatious, that we are threatened with a lack of water."

"But we'll find some," said Joe. "It is not to be thought of that we shouldn't discover some river, some stream, or pond, in all this vast extent of country."

"I hope so."

"Now don't you think that it's Joe's cargo of stone that is keeping us back?"

Kennedy asked this question only to tease Joe; and he did so the more willingly because he had, for a moment, shared the poor lad's hallucinations; but, not finding any thing in them, he had fallen back into the attitude of a strong-minded looker-on, and turned the affair off with a laugh.

Joe cast a mournful glance at him; but the doctor made no reply. He was thinking, not without secret terror, probably, of the vast solitudes of Sahara—for there whole weeks sometimes pass without the caravans meeting with a single spring of water. Occupied with these thoughts, he scrutinized every depression of the soil with the closest attention.

These anxieties, and the incidents recently occurring, had not been without their effect upon the spirits of our three travellers. They conversed less, and were more wrapt in their own thoughts.

Joe, clever lad as he was, seemed no longer the same person since his gaze had plunged into that ocean of gold. He kept entirely silent, and gazed incessantly upon the stony fragments heaped up in the car—worthless to-day, but of inestimable value to-morrow.

The appearance of this part of Africa was, moreover, quite calculated to inspire alarm: the desert was gradually expanding around them; not another village was to be seen—not even a collection of a few huts; and vegetation also was disappearing. Barely a few dwarf plants could now be noticed, like those on the wild heaths of Scotland; then came the first tract of grayish sand and flint, with here and there a lentisk tree and brambles. In the midst of this sterility, the rudimental carcass of the Globe appeared in ridges of sharply-jutting rock. These symptoms of a totally dry and barren region greatly disquieted Dr. Ferguson.

It seemed as though no caravan had ever braved this desert expanse, or it would have left visible traces of its encampments, or the whitened bones of men and animals. But nothing of the kind was to be seen, and the aeronauts felt that, ere long, an immensity of sand would cover the whole of this desolate region.

However, there was no going back; they must go forward; and, indeed, the doctor asked for nothing better; he would even have welcomed a tempest to carry him beyond this country. But, there was not a cloud in the sky. At the close of the day, the balloon had not made thirty miles.

If there had been no lack of water! But, there remained only three gallons in all! The doctor put aside one gallon, destined to quench the burning thirst that a heat of ninety degrees rendered intolerable. Two gallons only then remained to supply the cylinder. Hence, they could produce no more than four hundred and eighty cubic feet of gas; yet the cylinder consumed about nine cubic feet per hour. Consequently, they could not keep on longer than fifty-four hours—and all this was a mathematical calculation!

"Fifty-four hours!" said the doctor to his companions. "Therefore, as I am determined not to travel by night, for fear of passing some stream or pool, we have but three days and a half of journeying during which we must find water, at all hazards. I have thought it my duty to make you aware of the real state of the case, as I have retained only one gallon for drinking, and we shall have to put ourselves on the shortest allowance."

"Put us on short allowance, then, doctor," responded Kennedy, "but we must not despair. We have three days left, you say?"

"Yes, my dear Dick!"

"Well, as grieving over the matter won't help us, in three days there will be time enough to decide upon what is to be done; in the meanwhile, let us redouble our vigilance!"

At their evening meal, the water was strictly measured out, and the brandy was increased in quantity in the punch they drank. But they had to be careful with the spirits, the latter being more likely to produce than to quench thirst.

The car rested, during the night, upon an immense plateau, in which there was a deep hollow; its height was scarcely eight hundred feet above the level of the sea. This circumstance gave the doctor some hope, since it recalled to his mind the conjectures of geographers concerning the existence of a vast stretch of water in the centre of Africa. But, if such a lake really existed, the point was to reach it, and not a sign of change was visible in the motionless sky.

To the tranquil night and its starry magnificence succeeded the unchanging daylight and the blazing rays of the sun; and, from the earliest dawn, the temperature became scorching. At five o'clock in the morning, the doctor gave the signal for departure, and, for a considerable time, the balloon remained immovable in the leaden atmosphere.

The doctor might have escaped this intense heat by rising into a higher range, but, in order to do so, he would have had to consume a large quantity of water, a thing that had now become impossible. He contented himself, therefore, with keeping the balloon at one hundred feet from the ground, and, at that elevation, a feeble current drove it toward the western horizon.

The breakfast consisted of a little dried meat and pemmican. By noon, the Victoria had advanced only a few miles.

"We cannot go any faster," said the doctor; "we no longer command— we have to obey."

"Ah! doctor, here is one of those occasions when a propeller would not be a thing to be despised."

"Undoubtedly so, Dick, provided it would not require an expenditure of water to put it in motion, for, in that case, the situation would be precisely the same; moreover, up to this time, nothing practical of the sort has been invented. Balloons are still at that point where ships were before the invention of steam. It took six thousand years to invent propellers and screws; so we have time enough yet."

"Confounded heat!" said Joe, wiping away the perspiration that was streaming from his forehead.

"If we had water, this heat would be of service to us, for it dilates the hydrogen in the balloon, and diminishes the amount required in the spiral, although it is true that, if we were not short of the useful liquid, we should not have to economize it. Ah! that rascally savage who cost us the tank!"*

"You don't regret, though, what you did, doctor?"

"No, Dick, since it was in our power to save that unfortunate missionary from a horrible death. But, the hundred pounds of water that we threw overboard would be very useful to us now; it would be thirteen or fourteen days more of progress secured, or quite enough to carry us over this desert."

"We've made at least half the journey, haven't we?" asked Joe.

"In distance, yes; but in duration, no, should the wind leave us; and it, even now, has a tendency to die away altogether."

"Come, sir," said Joe, again, "we must not complain; we've got along pretty well, thus far, and whatever happens to me, I can't get desperate. We'll find water; mind, I tell you so."

The soil, however, ran lower from mile to mile; the undulations of the gold-bearing mountains they had left died away into the plain, like the last throes of exhausted Nature. Scanty grass took the place of the fine trees of the east; only a few belts of half-scorched herbage still contended against the invasion of the sand, and the huge rocks, that had rolled down from the distant summits, crushed in their fall, had scattered in sharp-edged pebbles which soon again became coarse sand, and finally impalpable dust.

"Here, at last, is Africa, such as you pictured it to yourself, Joe! Was I not right in saying, 'Wait a little?' eh?"

"Well, master, it's all natural, at least—heat and dust. It would be foolish to look for any thing else in such a country. Do you see," he added, laughing, "I had no confidence, for my part, in your forests and your prairies; they were out of reason. What was the use of coming so far to find scenery just like England? Here's the first time that I believe in Africa, and I'm not sorry to get a taste of it."

---

* The water-tank had been thrown overboard when the native clung to the car.

Toward evening, the doctor calculated that the balloon had not made twenty miles during that whole burning day, and a heated gloom closed in upon it, as soon as the sun had disappeared behind the horizon, which was traced against the sky with all the precision of a straight line.

The next day was Thursday, the 1st of May, but the days followed each other with desperate monotony. Each morning was like the one that had preceded it; noon poured down the same exhaustless rays, and night condensed in its shadow the scattered heat which the ensuing day would again bequeath to the succeeding night. The wind, now scarcely observable, was rather a gasp than a breath, and the morning could almost be foreseen when even that gasp would cease.

The doctor reacted against the gloominess of the situation and retained all the coolness and self-possession of a disciplined heart. With his glass he scrutinized every quarter of the horizon; he saw the last rising ground gradually melting to the dead level, and the last vegetation disappearing, while, before him, stretched the immensity of the desert.

The responsibility resting upon him pressed sorely, but he did not allow his disquiet to appear. Those two men, Dick and Joe, friends of his, both of them, he had induced to come with him almost by the force alone of friendship and of duty. Had he done well in that? Was it not like attempting to tread forbidden paths? Was he not, in this trip, trying to pass the borders of the impossible? Had not the Almighty reserved for later ages the knowledge of this inhospitable continent?

All these thoughts, of the kind that arise in hours of discouragement, succeeded each other and multiplied in his mind, and, by an irresistible association of ideas, the doctor allowed himself to be carried beyond the bounds of logic and of reason. After having established in his own mind what he should *not* have done, the next question was, what he should do, then. Would it be impossible to retrace his steps? Were there not currents higher up that would waft him to less arid regions? Well informed with regard to the countries over which he had passed, he was utterly ignorant of those to come, and thus his conscience speaking aloud to him, he resolved, in his turn, to speak frankly to his two companions. He thereupon laid the whole state of the case plainly before them; he showed them what had been done, and what there was yet to do; at the worst, they could return, or attempt it, at least.—What did they think about it?

"I have no other opinion than that of my excellent master," said Joe; "what he may have to suffer, I can suffer, and that better than he can, perhaps. Where he goes, there I'll go!"

"And you, Kennedy?"

"I, doctor, I'm not the man to despair; no one was less ignorant than I of the perils of the enterprise, but I did not want to see them, from the moment that you determined to brave them. Under present circumstances, my opinion is, that we should persevere—go clear to the end. Besides, to return looks to me quite as perilous as the other course. So onward, then! you may count upon us!"

"Thanks, my gallant friends!" replied the doctor, with much real feeling, "I expected such devotion as this; but I needed these encouraging words. Yet, once again, thank you, from the bottom of my heart!"

And, with this, the three friends warmly grasped each other by the hand.

"Now, hear me!" said the doctor. "According to my solar observations, we are not more than three hundred miles from the Gulf of Guinea; the desert, therefore, cannot extend indefinitely, since the coast is inhabited, and the country has been explored for some distance back into the interior. If needs be, we can direct our course to that quarter, and it seems out of the question that we should not come across some oasis, or some well, where we could replenish our stock of water. But, what we want now, is the wind, for without it we are held here suspended in the air at a dead calm.

"Let us wait with resignation," said the hunter.

But, each of the party, in his turn, vainly scanned the space around him during that long wearisome day. Nothing could be seen to form the basis of a hope. The very last inequalities of the soil disappeared with the setting sun, whose horizontal rays stretched in long lines of fire over the flat immensity. It was the Desert!

Our aeronauts had scarcely gone a distance of fifteen miles, having expended, as on the preceding day, one hundred and thirty-five cubic feet of gas to feed the cylinder, and two pints of water out of the remaining eight had been sacrificed to the demands of intense thirst.

The night passed quietly—too quietly, indeed, but the doctor did not sleep!

Chapter 25

On the morrow, there was the same purity of sky, the same stillness of the atmosphere. The balloon rose to an elevation of five hundred feet, but it had scarcely changed its position to the westward in any perceptible degree.

"We are right in the open desert," said the doctor. "Look at that vast reach of sand! What a strange spectacle! What a singular arrangement of nature! Why should there be, in one place, such extreme luxuriance of vegetation yonder, and here, this extreme aridity, and that in the same latitude, and under the same rays of the sun?"

"The why concerns me but little," answered Kennedy, "the reason interests me less than the fact. The thing is so; that's the important part of it!"

"Oh, it is well to philosophize a little, Dick; it does no harm."

"Let us philosophize, then, if you will; we have time enough before us; we are hardly moving; the wind is afraid to blow; it sleeps."

"That will not last forever," put in Joe; "I think I see some banks of clouds in the east."

"Joe's right!" said the doctor, after he had taken a look.

"Good!" said Kennedy; "now for our clouds, with a fine rain, and a fresh wind to dash it into our faces!"

"Well, we'll see, Dick, we'll see!"

"But this is Friday, master, and I'm afraid of Fridays!"

"Well, I hope that this very day you'll get over those notions."

"I hope so, master, too. Whew!" he added, mopping his face, "heat's a good thing, especially in winter, but in summer it don't do to take too much of it."

"Don't you fear the effect of the sun's heat on our balloon?" asked Kennedy, addressing the doctor.

"No! the gutta-percha coating resists much higher temperatures than even this. With my spiral I have subjected it inside to as much as one hundred and fifty-eight degrees sometimes, and the covering does not appear to have suffered."

"A cloud! a real cloud!" shouted Joe at this moment, for that piercing eyesight of his beat all the glasses.

And, in fact, a thick bank of vapor, now quite distinct, could be seen slowly emerging above the horizon. It appeared to be very deep, and, as it were, puffed out. It was, in reality, a conglomeration of smaller clouds. The latter invariably retained their original formation, and from this circumstance the doctor concluded that there was no current of air in their collected mass.

This compact body of vapor had appeared about eight o'clock in the morning, and, by eleven, it had already reached the height of the sun's disk. The latter then disappeared entirely behind the murky veil, and the lower belt of cloud, at the same moment, lifted above the line of the horizon, which was again disclosed in a full blaze of daylight.

"It's only an isolated cloud," remarked the doctor. "It won't do to count much upon that."

"Look, Dick, its shape is just the same as when we saw it this morning!"

"Then, doctor, there's to be neither rain nor wind, at least for us!"

"I fear so; the cloud keeps at a great height."

"Well, doctor, suppose we were to go in pursuit of this cloud, since it refuses to burst upon us?"

"I fancy that to do so wouldn't help us much; it would be a consumption of gas, and, consequently, of water, to little purpose; but, in our situation, we must not leave anything untried; therefore, let us ascend!"

And with this, the doctor put on a full head of flame from the cylinder, and the dilation of the hydrogen, occasioned by such sudden and intense heat, sent the balloon rapidly aloft.

About fifteen hundred feet from the ground, it encountered an opaque mass of cloud, and entered a dense fog, suspended at that elevation; but it did not meet with the least breath of wind. This fog seemed even destitute of humidity, and the articles brought in contact with it were scarcely dampened in the slightest degree. The balloon, completely enveloped in the vapor, gained a little increase of speed, perhaps, and that was all.

The doctor gloomily recognized what trifling success he had obtained from his manoeuvre, and was relapsing into deep meditation, when he heard Joe exclaim, in tones of most intense astonishment:

"Ah! by all that's beautiful!"

"What's the matter, Joe?"

"Doctor! Mr. Kennedy! Here's something curious!"

"What is it, then?"

"We are not alone, up here! There are rogues about! They've stolen our invention!"

"Has he gone crazy?" asked Kennedy.

Joe stood there, perfectly motionless, the very picture of amazement.

"Can the hot sun have really affected the poor fellow's brain?" said the doctor, turning toward him.

"Will you tell me?—"

"Look!" said Joe, pointing to a certain quarter of the sky.

"By St. James!" exclaimed Kennedy, in turn, "why, who would have believed it? Look, look! doctor!"

"I see it!" said the doctor, very quietly.

"Another balloon! and other passengers, like ourselves!"

And, sure enough, there was another balloon about two hundred paces from them, floating in the air with its car and its aeronauts. It was following exactly the same route as the Victoria.

"Well," said the doctor, "nothing remains for us but to make signals; take the flag, Kennedy, and show them our colors."

It seemed that the travellers by the other balloon had just the same idea, at the same moment, for the same kind of flag repeated precisely the same salute with a hand that moved in just the same manner.

"What does that mean?" asked Kennedy.

"They are apes," said Joe, "imitating us."

"It means," said the doctor, laughing, "that it is you, Dick, yourself, making that signal to yourself; or, in other words, that we see ourselves in the second balloon, which is no other than the Victoria."

"As to that, master, with all respect to you," said Joe, "you'll never make me believe it."

"Climb up on the edge of the car, Joe; wave your arms, and then you'll see."

Joe obeyed, and all his gestures were instantaneously and exactly repeated.

"It is merely the effect of the *mirage*," said the doctor, "and nothing else—a simple optical phenomenon due to the unequal refraction of light by different layers of the atmosphere, and that is all."

"It's wonderful," said Joe, who could not make up his mind to surrender, but went on repeating his gesticulations.

"What a curious sight! Do you know," said Kennedy, "that it's a real pleasure to have a view of our noble balloon in that style? She's a beauty, isn't she?—and how stately her movements as she sweeps along!"

"You may explain the matter as you like," continued Joe, "it's a strange thing, anyhow!"

But ere long this picture began to fade away; the clouds rose higher, leaving the balloon, which made no further attempt to follow them, and in about an hour they disappeared in the open sky.

The wind, which had been scarcely perceptible, seemed still to diminish, and the doctor in perfect desperation descended toward the ground, and all three of the travellers, whom the incident just recorded had, for a few moments, diverted from their anxieties, relapsed into gloomy meditation, sweltering the while beneath the scorching heat.

About four o'clock, Joe descried some object standing out against the vast background of sand, and soon was able to declare positively that there were two palm-trees at no great distance.

"Palm-trees!" exclaimed Ferguson; "why, then there's a spring—a well!"

He took up his glass and satisfied himself that Joe's eyes had not been mistaken.

"At length!" he said, over and over again, "water! water! and we are saved; for if we do move slowly, still we move, and we shall arrive at last!"

"Good, master! but suppose we were to drink a mouthful in the mean time, for this air is stifling?"

"Let us drink then, my boy!"

No one waited to be coaxed. A whole pint was swallowed then and there, reducing the total remaining supply to three pints and a half.

"Ah! that does one good!" said Joe; "wasn't it fine? Barclay and Perkins never turned out ale equal to that!"

"See the advantage of being put on short allowance!" moralized the doctor.

"It is not great, after all," retorted Kennedy; "and if I were never again to have the pleasure of drinking water, I should agree on condition that I should never be deprived of it."

At six o'clock the balloon was floating over the palm-trees.

They were two shrivelled, stunted, dried-up specimens of trees—two ghosts of palms—without foliage, and more dead than alive. Ferguson examined them with terror.

At their feet could be seen the half-worn stones of a spring, but these stones, pulverized by the baking heat of the sun, seemed to be nothing now but impalpable dust. There was not the slightest sign of moisture. The doctor's heart shrank within him, and he was about to communicate his thoughts to his companions, when their exclamations attracted his attention. As far as the eye could reach to the eastward, extended a long line of whitened bones; pieces of skeletons surrounded the fountain; a caravan had evidently made its way to that point, marking its progress by its bleaching remains; the weaker had fallen one by one upon the sand; the stronger, having at length reached this spring for which they panted, had there found a horrible death.

Our travellers looked at each other and turned pale.

"Let us not alight!" said Kennedy, "let us fly from this hideous spectacle! There's not a drop of water here!"

"No, Dick, as well pass the night here as elsewhere; let us have a clear conscience in the matter. We'll dig down to the very bottom of the well. There has been a spring here, and perhaps there's something left in it!"

The Victoria touched the ground; Joe and Kennedy put into the car a quantity of sand equal to their weight, and leaped out. They then hastened to the well, and penetrated to the interior by a flight of steps that was now nothing but dust. The spring appeared to have been dry for years. They dug down into a parched and powdery sand—the very dryest of all sand, indeed—there was not one trace of moisture!

The doctor saw them come up to the surface of the desert, saturated with perspiration, worn out, covered with fine dust, exhausted, discouraged and despairing.

He then comprehended that their search had been fruitless. He had expected as much, and he kept silent, for he felt that, from this moment forth, he must have courage and energy enough for three.

Joe brought up with him some pieces of a leathern bottle that had grown hard and horn-like with age, and angrily flung them away among the bleaching bones of the caravan.

At supper, not a word was spoken by our travellers, and they even ate without appetite. Yet they had not, up to this moment, endured the real agonies of thirst, and were in no desponding mood, excepting for the future.

Chapter 26

ONE HUNDRED AND THIRTEEN DEGREES.—THE DOCTOR'S
REFLECTIONS.—A DESPERATE SEARCH.—THE CYLINDER
GOES OUT.—ONE HUNDRED AND TWENTY-TWO DEGREES.—
CONTEMPLATION OF THE DESERT.—A NIGHT WALK.—SOLITUDE.—
DEBILITY.—JOE'S PROSPECTS.—HE GIVES HIMSELF ONE DAY MORE.

The distance made by the balloon during the preceding day did not exceed ten miles, and, to keep it afloat, one hundred and sixty-two cubic feet of gas had been consumed.

On Saturday morning the doctor again gave the signal for departure.

"The cylinder can work only six hours longer; and, if in that time we shall not have found either a well or a spring of water, God alone knows what will become of us!"

"Not much wind this morning, master," said Joe; "but it will come up, perhaps," he added, suddenly remarking the doctor's ill-concealed depression.

Vain hope! The atmosphere was in a dead calm—one of those calms which hold vessels captive in tropical seas. The heat had become intolerable; and the thermometer, in the shade under the awning, indicated one hundred and thirteen degrees.

Joe and Kennedy, reclining at full length near each other, tried, if not in slumber, at least in torpor, to forget their situation, for their forced inactivity gave them periods of leisure far from pleasant. That man is to be pitied the most who cannot wean himself from gloomy reflections by actual work, or some practical pursuit. But here there was nothing to look after, nothing to undertake, and they had to submit to the situation, without having it in their power to ameliorate it.

The pangs of thirst began to be severely felt; brandy, far from appeasing this imperious necessity, augmented it, and richly merited the name of "tiger's milk" applied to it by the African natives. Scarcely two pints of water remained, and that was heated. Each of the party devoured the few precious drops with his gaze, yet neither of them dared to moisten his lips with them. Two pints of water in the midst of the desert!

Then it was that Dr. Ferguson, buried in meditation, asked himself whether he had acted with prudence. Would he not have done better to have kept the water that he had decomposed in pure loss, in order to sustain him in the air? He had gained a little distance, to be sure; but was he any nearer to his journey's end? What difference did sixty miles to the rear make in this region, when there was no water to be had where they were? The wind, should it rise, would blow there as it did here, only less strongly at this point, if it came from the east. But hope urged him onward. And yet those two gallons of water, expended in vain, would have sufficed for nine days' halt in the desert. And what changes might not have occurred in nine days! Perhaps, too, while retaining the water, he might have ascended by throwing out ballast, at the cost merely of discharging some gas, when he had again to descend. But the gas in his balloon was his blood, his very life!

A thousand one such reflections whirled in succession through his brain; and, resting his head between his hands, he sat there for hours without raising it.

"We must make one final effort," he said, at last, about ten o'clock in the morning. "We must endeavor, just once more, to find an atmospheric current to bear us away from here, and, to that end, must risk our last resources."

Therefore, while his companions slept, the doctor raised the hydrogen in the balloon to an elevated temperature, and the huge globe, filling out by the dilation of the gas, rose straight up in the perpendicular rays of the sun. The doctor searched vainly for a breath of wind, from the height of one hundred feet to that of five miles; his starting-point remained fatally right below him, and absolute calm seemed to reign, up to the extreme limits of the breathing atmosphere.

At length the feeding-supply of water gave out; the cylinder was extinguished for lack of gas; the Buntzen battery ceased to work, and the balloon, shrinking together, gently descended to the sand, in the very place that the car had hollowed out there.

It was noon; and solar observations gave nineteen degrees thirty-five minutes east longitude, and six degrees fifty-one minutes north latitude, or nearly five hundred miles from Lake Tchad, and more than four hundred miles from the western coast of Africa.

On the balloon taking ground, Kennedy and Joe awoke from their stupor.

"We have halted," said the Scot.

"We had to do so," replied the doctor, gravely.

His companions understood him. The level of the soil at that point corresponded with the level of the sea, and, consequently, the balloon remained in perfect equilibrium, and absolutely motionless.

The weight of the three travellers was replaced with an equivalent quantity of sand, and they got out of the car. Each was absorbed in his own thoughts; and for many hours neither of them spoke. Joe prepared their evening meal, which consisted of biscuit and pemmican, and was hardly tasted by either of the party. A mouthful of scalding water from their little store completed this gloomy repast.

During the night none of them kept awake; yet none could be precisely said to have slept. On the morrow there remained only half a pint of water, and this the doctor put away, all three having resolved not to touch it until the last extremity.

It was not long, however, before Joe exclaimed:

"I'm choking, and the heat is getting worse! I'm not surprised at that, though," he added, consulting the thermometer; "one hundred and forty degrees!"

"The sand scorches me," said the hunter, "as though it had just come out of a furnace; and not a cloud in this sky of fire. It's enough to drive one mad!"

"Let us not despair," responded the doctor. "In this latitude these intense heats are invariably followed by storms, and the latter come with the suddenness of lightning. Notwithstanding this disheartening clearness of the sky, great atmospheric changes may take place in less than an hour."

"But," asked Kennedy, "is there any sign whatever of that?"

"Well," replied the doctor, "I think that there is some slight symptom of a fall in the barometer."

"May Heaven hearken to you, Samuel! for here we are pinned to the ground, like a bird with broken wings."

"With this difference, however, my dear Dick, that our wings are unhurt, and I hope that we shall be able to use them again."

"Ah! wind! wind!" exclaimed Joe; "enough to carry us to a stream or a well, and we'll be all right. We have provisions enough, and, with water, we could wait a month without suffering; but thirst is a cruel thing!"

It was not thirst alone, but the unchanging sight of the desert, that fatigued the mind. There was not a variation in the surface of the soil, not a hillock of sand, not a pebble, to relieve the gaze. This unbroken level discouraged the beholder, and gave him that kind of malady called the "desert-sickness." The impassible monotony of the arid blue sky, and the vast yellow expanse of the desert-sand, at length produced a sensation of terror. In this inflamed atmosphere the heat appeared to vibrate as it does above a blazing hearth, while the mind grew desperate in contemplating the limitless calm, and could see no reason why the thing should ever end, since immensity is a species of eternity.

Thus, at last, our hapless travellers, deprived of water in this torrid heat, began to feel symptoms of mental disorder. Their eyes swelled in their sockets, and their gaze became confused.

When night came on, the doctor determined to combat this alarming tendency by rapid walking. His idea was to pace the sandy plain for a few hours, not in search of any thing, but simply for exercise.

"Come along!" he said to his companions; "believe me, it will do you good."

"Out of the question!" said Kennedy; "I could not walk a step."

"And I," said Joe, "would rather sleep!"

"But sleep, or even rest, would be dangerous to you, my friends; you must react against this tendency to stupor. Come with me!"

But the doctor could do nothing with them, and, therefore, set off alone, amid the starry clearness of the night. The first few steps he took were painful, for they were the steps of an enfeebled man quite out of practice in walking. However, he quickly saw that the exercise would be beneficial to him, and pushed on several miles to the westward. Once in rapid motion, he felt his spirits greatly cheered, when, suddenly, a vertigo came over him; he seemed to be poised on the edge of an abyss; his knees bent under him; the vast solitude struck terror to his heart; he found himself the minute mathematical point, the centre of an infinite circumference, that is to say—a nothing! The balloon had disappeared entirely in the deepening gloom. The doctor, cool, impassible, reckless explorer that he was, felt himself at last seized with a nameless dread. He strove to retrace his steps, but in vain. He called aloud. Not even an echo replied, and his voice died out in the empty vastness of surrounding space, like a pebble cast into a bottomless gulf; then, down he sank, fainting, on the sand, alone, amid the eternal silence of the desert.

At midnight he came to, in the arms of his faithful follower, Joe. The latter, uneasy at his master's prolonged absence, had set out after him, easily tracing him by the clear imprint of his feet in the sand, and had found him lying in a swoon.

"What has been the matter, sir?" was the first inquiry.

"Nothing, Joe, nothing! Only a touch of weakness, that's all. It's over now."

"Oh! it won't amount to any thing, sir, I'm sure of that; but get up on your feet, if you can. There! lean upon me, and let us get back to the balloon."

And the doctor, leaning on Joe's arm, returned along the track by which he had come.

"You were too bold, sir; it won't do to run such risks. You might have been robbed," he added, laughing. "But, sir, come now, let us talk seriously."

"Speak! I am listening to you."

"We must positively make up our minds to do something. Our present situation cannot last more than a few days longer, and if we get no wind, we are lost."

The doctor made no reply.

"Well, then, one of us must sacrifice himself for the good of all, and it is most natural that it should fall to me to do so."

"What have you to propose? What is your plan?"

"A very simple one! It is to take provisions enough, and to walk right on until I come to some place, as I must do, sooner or later. In the mean time, if Heaven sends you a good wind, you need not wait, but can start again. For my part, if I come to a village, I'll work my way through with a few Arabic words that you can write for me on a slip of paper, and I'll bring you help or lose my hide. What do you think of my plan?"

"It is absolute folly, Joe, but worthy of your noble heart. The thing is impossible. You will not leave us."

"But, sir, we must do something, and this plan can't do you any harm, for, I say again, you need not wait; and then, after all, I may succeed."

"No, Joe, no! We will not separate. That would only be adding sorrow to trouble. It was written that matters should be as they are; and it is very probably written that it shall be quite otherwise by-and-by. Let us wait, then, with resignation."

"So be it, master; but take notice of one thing: I give you a day longer, and I'll not wait after that. To-day is Sunday; we might say Monday, as it is one o'clock in the morning, and if we don't get off by Tuesday, I'll run the risk. I've made up my mind to that!"

The doctor made no answer, and in a few minutes they got back to the car, where he took his place beside Kennedy, who lay there plunged in silence so complete that it could not be considered sleep.

JULES VERNE

Chapter 27

TERRIFIC HEAT.—HALLUCINATIONS.—THE LAST DROPS OF
WATER.—NIGHTS OF DESPAIR.—AN ATTEMPT AT SUICIDE.—THE
SIMOOM.—THE OASIS.—THE LION AND LIONESS.

The doctor's first care, on the morrow, was to consult the barometer. He found that the mercury had scarcely undergone any perceptible depression.

"Nothing!" he murmured, "nothing!"

He got out of the car and scrutinized the weather; there was only the same heat, the same cloudless sky, the same merciless drought.

"Must we, then, give up to despair?" he exclaimed, in agony.

Joe did not open his lips. He was buried in his own thoughts, and planning the expedition he had proposed.

Kennedy got up, feeling very ill, and a prey to nervous agitation. He was suffering horribly with thirst, and his swollen tongue and lips could hardly articulate a syllable.

There still remained a few drops of water. Each of them knew this, and each was thinking of it, and felt himself drawn toward them; but neither of the three dared to take a step.

Those three men, friends and companions as they were, fixed their haggard eyes upon each other with an instinct of ferocious longing, which was most plainly revealed in the hardy Scot, whose vigorous constitution yielded the soonest to these unnatural privations.

Throughout the day he was delirious, pacing up and down, uttering hoarse cries, gnawing his clinched fists, and ready to open his veins and drink his own hot blood.

"Ah!" he cried, "land of thirst! Well might you be called the land of despair!"

At length he sank down in utter prostration, and his friends heard no other sound from him than the hissing of his breath between his parched and swollen lips.

Toward evening, Joe had his turn of delirium. The vast expanse of sand appeared to him an immense pond, full of clear and limpid water; and, more than once, he dashed himself upon the scorching waste to drink long draughts, and rose again with his mouth clogged with hot dust.

"Curses on it!" he yelled, in his madness, "it's nothing but salt water!"

Then, while Ferguson and Kennedy lay there motionless, the resistless longing came over him to drain the last few drops of water that had been kept in reserve. The natural instinct proved too strong. He dragged himself toward the car, on his knees; he glared at the bottle containing the precious fluid; he gave one wild, eager glance, seized the treasured store, and bore it to his lips.

At that instant he heard a heart-rending cry close beside him— "Water! water!"

It was Kennedy, who had crawled up close to him, and was begging there, upon his knees, and weeping piteously.

Joe, himself in tears, gave the poor wretch the bottle, and Kennedy drained the last drop with savage haste.

"Thanks!" he murmured hoarsely, but Joe did not hear him, for both alike had dropped fainting on the sand.

What took place during that fearful night neither of them knew, but, on Tuesday morning, under those showers of heat which the sun poured down upon them, the unfortunate men felt their limbs gradually drying up, and when Joe attempted to rise he found it impossible.

He looked around him. In the car, the doctor, completely overwhelmed, sat with his arms folded on his breast, gazing with idiotic fixedness upon some imaginary point in space. Kennedy was frightful to behold. He was rolling his head from right to left like a wild beast in a cage.

All at once, his eyes rested on the butt of his rifle, which jutted above the rim of the car.

"Ah!" he screamed, raising himself with a superhuman effort.

Desperate, mad, he snatched at the weapon, and turned the barrel toward his mouth.

"Kennedy!" shouted Joe, throwing himself upon his friend.

"Let go! hands off!" moaned the Scot, in a hoarse, grating voice— and then the two struggled desperately for the rifle.

"Let go, or I'll kill you!" repeated Kennedy. But Joe clung to him only the more fiercely, and they had been contending thus without the doctor seeing them for many seconds, when, suddenly the rifle went off. At the sound of its discharge, the doctor rose up erect, like a spectre, and glared around him.

But all at once his glance grew more animated; he extended his hand toward the horizon, and in a voice no longer human shrieked:

"There! there—off there!"

JULES VERNE

There was such fearful force in the cry that Kennedy and Joe released each other, and both looked where the doctor pointed.

The plain was agitated like the sea shaken by the fury of a tempest; billows of sand went tossing over each other amid blinding clouds of dust; an immense pillar was seen whirling toward them through the air from the southeast, with terrific velocity; the sun was disappearing behind an opaque veil of cloud whose enormous barrier extended clear to the horizon, while the grains of fine sand went gliding together with all the supple ease of liquid particles, and the rising dust-tide gained more and more with every second.

Ferguson's eyes gleamed with a ray of energetic hope.

"The simoom!" he exclaimed.

"The simoom!" repeated Joe, without exactly knowing what it meant.

"So much the better!" said Kennedy, with the bitterness of despair. "So much the better—we shall die!"

"So much the better!" echoed the doctor, "for we shall live!" and, so saying, he began rapidly to throw out the sand that encumbered the car.

At length his companions understood him, and took their places at his side.

"And now, Joe," said the doctor, "throw out some fifty pounds of your ore, there!"

Joe no longer hesitated, although he still felt a fleeting pang of regret. The balloon at once began to ascend.

"It was high time!" said the doctor.

The simoom, in fact, came rushing on like a thunderbolt, and a moment later the balloon would have been crushed, torn to atoms, annihilated. The awful whirlwind was almost upon it, and it was already pelted with showers of sand driven like hail by the storm.

"Out with more ballast!" shouted the doctor.

"There!" responded Joe, tossing over a huge fragment of quartz.

With this, the Victoria rose swiftly above the range of the whirling column, but, caught in the vast displacement of the atmosphere thereby occasioned, it was borne along with incalculable rapidity away above this foaming sea.

The three travellers did not speak. They gazed, and hoped, and even felt refreshed by the breath of the tempest.

About three o'clock, the whirlwind ceased; the sand, falling again upon the desert, formed numberless little hillocks, and the sky resumed its former tranquillity.

The balloon, which had again lost its momentum, was floating in sight of an oasis, a sort of islet studded with green trees, thrown up upon the surface of this sandy ocean.

"Water! we'll find water there!" said the doctor.

And, instantly, opening the upper valve, he let some hydrogen escape, and slowly descended, taking the ground at about two hundred feet from the edge of the oasis.

In four hours the travellers had swept over a distance of two hundred and forty miles!

The car was at once ballasted, and Kennedy, closely followed by Joe, leaped out.

"Take your guns with you!" said the doctor; "take your guns, and be careful!"

Dick grasped his rifle, and Joe took one of the fowling-pieces. They then rapidly made for the trees, and disappeared under the fresh verdure, which announced the presence of abundant springs. As they hurried on, they had not taken notice of certain large footprints and fresh tracks of some living creature marked here and there in the damp soil.

Suddenly, a dull roar was heard not twenty paces from them.

"The roar of a lion!" said Joe.

"Good for that!" said the excited hunter; "we'll fight him. A man feels strong when only a fight's in question."

"But be careful, Mr. Kennedy; be careful! The lives of all depend upon the life of one."

But Kennedy no longer heard him; he was pushing on, his eye blazing; his rifle cocked; fearful to behold in his daring rashness. There, under a palm-tree, stood an enormous black-maned lion, crouching for a spring on his antagonist. Scarcely had he caught a glimpse of the hunter, when he bounded through the air; but he had not touched the ground ere a bullet pierced his heart, and he fell to the earth dead.

"Hurrah! hurrah!" shouted Joe, with wild exultation.

Kennedy rushed toward the well, slid down the dampened steps, and flung himself at full length by the side of a fresh spring, in which he plunged his parched lips. Joe followed suit, and for some minutes nothing was heard but the sound they made with their mouths, drinking more like maddened beasts than men.

"Take care, Mr. Kennedy," said Joe at last; "let us not overdo the thing!" and he panted for breath.

But Kennedy, without a word, drank on. He even plunged his

hands, and then his head, into the delicious tide—he fairly revelled in its coolness.

"But the doctor?" said Joe; "our friend, Dr. Ferguson?"

That one word recalled Kennedy to himself, and, hastily filling a flask that he had brought with him, he started on a run up the steps of the well.

But what was his amazement when he saw an opaque body of enormous dimensions blocking up the passage! Joe, who was close upon Kennedy's heels, recoiled with him.

"We are blocked in—entrapped!"

"Impossible! What does that mean?—"

Dick had no time to finish; a terrific roar made him only too quickly aware what foe confronted him.

"Another lion!" exclaimed Joe.

"A lioness, rather," said Kennedy. "Ah! ferocious brute!" he added, "I'll settle you in a moment more!" and swiftly reloaded his rifle.

In another instant he fired, but the animal had disappeared.

"Onward!" shouted Kennedy.

"No!" interposed the other, "that shot did not kill her; her body would have rolled down the steps; she's up there, ready to spring upon the first of us who appears, and he would be a lost man!"

"But what are we to do? We must get out of this, and the doctor is expecting us."

"Let us decoy the animal. Take my piece, and give me your rifle."

"What is your plan?"

"You'll see."

And Joe, taking off his linen jacket, hung it on the end of the rifle, and thrust it above the top of the steps. The lioness flung herself furiously upon it. Kennedy was on the alert for her, and his bullet broke her shoulder. The lioness, with a frightful howl of agony, rolled down the steps, overturning Joe in her fall. The poor fellow imagined that he could already feel the enormous paws of the savage beast in his flesh, when a second detonation resounded in the narrow passage, and Dr. Ferguson appeared at the opening above with his gun in hand, and still smoking from the discharge.

Joe leaped to his feet, clambered over the body of the dead lioness, and handed up the flask full of sparkling water to his master.

To carry it to his lips, and to half empty it at a draught, was the work of an instant, and the three travellers offered up thanks from the depths of their hearts to that Providence who had so miraculously saved them.

Chapter 28

AN EVENING OF DELIGHT.—JOE'S CULINARY PERFORMANCES.—
A DISSERTATION ON RAW MEAT.—THE NARRATIVE OF JAMES
BRUCE.—CAMPING OUT.—JOE'S DREAMS.—THE BAROMETER
BEGINS TO FALL.—THE BAROMETER RISES AGAIN.—
PREPARATIONS FOR DEPARTURE.—THE TEMPEST.

The evening was lovely, and our three friends enjoyed it in the cool shade of the mimosas, after a substantial repast, at which the tea and the punch were dealt out with no niggardly hand.

Kennedy had traversed the little domain in all directions. He had ransacked every thicket and satisfied himself that the balloon party were the only living creatures in this terrestrial paradise; so they stretched themselves upon their blankets and passed a peaceful night that brought them forgetfulness of their past sufferings.

On the morrow, May 7th, the sun shone with all his splendor, but his rays could not penetrate the dense screen of the palm-tree foliage, and as there was no lack of provisions, the doctor resolved to remain where he was while waiting for a favorable wind.

Joe had conveyed his portable kitchen to the oasis, and proceeded to indulge in any number of culinary combinations, using water all the time with the most profuse extravagance.

"What a strange succession of annoyances and enjoyments!" moralized Kennedy. "Such abundance as this after such privations; such luxury after such want! Ah! I nearly went mad!"

"My dear Dick," replied the doctor, "had it not been for Joe, you would not be sitting here, to-day, discoursing on the instability of human affairs."

"Whole-hearted friend!" said Kennedy, extending his hand to Joe.

"There's no occasion for all that," responded the latter; "but you can take your revenge some time, Mr. Kennedy, always hoping though that you may never have occasion to do the same for me!"

"It's a poor constitution this of ours to succumb to so little," philosophized Dr. Ferguson.

"So little water, you mean, doctor," interposed Joe; "that element must be very necessary to life."

"Undoubtedly, and persons deprived of food hold out longer than those deprived of water."

"I believe it. Besides, when needs must, one can eat any thing he comes across, even his fellow-creatures, although that must be a kind of food that's pretty hard to digest."

"The savages don't boggle much about it!" said Kennedy.

"Yes; but then they are savages, and accustomed to devouring raw meat; it's something that I'd find very disgusting, for my part."

"It is disgusting enough," said the doctor, "that's a fact; and so much so, indeed, that nobody believed the narratives of the earliest travellers in Africa who brought back word that many tribes on that continent subsisted upon raw meat, and people generally refused to credit the statement. It was under such circumstances that a very singular adventure befell James Bruce."

"Tell it to us, doctor; we've time enough to hear it," said Joe, stretching himself voluptuously on the cool greensward.

"By all means.—James Bruce was a Scotchman, of Stirlingshire, who, between 1768 and 1772, traversed all Abyssinia, as far as Lake Tyana, in search of the sources of the Nile. He afterward returned to England, but did not publish an account of his journeys until 1790. His statements were received with extreme incredulity, and such may be the reception accorded to our own. The manners and customs of the Abyssinians seemed so different from those of the English, that no one would credit the description of them. Among other details, Bruce had put forward the assertion that the tribes of Eastern Africa fed upon raw flesh, and this set everybody against him. He might say so as much as he pleased; there was no one likely to go and see! One day, in a parlor at Edinburgh, a Scotch gentleman took up the subject in his presence, as it had become the topic of daily pleasantry, and, in reference to the eating of raw flesh, said that the thing was neither possible nor true. Bruce made no reply, but went out and returned a few minutes later with a raw steak, seasoned with pepper and salt, in the African style.

"'Sir,' said he to the Scotchman, 'in doubting my statements, you have grossly affronted me; in believing the thing to be impossible, you have been egregiously mistaken; and, in proof thereof, you will now eat this beef-steak raw, or you will give me instant satisfaction!' The Scotchman had a wholesome dread of the brawny traveller, and *did* eat the steak, although not without a good many wry faces. Thereupon, with the utmost coolness, James Bruce added: 'Even admitting, sir, that the thing were untrue, you will, at least, no longer maintain that it is impossible.'"

"Well put in!" said Joe, "and if the Scotchman found it lie heavy on his stomach, he got no more than he deserved. If, on our return to England, they dare to doubt what we say about our travels—"

"Well, Joe, what would you do?"

"Why, I'll make the doubters swallow the pieces of the balloon, without either salt or pepper!"

All burst out laughing at Joe's queer notions, and thus the day slipped by in pleasant chat. With returning strength, hope had revived, and with hope came the courage to do and to dare. The past was obliterated in the presence of the future with providential rapidity.

Joe would have been willing to remain forever in this enchanting asylum; it was the realm he had pictured in his dreams; he felt himself at home; his master had to give him his exact location, and it was with the gravest air imaginable that he wrote down on his tablets fifteen degrees forty-three minutes east longitude, and eight degrees thirty-two minutes north latitude.

Kennedy had but one regret, to wit, that he could not hunt in that miniature forest, because, according to his ideas, there was a slight deficiency of ferocious wild beasts in it.

"But, my dear Dick," said the doctor, "haven't you rather a short memory? How about the lion and the lioness?"

"Oh, that!" he exclaimed with the contempt of a thorough-bred sportsman for game already killed. "But the fact is, that finding them here would lead one to suppose that we can't be far from a more fertile country."

"It don't prove much, Dick, for those animals, when goaded by hunger or thirst, will travel long distances, and I think that, to-night, we had better keep a more vigilant lookout, and light fires, besides."

"What, in such heat as this?" said Joe. "Well, if it's necessary, we'll have to do it, but I do think it a real pity to burn this pretty grove that has been such a comfort to us!"

"Oh! above all things, we must take the utmost care not to set it on fire," replied the doctor, "so that others in the same strait as ourselves may some day find shelter here in the middle of the desert."

"I'll be very careful, indeed, doctor; but do you think that this oasis is known?"

"Undoubtedly; it is a halting-place for the caravans that frequent the centre of Africa, and a visit from one of them might be any thing but pleasant to you, Joe."

"Why, are there any more of those rascally Nyam-Nyams around here?"

"Certainly; that is the general name of all the neighboring tribes, and, under the same climates, the same races are likely to have similar manners and customs."

"Pah!" said Joe, "but, after all, it's natural enough. If savages had the ways of gentlemen, where would be the difference? By George, these fine fellows wouldn't have to be coaxed long to eat the Scotchman's raw steak, nor the Scotchman either, into the bargain!"

With this very sensible observation, Joe began to get ready his firewood for the night, making just as little of it as possible. Fortunately, these precautions were superfluous; and each of the party, in his turn, dropped off into the soundest slumber.

On the next day the weather still showed no sign of change, but kept provokingly and obstinately fair. The balloon remained motionless, without any oscillation to betray a breath of wind.

The doctor began to get uneasy again. If their stay in the desert were to be prolonged like this, their provisions would give out. After nearly perishing for want of water, they would, at last, have to starve to death!

But he took fresh courage as he saw the mercury fall considerably in the barometer, and noticed evident signs of an early change in the atmosphere. He therefore resolved to make all his preparations for a start, so as to avail himself of the first opportunity. The feeding-tank and the water-tank were both completely filled.

Then he had to reestablish the equilibrium of the balloon, and Joe was obliged to part with another considerable portion of his precious quartz. With restored health, his ambitious notions had come back to him, and he made more than one wry face before obeying his master; but the latter convinced him that he could not carry so considerable a weight with him through the air, and gave him his choice between the water and the gold. Joe hesitated no longer, but flung out the requisite quantity of his much-prized ore upon the sand.

"The next people who come this way," he remarked, "will be rather surprised to find a fortune in such a place."

"And suppose some learned traveller should come across these specimens, eh?" suggested Kennedy.

"You may be certain, Dick, that they would take him by surprise, and that he would publish his astonishment in several folios; so that some day we shall hear of a wonderful deposit of gold-bearing quartz in the midst of the African sands!"

"And Joe there, will be the cause of it all!"

This idea of mystifying some learned sage tickled Joe hugely, and made him laugh.

During the rest of the day the doctor vainly kept on the watch for a change of weather. The temperature rose, and, had it not been for the shade of the oasis, would have been insupportable. The thermometer marked a hundred and forty-nine degrees in the sun, and a veritable rain of fire filled the air. This was the most intense heat that they had yet noted.

Joe arranged their bivouac for that evening, as he had done for the previous night; and during the watches kept by the doctor and Kennedy there was no fresh incident.

But, toward three o'clock in the morning, while Joe was on guard, the temperature suddenly fell; the sky became overcast with clouds, and the darkness increased.

"Turn out!" cried Joe, arousing his companions. "Turn out! Here's the wind!"

"At last!" exclaimed the doctor, eying the heavens. "But it is a storm! The balloon! Let us hasten to the balloon!"

It was high time for them to reach it. The Victoria was bending to the force of the hurricane, and dragging along the car, the latter grazing the sand. Had any portion of the ballast been accidentally thrown out, the balloon would have been swept away, and all hope of recovering it have been forever lost.

But fleet-footed Joe put forth his utmost speed, and checked the car, while the balloon beat upon the sand, at the risk of being torn to pieces. The doctor, followed by Kennedy, leaped in, and lit his cylinder, while his companions threw out the superfluous ballast.

The travellers took one last look at the trees of the oasis bowing to the force of the hurricane, and soon, catching the wind at two hundred feet above the ground, disappeared in the gloom.

Chapter 29

SIGNS OF VEGETATION.—THE FANTASTIC NOTION OF A FRENCH
AUTHOR.—A MAGNIFICENT COUNTRY.—THE KINGDOM OF
ADAMOVA.—THE EXPLORATIONS OF SPEKE AND BURTON
CONNECTED WITH THOSE OF DR. BARTH.—THE ATLANTIKA
MOUNTAINS.—THE RIVER BENOUE.—THE CITY OF YOLA.—
THE BAGELE.—MOUNT MENDIF.

From the moment of their departure, the travellers moved with great velocity. They longed to leave behind them the desert, which had so nearly been fatal to them.

About a quarter-past nine in the morning, they caught a glimpse of some signs of vegetation: herbage floating on that sea of sand, and announcing, as the weeds upon the ocean did to Christopher Columbus, the nearness of the shore—green shoots peeping up timidly between pebbles that were, in their turn, to be the rocks of that vast expanse.

Hills, but of trifling height, were seen in wavy lines upon the horizon. Their profile, muffled by the heavy mist, was defined but vaguely. The monotony, however, was beginning to disappear.

The doctor hailed with joy the new country thus disclosed, and, like a seaman on lookout at the mast-head, he was ready to shout aloud:

"Land, ho! land!"

An hour later the continent spread broadly before their gaze, still wild in aspect, but less flat, less denuded, and with a few trees standing out against the gray sky.

"We are in a civilized country at last!" said the hunter.

"Civilized? Well, that's one way of speaking; but there are no people to be seen yet."

"It will not be long before we see them," said Ferguson, "at our present rate of travel."

"Are we still in the negro country, doctor?"

"Yes, and on our way to the country of the Arabs."

"What! real Arabs, sir, with their camels?"

"No, not many camels; they are scarce, if not altogether unknown, in these regions. We must go a few degrees farther north to see them."

"What a pity!"

"And why, Joe?"

"Because, if the wind fell contrary, they might be of use to us."

"How so?"

"Well, sir, it's just a notion that's got into my head: we might hitch them to the car, and make them tow us along. What do you say to that, doctor?"

"Poor Joe! Another person had that idea in advance of you. It was used by a very gifted French author—M. Mery—in a romance, it is true. He has his travellers drawn along in a balloon by a team of camels; then a lion comes up, devours the camels, swallows the tow-rope, and hauls the balloon in their stead; and so on through the story. You see that the whole thing is the top-flower of fancy, but has nothing in common with our style of locomotion."

Joe, a little cut down at learning that his idea had been used already, cudgelled his wits to imagine what animal could have devoured the lion; but he could not guess it, and so quietly went on scanning the appearance of the country.

A lake of medium extent stretched away before him, surrounded by an amphitheatre of hills, which yet could not be dignified with the name of mountains. There were winding valleys, numerous and fertile, with their tangled thickets of the most various trees. The African oil-tree rose above the mass, with leaves fifteen feet in length upon its stalk, the latter studded with sharp thorns; the bombax, or silk-cotton-tree, filled the wind, as it swept by, with the fine down of its seeds; the pungent odors of the pendanus, the "kenda" of the Arabs, perfumed the air up to the height where the Victoria was sailing; the papaw-tree, with its palm-shaped leaves; the sterculier, which produces the Soudan-nut; the baobab, and the banana-tree, completed the luxuriant flora of these inter-tropical regions.

"The country is superb!" said the doctor.

"Here are some animals," added Joe. "Men are not far away."

"Oh, what magnificent elephants!" exclaimed Kennedy. "Is there no way to get a little shooting?"

"How could we manage to halt in a current as strong as this? No, Dick; you must taste a little of the torture of Tantalus just now. You shall make up for it afterward."

And, in truth, there was enough to excite the fancy of a sportsman. Dick's heart fairly leaped in his breast as he grasped the butt of his Purdy.

The fauna of the region were as striking as its flora. The wild-ox revelled in dense herbage that often concealed his whole body; gray, black, and yellow elephants of the most gigantic size burst headlong, like a living hurricane, through the forests, breaking, rending, tearing down, devastating every thing in their path; upon the woody slopes of the hills trickled cascades and springs flowing northward; there, too, the hippopotami bathed their huge forms, splashing and snorting as they frolicked in the water, and lamantines, twelve feet long, with bodies like seals, stretched themselves along the banks, turning up toward the sun their rounded teats swollen with milk.

It was a whole menagerie of rare and curious beasts in a wondrous hot-house, where numberless birds with plumage of a thousand hues gleamed and fluttered in the sunshine.

By this prodigality of Nature, the doctor recognized the splendid kingdom of Adamova.

"We are now beginning to trench upon the realm of modern discovery. I have taken up the lost scent of preceding travellers. It is a happy chance, my friends, for we shall be enabled to link the toils of Captains Burton and Speke with the explorations of Dr. Barth. We have left the Englishmen behind us, and now have caught up with the Hamburger. It will not be long, either, before we arrive at the extreme point attained by that daring explorer."

"It seems to me that there is a vast extent of country between the two explored routes," remarked Kennedy; "at least, if I am to judge by the distance that we have made."

"It is easy to determine: take the map and see what is the longitude of the southern point of Lake Ukereoue, reached by Speke."

"It is near the thirty-seventh degree."

"And the city of Yola, which we shall sight this evening, and to which Barth penetrated, what is its position?"

"It is about in the twelfth degree of east longitude."

"Then there are twenty-five degrees, or, counting sixty miles to each, about fifteen hundred miles in all."

"A nice little walk," said Joe, "for people who have to go on foot."

"It will be accomplished, however. Livingstone and Moffat are pushing on up this line toward the interior. Nyassa, which they have discovered, is not far from Lake Tanganayika, seen by Burton. Ere the close of the century these regions will, undoubtedly, be explored. But," added the doctor, consulting his compass, "I regret that the wind is carrying us so far to the westward. I wanted to get to the north."

After twelve hours of progress, the Victoria found herself on the confines of Nigritia. The first inhabitants of this region, the Chouas Arabs, were feeding their wandering flocks. The immense summits of the Atlantika Mountains seen above the horizon—mountains that no European foot had yet scaled, and whose height is computed to be ten thousand feet! Their western slope determines the flow of all the waters in this region of Africa toward the ocean. They are the Mountains of the Moon to this part of the continent.

At length a real river greeted the gaze of our travellers, and, by the enormous ant-hills seen in its vicinity, the doctor recognized the Benoue, one of the great tributaries of the Niger, the one which the natives have called "The Fountain of the Waters."

"This river," said the doctor to his companions, "will, one day, be the natural channel of communication with the interior of Nigritia. Under the command of one of our brave captains, the steamer Pleiad has already ascended as far as the town of Yola. You see that we are not in an unknown country."

Numerous slaves were engaged in the labors of the field, cultivating sorgho, a kind of millet which forms the chief basis of their diet; and the most stupid expressions of astonishment ensued as the Victoria sped past like a meteor. That evening the balloon halted about forty miles from Yola, and ahead of it, but in the distance, rose the two sharp cones of Mount Mendif.

The doctor threw out his anchors and made fast to the top of a high tree; but a very violent wind beat upon the balloon with such force as to throw it over on its side, thus rendering the position of the car sometimes extremely dangerous. Ferguson did not close his all night, and he was repeatedly on the point of cutting the anchor-rope and scudding away before the gale. At length, however, the storm abated, and the oscillations of the balloon ceased to be alarming.

On the morrow the wind was more moderate, but it carried our travellers away from the city of Yola, which recently rebuilt by the Fouillans, excited Ferguson's curiosity. However, he had to make up his mind to being borne farther to the northward and even a little to the east.

Kennedy proposed to halt in this fine hunting-country, and Joe declared that the need of fresh meat was beginning to be felt; but the savage customs of the country, the attitude of the population, and some shots fired at the Victoria, admonished the doctor to continue his journey. They were then crossing a region that was the scene of massacres and burnings, and where warlike conflicts between the barbarian sultans, contending for their power amid the most atrocious carnage, never cease.

Numerous and populous villages of long low huts stretched away between broad pasture-fields whose dense herbage was besprinkled with violet-colored blossoms. The huts, looking like huge beehives, were sheltered behind bristling palisades. The wild hill-sides and hollows frequently reminded the beholder of the glens in the Highlands of Scotland, as Kennedy more than once remarked.

In spite of all he could do, the doctor bore directly to the northeast, toward Mount Mendif, which was lost in the midst of environing clouds. The lofty summits of these mountains separate the valley of the Niger from the basin of Lake Tchad.

Soon afterward was seen the Bagele, with its eighteen villages clinging to its flanks like a whole brood of children to their mother's bosom—a magnificent spectacle for the beholder whose gaze commanded and took in the entire picture at one view. Even the ravines were seen to be covered with fields of rice and of arachides.

By three o'clock the Victoria was directly in front of Mount Mendif. It had been impossible to avoid it; the only thing to be done was to cross it. The doctor, by means of a temperature increased to one hundred and eighty degrees, gave the balloon a fresh ascensional force of nearly sixteen hundred pounds, and it went up to an elevation of more than eight thousand feet, the greatest height attained during the journey. The temperature of the atmosphere was so much cooler at that point that the aeronauts had to resort to their blankets and thick coverings.

Ferguson was in haste to descend; the covering of the balloon gave indications of bursting, but in the meanwhile he had time to satisfy himself of the volcanic origin of the mountain, whose extinct craters are now but deep abysses. Immense accumulations of bird-guano gave the sides of Mount Mendif the appearance of calcareous rocks, and there was enough of the deposit there to manure all the lands in the United Kingdom.

At five o'clock the Victoria, sheltered from the south winds, went gently gliding along the slopes of the mountain, and stopped in a wide clearing remote from any habitation. The instant it touched the soil, all needful precautions were taken to hold it there firmly; and Kennedy, fowling-piece in hand, sallied out upon the sloping plain. Ere long, he returned with half a dozen wild ducks and a kind of snipe, which Joe served up in his best style. The meal was heartily relished, and the night was passed in undisturbed and refreshing slumber.

Chapter 30

MOSFEIA.—THE SHEIK.—DENHAM, CLAPPERTON, AND OUDNEY.—
VOGEL.—THE CAPITAL OF LOGGOUM.—TOOLE.—BECALMED ABOVE
KERNAK.—THE GOVERNOR AND HIS COURT.—THE ATTACK.—THE
INCENDIARY PIGEONS.

On the next day, May 11th, the Victoria resumed her adventurous
journey. Her passengers had the same confidence in her that a
good seaman has in his ship.

In terrific hurricanes, in tropical heats, when making dangerous
departures, and descents still more dangerous, it had, at all times and in
all places, come out safely. It might almost have been said that Ferguson
managed it with a wave of the hand; and hence, without knowing in
advance, where the point of arrival would be, the doctor had no fears
concerning the successful issue of his journey. However, in this country
of barbarians and fanatics, prudence obliged him to take the strictest
precautions. He therefore counselled his companions to have their eyes
wide open for every thing and at all hours.

The wind drifted a little more to the northward, and, toward nine
o'clock, they sighted the larger city of Mosfeia, built upon an eminence
which was itself enclosed between two lofty mountains. Its position
was impregnable, a narrow road running between a marsh and a thick
wood being the only channel of approach to it.

At the moment of which we write, a sheik, accompanied by a
mounted escort, and clad in a garb of brilliant colors, preceded by
couriers and trumpeters, who put aside the boughs of the trees as he
rode up, was making his grand entry into the place.

The doctor lowered the balloon in order to get a better look at this
cavalcade of natives; but, as the balloon grew larger to their eyes, they began
to show symptoms of intense affright, and at length made off in different
directions as fast as their legs and those of their horses could carry them.

The sheik alone did not budge an inch. He merely grasped his long
musket, cocked it, and proudly waited in silence. The doctor came on to
within a hundred and fifty feet of him, and then, with his roundest and
fullest voice, saluted him courteously in the Arabic tongue.

But, upon hearing these words falling, as it seemed, from the sky,
the sheik dismounted and prostrated himself in the dust of the highway,

where the doctor had to leave him, finding it impossible to divert him from his adoration.

"Unquestionably," Ferguson remarked, "those people take us for supernatural beings. When Europeans came among them for the first time, they were mistaken for creatures of a higher race. When this sheik comes to speak of to-day's meeting, he will not fail to embellish the circumstance with all the resources of an Arab imagination. You may, therefore, judge what an account their legends will give of us some day."

"Not such a desirable thing, after all," said the Scot, "in the point of view that affects civilization; it would be better to pass for mere men. That would give these negro races a superior idea of European power."

"Very good, my dear Dick; but what can we do about it? You might sit all day explaining the mechanism of a balloon to the savants of this country, and yet they would not comprehend you, but would persist in ascribing it to supernatural aid."

"Doctor, you spoke of the first time Europeans visited these regions. Who were the visitors?" inquired Joe.

"My dear fellow, we are now upon the very track of Major Denham. It was at this very city of Mosfeia that he was received by the Sultan of Mandara; he had quitted the Bornou country; he accompanied the sheik in an expedition against the Fellatahs; he assisted in the attack on the city, which, with its arrows alone, bravely resisted the bullets of the Arabs, and put the sheik's troops to flight. All this was but a pretext for murders, raids, and pillage. The major was completely plundered and stripped, and had it not been for his horse, under whose stomach he clung with the skill of an Indian rider, and was borne with a headlong gallop from his barbarous pursuers, he never could have made his way back to Kouka, the capital of Bornou."

"Who was this Major Denham?"

"A fearless Englishman, who, between 1822 and 1824, commanded an expedition into the Bornou country, in company with Captain Clapperton and Dr. Oudney. They set out from Tripoli in the month of March, reached Mourzouk, the capital of Fez, and, following the route which at a later period Dr. Barth was to pursue on his way back to Europe, they arrived, on the 16th of February, 1823, at Kouka, near Lake Tchad. Denham made several explorations in Bornou, in Mandara, and to the eastern shores of the lake. In the mean time, on the 15th of December, 1823, Captain Clapperton and Dr. Oudney had pushed their way through the Soudan country as far as Sackatoo, and Oudney died of fatigue and exhaustion in the town of Murmur."

"This part of Africa has, therefore, paid a heavy tribute of victims to the cause of science," said Kennedy.

"Yes, this country is fatal to travellers. We are moving directly toward the kingdom of Baghirmi, which Vogel traversed in 1856, so as to reach the Wadai country, where he disappeared. This young man, at the age of twenty-three, had been sent to cooperate with Dr. Barth. They met on the 1st of December, 1854, and thereupon commenced his explorations of the country. Toward 1856, he announced, in the last letters received from him, his intention to reconnoitre the kingdom of Wadai, which no European had yet penetrated. It appears that he got as far as Wara, the capital, where, according to some accounts, he was made prisoner, and, according to others, was put to death for having attempted to ascend a sacred mountain in the environs. But, we must not too lightly admit the death of travellers, since that does away with the necessity of going in search of them. For instance, how often was the death of Dr. Barth reported, to his own great annoyance! It is, therefore, very possible that Vogel may still be held as a prisoner by the Sultan of Wadai, in the hope of obtaining a good ransom for him.

"Baron de Neimans was about starting for the Wadai country when he died at Cairo, in 1855; and we now know that De Heuglin has set out on Vogel's track with the expedition sent from Leipsic, so that we shall soon be accurately informed as to the fate of that young and interesting explorer."*

Mosfeia had disappeared from the horizon long ere this, and the Mandara country was developing to the gaze of our aeronauts its astonishing fertility, with its forests of acacias, its locust-trees covered with red flowers, and the herbaceous plants of its fields of cotton and indigo trees. The river Shari, which eighty miles farther on rolled its impetuous waters into Lake Tchad, was quite distinctly seen.

The doctor got his companions to trace its course upon the maps drawn by Dr. Barth.

"You perceive," said he, "that the labors of this savant have been conducted with great precision; we are moving directly toward the

---

* Since the doctor's departure, letters written from El'Obeid by Mr. Muntzinger, the newly-appointed head of the expedition, unfortunately place the death of Vogel beyond a doubt.

Loggoum region, and perhaps toward Kernak, its capital. It was there that poor Toole died, at the age of scarcely twenty-two. He was a young Englishman, an ensign in the 80th regiment, who, a few weeks before, had joined Major Denham in Africa, and it was not long ere he there met his death. Ah! this vast country might well be called the graveyard of European travellers."

Some boats, fifty feet long, were descending the current of the Shari. The Victoria, then one thousand feet above the soil, hardly attracted the attention of the natives; but the wind, which until then had been blowing with a certain degree of strength, was falling off.

"Is it possible that we are to be caught in another dead calm?" sighed the doctor.

"Well, we've no lack of water, nor the desert to fear, anyhow, master," said Joe.

"No; but there are races here still more to be dreaded."

"Why!" said Joe, again, "there's something like a town."

"That is Kernak. The last puffs of the breeze are wafting us to it, and, if we choose, we can take an exact plan of the place."

"Shall we not go nearer to it?" asked Kennedy.

"Nothing easier, Dick! We are right over it. Allow me to turn the stopcock of the cylinder, and we'll not be long in descending."

Half an hour later the balloon hung motionless about two hundred feet from the ground.

"Here we are!" said the doctor, "nearer to Kernak than a man would be to London, if he were perched in the cupola of St. Paul's. So we can take a survey at our ease."

"What is that tick-tacking sound that we hear on all sides?"

Joe looked attentively, and at length discovered that the noise they heard was produced by a number of weavers beating cloth stretched in the open air, on large trunks of trees.

The capital of Loggoum could then be seen in its entire extent, like an unrolled chart. It is really a city with straight rows of houses and quite wide streets. In the midst of a large open space there was a slave-market, attended by a great crowd of customers, for the Mandara women, who have extremely small hands and feet, are in excellent request, and can be sold at lucrative rates.

At the sight of the Victoria, the scene so often produced occurred again. At first there were outcries, and then followed general stupefaction; business was abandoned; work was flung aside, and all noise ceased. The aeronauts remained as they were, completely motionless, and lost not a detail of the populous city. They even went down to within sixty feet of the ground.

Hereupon the Governor of Loggoum came out from his residence, displaying his green standard, and accompanied by his musicians, who blew on hoarse buffalo-horns, as though they would split their cheeks or any thing else, excepting their own lungs. The crowd at once gathered around him. In the mean while Dr. Ferguson tried to make himself heard, but in vain.

This population looked like proud and intelligent people, with their high foreheads, their almost aquiline noses, and their curling hair; but the presence of the Victoria troubled them greatly. Horsemen could be seen galloping in all directions, and it soon became evident that the governor's troops were assembling to oppose so extraordinary a foe. Joe wore himself out waving handkerchiefs of every color and shape to them; but his exertions were all to no purpose.

However, the sheik, surrounded by his court, proclaimed silence, and pronounced a discourse, of which the doctor could not understand a word. It was Arabic, mixed with Baghirmi. He could make out enough, however, by the universal language of gestures, to be aware that he was receiving a very polite invitation to depart. Indeed, he would have asked for nothing better, but for lack of wind, the thing had become impossible. His noncompliance, therefore, exasperated the governor, whose courtiers and attendants set up a furious howl to enforce immediate obedience on the part of the aerial monster.

They were odd-looking fellows those courtiers, with their five or six shirts swathed around their bodies! They had enormous stomachs, some of which actually seemed to be artificial. The doctor surprised his companions by informing them that this was the way to pay court to the sultan. The rotundity of the stomach indicated the ambition of its possessor. These corpulent gentry gesticulated and bawled at the top of their voices—one of them particularly distinguishing himself above the rest—to such an extent, indeed, that he must have been a prime minister—at least, if the disturbance he made was any criterion of his rank. The common rabble of dusky denizens united their howlings with the uproar of the court, repeating their gesticulations like so many monkeys, and thereby producing a single and instantaneous movement of ten thousand arms at one time.

To these means of intimidation, which were presently deemed insufficient, were added others still more formidable. Soldiers, armed with bows and arrows, were drawn up in line of battle; but by this time the balloon was expanding, and rising quietly beyond their reach. Upon this the governor seized a musket and aimed it at the balloon; but, Kennedy, who was watching him, shattered the uplifted weapon in the sheik's grasp.

At this unexpected blow there was a general rout. Every mother's son of them scampered for his dwelling with the utmost celerity, and stayed there, so that the streets of the town were absolutely deserted for the remainder of that day.

Night came, and not a breath of wind was stirring. The aeronauts had to make up their minds to remain motionless at the distance of but three hundred feet above the ground. Not a fire or light shone in the deep gloom, and around reigned the silence of death; but the doctor only redoubled his vigilance, as this apparent quiet might conceal some snare.

And he had reason to be watchful. About midnight, the whole city seemed to be in a blaze. Hundreds of streaks of flame crossed each other, and shot to and fro in the air like rockets, forming a regular network of fire.

"That's really curious!" said the doctor, somewhat puzzled to make out what it meant.

"By all that's glorious!" shouted Kennedy, "it looks as if the fire were ascending and coming up toward us!"

And, sure enough, with an accompaniment of musket-shots, yelling, and din of every description, the mass of fire was, indeed, mounting toward the Victoria. Joe got ready to throw out ballast, and Ferguson was not long at guessing the truth. Thousands of pigeons, their tails garnished with combustibles, had been set loose and driven toward the Victoria; and now, in their terror, they were flying high up, zigzagging the atmosphere with lines of fire. Kennedy was preparing to discharge all his batteries into the middle of the ascending multitude, but what could he have done against such a numberless army? The pigeons were already whisking around the car; they were even surrounding the balloon, the sides of which, reflecting their illumination, looked as though enveloped with a network of fire.

The doctor dared hesitate no longer; and, throwing out a fragment of quartz, he kept himself beyond the reach of these dangerous assailants;

and, for two hours afterward, he could see them wandering hither and thither through the darkness of the night, until, little by little, their light diminished, and they, one by one, died out.

"Now we may sleep in quiet," said the doctor.

"Not badly got up for barbarians," mused friend Joe, speaking his thoughts aloud.

"Oh, they employ these pigeons frequently, to set fire to the thatch of hostile villages; but this time the village mounted higher than they could go."

"Why, positively, a balloon need fear no enemies!"

"Yes, indeed, it may!" objected Ferguson.

"What are they, then, doctor?"

"They are the careless people in the car! So, my friends, let us have vigilance in all places and at all times."

Chapter 31

DEPARTURE IN THE NIGHT-TIME.—ALL THREE.—KENNEDY'S
INSTINCTS.—PRECAUTIONS.—THE COURSE OF THE SHARI RIVER.—
LAKE TCHAD.—THE WATER OF THE LAKE.—THE HIPPOPOTAMUS.—
ONE BULLET THROWN AWAY.

About three o'clock in the morning, Joe, who was then on watch, at length saw the city move away from beneath his feet. The Victoria was once again in motion, and both the doctor and Kennedy awoke.

The former consulted his compass, and saw, with satisfaction, that the wind was carrying them toward the north-northeast.

"We are in luck!" said he; "every thing works in our favor: we shall discover Lake Tchad this very day."

"Is it a broad sheet of water?" asked Kennedy.

"Somewhat, Dick. At its greatest length and breadth, it measures about one hundred and twenty miles."

"It will spice our trip with a little variety to sail over a spacious sheet of water."

"After all, though, I don't see that we have much to complain of on that score. Our trip has been very much varied, indeed; and, moreover, we are getting on under the best possible conditions."

"Unquestionably so; excepting those privations on the desert, we have encountered no serious danger."

"It is not to be denied that our noble balloon has behaved wonderfully well. To-day is May 12th, and we started on the 18th of April. That makes twenty-five days of journeying. In ten days more we shall have reached our destination."

"Where is that?"

"I do not know. But what does that signify?"

"You are right again, Samuel! Let us intrust to Providence the care of guiding us and of keeping us in good health as we are now. We don't look much as though we had been crossing the most pestilential country in the world!"

"We had an opportunity of getting up in life, and that's what we have done!"

"Hurrah for trips in the air!" cried Joe. "Here we are at the end of twenty-five days in good condition, well fed, and well rested. We've had too much rest in fact, for my legs begin to feel rusty, and I wouldn't be vexed a bit to stretch them with a run of thirty miles or so!"

"You can do that, Joe, in the streets of London, but in fine we set out three together, like Denham, Clapperton, and Overweg; like Barth, Richardson, and Vogel, and, more fortunate than our predecessors here, we are three in number still. But it is most important for us not to separate. If, while one of us was on the ground, the Victoria should have to ascend in order to escape some sudden danger, who knows whether we should ever see each other again? Therefore it is that I say again to Kennedy frankly that I do not like his going off alone to hunt."

"But still, Samuel, you will permit me to indulge that fancy a little. There is no harm in renewing our stock of provisions. Besides, before our departure, you held out to me the prospect of some superb hunting, and thus far I have done but little in the line of the Andersons and Cummings."

"But, my dear Dick, your memory fails you, or your modesty makes you forget your own exploits. It really seems to me that, without mentioning small game, you have already an antelope, an elephant, and two lions on your conscience."

"But what's all that to an African sportsman who sees all the animals in creation strutting along under the muzzle of his rifle? There! there! look at that troop of giraffes!"

"Those giraffes," roared Joe; "why, they're not as big as my fist."

"Because we are a thousand feet above them; but close to them you would discover that they are three times as tall as you are!"

"And what do you say to yon herd of gazelles, and those ostriches, that run with the speed of the wind?" resumed Kennedy.

"Those ostriches?" remonstrated Joe, again; "those are chickens, and the greatest kind of chickens!"

"Come, doctor, can't we get down nearer to them?" pleaded Kennedy.

"We can get closer to them, Dick, but we must not land. And what good will it do you to strike down those poor animals when they can be of no use to you? Now, if the question were to destroy a lion, a tiger, a cat, a hyena, I could understand it; but to deprive an antelope or a gazelle of life, to no other purpose than the gratification of your instincts as a sportsman, seems hardly worth the trouble. But, after all, my friend, we are going to keep at about one hundred feet only from the soil, and, should you see any ferocious wild beast, oblige us by sending a ball through its heart!"

The Victoria descended gradually, but still keeping at a safe height, for, in a barbarous, yet very populous country, it was necessary to keep on the watch for unexpected perils.

The travellers were then directly following the course of the Shari. The charming banks of this river were hidden beneath the foliage of trees of various dyes; lianas and climbing plants wound in and out on all sides and formed the most curious combinations of color. Crocodiles were seen basking in the broad blaze of the sun or plunging beneath the waters with the agility of lizards, and in their gambols they sported about among the many green islands that intercept the current of the stream.

It was thus, in the midst of rich and verdant landscapes that our travellers passed over the district of Maffatay, and about nine o'clock in the morning reached the southern shore of Lake Tchad.

There it was at last, outstretched before them, that Caspian Sea of Africa, the existence of which was so long consigned to the realms of fable—that interior expanse of water to which only Denham's and Barth's expeditions had been able to force their way.

The doctor strove in vain to fix its precise configuration upon paper. It had already changed greatly since 1847. In fact, the chart of Lake Tchad is very difficult to trace with exactitude, for it is surrounded by muddy and almost impassable morasses, in which Barth thought that he was doomed to perish. From year to year these marshes, covered with reeds and papyrus fifteen feet high, become the lake itself. Frequently, too, the villages on its shores are half submerged, as was the case with Ngornou in 1856, and now the hippopotamus and the alligator frisk and dive where the dwellings of Bornou once stood.

The sun shot his dazzling rays over this placid sheet of water, and toward the north the two elements merged into one and the same horizon.

The doctor was desirous of determining the character of the water, which was long believed to be salt. There was no danger in descending close to the lake, and the car was soon skimming its surface like a bird at the distance of only five feet.

Joe plunged a bottle into the lake and drew it up half filled. The water was then tasted and found to be but little fit for drinking, with a certain carbonate-of-soda flavor.

While the doctor was jotting down the result of this experiment, the loud report of a gun was heard close beside him. Kennedy had not been able to resist the temptation of firing at a huge hippopotamus. The latter, who had been basking quietly, disappeared at the sound of the explosion, but did not seem to be otherwise incommoded by Kennedy's conical bullet.

"You'd have done better if you had harpooned him," said Joe.

"But how?"

"With one of our anchors. It would have been a hook just big enough for such a rousing beast as that!"

"Humph!" exclaimed Kennedy, "Joe really has an idea this time—"

"Which I beg of you not to put into execution," interposed the doctor. "The animal would very quickly have dragged us where we could not have done much to help ourselves, and where we have no business to be."

"Especially now since we've settled the question as to what kind of water there is in Lake Tchad. Is that sort of fish good to eat, Dr. Ferguson?"

"That fish, as you call it, Joe, is really a mammiferous animal of the pachydermal species. Its flesh is said to be excellent and is an article of important trade between the tribes living along the borders of the lake."

"Then I'm sorry that Mr. Kennedy's shot didn't do more damage."

"The animal is vulnerable only in the stomach and between the thighs. Dick's ball hasn't even marked him; but should the ground strike me as favorable, we shall halt at the northern end of the lake, where Kennedy will find himself in the midst of a whole menagerie, and can make up for lost time."

"Well," said Joe, "I hope then that Mr. Kennedy will hunt the hippopotamus a little; I'd like to taste the meat of that queer-looking beast. It doesn't look exactly natural to get away into the centre of Africa, to feed on snipe and partridge, just as if we were in England."

Chapter 32

Since its arrival at Lake Tchad, the balloon had struck a current that edged it farther to the westward. A few clouds tempered the heat of the day, and, besides, a little air could be felt over this vast expanse of water; but about one o'clock, the Victoria, having slanted across this part of the lake, again advanced over the land for a space of seven or eight miles.

The doctor, who was somewhat vexed at first at this turn of his course, no longer thought of complaining when he caught sight of the city of Kouka, the capital of Bornou. He saw it for a moment, encircled by its walls of white clay, and a few rudely-constructed mosques rising clumsily above that conglomeration of houses that look like playing-dice, which form most Arab towns. In the court-yards of the private dwellings, and on the public squares, grew palms and caoutchouc-trees topped with a dome of foliage more than one hundred feet in breadth. Joe called attention to the fact that these immense parasols were in proper accordance with the intense heat of the sun, and made thereon some pious reflections which it were needless to repeat.

Kouka really consists of two distinct towns, separated by the "Dendal," a large boulevard three hundred yards wide, at that hour crowded with horsemen and foot passengers. On one side, the rich quarter stands squarely with its airy and lofty houses, laid out in regular order; on the other, is huddled together the poor quarter, a miserable collection of low hovels of a conical shape, in which a poverty-stricken multitude vegetate rather than live, since Kouka is neither a trading nor a commercial city.

Kennedy thought it looked something like Edinburgh, were that city extended on a plain, with its two distinct boroughs.

But our travellers had scarcely the time to catch even this glimpse of it, for, with the fickleness that characterizes the air-currents of this region, a contrary wind suddenly swept them some forty miles over the surface of Lake Tchad.

Then then were regaled with a new spectacle. They could count the numerous islets of the lake, inhabited by the Biddiomahs, a race of bloodthirsty and formidable pirates, who are as greatly feared when neighbors as are the Touaregs of Sahara.

These estimable people were in readiness to receive the Victoria bravely with stones and arrows, but the balloon quickly passed their islands, fluttering over them, from one to the other with butterfly motion, like a gigantic beetle.

At this moment, Joe, who was scanning the horizon, said to Kennedy:

"There, sir, as you are always thinking of good sport, yonder is just the thing for you!"

"What is it, Joe?"

"This time, the doctor will not disapprove of your shooting."

"But what is it?"

"Don't you see that flock of big birds making for us?"

"Birds?" exclaimed the doctor, snatching his spyglass.

"I see them," replied Kennedy; "there are at least a dozen of them."

"Fourteen, exactly!" said Joe.

"Heaven grant that they may be of a kind sufficiently noxious for the doctor to let me peg away at them!"

"I should not object, but I would much rather see those birds at a distance from us!"

"Why, are you afraid of those fowls?"

"They are condors, and of the largest size. Should they attack us—"

"Well, if they do, we'll defend ourselves. We have a whole arsenal at our disposal. I don't think those birds are so very formidable."

"Who can tell?" was the doctor's only remark.

Ten minutes later, the flock had come within gunshot, and were making the air ring with their hoarse cries. They came right toward the Victoria, more irritated than frightened by her presence.

"How they scream! What a noise!" said Joe.

"Perhaps they don't like to see anybody poaching in their country up in the air, or daring to fly like themselves!"

"Well, now, to tell the truth, when I take a good look at them, they are an ugly, ferocious set, and I should think them dangerous enough if they were armed with Purdy-Moore rifles," admitted Kennedy.

"They have no need of such weapons," said Ferguson, looking very grave.

The condors flew around them in wide circles, their flight growing gradually closer and closer to the balloon. They swept through the air in rapid, fantastic curves, occasionally precipitating themselves headlong with the speed of a bullet, and then breaking their line of projection by an abrupt and daring angle.

The doctor, much disquieted, resolved to ascend so as to escape this dangerous proximity. He therefore dilated the hydrogen in his balloon, and it rapidly rose.

But the condors mounted with him, apparently determined not to part company.

"They seem to mean mischief!" said the hunter, cocking his rifle.

And, in fact, they were swooping nearer, and more than one came within fifty feet of them, as if defying the fire-arms.

"By George, I'm itching to let them have it!" exclaimed Kennedy.

"No, Dick; not now! Don't exasperate them needlessly. That would only be exciting them to attack us!"

"But I could soon settle those fellows!"

"You may think so, Dick. But you are wrong!"

"Why, we have a bullet for each of them!"

"And suppose that they were to attack the upper part of the balloon, what would you do? How would you get at them? Just imagine yourself in the presence of a troop of lions on the plain, or a school of sharks in the open ocean! For travellers in the air, this situation is just as dangerous."

"Are you speaking seriously, doctor?"

"Very seriously, Dick."

"Let us wait, then!"

"Wait! Hold yourself in readiness in case of an attack, but do not fire without my orders."

The birds then collected at a short distance, yet to near that their naked necks, entirely bare of feathers, could be plainly seen, as they stretched them out with the effort of their cries, while their gristly crests, garnished with a comb and gills of deep violet, stood erect with rage. They were of the very largest size, their bodies being more than three feet in length, and the lower surface of their white wings glittering in the sunlight. They might well have been considered winged sharks, so striking was their resemblance to those ferocious rangers of the deep.

"They are following us!" said the doctor, as he saw them ascending with him, "and, mount as we may, they can fly still higher!"

"Well, what are we to do?" asked Kennedy.

The doctor made no answer.

"Listen, Samuel!" said the sportsman. "There are fourteen of those birds; we have seventeen shots at our disposal if we discharge all our weapons. Have we not the means, then, to destroy them or disperse them? I will give a good account of some of them!"

"I have no doubt of your skill, Dick; I look upon all as dead that may come within range of your rifle, but I repeat that, if they attack the upper part of the balloon, you could not get a sight at them. They would tear the silk covering that sustains us, and we are three thousand feet up in the air!"

At this moment, one of the ferocious birds darted right at the balloon, with outstretched beak and claws, ready to rend it with either or both.

"Fire! fire at once!" cried the doctor.

He had scarcely ceased, ere the huge creature, stricken dead, dropped headlong, turning over and over in space as he fell.

Kennedy had already grasped one of the two-barrelled fowling-pieces and Joe was taking aim with another.

Frightened by the report, the condors drew back for a moment, but they almost instantly returned to the charge with extreme fury. Kennedy severed the head of one from its body with his first shot, and Joe broke the wing of another.

"Only eleven left," said he.

Thereupon the birds changed their tactics, and by common consent soared above the balloon. Kennedy glanced at Ferguson. The latter, in spite of his imperturbability, grew pale. Then ensued a moment of terrifying silence. In the next they heard a harsh tearing noise, as of something rending the silk, and the car seemed to sink from beneath the feet of our three aeronauts.

"We are lost!" exclaimed Ferguson, glancing at the barometer, which was now swiftly rising.

"Over with the ballast!" he shouted, "over with it!"

And in a few seconds the last lumps of quartz had disappeared.

"We are still falling! Empty the water-tanks! Do you hear me, Joe? We are pitching into the lake!"

Joe obeyed. The doctor leaned over and looked out. The lake seemed to come up toward him like a rising tide. Every object around grew rapidly in size while they were looking at it. The car was not two hundred feet from the surface of Lake Tchad.

"The provisions! the provisions!" cried the doctor.

And the box containing them was launched into space.

Their descent became less rapid, but the luckless aeronauts were still falling, and into the lake.

"Throw out something—something more!" cried the doctor.

"There is nothing more to throw!" was Kennedy's despairing response.

"Yes, there is!" called Joe, and with a wave of the hand he disappeared like a flash, over the edge of the car.

"Joe! Joe!" exclaimed the doctor, horror-stricken.

The Victoria thus relieved resumed her ascending motion, mounted a thousand feet into the air, and the wind, burying itself in the disinflated covering, bore them away toward the northern part of the lake.

"Lost!" exclaimed the sportsman, with a gesture of despair.

"Lost to save us!" responded Ferguson.

And these men, intrepid as they were, felt the large tears streaming down their cheeks. They leaned over with the vain hope of seeing some trace of their heroic companion, but they were already far away from him.

"What course shall we pursue?" asked Kennedy.

"Alight as soon as possible, Dick, and then wait."

After a sweep of some sixty miles the Victoria halted on a desert shore, on the north of the lake. The anchors caught in a low tree and the sportsman fastened it securely. Night came, but neither Ferguson nor Kennedy could find one moment's sleep.

Chapter 33

CONJECTURES.—REESTABLISHMENT OF THE VICTORIA'S
EQUILIBRIUM.—DR. FERGUSON'S NEW CALCULATIONS.—KENNEDY'S
HUNT.—A COMPLETE EXPLORATION OF LAKE TCHAD.—TANGALIA.—
THE RETURN.—LARI.

On the morrow, the 13th of May, our travellers, for the first time, reconnoitred the part of the coast on which they had landed. It was a sort of island of solid ground in the midst of an immense marsh. Around this fragment of terra firma grew reeds as lofty as trees are in Europe, and stretching away out of sight.

These impenetrable swamps gave security to the position of the balloon. It was necessary to watch only the borders of the lake. The vast stretch of water broadened away from the spot, especially toward the east, and nothing could be seen on the horizon, neither mainland nor islands.

The two friends had not yet ventured to speak of their recent companion. Kennedy first imparted his conjectures to the doctor.

"Perhaps Joe is not lost after all," he said. "He was a skilful lad, and had few equals as a swimmer. He would find no difficulty in swimming across the Firth of Forth at Edinburgh. We shall see him again—but how and where I know not. Let us omit nothing on our part to give him the chance of rejoining us."

"May God grant it as you say, Dick!" replied the doctor, with much emotion. "We shall do everything in the world to find our lost friend again. Let us, in the first place, see where we are. But, above all things, let us rid the Victoria of this outside covering, which is of no further use. That will relieve us of six hundred and fifty pounds, a weight not to be despised—and the end is worth the trouble!"

The doctor and Kennedy went to work at once, but they encountered great difficulty. They had to tear the strong silk away piece by piece, and then cut it in narrow strips so as to extricate it from the meshes of the network. The tear made by the beaks of the condors was found to be several feet in length.

This operation took at least four hours, but at length the inner balloon once completely extricated did not appear to have suffered in the least degree. The Victoria was thus diminished in size by one fifth, and this difference was sufficiently noticeable to excite Kennedy's surprise.

"Will it be large enough?" he asked.

"Have no fears on that score, I will reestablish the equilibrium, and should our poor Joe return we shall find a way to start off with him again on our old route."

"At the moment of our fall, unless I am mistaken, we were not far from an island."

"Yes, I recollect it," said the doctor, "but that island, like all the islands on Lake Tchad, is, no doubt, inhabited by a gang of pirates and murderers. They certainly witnessed our misfortune, and should Joe fall into their hands, what will become of him unless protected by their superstitions?"

"Oh, he's just the lad to get safely out of the scrape, I repeat. I have great confidence in his shrewdness and skill."

"I hope so. Now, Dick, you may go and hunt in the neighborhood, but don't get far away whatever you do. It has become a pressing necessity for us to renew our stock of provisions, since we had to sacrifice nearly all the old lot."

"Very good, doctor, I shall not be long absent."

Hereupon, Kennedy took a double-barrelled fowling-piece, and strode through the long grass toward a thicket not far off, where the frequent sound of shooting soon let the doctor know that the sportsman was making a good use of his time.

Meanwhile Ferguson was engaged in calculating the relative weight of the articles still left in the car, and in establishing the equipoise of the second balloon. He found that there were still left some thirty pounds of pemmican, a supply of tea and coffee, about a gallon and a half of brandy, and one empty water-tank. All the dried meat had disappeared.

The doctor was aware that, by the loss of the hydrogen in the first balloon, the ascensional force at his disposal was now reduced to about nine hundred pounds. He therefore had to count upon this difference in order to rearrange his equilibrium. The new balloon measured sixty-seven thousand cubic feet, and contained thirty-three thousand four hundred and eighty feet of gas. The dilating apparatus appeared to be in good condition, and neither the battery nor the spiral had been injured.

The ascensional force of the new balloon was then about three thousand pounds, and, in adding together the weight of the apparatus, of the passengers, of the stock of water, of the car and its accessories, and putting aboard fifty gallons of water, and one hundred pounds of fresh meat, the doctor got a total weight of twenty-eight hundred and thirty pounds. He could then take with him one hundred and seventy pounds of ballast, for unforeseen emergencies, and the balloon would be in exact balance with the surrounding atmosphere.

His arrangements were completed accordingly, and he made up for Joe's weight with a surplus of ballast. He spent the whole day in these preparations, and the latter were finished when Kennedy returned. The hunter had been successful, and brought back a regular cargo of geese, wild-duck, snipe, teal, and plover. He went to work at once to draw and smoke the game. Each piece, suspended on a small, thin skewer, was hung over a fire of green wood. When they seemed in good order, Kennedy, who was perfectly at home in the business, packed them away in the car.

On the morrow, the hunter was to complete his supplies.

Evening surprised our travellers in the midst of this work. Their supper consisted of pemmican, biscuit, and tea; and fatigue, after having given them appetite, brought them sleep. Each of them strained eyes and ears into the gloom during his watch, sometimes fancying that they heard the voice of poor Joe; but, alas! the voice that they so longed to hear, was far away.

"At the first streak of day, the doctor aroused Kennedy.

"I have been long and carefully considering what should be done," said he, "to find our companion."

"Whatever your plan may be, doctor, it will suit me. Speak!"

"Above all things, it is important that Joe should hear from us in some way."

"Undoubtedly. Suppose the brave fellow should take it into his head that we have abandoned him?"

"He! He knows us too well for that. Such a thought would never come into his mind. But he must be informed as to where we are."

"How can that be managed?"

"We shall get into our car and be off again through the air."

"But, should the wind bear us away?"

"Happily, it will not. See, Dick! it is carrying us back to the lake; and this circumstance, which would have been vexatious yesterday, is fortunate now. Our efforts, then, will be limited to keeping ourselves above that vast sheet of water throughout the day. Joe cannot fail to see us, and his eyes will be constantly on the lookout in that direction. Perhaps he will even manage to let us know the place of his retreat."

"If he be alone and at liberty, he certainly will."

"And if a prisoner," resumed the doctor, "it not being the practice of the natives to confine their captives, he will see us, and comprehend the object of our researches."

"But, at last," put in Kennedy—"for we must anticipate every thing—should we find no trace—if he should have left no mark to follow him by, what are we to do?"

"We shall endeavor to regain the northern part of the lake, keeping ourselves as much in sight as possible. There we'll wait; we'll explore the banks; we'll search the water's edge, for Joe will assuredly try to reach the shore; and we will not leave the country without having done every thing to find him."

"Let us set out, then!" said the hunter.

The doctor hereupon took the exact bearings of the patch of solid land they were about to leave, and arrived at the conclusion that it lay on the north shore of Lake Tchad, between the village of Lari and the village of Ingemini, both visited by Major Denham. During this time Kennedy was completing his stock of fresh meat. Although the neighboring marshes showed traces of the rhinoceros, the lamantine (or manatee), and the hippopotamus, he had no opportunity to see a single specimen of those animals.

At seven in the morning, but not without great difficulty—which to Joe would have been nothing—the balloon's anchor was detached from its hold, the gas dilated, and the new Victoria rose two hundred feet into the air. It seemed to hesitate at first, and went spinning around, like a top; but at last a brisk current caught it, and it advanced over the lake, and was soon borne away at a speed of twenty miles per hour.

The doctor continued to keep at a height of from two hundred to five hundred feet. Kennedy frequently discharged his rifle; and, when passing over islands, the aeronauts approached them even imprudently, scrutinizing the thickets, the bushes, the underbrush—in fine, every spot where a mass of shade or jutting rock could have afforded a retreat to their companion. They swooped down close to the long pirogues that navigated the lake; and the wild fishermen, terrified at the sight of the balloon, would plunge into the water and regain their islands with every symptom of undisguised affright.

"We can see nothing," said Kennedy, after two hours of search.

"Let us wait a little longer, Dick, and not lose heart. We cannot be far away from the scene of our accident."

By eleven o'clock the balloon had gone ninety miles. It then fell in with a new current, which, blowing almost at right angles to the other, drove them eastward about sixty miles. It next floated over a very large and populous island, which the doctor took to be Farram, on which the capital of the Biddiomahs is situated. Ferguson expected at every moment to see Joe spring up out of some thicket, flying for his life, and calling for help. Were he free, they could pick him up without trouble; were he a prisoner, they could rescue him by repeating the manoeuvre they had practised to save the missionary, and he would soon be with his friends again; but nothing was seen, not a sound was heard. The case seemed desperate.

About half-past two o'clock, the Victoria hove in sight of Tangalia, a village situated on the eastern shore of Lake Tchad, where it marks the extreme point attained by Denham at the period of his exploration.

The doctor became uneasy at this persistent setting of the wind in that direction, for he felt that he was being thrown back to the eastward, toward the centre of Africa, and the interminable deserts of that region.

"We must absolutely come to a halt," said he, "and even alight. For Joe's sake, particularly, we ought to go back to the lake; but, to begin with, let us endeavor to find an opposite current."

During more than an hour he searched at different altitudes: the balloon always came back toward the mainland. But at length, at the height of a thousand feet, a very violent breeze swept to the northwestward.

It was out of the question that Joe should have been detained on one of the islands of the lake; for, in such case he would certainly have found means to make his presence there known. Perhaps he had been dragged to the mainland. The doctor was reasoning thus to himself, when he again came in sight of the northern shore of Lake Tchad.

As for supposing that Joe had been drowned, that was not to be believed for a moment. One horrible thought glanced across the minds of both Kennedy and the doctor: caymans swarm in these waters! But neither one nor the other had the courage to distinctly communicate this impression. However, it came up to them so forcibly at last that the doctor said, without further preface:

"Crocodiles are found only on the shores of the islands or of the lake, and Joe will have skill enough to avoid them. Besides, they are not very dangerous; and the Africans bathe with impunity, and quite fearless of their attacks."

Kennedy made no reply. He preferred keeping quiet to discussing this terrible possibility.

The doctor made out the town of Lari about five o'clock in the evening. The inhabitants were at work gathering in their cotton-crop in front of their huts, constructed of woven reeds, and standing in the midst of clean and neatly-kept enclosures. This collection of about fifty habitations occupied a slight depression of the soil, in a valley extending between two low mountains. The force of the wind carried the doctor farther onward than he wanted to go; but it changed a second time, and bore him back exactly to his starting-point, on the sort of enclosed island where he had passed the preceding night. The anchor, instead of catching the branches of the tree, took hold in the masses of reeds mixed with the thick mud of the marshes, which offered considerable resistance.

The doctor had much difficulty in restraining the balloon; but at length the wind died away with the setting in of nightfall; and the two friends kept watch together in an almost desperate state of mind.

Chapter 34

THE HURRICANE.—A FORCED DEPARTURE.—LOSS OF AN ANCHOR.—
MELANCHOLY REFLECTIONS.—THE RESOLUTION ADOPTED.—THE
SAND-STORM.—THE BURIED CARAVAN.—A CONTRARY YET
FAVORABLE WIND.—THE RETURN SOUTHWARD.—KENNEDY
AT HIS POST.

At three o'clock in the morning the wind was raging. It beat down with such violence that the Victoria could not stay near the ground without danger. It was thrown almost flat over upon its side, and the reeds chafed the silk so roughly that it seemed as though they would tear it.

"We must be off, Dick," said the doctor; "we cannot remain in this situation."

"But, doctor, what of Joe?"

"I am not likely to abandon him. No, indeed! and should the hurricane carry me a thousand miles to the northward, I will return! But here we are endangering the safety of all."

"Must we go without him?" asked the Scot, with an accent of profound grief.

"And do you think, then," rejoined Ferguson, "that my heart does not bleed like your own? Am I not merely obeying an imperious necessity?"

"I am entirely at your orders," replied the hunter; "let us start!"

But their departure was surrounded with unusual difficulty. The anchor, which had caught very deeply, resisted all their efforts to disengage it; while the balloon, drawing in the opposite direction, increased its tension. Kennedy could not get it free. Besides, in his present position, the manoeuvre had become a very perilous one, for the Victoria threatened to break away before he should be able to get into the car again.

The doctor, unwilling to run such a risk, made his friend get into his place, and resigned himself to the alternative of cutting the anchor-rope. The Victoria made one bound of three hundred feet into the air, and took her route directly northward.

Ferguson had no other choice than to scud before the storm. He folded his arms, and soon became absorbed in his own melancholy reflections.

After a few moments of profound silence, he turned to Kennedy, who sat there no less taciturn.

"We have, perhaps, been tempting Providence," said he; "it does not belong to man to undertake such a journey!"—and a sigh of grief escaped him as he spoke.

"It is but a few days," replied the sportsman, "since we were congratulating ourselves upon having escaped so many dangers! All three of us were shaking hands!"

"Poor Joe! kindly and excellent disposition! brave and candid heart! Dazzled for a moment by his sudden discovery of wealth, he willingly sacrificed his treasures! And now, he is far from us; and the wind is carrying us still farther away with resistless speed!"

"Come, doctor, admitting that he may have found refuge among the lake tribes, can he not do as the travellers who visited them before us, did;—like Denham, like Barth? Both of those men got back to their own country."

"Ah! my dear Dick! Joe doesn't know one word of the language; he is alone, and without resources. The travellers of whom you speak did not attempt to go forward without sending many presents in advance of them to the chiefs, and surrounded by an escort armed and trained for these expeditions. Yet, they could not avoid sufferings of the worst description! What, then, can you expect the fate of our companion to be? It is horrible to think of, and this is one of the worst calamities that it has ever been my lot to endure!"

"But, we'll come back again, doctor!"

"Come back, Dick? Yes, if we have to abandon the balloon! if we should be forced to return to Lake Tchad on foot, and put ourselves in communication with the Sultan of Bornou! The Arabs cannot have retained a disagreeable remembrance of the first Europeans."

"I will follow you, doctor," replied the hunter, with emphasis. "You may count upon me! We would rather give up the idea of prosecuting this journey than not return. Joe forgot himself for our sake; we will sacrifice ourselves for his!"

This resolve revived some hope in the hearts of these two men; they felt strong in the same inspiration. Ferguson forthwith set every thing at work to get into a contrary current, that might bring him back again to Lake Tchad; but this was impracticable at that moment, and even to alight was out of the question on ground completely bare of trees, and with such a hurricane blowing.

The Victoria thus passed over the country of the Tibbous, crossed the Belad el Djerid, a desert of briers that forms the border of the Soudan, and advanced into the desert of sand streaked with the long tracks of the many caravans that pass and repass there. The last line of vegetation was speedily lost in the dim southern horizon, not far from the principal oasis in this part of Africa, whose fifty wells are shaded by magnificent trees; but it was impossible to stop. An Arab encampment, tents of striped stuff, some camels, stretching out their viper-like heads and necks along the sand, gave life to this solitude, but the Victoria sped by like a shooting-star, and in this way traversed a distance of sixty miles in three hours, without Ferguson being able to check or guide her course.

"We cannot halt, we cannot alight!" said the doctor; "not a tree, not an inequality of the ground! Are we then to be driven clear across Sahara? Surely, Heaven is indeed against us!"

He was uttering these words with a sort of despairing rage, when suddenly he saw the desert sands rising aloft in the midst of a dense cloud of dust, and go whirling through the air, impelled by opposing currents.

Amid this tornado, an entire caravan, disorganized, broken, and overthrown, was disappearing beneath an avalanche of sand. The camels, flung pell-mell together, were uttering dull and pitiful groans; cries and howls of despair were heard issuing from that dusty and stifling cloud, and, from time to time, a parti-colored garment cut the chaos of the scene with its vivid hues, and the moaning and shrieking sounded over all, a terrible accompaniment to this spectacle of destruction.

Ere long the sand had accumulated in compact masses; and there, where so recently stretched a level plain as far as the eye could see, rose now a ridgy line of hillocks, still moving from beneath—the vast tomb of an entire caravan!

The doctor and Kennedy, pallid with emotion, sat transfixed by this fearful spectacle. They could no longer manage their balloon, which went whirling round and round in contending currents, and refused to obey the different dilations of the gas. Caught in these eddies of the atmosphere, it spun about with a rapidity that made their heads reel, while the car oscillated and swung to and fro violently at the same time. The instruments suspended under the awning clattered together as though they would be dashed to pieces; the pipes of the spiral bent to and fro, threatening to break at every instant; and the water-tanks jostled and jarred with tremendous din. Although but two feet apart, our aeronauts could not hear each other speak, but with firmly-clinched hands they clung convulsively to the cordage, and endeavored to steady themselves against the fury of the tempest.

Kennedy, with his hair blown wildly about his face, looked on without speaking; but the doctor had regained all his daring in the midst of this deadly peril, and not a sign of his emotion was betrayed in his countenance, even when, after a last violent twirl, the Victoria stopped suddenly in the midst of a most unlooked-for calm; the north wind had abruptly got the upper hand, and now drove her back with equal rapidity over the route she had traversed in the morning.

"Whither are we going now?" cried Kennedy.

"Let us leave that to Providence, my dear Dick; I was wrong in doubting it. It knows better than we, and here we are, returning to places that we had expected never to see again!"

The surface of the country, which had looked so flat and level when they were coming, now seemed tossed and uneven, like the ocean-billows after a storm; a long succession of hillocks, that had scarcely settled to their places yet, indented the desert; the wind blew furiously, and the balloon fairly flew through the atmosphere.

The direction taken by our aeronauts differed somewhat from that of the morning, and thus about nine o'clock, instead of finding themselves again near the borders of Lake Tchad, they saw the desert still stretching away before them.

Kennedy remarked the circumstance.

"It matters little," replied the doctor, "the important point is to return southward; we shall come across the towns of Bornou, Wouddie, or Kouka, and I should not hesitate to halt there."

"If you are satisfied, I am content," replied the Scot, "but Heaven grant that we may not be reduced to cross the desert, as those unfortunate Arabs had to do! What we saw was frightful!"

"It often happens, Dick; these trips across the desert are far more perilous than those across the ocean. The desert has all the dangers of the sea, including the risk of being swallowed up, and added thereto are unendurable fatigues and privations."

"I think the wind shows some symptoms of moderating; the sand-dust is less dense; the undulations of the surface are diminishing, and the sky is growing clearer."

"So much the better! We must now reconnoitre attentively with our glasses, and take care not to omit a single point."

"I will look out for that, doctor, and not a tree shall be seen without my informing you of it."

And, suiting the action to the word, Kennedy took his station, spyglass in hand, at the forward part of the car.

Chapter 35

What had become of Joe, while his master was thus vainly seeking for him?

When he had dashed headlong into the lake, his first movement on coming to the surface was to raise his eyes and look upward. He saw the Victoria already risen far above the water, still rapidly ascending and growing smaller and smaller. It was soon caught in a rapid current and disappeared to the northward. His master—both his friends were saved!

"How lucky it was," thought he, "that I had that idea to throw myself out into the lake! Mr. Kennedy would soon have jumped at it, and he would not have hesitated to do as I did, for nothing's more natural than for one man to give himself up to save two others. That's mathematics!"

Satisfied on this point, Joe began to think of himself. He was in the middle of a vast lake, surrounded by tribes unknown to him, and probably ferocious. All the greater reason why he should get out of the scrape by depending only on himself. And so he gave himself no farther concern about it.

Before the attack by the birds of prey, which, according to him, had behaved like real condors, he had noticed an island on the horizon, and determining to reach it, if possible, he put forth all his knowledge and skill in the art of swimming, after having relieved himself of the most troublesome part of his clothing. The idea of a stretch of five or six miles by no means disconcerted him; and therefore, so long as he was in the open lake, he thought only of striking out straight ahead and manfully.

In about an hour and a half the distance between him and the island had greatly diminished.

But as he approached the land, a thought, at first fleeting and then tenacious, arose in his mind. He knew that the shores of the lake were frequented by huge alligators, and was well aware of the voracity of those monsters.

Now, no matter how much he was inclined to find every thing in this world quite natural, the worthy fellow was no little disturbed by this reflection. He feared greatly lest white flesh like his might be particularly acceptable to the dreaded brutes, and advanced only with extreme precaution, his eyes on the alert on both sides and all around him. At length, he was not more than one hundred yards from a bank, covered with green trees, when a puff of air strongly impregnated with a musky odor reached him.

"There!" said he to himself, "just what I expected. The crocodile isn't far off!"

With this he dived swiftly, but not sufficiently so to avoid coming into contact with an enormous body, the scaly surface of which scratched him as he passed. He thought himself lost and swam with desperate energy. Then he rose again to the top of the water, took breath and dived once more. Thus passed a few minutes of unspeakable anguish, which all his philosophy could not overcome, for he thought, all the while, that he heard behind him the sound of those huge jaws ready to snap him up forever. In this state of mind he was striking out under the water as noiselessly as possible when he felt himself seized by the arm and then by the waist.

Poor Joe! he gave one last thought to his master; and began to struggle with all the energy of despair, feeling himself the while drawn along, but not toward the bottom of the lake, as is the habit of the crocodile when about to devour its prey, but toward the surface.

So soon as he could get breath and look around him, he saw that he was between two natives as black as ebony, who held him, with a firm gripe, and uttered strange cries.

"Ha!" said Joe, "blacks instead of crocodiles! Well, I prefer it as it is; but how in the mischief dare these fellows go in bathing in such places?"

Joe was not aware that the inhabitants of the islands of Lake Tchad, like many other negro tribes, plunge with impunity into sheets of water infested with crocodiles and caymans, and without troubling their heads about them. The amphibious denizens of this lake enjoy the well-deserved reputation of being quite inoffensive.

But had not Joe escaped one peril only to fall into another? That was a question which he left events to decide; and, since he could not do otherwise, he allowed himself to be conducted to the shore without manifesting any alarm.

"Evidently," thought he, "these chaps saw the Victoria skimming the waters of the lake, like a monster of the air. They were the distant witnesses of my tumble, and they can't fail to have some respect for a man that fell from the sky! Let them have their own way, then."

Joe was at this stage of his meditations, when he was landed amid a yelling crowd of both sexes, and all ages and sizes, but not of all colors. In fine, he was surrounded by a tribe of Biddiomahs as black as jet. Nor had he to blush for the scantiness of his costume, for he saw that he was in "undress" in the highest style of that country.

But before he had time to form an exact idea of the situation, there was no mistaking the agitation of which he instantly became the object, and this soon enabled him to pluck up courage, although the adventure of Kazah did come back rather vividly to his memory.

"I foresee that they are going to make a god of me again," thought he, "some son of the moon most likely. Well, one trade's as good as another when a man has no choice. The main thing is to gain time. Should the Victoria pass this way again, I'll take advantage of my new position to treat my worshippers here to a miracle when I go sailing up into the sky!"

While Joe's thoughts were running thus, the throng pressed around him. They prostrated themselves before him; they howled; they felt him; they became even annoyingly familiar; but at the same time they had the consideration to offer him a superb banquet consisting of sour milk and rice pounded in honey. The worthy fellow, making the best of every thing, took one of the heartiest luncheons he ever ate in his life, and gave his new adorers an exalted idea of how the gods tuck away their food upon grand occasions.

When evening came, the sorcerers of the island took him respectfully by the hand, and conducted him to a sort of house surrounded with talismans; but, as he was entering it, Joe cast an uneasy look at the heaps of human bones that lay scattered around this sanctuary. But he had still more time to think about them when he found himself at last shut up in the cabin.

During the evening and through a part of the night, he heard festive chantings, the reverberations of a kind of drum, and a clatter of old iron, which were very sweet, no doubt, to African ears. Then there were howling choruses, accompanied by endless dances by gangs of natives who circled round and round the sacred hut with contortions and grimaces.

Joe could catch the sound of this deafening orchestra, through the mud and reeds of which his cabin was built; and perhaps under other circumstances he might have been amused by these strange ceremonies; but his mind was soon disturbed by quite different and less agreeable reflections. Even looking at the bright side of things, he found it both stupid and sad to be left alone in the midst of this savage country and among these wild tribes. Few travellers who had penetrated to these regions had ever again seen their native land. Moreover, could he trust to the worship of which he saw himself the object? He had good reason to believe in the vanity of human greatness; and he asked himself whether, in this country, adoration did not sometimes go to the length of eating the object adored!

But, notwithstanding this rather perplexing prospect, after some hours of meditation, fatigue got the better of his gloomy thoughts, and Joe fell into a profound slumber, which would have lasted no doubt until sunrise, had not a very unexpected sensation of dampness awakened the sleeper. Ere long this dampness became water, and that water gained so rapidly that it had soon mounted to Joe's waist.

"What can this be?" said he; "a flood! a water-spout! or a new torture invented by these blacks? Faith, though, I'm not going to wait here till it's up to my neck!"

And, so saying, he burst through the frail wall with a jog of his powerful shoulder, and found himself—where?—in the open lake! Island there was none. It had sunk during the night. In its place, the watery immensity of Lake Tchad!

"A poor country for the land-owners!" said Joe, once more vigorously resorting to his skill in the art of natation.

One of those phenomena, which are by no means unusual on Lake Tchad, had liberated our brave Joe. More than one island, that previously seemed to have the solidity of rock, has been submerged in this way; and the people living along the shores of the mainland have had to pick up the unfortunate survivors of these terrible catastrophes.

Joe knew nothing about this peculiarity of the region, but he was none the less ready to profit by it. He caught sight of a boat drifting about, without occupants, and was soon aboard of it. He found it to be but the trunk of a tree rudely hollowed out; but there were a couple of paddles in it, and Joe, availing himself of a rapid current, allowed his craft to float along.

"But let us see where we are," he said. "The polar-star there, that does its work honorably in pointing out the direction due north to everybody else, will, most likely, do me that service."

He discovered, with satisfaction, that the current was taking him toward the northern shore of the lake, and he allowed himself to glide with it. About two o'clock in the morning he disembarked upon a promontory covered with prickly reeds, that proved very provoking and inconvenient even to a philosopher like him; but a tree grew there expressly to offer him a bed among its branches, and Joe climbed up into it for greater security, and there, without sleeping much, however, awaited the dawn of day.

When morning had come with that suddenness which is peculiar to the equatorial regions, Joe cast a glance at the tree which had sheltered him during the last few hours, and beheld a sight that chilled the marrow in his bones. The branches of the tree were literally covered with snakes and chameleons! The foliage actually was hidden beneath their coils, so that the beholder might have fancied that he saw before him a new kind of tree that bore reptiles for its leaves and fruit. And all this horrible living mass writhed and twisted in the first rays of the morning sun! Joe experienced a keen sensation or terror mingled with disgust, as he looked at it, and he leaped precipitately from the tree amid the hissings of these new and unwelcome bedfellows.

"Now, there's something that I would never have believed!" said he.

He was not aware that Dr. Vogel's last letters had made known this singular feature of the shores of Lake Tchad, where reptiles are more numerous than in any other part of the world. But after what he had just seen, Joe determined to be more circumspect for the future; and, taking his bearings by the sun, he set off afoot toward the northeast, avoiding with the utmost care cabins, huts, hovels, and dens of every description, that might serve in any manner as a shelter for human beings.

How often his gaze was turned upward to the sky! He hoped to catch a glimpse, each time, of the Victoria; and, although he looked vainly during all that long, fatiguing day of sore foot-travel, his confident reliance on his master remained undiminished. Great energy of character was needed to enable him thus to sustain the situation with philosophy. Hunger conspired with fatigue to crush him, for a man's system is not greatly restored and fortified by a diet of roots, the pith of plants, such as the Mele, or the fruit of the doum palm-tree; and yet, according to his own calculations, Joe was enabled to push on about twenty miles to the westward.

His body bore in scores of places the marks of the thorns with which the lake-reeds, the acacias, the mimosas, and other wild shrubbery through which he had to force his way, are thickly studded; and his torn and bleeding feet rendered walking both painful and difficult. But at length he managed to react against all these sufferings; and when evening came again, he resolved to pass the night on the shores of Lake Tchad.

There he had to endure the bites of myriads of insects—gnats, mosquitoes, ants half an inch long, literally covered the ground; and, in less than two hours, Joe had not a rag remaining of the garments that had covered him, the insects having devoured them! It was a terrible night, that did not yield our exhausted traveller an hour of sleep. During all this time the wild-boars and native buffaloes, reenforced by the ajoub—a very dangerous species of lamantine—carried on their ferocious revels in the bushes and under the waters of the lake, filling the night with a hideous concert. Joe dared scarcely breathe. Even his courage and coolness had hard work to bear up against so terrible a situation.

At length, day came again, and Joe sprang to his feet precipitately; but judge of the loathing he felt when he saw what species of creature had shared his couch—a toad!—but a toad five inches in length, a monstrous, repulsive specimen of vermin that sat there staring at him with huge round eyes. Joe felt his stomach revolt at the sight, and, regaining a little strength from the intensity of his repugnance, he rushed at the top of his speed and plunged into the lake. This sudden bath somewhat allayed the pangs of the itching that tortured his whole body; and, chewing a few leaves, he set forth resolutely, again feeling an obstinate resolution in the act, for which he could hardly account even to his own mind. He no longer seemed to have entire control of his own acts, and, nevertheless, he felt within him a strength superior to despair.

However, he began now to suffer terribly from hunger. His stomach, less resigned than he was, rebelled, and he was obliged to fasten a tendril of wild-vine tightly about his waist. Fortunately, he could quench his thirst at any moment, and, in recalling the sufferings he had undergone in the desert, he experienced comparative relief in his exemption from that other distressing want.

"What can have become of the Victoria?" he wondered. "The wind blows from the north, and she should be carried back by it toward the lake. No doubt the doctor has gone to work to right her balance, but yesterday would have given him time enough for that, so that may be to-day—but I must act just as if I was never to see him again. After all, if I only get to one of the large towns on the lake, I'll find myself no worse off than the travellers my master used to talk about. Why shouldn't I work my way out of the scrape as well as they did? Some of them got back home again. Come, then! the deuce! Cheer up, my boy!"

Thus talking to himself and walking on rapidly, Joe came right upon a horde of natives in the very depths of the forest, but he halted in time and was not seen by them. The negroes were busy poisoning arrows with the juice of the euphorbium—a piece of work deemed a great affair among these savage tribes, and carried on with a sort of ceremonial solemnity.

Joe, entirely motionless and even holding his breath, was keeping himself concealed in a thicket, when, happening to raise his eyes, he saw through an opening in the foliage the welcome apparition of the balloon—the Victoria herself—moving toward the lake, at a height of only about one hundred feet above him. But he could not make himself heard; he dared not, could not make his friends even see him!

Tears came to his eyes, not of grief but of thankfulness; his master was then seeking him; his master had not left him to perish! He would have to wait for the departure of the blacks; then he could quit his hiding-place and run toward the borders of Lake Tchad!

But by this time the Victoria was disappearing in the distant sky. Joe still determined to wait for her; she would come back again, undoubtedly. She did, indeed, return, but farther to the eastward. Joe ran, gesticulated, shouted—but all in vain! A strong breeze was sweeping the balloon away with a speed that deprived him of all hope.

For the first time, energy and confidence abandoned the heart of the unfortunate man. He saw that he was lost. He thought his master gone beyond all prospect of return. He dared no longer think; he would no longer reflect!

Like a crazy man, his feet bleeding, his body cut and torn, he walked on during all that day and a part of the next night. He even dragged himself along, sometimes on his knees, sometimes with his hands. He saw the moment nigh when all his strength would fail, and nothing would be left to him but to sink upon the ground and die.

Thus working his way along, he at length found himself close to a marsh, or what he knew would soon become a marsh, for night had set in some hours before, and he fell by a sudden misstep into a thick, clinging mire. In spite of all his efforts, in spite of his desperate struggles, he felt himself sinking gradually in the swampy ooze, and in a few minutes he was buried to his waist.

"Here, then, at last, is death!" he thought, in agony, "and what a death!"

He now began to struggle again, like a madman; but his efforts only served to bury him deeper in the tomb that the poor doomed lad was hollowing for himself; not a log of wood or a branch to buoy him up; not a reed to which he might cling! He felt that all was over! His eyes convulsively closed!

"Master! master!—Help!" were his last words; but his voice, despairing, unaided, half stifled already by the rising mire, died away feebly on the night.

Chapter 36

A Throng of People on the Horizon.—A Troop of Arabs.—The Pursuit.—It Is He.—Fall from Horseback.—The Strangled Arab.—A Ball from Kennedy.—Adroit Manoeuvres.—Caught Up Flying.—Joe Saved at Last.

From the moment when Kennedy resumed his post of observation in the front of the car, he had not ceased to watch the horizon with his utmost attention.

After the lapse of some time he turned toward the doctor and said:

"If I am not greatly mistaken I can see, off yonder in the distance, a throng of men or animals moving. It is impossible to make them out yet, but I observe that they are in violent motion, for they are raising a great cloud of dust."

"May it not be another contrary breeze?" said the doctor, "another whirlwind coming to drive us back northward again?" and while speaking he stood up to examine the horizon.

"I think not, Samuel; it is a troop of gazelles or of wild oxen."

"Perhaps so, Dick; but yon throng is some nine or ten miles from us at least, and on my part, even with the glass, I can make nothing of it!"

"At all events I shall not lose sight of it. There is something remarkable about it that excites my curiosity. Sometimes it looks like a body of cavalry manoeuvring. Ah! I was not mistaken. It is, indeed, a squadron of horsemen. Look—look there!"

The doctor eyed the group with great attention, and, after a moment's pause, remarked:

"I believe that you are right. It is a detachment of Arabs or Tibbous, and they are galloping in the same direction with us, as though in flight, but we are going faster than they, and we are rapidly gaining on them. In half an hour we shall be near enough to see them and know what they are."

Kennedy had again lifted his glass and was attentively scrutinizing them. Meanwhile the crowd of horsemen was becoming more distinctly visible, and a few were seen to detach themselves from the main body.

"It is some hunting manoeuvre, evidently," said Kennedy. "Those fellows seem to be in pursuit of something. I would like to know what they are about."

"Patience, Dick! In a little while we shall overtake them, if they continue on the same route. We are going at the rate of twenty miles per hour, and no horse can keep up with that."

Kennedy again raised his glass, and a few minutes later he exclaimed:

"They are Arabs, galloping at the top of their speed; I can make them out distinctly. They are about fifty in number. I can see their bournouses puffed out by the wind. It is some cavalry exercise that they are going through. Their chief is a hundred paces ahead of them and they are rushing after him at headlong speed."

"Whoever they may be, Dick, they are not to be feared, and then, if necessary, we can go higher."

"Wait, doctor—wait a little!"

"It's curious," said Kennedy again, after a brief pause, "but there's something going on that I can't exactly explain. By the efforts they make, and the irregularity of their line, I should fancy that those Arabs are pursuing some one, instead of following."

"Are you certain of that, Dick?"

"Oh! yes, it's clear enough now. I am right! It is a pursuit—a hunt—but a man-hunt! That is not their chief riding ahead of them, but a fugitive."

"A fugitive!" exclaimed the doctor, growing more and more interested.

"Yes!"

"Don't lose sight of him, and let us wait!"

Three or four miles more were quickly gained upon these horsemen, who nevertheless were dashing onward with incredible speed.

"Doctor! doctor!" shouted Kennedy in an agitated voice.

"What is the matter, Dick?"

"Is it an illusion? Can it be possible?"

"What do you mean?"

"Wait!" and so saying, the Scot wiped the sights of his spy-glass carefully, and looked through it again intently.

"Well?" questioned the doctor.

"It is he, doctor!"

"He!" exclaimed Ferguson with emotion.

"It is he! no other!" and it was needless to pronounce the name.

"Yes! it is he! on horseback, and only a hundred paces in advance of his enemies! He is pursued!"

"It is Joe—Joe himself!" cried the doctor, turning pale.

"He cannot see us in his flight!"

"He will see us, though!" said the doctor, lowering the flame of his blow-pipe.

"But how?"

"In five minutes we shall be within fifty feet of the ground, and in fifteen we shall be right over him!"

"We must let him know it by firing a gun!"

"No! he can't turn back to come this way. He's headed off!"

"What shall we do, then?"

"We must wait."

"Wait?—and these Arabs!"

"We shall overtake them. We'll pass them. We are not more than two miles from them, and provided that Joe's horse holds out!"

"Great God!" exclaimed Kennedy, suddenly.

"What is the matter?"

Kennedy had uttered a cry of despair as he saw Joe fling himself to the ground. His horse, evidently exhausted, had just fallen headlong.

"He sees us!" cried the doctor, "and he motions to us, as he gets upon his feet!"

"But the Arabs will overtake him! What is he waiting for? Ah! the brave lad! Huzza!" shouted the sportsman, who could no longer restrain his feelings.

Joe, who had immediately sprung up after his fall, just as one of the swiftest horsemen rushed upon him, bounded like a panther, avoided his assailant by leaping to one side, jumped up behind him on the crupper, seized the Arab by the throat, and, strangling him with his sinewy hands and fingers of steel, flung him on the sand, and continued his headlong flight.

A tremendous howl was heard from the Arabs, but, completely engrossed by the pursuit, they had not taken notice of the balloon, which was now but five hundred paces behind them, and only about thirty feet from the ground. On their part, they were not twenty lengths of their horses from the fugitive.

One of them was very perceptibly gaining on Joe, and was about to pierce him with his lance, when Kennedy, with fixed eye and steady hand, stopped him short with a ball, that hurled him to the earth.

Joe did not even turn his head at the report. Some of the horsemen reined in their barbs, and fell on their faces in the dust as they caught sight of the Victoria; the rest continued their pursuit.

"But what is Joe about?" said Kennedy; "he don't stop!"

"He's doing better than that, Dick! I understand him! He's keeping on in the same direction as the balloon. He relies upon our intelligence. Ah! the noble fellow! We'll carry him off in the very teeth of those Arab rascals! We are not more than two hundred paces from him!"

"What are we to do?" asked Kennedy.

"Lay aside your rifle, Dick."

And the Scot obeyed the request at once.

"Do you think that you can hold one hundred and fifty pounds of ballast in your arms?"

"Ay, more than that!"

"No! That will be enough!"

And the doctor proceeded to pile up bags of sand in Kennedy's arms.

"Hold yourself in readiness in the back part of the car, and be prepared to throw out that ballast at a single effort. But, for your life, don't do so until I give the word!"

"Be easy on that point."

"Otherwise, we should miss Joe, and he would be lost."

"Count upon me!"

The Victoria at that moment almost commanded the troop of horsemen who were still desperately urging their steeds at Joe's heels. The doctor, standing in the front of the car, held the ladder clear, ready to throw it at any moment. Meanwhile, Joe had still maintained the distance between himself and his pursuers—say about fifty feet. The Victoria was now ahead of the party.

"Attention!" exclaimed the doctor to Kennedy.

"I'm ready!"

"Joe, look out for yourself!" shouted the doctor in his sonorous, ringing voice, as he flung out the ladder, the lowest ratlines of which tossed up the dust of the road.

As the doctor shouted, Joe had turned his head, but without checking his horse. The ladder dropped close to him, and at the instant he grasped it the doctor again shouted to Kennedy:

"Throw ballast!"

"It's done!"

And the Victoria, lightened by a weight greater than Joe's, shot up one hundred and fifty feet into the air.

Joe clung with all his strength to the ladder during the wide oscillations that it had to describe, and then making an indescribable gesture to the Arabs, and climbing with the agility of a monkey, he sprang up to his companions, who received him with open arms.

The Arabs uttered a scream of astonishment and rage. The fugitive had been snatched from them on the wing, and the Victoria was rapidly speeding far beyond their reach.

"Master! Kennedy!" exclaimed Joe, and overwhelmed, at last, with fatigue and emotion, the poor fellow fainted away, while Kennedy, almost beside himself, kept exclaiming:

"Saved—saved!"

"Saved indeed!" murmured the doctor, who had recovered all his phlegmatic coolness.

Joe was almost naked. His bleeding arms, his body covered with cuts and bruises, told what his sufferings had been. The doctor quietly dressed his wounds, and laid him comfortably under the awning.

Joe soon returned to consciousness, and asked for a glass of brandy, which the doctor did not see fit to refuse, as the faithful fellow had to be indulged.

After he had swallowed the stimulant, Joe grasped the hands of his two friends and announced that he was ready to relate what had happened to him.

But they would not allow him to talk at that time, and he sank back into a profound sleep, of which he seemed to have the greatest possible need.

The Victoria was then taking an oblique line to the westward. Driven by a tempestuous wind, it again approached the borders of the thorny desert, which the travellers descried over the tops of palm-trees, bent and broken by the storm; and, after having made a run of two hundred miles since rescuing Joe, it passed the tenth degree of east longitude about nightfall.

Chapter 37

The Western Route.—Joe Wakes Up.—His Obstinacy.—End of Joe's Narrative.—Tagelei.—Kennedy's Anxieties.—The Route to the North.—A Night Near Aghades.

During the night the wind lulled as though reposing after the boisterousness of the day, and the Victoria remained quietly at the top of the tall sycamore. The doctor and Kennedy kept watch by turns, and Joe availed himself of the chance to sleep most sturdily for twenty-four hours at a stretch.

"That's the remedy he needs," said Dr. Ferguson. "Nature will take charge of his care."

With the dawn the wind sprang up again in quite strong, and moreover capricious gusts. It shifted abruptly from south to north, but finally the Victoria was carried away by it toward the west.

The doctor, map in hand, recognized the kingdom of Damerghou, an undulating region of great fertility, in which the huts that compose the villages are constructed of long reeds interwoven with branches of the asclepia. The grain-mills were seen raised in the cultivated fields, upon small scaffoldings or platforms, to keep them out of the reach of the mice and the huge ants of that country.

They soon passed the town of Zinder, recognized by its spacious place of execution, in the centre of which stands the "tree of death." At its foot the executioner stands waiting, and whoever passes beneath its shadow is immediately hung!

Upon consulting his compass, Kennedy could not refrain from saying:

"Look! we are again moving northward."

"No matter; if it only takes us to Timbuctoo, we shall not complain. Never was a finer voyage accomplished under better circumstances!"

"Nor in better health," said Joe, at that instant thrusting his jolly countenance from between the curtains of the awning.

"There he is! there's our gallant friend—our preserver!" exclaimed Kennedy, cordially.—"How goes it, Joe?"

"Oh! why, naturally enough, Mr. Kennedy, very naturally! I never felt better in my life! Nothing sets a man up like a little pleasure-trip with a bath in Lake Tchad to start on—eh, doctor?"

"Brave fellow!" said Ferguson, pressing Joe's hand, "what terrible anxiety you caused us!"

"Humph! and you, sir? Do you think that I felt easy in my mind about you, gentlemen? You gave me a fine fright, let me tell you!"

"We shall never agree in the world, Joe, if you take things in that style."

"I see that his tumble hasn't changed him a bit," added Kennedy.

"Your devotion and self-forgetfulness were sublime, my brave lad, and they saved us, for the Victoria was falling into the lake, and, once there, nobody could have extricated her."

"But, if my devotion, as you are pleased to call my summerset, saved you, did it not save me too, for here we are, all three of us, in first-rate health? Consequently we have nothing to squabble about in the whole affair."

"Oh! we can never come to a settlement with that youth," said the sportsman.

"The best way to settle it," replied Joe, "is to say nothing more about the matter. What's done is done. Good or bad, we can't take it back."

"You obstinate fellow!" said the doctor, laughing; "you can't refuse, though, to tell us your adventures, at all events."

"Not if you think it worth while. But, in the first place, I'm going to cook this fat goose to a turn, for I see that Mr. Kennedy has not wasted his time."

"All right, Joe!"

"Well, let us see then how this African game will sit on a European stomach!"

The goose was soon roasted by the flame of the blow-pipe, and not long afterward was comfortably stowed away. Joe took his own good share, like a man who had eaten nothing for several days. After the tea and the punch, he acquainted his friends with his recent adventures. He spoke with some emotion, even while looking at things with his usual philosophy. The doctor could not refrain from frequently pressing his hand when he saw his worthy servant more considerate of his master's safety than of his own, and, in relation to the sinking of the island of the Biddiomahs, he explained to him the frequency of this phenomenon upon Lake Tchad.

At length Joe, continuing his recital, arrived at the point where, sinking in the swamp, he had uttered a last cry of despair.

"I thought I was gone," said he, "and as you came right into my mind, I made a hard fight for it. How, I couldn't tell you—but I'd made up my mind that I wouldn't go under without knowing why. Just then, I saw—two or three feet from me—what do you think? the end of a rope that had been fresh cut; so I took leave to make another jerk, and, by hook or by crook, I got to the rope. When I pulled, it didn't give; so I pulled again and hauled away and there I was on dry ground! At the end of the rope, I found an anchor! Ah, master, I've a right to call that the anchor of safety, anyhow, if you have no objection. I knew it again! It was the anchor of the Victoria! You had grounded there! So I followed the direction of the rope and that gave me your direction, and, after trying hard a few times more, I got out of the swamp. I had got my strength back with my spunk, and I walked on part of the night away from the lake, until I got to the edge of a very big wood. There I saw a fenced-in place, where some horses were grazing, without thinking of any harm. Now, there are times when everybody knows how to ride a horse, are there not, doctor? So I didn't spend much time thinking about it, but jumped right on the back of one of those innocent animals and away we went galloping north as fast as our legs could carry us. I needn't tell you about the towns that I didn't see nor the villages that I took good care to go around. No! I crossed the ploughed fields; I leaped the hedges; I scrambled over the fences; I dug my heels into my nag; I thrashed him; I fairly lifted the poor fellow off his feet! At last I got to the end of the tilled land. Good! There was the desert. 'That suits me!' said I, 'for I can see better ahead of me and farther too.' I was hoping all the time to see the balloon tacking about and waiting for me. But not a bit of it; and so, in about three hours, I go plump, like a fool, into a camp of Arabs! Whew! what a hunt that was! You see, Mr. Kennedy, a hunter don't know what a real hunt is until he's been hunted himself! Still I advise him not to try it if he can keep out of it! My horse was so tired, he was ready to drop off his legs; they were close on me; I threw myself to the ground; then I jumped up again behind an Arab! I didn't mean the fellow any harm, and I hope he has no grudge against me for choking him, but I saw you—and you know the rest. The Victoria came on at my heels, and you caught me up flying, as a circus-rider does a ring. Wasn't I right in counting on you? Now, doctor, you see how simple all that was! Nothing more natural in the world! I'm ready to begin over again, if it would be of any service to you. And besides, master, as I said a while ago, it's not worth mentioning."

"My noble, gallant Joe!" said the doctor, with great feeling. "Heart of gold! we were not astray in trusting to your intelligence and skill."

"Poh! doctor, one has only just to follow things along as they happen, and he can always work his way out of a scrape! The safest plan, you see, is to take matters as they come."

While Joe was telling his experience, the balloon had rapidly passed over a long reach of country, and Kennedy soon pointed out on the horizon a collection of structures that looked like a town. The doctor glanced at his map and recognized the place as the large village of Tagelei, in the Damerghou country.

"Here," said he, "we come upon Dr. Barth's route. It was at this place that he parted from his companions, Richardson and Overweg; the first was to follow the Zinder route, and the second that of Maradi; and you may remember that, of these three travellers, Barth was the only one who ever returned to Europe."

"Then," said Kennedy, following out on the map the direction of the Victoria, "we are going due north."

"Due north, Dick."

"And don't that give you a little uneasiness?"

"Why should it?"

"Because that line leads to Tripoli, and over the Great Desert."

"Oh, we shall not go so far as that, my friend—at least, I hope not."

"But where do you expect to halt?"

"Come, Dick, don't you feel some curiosity to see Timbuctoo?"

"Timbuctoo?"

"Certainly," said Joe; "nobody nowadays can think of making the trip to Africa without going to see Timbuctoo."

"You will be only the fifth or sixth European who has ever set eyes on that mysterious city."

"Ho, then, for Timbuctoo!"

"Well, then, let us try to get as far as between the seventeenth and eighteenth degrees of north latitude, and there we will seek a favorable wind to carry us westward."

"Good!" said the hunter. "But have we still far to go to the northward?"

"One hundred and fifty miles at least."

"In that case," said Kennedy, "I'll turn in and sleep a bit."

"Sleep, sir; sleep!" urged Joe. "And you, doctor, do the same yourself: you must have need of rest, for I made you keep watch a little out of time."

The sportsman stretched himself under the awning; but Ferguson, who was not easily conquered by fatigue, remained at his post.

In about three hours the Victoria was crossing with extreme rapidity an expanse of stony country, with ranges of lofty, naked mountains of granitic formation at the base. A few isolated peaks attained the height of even four thousand feet. Giraffes, antelopes, and ostriches were seen running and bounding with marvellous agility in the midst of forests of acacias, mimosas, souahs, and date-trees. After the barrenness of the desert, vegetation was now resuming its empire. This was the country of the Kailouas, who veil their faces with a bandage of cotton, like their dangerous neighbors, the Touaregs.

At ten o'clock in the evening, after a splendid trip of two hundred and fifty miles, the Victoria halted over an important town. The moonlight revealed glimpses of one district half in ruins; and some pinnacles of mosques and minarets shot up here and there, glistening in the silvery rays. The doctor took a stellar observation, and discovered that he was in the latitude of Aghades.

This city, once the seat of an immense trade, was already falling into ruin when Dr. Barth visited it.

The Victoria, not being seen in the obscurity of night, descended about two miles above Aghades, in a field of millet. The night was calm, and began to break into dawn about three o'clock A.M.; while a light wind coaxed the balloon westward, and even a little toward the south.

Dr. Ferguson hastened to avail himself of such good fortune, and rapidly ascending resumed his aerial journey amid a long wake of golden morning sunshine.

Chapter 38

A Rapid Passage.—Prudent Resolves.—Caravans in
Sight.—Incessant Rains.—Goa.—The Niger.—Golberry,
Geoffroy, and Gray.—Mungo Park.—Laing.—Rene Caillie.—
Clapperton.—John and Richard Lander.

The 17th of May passed tranquilly, without any remarkable incident; the desert gained upon them once more; a moderate wind bore the Victoria toward the southwest, and she never swerved to the right or to the left, but her shadow traced a perfectly straight line on the sand.

Before starting, the doctor had prudently renewed his stock of water, having feared that he should not be able to touch ground in these regions, infested as they are by the Aouelim-Minian Touaregs. The plateau, at an elevation of eighteen hundred feet above the level of the sea, sloped down toward the south. Our travellers, having crossed the Aghades route at Murzouk—a route often pressed by the feet of camels—arrived that evening, in the sixteenth degree of north latitude, and four degrees fifty-five minutes east longitude, after having passed over one hundred and eighty miles of a long and monotonous day's journey.

During the day Joe dressed the last pieces of game, which had been only hastily prepared, and he served up for supper a mess of snipe, that were greatly relished. The wind continuing good, the doctor resolved to keep on during the night, the moon, still nearly at the full, illumining it with her radiance. The Victoria ascended to a height of five hundred feet, and, during her nocturnal trip of about sixty miles, the gentle slumbers of an infant would not have been disturbed by her motion.

On Sunday morning, the direction of the wind again changed, and it bore to the northwestward. A few crows were seen sweeping through the air, and, off on the horizon, a flock of vultures which, fortunately, however, kept at a distance.

The sight of these birds led Joe to compliment his master on the idea of having two balloons.

"Where would we be," said he, "with only one balloon? The second balloon is like the life-boat to a ship; in case of wreck we could always take to it and escape."

"You are right, friend Joe," said the doctor, "only that my life-boat gives me some uneasiness. It is not so good as the main craft."

"What do you mean by that, doctor?" asked Kennedy.

"I mean to say that the new Victoria is not so good as the old one. Whether it be that the stuff it is made of is too much worn, or that the heat of the spiral has melted the gutta-percha, I can observe a certain loss of gas. It don't amount to much thus far, but still it is noticeable. We have a tendency to sink, and, in order to keep our elevation, I am compelled to give greater dilation to the hydrogen."

"The deuce!" exclaimed Kennedy with concern; "I see no remedy for that."

"There is none, Dick, and that is why we must hasten our progress, and even avoid night halts."

"Are we still far from the coast?" asked Joe.

"Which coast, my boy? How are we to know whither chance will carry us? All that I can say is, that Timbuctoo is still about four hundred miles to the westward.

"And how long will it take us to get there?"

"Should the wind not carry us too far out of the way, I hope to reach that city by Tuesday evening."

"Then," remarked Joe, pointing to a long file of animals and men winding across the open desert, "we shall arrive there sooner than that caravan."

Ferguson and Kennedy leaned over and saw an immense cavalcade. There were at least one hundred and fifty camels of the kind that, for twelve mutkals of gold, or about twenty-five dollars, go from Timbuctoo to Tafilet with a load of five hundred pounds upon their backs. Each animal had dangling to its tail a bag to receive its excrement, the only fuel on which the caravans can depend when crossing the desert.

These Touareg camels are of the very best race. They can go from three to seven days without drinking, and for two without eating. Their speed surpasses that of the horse, and they obey with intelligence the voice of the khabir, or guide of the caravan. They are known in the country under the name of mehari.

Such were the details given by the doctor while his companions continued to gaze upon that multitude of men, women, and children, advancing on foot and with difficulty over a waste of sand half in motion, and scarcely kept in its place by scanty nettles, withered grass, and stunted bushes that grew upon it. The wind obliterated the marks of their feet almost instantly.

Joe inquired how the Arabs managed to guide themselves across the desert, and come to the few wells scattered far between throughout this vast solitude.

"The Arabs," replied Dr. Ferguson, "are endowed by nature with a wonderful instinct in finding their way. Where a European would be at a loss, they never hesitate for a moment. An insignificant fragment of rock, a pebble, a tuft of grass, a different shade of color in the sand, suffice to guide them with accuracy. During the night they go by the polar star. They never travel more than two miles per hour, and always rest during the noonday heat. You may judge from that how long it takes them to cross Sahara, a desert more than nine hundred miles in breadth."

But the Victoria had already disappeared from the astonished gaze of the Arabs, who must have envied her rapidity. That evening she passed two degrees twenty minutes east longitude, and during the night left another degree behind her.

On Monday the weather changed completely. Rain began to fall with extreme violence, and not only had the balloon to resist the power of this deluge, but also the increase of weight which it caused by wetting the whole machine, car and all. This continuous shower accounted for the swamps and marshes that formed the sole surface of the country. Vegetation reappeared, however, along with the mimosas, the baobabs, and the tamarind-trees.

Such was the Sonray country, with its villages topped with roofs turned over like Armenian caps. There were few mountains, and only such hills as were enough to form the ravines and pools where the pintadoes and snipes went sailing and diving through. Here and there, an impetuous torrent cut the roads, and had to be crossed by the natives on long vines stretched from tree to tree. The forests gave place to jungles, which alligators, hippopotami, and the rhinoceros, made their haunts.

"It will not be long before we see the Niger," said the doctor. "The face of the country always changes in the vicinity of large rivers. These moving highways, as they are sometimes correctly called, have first brought vegetation with them, as they will at last bring civilization. Thus, in its course of twenty-five hundred miles, the Niger has scattered along its banks the most important cities of Africa."

"By-the-way," put in Joe, "that reminds me of what was said by an admirer of the goodness of Providence, who praised the foresight with which it had generally caused rivers to flow close to large cities!"

At noon the Victoria was passing over a petty town, a mere assemblage of miserable huts, which once was Goa, a great capital.

"It was there," said the doctor, "that Barth crossed the Niger, on his return from Timbuctoo. This is the river so famous in antiquity, the rival of the Nile, to which pagan superstition ascribed a celestial origin. Like the Nile, it has engaged the attention of geographers in all ages; and like it, also, its exploration has cost the lives of many victims; yes, even more of them than perished on account of the other."

The Niger flowed broadly between its banks, and its waters rolled southward with some violence of current; but our travellers, borne swiftly by as they were, could scarcely catch a glimpse of its curious outline.

"I wanted to talk to you about this river," said Dr. Ferguson, "and it is already far from us. Under the names of Dhiouleba, Mayo, Egghirreou, Quorra, and other titles besides, it traverses an immense extent of country, and almost competes in length with the Nile. These appellations signify simply 'the River,' according to the dialects of the countries through which it passes."

"Did Dr. Barth follow this route?" asked Kennedy.

"No, Dick: in quitting Lake Tchad, he passed through the different towns of Bornou, and intersected the Niger at Say, four degrees below Goa; then he penetrated to the bosom of those unexplored countries which the Niger embraces in its elbow; and, after eight months of fresh fatigues, he arrived at Timbuctoo; all of which we may do in about three days with as swift a wind as this."

"Have the sources of the Niger been discovered?" asked Joe.

"Long since," replied the doctor. "The exploration of the Niger and its tributaries was the object of several expeditions, the principal of which I shall mention: Between 1749 and 1758, Adamson made a reconnoissance of the river, and visited Gorea; from 1785 to 1788, Golberry and Geoffroy travelled across the deserts of Senegambia, and ascended as far as the country of the Moors, who assassinated Saugnier, Brisson, Adam, Riley, Cochelet, and so many other unfortunate men. Then came the illustrious Mungo Park, the friend of Sir Walter Scott, and, like him, a Scotchman by birth. Sent out in 1795 by the African Society of London, he got as far as Bambarra, saw the Niger, travelled five hundred miles with a slave-merchant, reconnoitred the Gambia River, and returned to England in 1797. He again set out, on the 30th of January, 1805, with his brother-in-law Anderson, Scott, the designer, and a gang of workmen; he reached Gorea, there added a detachment of thirty-five soldiers to his party, and saw the Niger again on the 19th of August. But, by that time, in consequence of fatigue, privations, ill-usage, the inclemencies of the weather, and the unhealthiness of the country, only eleven persons remained alive of the forty Europeans in the party. On the 16th of November, the last letters from Mungo Park reached his wife; and, a year later a trader from that country gave information that, having got as far as Boussa, on the Niger, on the 23d of December, the unfortunate traveller's boat was upset by the cataracts in that part of the river, and he was murdered by the natives."

"And his dreadful fate did not check the efforts of others to explore that river?"

"On the contrary, Dick. Since then, there were two objects in view: namely, to recover the lost man's papers, as well as to pursue the exploration. In 1816, an expedition was organized, in which Major Grey took part. It arrived in Senegal, penetrated to the Fonta-Jallon, visited the Foullah and Mandingo populations, and returned to England without further results. In 1822, Major Laing explored all the western part of Africa near to the British possessions; and he it was who got so far as the sources of the Niger; and, according to his documents, the spring in which that immense river takes its rise is not two feet broad.

"Easy to jump over," said Joe.

"How's that? Easy you think, eh?" retorted the doctor. "If we are to believe tradition, whoever attempts to pass that spring, by leaping over it, is immediately swallowed up; and whoever tries to draw water from it, feels himself repulsed by an invisible hand."

"I suppose a man has a right not to believe a word of that!" persisted Joe.

"Oh, by all means!—Five years later, it was Major Laing's destiny to force his way across the desert of Sahara, penetrate to Timbuctoo, and perish a few miles above it, by strangling, at the hands of the Oueladshiman, who wanted to compel him to turn Mussulman."

"Still another victim!" said the sportsman.

"It was then that a brave young man, with his own feeble resources, undertook and accomplished the most astonishing of modern journeys—I mean the Frenchman Rene Caillie, who, after sundry attempts in 1819 and 1824, set out again on the 19th of April, 1827, from Rio Nunez. On the 3d of August he arrived at Time, so thoroughly exhausted and ill that he could not resume his journey until six months later, in January, 1828. He then joined a caravan, and, protected by his Oriental dress, reached the Niger on the 10th of March, penetrated to the city of Jenne, embarked on the river, and descended it, as far as Timbuctoo, where he arrived on the 30th of April. In 1760, another Frenchman, Imbert by name, and, in 1810, an Englishman, Robert Adams, had seen this curious place; but Rene Caillie was to be the first European who could bring back any authentic data concerning it. On the 4th of May he quitted this 'Queen of the desert;' on the 9th, he surveyed the very spot where Major Laing had been murdered; on the 19th, he arrived at El-Arouan, and left that commercial town to brave a thousand dangers in crossing the vast solitudes comprised between the Soudan and the northern regions of Africa. At length he entered Tangiers, and on the 28th of September sailed for Toulon. In nineteen months, notwithstanding one hundred and eighty days' sickness, he had traversed Africa from west to north. Ah! had Callie been born in England, he would have been honored as the most intrepid traveller of modern times, as was the case with Mungo Park. But in France he was not appreciated according to his worth."

"He was a sturdy fellow!" said Kennedy, "but what became of him?"

"He died at the age of thirty-nine, from the consequences of his long fatigues. They thought they had done enough in decreeing him the prize of the Geographical Society in 1828; the highest honors would have been paid to him in England.

"While he was accomplishing this remarkable journey, an Englishman had conceived a similar enterprise and was trying to push it through with equal courage, if not with equal good fortune. This was Captain Clapperton, the companion of Denham. In 1829 he reentered Africa by the western coast of the Gulf of Benin; he then followed in the track of Mungo Park and of Laing, recovered at Boussa the documents relative to the death of the former, and arrived on the 20th of August at Sackatoo, where he was seized and held as a prisoner, until he expired in the arms of his faithful attendant Richard Lander."

"And what became of this Lander?" asked Joe, deeply interested.

"He succeeded in regaining the coast and returned to London, bringing with him the captain's papers, and an exact narrative of his own journey. He then offered his services to the government to complete the reconnoissance of the Niger. He took with him his brother John, the second child of a poor couple in Cornwall, and, together, these men, between 1829 and 1831, redescended the river from Boussa to its mouth, describing it village by village, mile by mile."

"So both the brothers escaped the common fate?" queried Kennedy.

"Yes, on this expedition, at least; but in 1833 Richard undertook a third trip to the Niger, and perished by a bullet, near the mouth of the river. You see, then, my friends, that the country over which we are now passing has witnessed some noble instances of self-sacrifice which, unfortunately, have only too often had death for their reward."

Chapter 39

THE COUNTRY IN THE ELBOW OF THE NIGER.—A FANTASTIC VIEW
OF THE HOMBORI MOUNTAINS.—KABRA.—TIMBUCTOO.—THE
CHART OF DR. BARTH.—A DECAYING CITY.—WHITHER
HEAVEN WILLS.

During this dull Monday, Dr. Ferguson diverted his thoughts by giving his companions a thousand details concerning the country they were crossing. The surface, which was quite flat, offered no impediment to their progress. The doctor's sole anxiety arose from the obstinate northeast wind which continued to blow furiously, and bore them away from the latitude of Timbuctoo.

The Niger, after running northward as far as that city, sweeps around, like an immense water-jet from some fountain, and falls into the Atlantic in a broad sheaf. In the elbow thus formed the country is of varied character, sometimes luxuriantly fertile, and sometimes extremely bare; fields of maize succeeded by wide spaces covered with broom-corn and uncultivated plains. All kinds of aquatic birds—pelicans, wild-duck, kingfishers, and the rest—were seen in numerous flocks hovering about the borders of the pools and torrents.

From time to time there appeared an encampment of Touaregs, the men sheltered under their leather tents, while their women were busied with the domestic toil outside, milking their camels and smoking their huge-bowled pipes.

By eight o'clock in the evening the Victoria had advanced more than two hundred miles to the westward, and our aeronauts became the spectators of a magnificent scene.

A mass of moonbeams forcing their way through an opening in the clouds, and gliding between the long lines of falling rain, descended in a golden shower on the ridges of the Hombori Mountains. Nothing could be more weird than the appearance of these seemingly basaltic summits; they stood out in fantastic profile against the sombre sky, and the beholder might have fancied them to be the legendary ruins of some vast city of the middle ages, such as the icebergs of the polar seas sometimes mimic them in nights of gloom.

"An admirable landscape for the 'Mysteries of Udolpho'!" exclaimed the doctor. "Ann Radcliffe could not have depicted yon mountains in a more appalling aspect."

"Faith!" said Joe, "I wouldn't like to be strolling alone in the evening through this country of ghosts. Do you see now, master, if it wasn't so heavy, I'd like to carry that whole landscape home to Scotland! It would do for the borders of Loch Lomond, and tourists would rush there in crowds."

"Our balloon is hardly large enough to admit of that little experiment—but I think our direction is changing. Bravo!—the elves and fairies of the place are quite obliging. See, they've sent us a nice little southeast breeze, that will put us on the right track again."

In fact, the Victoria was resuming a more northerly route, and on the morning of the 20th she was passing over an inextricable network of channels, torrents, and streams, in fine, the whole complicated tangle of the Niger's tributaries. Many of these channels, covered with a thick growth of herbage, resembled luxuriant meadow-lands. There the doctor recognized the route followed by the explorer Barth when he launched upon the river to descend to Timbuctoo. Eight hundred fathoms broad at this point, the Niger flowed between banks richly grown with cruciferous plants and tamarind-trees. Herds of agile gazelles were seen skipping about, their curling horns mingling with the tall herbage, within which the alligator, half concealed, lay silently in wait for them with watchful eyes.

Long files of camels and asses laden with merchandise from Jenne were winding in under the noble trees. Ere long, an amphitheatre of low-built houses was discovered at a turn of the river, their roofs and terraces heaped up with hay and straw gathered from the neighboring districts.

"There's Kabra!" exclaimed the doctor, joyously; "there is the harbor of Timbuctoo, and the city is not five miles from here!"

"Then, sir, you are satisfied?" half queried Joe.

"Delighted, my boy!"

"Very good; then every thing's for the best!"

In fact, about two o'clock, the Queen of the Desert, mysterious Timbuctoo, which once, like Athens and Rome, had her schools of learned men, and her professorships of philosophy, stretched away before the gaze of our travellers.

Ferguson followed the most minute details upon the chart traced by Barth himself, and was enabled to recognize its perfect accuracy.

The city forms an immense triangle marked out upon a vast plain of white sand, its acute angle directed toward the north and piercing a corner of the desert. In the environs there was almost nothing, hardly even a few grasses, with some dwarf mimosas and stunted bushes.

As for the appearance of Timbuctoo, the reader has but to imagine a collection of billiard-balls and thimbles—such is the bird's-eye view! The streets, which are quite narrow, are lined with houses only one story in height, built of bricks dried in the sun, and huts of straw and reeds, the former square, the latter conical. Upon the terraces were seen some of the male inhabitants, carelessly lounging at full length in flowing apparel of bright colors, and lance or musket in hand; but no women were visible at that hour of the day.

"Yet they are said to be handsome," remarked the doctor. "You see the three towers of the three mosques that are the only ones left standing of a great number—the city has indeed fallen from its ancient splendor! At the top of the triangle rises the Mosque of Sankore, with its ranges of galleries resting on arcades of sufficiently pure design. Farther on, and near to the Sane-Gungu quarter, is the Mosque of Sidi-Yahia and some two-story houses. But do not look for either palaces or monuments: the sheik is a mere son of traffic, and his royal palace is a counting-house."

"It seems to me that I can see half-ruined ramparts," said Kennedy.

"They were destroyed by the Fouillanes in 1826; the city was one-third larger then, for Timbuctoo, an object generally coveted by all the tribes, since the eleventh century, has belonged in succession to the Touaregs, the Sonrayans, the Morocco men, and the Fouillanes; and this great centre of civilization, where a sage like Ahmed-Baba owned, in the sixteenth century, a library of sixteen hundred manuscripts, is now nothing but a mere half-way house for the trade of Central Africa."

The city, indeed, seemed abandoned to supreme neglect; it betrayed that indifference which seems epidemic to cities that are passing away. Huge heaps of rubbish encumbered the suburbs, and, with the hill on which the market-place stood, formed the only inequalities of the ground.

When the Victoria passed, there was some slight show of movement; drums were beaten; but the last learned man still lingering in the place had hardly time to notice the new phenomenon, for our travellers, driven onward by the wind of the desert, resumed the winding course of the river, and, ere long, Timbuctoo was nothing more than one of the fleeting reminiscences of their journey.

"And now," said the doctor, "Heaven may waft us whither it pleases!"

"Provided only that we go westward," added Kennedy.

"Bah!" said Joe; "I wouldn't be afraid if it was to go back to Zanzibar by the same road, or to cross the ocean to America."

"We would first have to be able to do that, Joe!"

"And what's wanting, doctor?"

"Gas, my boy; the ascending force of the balloon is evidently growing weaker, and we shall need all our management to make it carry us to the sea-coast. I shall even have to throw over some ballast. We are too heavy."

"That's what comes of doing nothing, doctor; when a man lies stretched out all day long in his hammock, he gets fat and heavy. It's a lazybones trip, this of ours, master, and when we get back every body will find us big and stout."

"Just like Joe," said Kennedy; "just the ideas for him: but wait a bit! Can you tell what we may have to go through yet? We are still far from the end of our trip. Where do you expect to strike the African coast, doctor?"

"I should find it hard to answer you, Kennedy. We are at the mercy of very variable winds; but I should think myself fortunate were we to strike it between Sierra Leone and Portendick. There is a stretch of country in that quarter where we should meet with friends."

"And it would be a pleasure to press their hands; but, are we going in the desirable direction?"

"Not any too well, Dick; not any too well! Look at the needle of the compass; we are bearing southward, and ascending the Niger toward its sources."

"A fine chance to discover them," said Joe, "if they were not known already. Now, couldn't we just find others for it, on a pinch?"

"Not exactly, Joe; but don't be alarmed: I hardly expect to go so far as that."

At nightfall the doctor threw out the last bags of sand. The Victoria rose higher, and the blow-pipe, although working at full blast, could scarcely keep her up. At that time she was sixty miles to the southward of Timbuctoo, and in the morning the aeronauts awoke over the banks of the Niger, not far from Lake Debo.

Chapter 40

DR. FERGUSON'S ANXIETIES.—PERSISTENT MOVEMENT SOUTHWARD.—A CLOUD OF GRASSHOPPERS.—A VIEW OF JENNE.—A VIEW OF SEGO.—CHANGE OF THE WIND.—JOE'S REGRETS.

The flow of the river was, at that point, divided by large islands into narrow branches, with a very rapid current. Upon one among them stood some shepherds' huts, but it had become impossible to take an exact observation of them, because the speed of the balloon was constantly increasing. Unfortunately, it turned still more toward the south, and in a few moments crossed Lake Debo.

Dr. Ferguson, forcing the dilation of his aerial craft to the utmost, sought for other currents of air at different heights, but in vain; and he soon gave up the attempt, which was only augmenting the waste of gas by pressing it against the well-worn tissue of the balloon.

He made no remark, but he began to feel very anxious. This persistence of the wind to head him off toward the southern part of Africa was defeating his calculations, and he no longer knew upon whom or upon what to depend. Should he not reach the English or French territories, what was to become of him in the midst of the barbarous tribes that infest the coasts of Guinea? How should he there get to a ship to take him back to England? And the actual direction of the wind was driving him along to the kingdom of Dahomey, among the most savage races, and into the power of a ruler who was in the habit of sacrificing thousands of human victims at his public orgies. There he would be lost!

On the other hand, the balloon was visibly wearing out, and the doctor felt it failing him. However, as the weather was clearing up a little, he hoped that the cessation of the rain would bring about a change in the atmospheric currents.

It was therefore a disagreeable reminder of the actual situation when Joe said aloud:

"There! the rain's going to pour down harder than ever; and this time it will be the deluge itself, if we're to judge by yon cloud that's coming up!"

"What! another cloud?" asked Ferguson.

"Yes, and a famous one," replied Kennedy.

"I never saw the like of it," added Joe.

"I breathe freely again!" said the doctor, laying down his spy-glass. "That's not a cloud!"

"Not a cloud?" queried Joe, with surprise.

"No; it is a swarm."

"Eh?"

"A swarm of grasshoppers!"

"That? Grasshoppers!"

"Myriads of grasshoppers, that are going to sweep over this country like a water-spout; and woe to it! for, should these insects alight, it will be laid waste."

"That would be a sight worth beholding!"

"Wait a little, Joe. In ten minutes that cloud will have arrived where we are, and you can then judge by the aid of your own eyes."

The doctor was right. The cloud, thick, opaque, and several miles in extent, came on with a deafening noise, casting its immense shadow over the fields. It was composed of numberless legions of that species of grasshopper called crickets. About a hundred paces from the balloon, they settled down upon a tract full of foliage and verdure. Fifteen minutes later, the mass resumed its flight, and our travellers could, even at a distance, see the trees and the bushes entirely stripped, and the fields as bare as though they had been swept with the scythe. One would have thought that a sudden winter had just descended upon the earth and struck the region with the most complete sterility.

"Well, Joe, what do you think of that?"

"Well, doctor, it's very curious, but quite natural. What one grasshopper does on a small scale, thousands do on a grand scale."

"It's a terrible shower," said the hunter; "more so than hail itself in the devastation it causes."

"It is impossible to prevent it," replied Ferguson. "Sometimes the inhabitants have had the idea to burn the forests, and even the standing crops, in order to arrest the progress of these insects; but the first ranks plunging into the flames would extinguish them beneath their mass, and the rest of the swarm would then pass irresistibly onward. Fortunately, in these regions, there is some sort of compensation for their ravages, since the natives gather these insects in great numbers and greedily eat them."

"They are the prawns of the air," said Joe, who added that he was sorry that he had never had the chance to taste them—just for information's sake!

The country became more marshy toward evening; the forests dwindled to isolated clumps of trees; and on the borders of the river could be seen plantations of tobacco, and swampy meadow-lands fat with forage. At last the city of Jenne, on a large island, came in sight, with the two towers of its clay-built mosque, and the putrid odor of the millions of swallows' nests accumulated in its walls. The tops of some baobabs, mimosas, and date-trees peeped up between the houses; and, even at night, the activity of the place seemed very great. Jenne is, in fact, quite a commercial city: it supplies all the wants of Timbuctoo. Its boats on the river, and its caravans along the shaded roads, bear thither the various products of its industry.

"Were it not that to do so would prolong our journey," said the doctor, "I should like to alight at this place. There must be more than one Arab there who has travelled in England and France, and to whom our style of locomotion is not altogether new. But it would not be prudent."

"Let us put off the visit until our next trip," said Joe, laughing.

"Besides, my friends, unless I am mistaken, the wind has a slight tendency to veer a little more to the eastward, and we must not lose such an opportunity."

The doctor threw overboard some articles that were no longer of use—some empty bottles, and a case that had contained preserved-meat—and thereby managed to keep the balloon in a belt of the atmosphere more favorable to his plans. At four o'clock in the morning the first rays of the sun lighted up Sego, the capital of Bambarra, which could be recognized at once by the four towns that compose it, by its Saracenic mosques, and by the incessant going and coming of the flat-bottomed boats that convey its inhabitants from one quarter to the other. But the travellers were not more seen than they saw. They sped rapidly and directly to the northwest, and the doctor's anxiety gradually subsided.

"Two more days in this direction, and at this rate of speed, and we'll reach the Senegal River."

"And we'll be in a friendly country?" asked the hunter.

"Not altogether; but, if the worst came to the worst, and the balloon were to fail us, we might make our way to the French settlements. But, let it hold out only for a few hundred miles, and we shall arrive without fatigue, alarm, or danger, at the western coast."

"And the thing will be over!" added Joe. "Heigh-ho! so much the worse. If it wasn't for the pleasure of telling about it, I would never want to set foot on the ground again! Do you think anybody will believe our story, doctor?"

"Who can tell, Joe? One thing, however, will be undeniable: a thousand witnesses saw us start on one side of the African Continent, and a thousand more will see us arrive on the other."

"And, in that case, it seems to me that it would be hard to say that we had not crossed it," added Kennedy.

"Ah, doctor!" said Joe again, with a deep sigh, "I'll think more than once of my lumps of solid gold-ore! There was something that would have given *weight* to our narrative! At a grain of gold per head, I could have got together a nice crowd to listen to me, and even to admire me!"

Chapter 41

THE APPROACHES TO SENEGAL.—THE BALLOON SINKS LOWER
AND LOWER.—THEY KEEP THROWING OUT, THROWING
OUT.—THE MARABOUT AL-HADJI.—MESSRS. PASCAL,
VINCENT, AND LAMBERT.—A RIVAL OF MOHAMMED.—THE
DIFFICULT MOUNTAINS.—KENNEDY'S WEAPONS.—ONE OF JOE'S
MANOEUVRES.—A HALT OVER A FOREST.

On the 27th of May, at nine o'clock in the morning, the country presented an entirely different aspect. The slopes, extending far away, changed to hills that gave evidence of mountains soon to follow. They would have to cross the chain which separates the basin of the Niger from the basin of the Senegal, and determines the course of the watershed, whether to the Gulf of Guinea on the one hand, or to the bay of Cape Verde on the other.

As far as Senegal, this part of Africa is marked down as dangerous. Dr. Ferguson knew it through the recitals of his predecessors. They had suffered a thousand privations and been exposed to a thousand dangers in the midst of these barbarous negro tribes. It was this fatal climate that had devoured most of the companions of Mungo Park. Ferguson, therefore, was more than ever decided not to set foot in this inhospitable region.

But he had not enjoyed one moment of repose. The Victoria was descending very perceptibly, so much so that he had to throw overboard a number more of useless articles, especially when there was a mountain-top to pass. Things went on thus for more than one hundred and twenty miles; they were worn out with ascending and falling again; the balloon, like another rock of Sisyphus, kept continually sinking back toward the ground. The rotundity of the covering, which was now but little inflated, was collapsing already. It assumed an elongated shape, and the wind hollowed large cavities in the silken surface.

Kennedy could not help observing this.

"Is there a crack or a tear in the balloon?" he asked.

"No, but the gutta percha has evidently softened or melted in the heat, and the hydrogen is escaping through the silk."

"How can we prevent that?"

"It is impossible. Let us lighten her. That is the only help. So let us throw out every thing we can spare."

"But what shall it be?" said the hunter, looking at the car, which was already quite bare.

"Well, let us get rid of the awning, for its weight is quite considerable."

Joe, who was interested in this order, climbed up on the circle which kept together the cordage of the network, and from that place easily managed to detach the heavy curtains of the awning and throw them overboard.

"There's something that will gladden the hearts of a whole tribe of blacks," said he; "there's enough to dress a thousand of them, for they're not very extravagant with cloth."

The balloon had risen a little, but it soon became evident that it was again approaching the ground.

"Let us alight," suggested Kennedy, "and see what can be done with the covering of the balloon."

"I tell you, again, Dick, that we have no means of repairing it."

"Then what shall we do?"

"We'll have to sacrifice every thing not absolutely indispensable; I am anxious, at all hazards, to avoid a detention in these regions. The forests over the tops of which we are skimming are any thing but safe."

"What! are there lions in them, or hyenas?" asked Joe, with an expression of sovereign contempt.

"Worse than that, my boy! There are men, and some of the most cruel, too, in all Africa."

"How is that known?"

"By the statements of travellers who have been here before us. Then the French settlers, who occupy the colony of Senegal, necessarily have relations with the surrounding tribes. Under the administration of Colonel Faidherbe, reconnaissances have been pushed far up into the country. Officers such as Messrs. Pascal, Vincent, and Lambert, have brought back precious documents from their expeditions. They have explored these countries formed by the elbow of the Senegal in places where war and pillage have left nothing but ruins."

"What, then, took place?"

"I will tell you. In 1854 a Marabout of the Senegalese Fouta, Al-Hadji by name, declaring himself to be inspired like Mohammed, stirred up all the tribes to war against the infidels—that is to say, against the Europeans. He carried destruction and desolation over the regions between the Senegal River and its tributary, the Fateme. Three hordes of fanatics led on by him scoured the country, sparing neither a village nor a hut in their pillaging, massacring career. He advanced in person on the town of Sego, which was a long time threatened. In 1857 he worked up farther to the northward, and invested the fortification of Medina, built by the French on the bank of the river. This stronghold was defended by Paul Holl, who, for several months, without provisions or ammunition, held out until Colonel Faidherbe came to his relief. Al-Hadji and his bands then repassed the Senegal, and reappeared in the Kaarta, continuing their rapine and murder.— Well, here below us is the very country in which he has found refuge with his hordes of banditti; and I assure you that it would not be a good thing to fall into his hands."

"We shall not," said Joe, "even if we have to throw overboard our clothes to save the Victoria."

"We are not far from the river," said the doctor, "but I foresee that our balloon will not be able to carry us beyond it."

"Let us reach its banks, at all events," said the Scot, "and that will be so much gained."

"That is what we are trying to do," rejoined Ferguson, "only that one thing makes me feel anxious."

"What is that?"

"We shall have mountains to pass, and that will be difficult to do, since I cannot augment the ascensional force of the balloon, even with the greatest possible heat that I can produce."

"Well, wait a bit," said Kennedy, "and we shall see!"

"The poor Victoria!" sighed Joe; "I had got fond of her as the sailor does of his ship, and I'll not give her up so easily. She may not be what she was at the start—granted; but we shouldn't say a word against her. She has done us good service, and it would break my heart to desert her."

"Be at your ease, Joe; if we leave her, it will be in spite of ourselves. She'll serve us until she's completely worn out, and I ask of her only twenty-four hours more!"

"Ah, she's getting used up! She grows thinner and thinner," said Joe, dolefully, while he eyed her. "Poor balloon!"

"Unless I am deceived," said Kennedy, "there on the horizon are the mountains of which you were speaking, doctor."

"Yes, there they are, indeed!" exclaimed the doctor, after having examined them through his spy-glass, "and they look very high. We shall have some trouble in crossing them."

"Can we not avoid them?"

"I am afraid not, Dick. See what an immense space they occupy— nearly one-half of the horizon!"

"They even seem to shut us in," added Joe. "They are gaining on both our right and our left."

"We must then pass over them."

These obstacles, which threatened such imminent peril, seemed to approach with extreme rapidity, or, to speak more accurately, the wind, which was very fresh, was hurrying the balloon toward the sharp peaks. So rise it must, or be dashed to pieces.

"Let us empty our tank of water," said the doctor, "and keep only enough for one day."

"There it goes," shouted Joe.

"Does the balloon rise at all?" asked Kennedy.

"A little—some fifty feet," replied the doctor, who kept his eyes fixed on the barometer. "But that is not enough."

In truth the lofty peaks were starting up so swiftly before the travellers that they seemed to be rushing down upon them. The balloon was far from rising above them. She lacked an elevation of more than five hundred feet more.

The stock of water for the cylinder was also thrown overboard and only a few pints were retained, but still all this was not enough.

"We must pass them though!" urged the doctor.

"Let us throw out the tanks—we have emptied them." said Kennedy.

"Over with them!"

"There they go!" panted Joe. "But it's hard to see ourselves dropping off this way by piecemeal."

"Now, for your part, Joe, make no attempt to sacrifice yourself as you did the other day! Whatever happens, swear to me that you will not leave us!"

"Have no fears, my master, we shall not be separated."

The Victoria had ascended some hundred and twenty feet, but the crest of the mountain still towered above it. It was an almost perpendicular ridge that ended in a regular wall rising abruptly in a straight line. It still rose more than two hundred feet over the aeronauts.

"In ten minutes," said the doctor to himself, "our car will be dashed against those rocks unless we succeed in passing them!"

"Well, doctor?" queried Joe.

"Keep nothing but our pemmican, and throw out all the heavy meat."

Thereupon the balloon was again lightened by some fifty pounds, and it rose very perceptibly, but that was of little consequence, unless it got above the line of the mountain-tops. The situation was terrifying. The Victoria was rushing on with great rapidity. They could feel that she would be dashed to pieces—that the shock would be fearful.

The doctor glanced around him in the car. It was nearly empty.

"If needs be, Dick, hold yourself in readiness to throw over your fire-arms!"

"Sacrifice my fire-arms?" repeated the sportsman, with intense feeling.

"My friend, I ask it; it will be absolutely necessary!"

"Samuel! Doctor!"

"Your guns, and your stock of powder and ball might cost us our lives."

"We are close to it!" cried Joe.

Sixty feet! The mountain still overtopped the balloon by sixty feet.

Joe took the blankets and other coverings and tossed them out; then, without a word to Kennedy, he threw over several bags of bullets and lead.

The balloon went up still higher; it surmounted the dangerous ridge, and the rays of the sun shone upon its uppermost extremity; but the car was still below the level of certain broken masses of rock, against which it would inevitably be dashed.

"Kennedy! Kennedy! throw out your fire-arms, or we are lost!" shouted the doctor.

"Wait, sir; wait one moment!" they heard Joe exclaim, and, looking around, they saw Joe disappear over the edge of the balloon.

"Joe! Joe!" cried Kennedy.

"Wretched man!" was the doctor's agonized expression.

The flat top of the mountain may have had about twenty feet in breadth at this point, and, on the other side, the slope presented a less declivity. The car just touched the level of this plane, which happened to be quite even, and it glided over a soil composed of sharp pebbles that grated as it passed.

"We're over it! we're over it! we're clear!" cried out an exulting voice that made Ferguson's heart leap to his throat.

The daring fellow was there, grasping the lower rim of the car, and running afoot over the top of the mountain, thus lightening the balloon of his whole weight. He had to hold on with all his strength, too, for it was likely to escape his grasp at any moment.

When he had reached the opposite declivity, and the abyss was before him, Joe, by a vigorous effort, hoisted himself from the ground, and, clambering up by the cordage, rejoined his friends.

"That was all!" he coolly exclaimed.

"My brave Joe! my friend!" said the doctor, with deep emotion.

"Oh! what I did," laughed the other, "was not for you; it was to save Mr. Kennedy's rifle. I owed him that good turn for the affair with the Arab! I like to pay my debts, and now we are even," added he, handing to the sportsman his favorite weapon. "I'd feel very badly to see you deprived of it."

Kennedy heartily shook the brave fellow's hand, without being able to utter a word.

The Victoria had nothing to do now but to descend. That was easy enough, so that she was soon at a height of only two hundred feet from the ground, and was then in equilibrium. The surface seemed very much broken as though by a convulsion of nature. It presented numerous inequalities, which would have been very difficult to avoid during the night with a balloon that could no longer be controlled. Evening was coming on rapidly, and, notwithstanding his repugnance, the doctor had to make up his mind to halt until morning.

"We'll now look for a favorable stopping-place," said he.

"Ah!" replied Kennedy, "you have made up your mind, then, at last?"

"Yes, I have for a long time been thinking over a plan which we'll try to put into execution; it is only six o'clock in the evening, and we shall have time enough. Throw out your anchors, Joe!"

Joe immediately obeyed, and the two anchors dangled below the balloon.

"I see large forests ahead of us," said the doctor; "we are going to sweep along their tops, and we shall grapple to some tree, for nothing would make me think of passing the night below, on the ground."

"But can we not descend?" asked Kennedy.

"To what purpose? I repeat that it would be dangerous for us to separate, and, besides, I claim your help for a difficult piece of work."

The Victoria, which was skimming along the tops of immense forests, soon came to a sharp halt. Her anchors had caught, and, the wind falling as dusk came on, she remained motionlessly suspended above a vast field of verdure, formed by the tops of a forest of sycamores.

Chapter 42

A Struggle of Generosity.—The Last Sacrifice.—The Dilating Apparatus.—Joe's Adroitness.—Midnight.—The Doctor's Watch.—Kennedy's Watch.—The Latter Falls Asleep at His Post.—The Fire.—The Howlings of the Natives.—Out of Range.

Doctor Ferguson's first care was to take his bearings by stellar observation, and he discovered that he was scarcely twenty-five miles from Senegal.

"All that we can manage to do, my friends," said he, after having pointed his map, "is to cross the river; but, as there is neither bridge nor boat, we must, at all hazards, cross it with the balloon, and, in order to do that, we must still lighten up."

"But I don't exactly see how we can do that?" replied Kennedy, anxious about his fire-arms, "unless one of us makes up his mind to sacrifice himself for the rest,—that is, to stay behind, and, in my turn, I claim that honor."

"You, indeed!" remonstrated Joe; "ain't I used to—"

"The question now is, not to throw ourselves out of the car, but simply to reach the coast of Africa on foot. I am a first-rate walker, a good sportsman, and—"

"I'll never consent to it!" insisted Joe.

"Your generous rivalry is useless, my brave friends," said Ferguson; "I trust that we shall not come to any such extremity: besides, if we did, instead of separating, we should keep together, so as to make our way across the country in company."

"That's the talk," said Joe; "a little tramp won't do us any harm."

"But before we try that," resumed the doctor, "we must employ a last means of lightening the balloon."

"What will that be? I should like to see it," said Kennedy, incredulously.

"We must get rid of the cylinder-chests, the spiral, and the Buntzen battery. Nine hundred pounds make a rather heavy load to carry through the air."

"But then, Samuel, how will you dilate your gas?"

"I shall not do so at all. We'll have to get along without it."

"But—"

"Listen, my friends: I have calculated very exactly the amount of ascensional force left to us, and it is sufficient to carry us every one with the few objects that remain. We shall make in all a weight of hardly five hundred pounds, including the two anchors which I desire to keep."

"Dear doctor, you know more about the matter than we do; you are the sole judge of the situation. Tell us what we ought to do, and we will do it."

"I am at your orders, master," added Joe.

"I repeat, my friends, that however serious the decision may appear, we must sacrifice our apparatus."

"Let it go, then!" said Kennedy, promptly.

"To work!" said Joe.

It was no easy job. The apparatus had to be taken down piece by piece. First, they took out the mixing reservoir, then the one belonging to the cylinder, and lastly the tank in which the decomposition of the water was effected. The united strength of all three travellers was required to detach these reservoirs from the bottom of the car in which they had been so firmly secured; but Kennedy was so strong, Joe so adroit, and the doctor so ingenious, that they finally succeeded. The different pieces were thrown out, one after the other, and they disappeared below, making huge gaps in the foliage of the sycamores.

"The black fellows will be mightily astonished," said Joe, "at finding things like those in the woods; they'll make idols of them!"

The next thing to be looked after was the displacement of the pipes that were fastened in the balloon and connected with the spiral. Joe succeeded in cutting the caoutchouc jointings above the car, but when he came to the pipes he found it more difficult to disengage them, because they were held by their upper extremity and fastened by wires to the very circlet of the valve.

Then it was that Joe showed wonderful adroitness. In his naked feet, so as not to scratch the covering, he succeeded by the aid of the network, and in spite of the oscillations of the balloon, in climbing to the upper extremity, and after a thousand difficulties, in holding on with one hand to that slippery surface, while he detached the outside screws that secured the pipes in their place. These were then easily taken out, and drawn away by the lower end, which was hermetically sealed by means of a strong ligature.

The Victoria, relieved of this considerable weight, rose upright in the air and tugged strongly at the anchor-rope.

About midnight this work ended without accident, but at the cost of most severe exertion, and the trio partook of a luncheon of pemmican and cold punch, as the doctor had no more fire to place at Joe's disposal.

Besides, the latter and Kennedy were dropping off their feet with fatigue.

"Lie down, my friends, and get some rest," said the doctor. "I'll take the first watch; at two o'clock I'll waken Kennedy; at four, Kennedy will waken Joe, and at six we'll start; and may Heaven have us in its keeping for this last day of the trip!"

Without waiting to be coaxed, the doctor's two companions stretched themselves at the bottom of the car and dropped into profound slumber on the instant.

The night was calm. A few clouds broke against the last quarter of the moon, whose uncertain rays scarcely pierced the darkness. Ferguson, resting his elbows on the rim of the car, gazed attentively around him. He watched with close attention the dark screen of foliage that spread beneath him, hiding the ground from his view. The least noise aroused his suspicions, and he questioned even the slightest rustling of the leaves.

He was in that mood which solitude makes more keenly felt, and during which vague terrors mount to the brain. At the close of such a journey, after having surmounted so many obstacles, and at the moment of touching the goal, one's fears are more vivid, one's emotions keener. The point of arrival seems to fly farther from our gaze.

Moreover, the present situation had nothing very consolatory about it. They were in the midst of a barbarous country, and dependent upon a vehicle that might fail them at any moment. The doctor no longer counted implicitly on his balloon; the time had gone by when he manoeuvred it boldly because he felt sure of it.

Under the influence of these impressions, the doctor, from time to time, thought that he heard vague sounds in the vast forests around him; he even fancied that he saw a swift gleam of fire shining between the trees. He looked sharply and turned his night-glass toward the spot; but there was nothing to be seen, and the profoundest silence appeared to return.

He had, no doubt, been under the dominion of a mere hallucination. He continued to listen, but without hearing the slightest noise. When his watch had expired, he woke Kennedy, and, enjoining upon him to observe the extremest vigilance, took his place beside Joe, and fell sound asleep.

Kennedy, while still rubbing his eyes, which he could scarcely keep open, calmly lit his pipe. He then ensconced himself in a corner, and began to smoke vigorously by way of keeping awake.

The most absolute silence reigned around him; a light wind shook the tree-tops and gently rocked the car, inviting the hunter to taste the sleep that stole over him in spite of himself. He strove hard to resist it, and repeatedly opened his eyes to plunge into the outer darkness one of those looks that see nothing; but at last, yielding to fatigue, he sank back and slumbered.

How long he had been buried in this stupor he knew not, but he was suddenly aroused from it by a strange, unexpected crackling sound.

He rubbed his eyes and sprang to his feet. An intense glare half-blinded him and heated his cheek—the forest was in flames!

"Fire! fire!" he shouted, scarcely comprehending what had happened.

His two companions started up in alarm.

"What's the matter?" was the doctor's immediate exclamation.

"Fire!" said Joe. "But who could—"

At this moment loud yells were heard under the foliage, which was now illuminated as brightly as the day.

"Ah! the savages!" cried Joe again; "they have set fire to the forest so as to be the more certain of burning us up."

"The Talabas! Al-Hadji's marabouts, no doubt," said the doctor.

A circle of fire hemmed the Victoria in; the crackling of the dry wood mingled with the hissing and sputtering of the green branches; the clambering vines, the foliage, all the living part of this vegetation, writhed in the destructive element. The eye took in nothing but one vast ocean of flame; the large trees stood forth in black relief in this huge furnace, their branches covered with glowing coals, while the whole blazing mass, the entire conflagration, was reflected on the clouds, and the travellers could fancy themselves enveloped in a hollow globe of fire.

"Let us escape to the ground!" shouted Kennedy, "it is our only chance of safety!"

But Ferguson checked him with a firm grasp, and, dashing at the anchor-rope, severed it with one well-directed blow of his hatchet. Meanwhile, the flames, leaping up at the balloon, already quivered on its illuminated sides; but the Victoria, released from her fastenings, spun upward a thousand feet into the air.

Frightful yells resounded through the forest, along with the report of fire-arms, while the balloon, caught in a current of air that rose with the dawn of day, was borne to the westward.

It was now four o'clock in the morning.

Chapter 43

THE TALABAS.—THE PURSUIT.—A DEVASTATED COUNTRY.—THE
WIND BEGINS TO FALL.—THE VICTORIA SINKS.—THE LAST OF THE
PROVISIONS.—THE LEAPS OF THE BALLOON.—A DEFENCE WITH
FIRE-ARMS.—THE WIND FRESHENS.—THE SENEGAL RIVER.—THE
CATARACTS OF GOUINA.—THE HOT AIR.—THE
PASSAGE OF THE RIVER.

H ad we not taken the precaution to lighten the balloon yesterday evening, we should have been lost beyond redemption," said the doctor, after a long silence.

"See what's gained by doing things at the right time!" replied Joe. "One gets out of scrapes then, and nothing is more natural."

"We are not out of danger yet," said the doctor.

"What do you still apprehend?" queried Kennedy. "The balloon can't descend without your permission, and even were it to do so—"

"Were it to do so, Dick? Look!"

They had just passed the borders of the forest, and the three friends could see some thirty mounted men clad in broad pantaloons and the floating bournouses. They were armed, some with lances, and others with long muskets, and they were following, on their quick, fiery little steeds, the direction of the balloon, which was moving at only moderate speed.

When they caught sight of the aeronauts, they uttered savage cries, and brandished their weapons. Anger and menace could be read upon their swarthy faces, made more ferocious by thin but bristling beards. Meanwhile they galloped along without difficulty over the low levels and gentle declivities that lead down to the Senegal.

"It is, indeed, they!" said the doctor; "the cruel Talabas! the ferocious marabouts of Al-Hadji! I would rather find myself in the middle of the forest encircled by wild beasts than fall into the hands of these banditti."

"They haven't a very obliging look!" assented Kennedy; "and they are rough, stalwart fellows."

"Happily those brutes can't fly," remarked Joe; "and that's something."

"See," said Ferguson, "those villages in ruins, those huts burned down—that is their work! Where vast stretches of cultivated land were once seen, they have brought barrenness and devastation."

"At all events, however," interposed Kennedy, "they can't overtake us; and, if we succeed in putting the river between us and them, we are safe."

"Perfectly, Dick," replied Ferguson; "but we must not fall to the ground!" and, as he said this, he glanced at the barometer.

"In any case, Joe," added Kennedy, "it would do us no harm to look to our fire-arms."

"No harm in the world, Mr. Dick! We are lucky that we didn't scatter them along the road."

"My rifle!" said the sportsman. "I hope that I shall never be separated from it!"

And so saying, Kennedy loaded the pet piece with the greatest care, for he had plenty of powder and ball remaining.

"At what height are we?" he asked the doctor.

"About seven hundred and fifty feet; but we no longer have the power of seeking favorable currents, either going up or coming down. We are at the mercy of the balloon!"

"That is vexatious!" rejoined Kennedy. "The wind is poor; but if we had come across a hurricane like some of those we met before, these vile brigands would have been out of sight long ago."

"The rascals follow us at their leisure," said Joe. "They're only at a short gallop. Quite a nice little ride!"

"If we were within range," sighed the sportsman, "I should amuse myself with dismounting a few of them."

"Exactly," said the doctor; "but then they would have you within range also, and our balloon would offer only too plain a target to the bullets from their long guns; and, if they were to make a hole in it, I leave you to judge what our situation would be!"

The pursuit of the Talabas continued all morning; and by eleven o'clock the aeronauts had made scarcely fifteen miles to the westward.

The doctor was anxiously watching for the least cloud on the horizon. He feared, above all things, a change in the atmosphere. Should he be thrown back toward the Niger, what would become of him? Besides, he remarked that the balloon tended to fall considerably. Since the start, he had already lost more than three hundred feet, and the Senegal must be about a dozen miles distant. At his present rate of speed, he could count upon travelling only three hours longer.

At this moment his attention was attracted by fresh cries. The Talabas appeared to be much excited, and were spurring their horses.

The doctor consulted his barometer, and at once discovered the cause of these symptoms.

"Are we descending?" asked Kennedy.

"Yes!" replied the doctor.

"The mischief!" thought Joe

In the lapse of fifteen minutes the Victoria was only one hundred and fifty feet above the ground; but the wind was much stronger than before.

The Talabas checked their horses, and soon a volley of musketry pealed out on the air.

"Too far, you fools!" bawled Joe. "I think it would be well to keep those scamps at a distance."

And, as he spoke, he aimed at one of the horsemen who was farthest to the front, and fired. The Talaba fell headlong, and, his companions halting for a moment, the balloon gained upon them.

"They are prudent!" said Kennedy.

"Because they think that they are certain to take us," replied the doctor; "and, they will succeed if we descend much farther. We must, absolutely, get higher into the air."

"What can we throw out?" asked Joe.

"All that remains of our stock of pemmican; that will be thirty pounds less weight to carry."

"Out it goes, sir!" said Joe, obeying orders.

The car, which was now almost touching the ground, rose again, amid the cries of the Talabas; but, half an hour later, the balloon was again falling rapidly, because the gas was escaping through the pores of the covering.

Ere long the car was once more grazing the soil, and Al-Hadji's black riders rushed toward it; but, as frequently happens in like cases, the balloon had scarcely touched the surface ere it rebounded, and only came down again a mile away.

"So we shall not escape!" said Kennedy, between his teeth.

"Throw out our reserved store of brandy, Joe," cried the doctor; "our instruments, and every thing that has any weight, even to our last anchor, because go they must!"

Joe flung out the barometers and thermometers, but all that amounted to little; and the balloon, which had risen for an instant, fell again toward the ground.

The Talabas flew toward it, and at length were not more than two hundred paces away.

"Throw out the two fowling-pieces!" shouted Ferguson.

"Not without discharging them, at least," responded the sportsman; and four shots in quick succession struck the thick of the advancing group of horsemen. Four Talabas fell, amid the frantic howls and imprecations of their comrades.

The Victoria ascended once more, and made some enormous leaps, like a huge gum-elastic ball, bounding and rebounding through the air. A strange sight it was to see these unfortunate men endeavoring to escape by those huge aerial strides, and seeming, like the giant Antaeus, to receive fresh strength every time they touched the earth. But this situation had to terminate. It was now nearly noon; the Victoria was getting empty and exhausted, and assuming a more and more elongated form every instant. Its outer covering was becoming flaccid, and floated loosely in the air, and the folds of the silk rustled and grated on each other.

"Heaven abandons us!" said Kennedy; "we have to fall!"

Joe made no answer. He kept looking intently at his master.

"No!" said the latter; "we have more than one hundred and fifty pounds yet to throw out."

"What can it be, then?" said Kennedy, thinking that the doctor must be going mad.

"The car!" was his reply; "we can cling to the network. There we can hang on in the meshes until we reach the river. Quick! quick!"

And these daring men did not hesitate a moment to avail themselves of this last desperate means of escape. They clutched the network, as the doctor directed, and Joe, holding on by one hand, with the other cut the cords that suspended the car; and the latter dropped to the ground just as the balloon was sinking for the last time.

"Hurrah! hurrah!" shouted the brave fellow exultingly, as the Victoria, once more relieved, shot up again to a height of three hundred feet.

The Talabas spurred their horses, which now came tearing on at a furious gallop; but the balloon, falling in with a much more favorable wind, shot ahead of them, and was rapidly carried toward a hill that stretched across the horizon to the westward. This was a circumstance favorable to the aeronauts, because they could rise over the hill, while Al-Hadji's horde had to diverge to the northward in order to pass this obstacle.

The three friends still clung to the network. They had been able to fasten it under their feet, where it had formed a sort of swinging pocket.

Suddenly, after they had crossed the hill, the doctor exclaimed: "The river! the river! the Senegal, my friends!"

And about two miles ahead of them, there was indeed the river rolling along its broad mass of water, while the farther bank, which was low and fertile, offered a sure refuge, and a place favorable for a descent.

"Another quarter of an hour," said Ferguson, "and we are saved!"

But it was not to happen thus; the empty balloon descended slowly upon a tract almost entirely bare of vegetation. It was made up of long slopes and stony plains, a few bushes and some coarse grass, scorched by the sun.

The Victoria touched the ground several times, and rose again, but her rebound was diminishing in height and length. At the last one, it caught by the upper part of the network in the lofty branches of a baobab, the only tree that stood there, solitary and alone, in the midst of the waste.

"It's all over," said Kennedy.

"And at a hundred paces only from the river!" groaned Joe.

The three hapless aeronauts descended to the ground, and the doctor drew his companions toward the Senegal.

At this point the river sent forth a prolonged roaring; and when Ferguson reached its bank, he recognized the falls of Gouina. But not a boat, not a living creature was to be seen. With a breadth of two thousand feet, the Senegal precipitates itself for a height of one hundred and fifty, with a thundering reverberation. It ran, where they saw it, from east to west, and the line of rocks that barred its course extended from north to south. In the midst of the falls, rocks of strange forms started up like huge ante-diluvian animals, petrified there amid the waters.

The impossibility of crossing this gulf was self-evident, and Kennedy could not restrain a gesture of despair.

But Dr. Ferguson, with an energetic accent of undaunted daring, exclaimed—

"All is not over!"

"I knew it," said Joe, with that confidence in his master which nothing could ever shake.

The sight of the dried-up grass had inspired the doctor with a bold idea. It was the last chance of escape. He led his friends quickly back to where they had left the covering of the balloon.

"We have at least an hour's start of those banditti," said he; "let us lose no time, my friends; gather a quantity of this dried grass; I want a hundred pounds of it, at least."

"For what purpose?" asked Kennedy, surprised.

"I have no more gas; well, I'll cross the river with hot air!"

"Ah, doctor," exclaimed Kennedy, "you are, indeed, a great man!"

Joe and Kennedy at once went to work, and soon had an immense pile of dried grass heaped up near the baobab.

In the mean time, the doctor had enlarged the orifice of the balloon by cutting it open at the lower end. He then was very careful to expel the last remnant of hydrogen through the valve, after which he heaped up a quantity of grass under the balloon, and set fire to it.

It takes but a little while to inflate a balloon with hot air. A head of one hundred and eighty degrees is sufficient to diminish the weight of the air it contains to the extent of one-half, by rarefying it. Thus, the Victoria quickly began to assume a more rounded form. There was no lack of grass; the fire was kept in full blast by the doctor's assiduous efforts, and the balloon grew fuller every instant.

It was then a quarter to four o'clock.

At this moment the band of Talabas reappeared about two miles to the northward, and the three friends could hear their cries, and the clatter of their horses galloping at full speed.

"In twenty minutes they will be here!" said Kennedy.

"More grass! more grass, Joe! In ten minutes we shall have her full of hot air."

"Here it is, doctor!"

The Victoria was now two-thirds inflated.

"Come, my friends, let us take hold of the network, as we did before."

"All right!" they answered together.

In about ten minutes a few jerking motions by the balloon indicated that it was disposed to start again. The Talabas were approaching. They were hardly five hundred paces away.

"Hold on fast!" cried Ferguson.

"Have no fear, master—have no fear!"

And the doctor, with his foot pushed another heap of grass upon the fire.

With this the balloon, now completely inflated by the increased temperature, moved away, sweeping the branches of the baobab in her flight.

"We're off!" shouted Joe.

A volley of musketry responded to his exclamation. A bullet even ploughed his shoulder; but Kennedy, leaning over, and discharging his rifle with one hand, brought another of the enemy to the ground.

Cries of fury exceeding all description hailed the departure of the balloon, which had at once ascended nearly eight hundred feet. A swift current caught and swept it along with the most alarming oscillations, while the intrepid doctor and his friends saw the gulf of the cataracts yawning below them.

Ten minutes later, and without having exchanged a word, they descended gradually toward the other bank of the river.

There, astonished, speechless, terrified, stood a group of men clad in the French uniform. Judge of their amazement when they saw the balloon rise from the right bank of the river. They had well-nigh taken it for some celestial phenomenon, but their officers, a lieutenant of marines and a naval ensign, having seen mention made of Dr. Ferguson's daring expedition, in the European papers, quickly explained the real state of the case.

The balloon, losing its inflation little by little, settled with the daring travellers still clinging to its network; but it was doubtful whether it would reach the land. At once some of the brave Frenchmen rushed into the water and caught the three aeronauts in their arms just as the Victoria fell at the distance of a few fathoms from the left bank of the Senegal.

"Dr. Ferguson!" exclaimed the lieutenant.

"The same, sir," replied the doctor, quietly, "and his two friends."

The Frenchmen escorted our travellers from the river, while the balloon, half-empty, and borne away by a swift current, sped on, to plunge, like a huge bubble, headlong with the waters of the Senegal, into the cataracts of Gouina.

"The poor Victoria!" was Joe's farewell remark.

The doctor could not restrain a tear, and extending his hands his two friends wrung them silently with that deep emotion which requires no spoken words.

Chapter 44

CONCLUSION.—THE CERTIFICATE.—THE FRENCH SETTLEMENTS.—
THE POST OF MEDINA.—THE BASILIC.—SAINT LOUIS.—THE
ENGLISH FRIGATE.—THE RETURN TO LONDON.

The expedition upon the bank of the river had been sent by the governor of Senegal. It consisted of two officers, Messrs. Dufraisse, lieutenant of marines, and Rodamel, naval ensign, and with these were a sergeant and seven soldiers. For two days they had been engaged in reconnoitring the most favorable situation for a post at Gouina, when they became witnesses of Dr. Ferguson's arrival.

The warm greetings and felicitations of which our travellers were the recipients may be imagined. The Frenchmen, and they alone, having had ocular proof of the accomplishment of the daring project, naturally became Dr. Ferguson's witnesses. Hence the doctor at once asked them to give their official testimony of his arrival at the cataracts of Gouina.

"You would have no objection to signing a certificate of the fact, would you?" he inquired of Lieutenant Dufraisse.

"At your orders!" the latter instantly replied.

The Englishmen were escorted to a provisional post established on the bank of the river, where they found the most assiduous attention, and every thing to supply their wants. And there the following certificate was drawn up in the terms in which it appears to-day, in the archives of the Royal Geographical Society of London:

"We, the undersigned, do hereby declare that, on the day herein mentioned, we witnessed the arrival of Dr. Ferguson and his two companions, Richard Kennedy and Joseph Wilson, clinging to the cordage and network of a balloon, and that the said balloon fell at a distance of a few paces from us into the river, and being swept away by the current was lost in the cataracts of Gouina. In testimony whereof, we have hereunto set our hands and seals beside those of the persons hereinabove named, for the information of all whom it may concern.

"Done at the Cataracts of Gouina, on the 24th of May, 1862.

(Signed),   SAMUEL FERGUSON
            RICHARD KENNEDY,
            JOSEPH WILSON,

DUFRAISSE, Lieutenant of Marines,
RODAMEL, Naval Ensign,
DUFAYS, Sergeant,
FLIPPEAU, MAYOR,
PELISSIER, LOROIS
RASCAGNET, GUILLON, LEBEL,
} Privates.

Here ended the astonishing journey of Dr. Ferguson and his brave companions, as vouched for by undeniable testimony; and they found themselves among friends in the midst of most hospitable tribes, whose relations with the French settlements are frequent and amicable.

They had arrived at Senegal on Saturday, the 24th of May, and on the 27th of the same month they reached the post of Medina, situated a little farther to the north, but on the river.

There the French officers received them with open arms, and lavished upon them all the resources of their hospitality. Thus aided, the doctor and his friends were enabled to embark almost immediately on the small steamer called the Basilic, which ran down to the mouth of the river.

Two weeks later, on the 10th of June, they arrived at Saint Louis, where the governor gave them a magnificent reception, and they recovered completely from their excitement and fatigue.

Besides, Joe said to every one who chose to listen:

"That was a stupid trip of ours, after all, and I wouldn't advise any body who is greedy for excitement to undertake it. It gets very tiresome at the last, and if it hadn't been for the adventures on Lake Tchad and at the Senegal River, I do believe that we'd have died of yawning."

An English frigate was just about to sail, and the three travellers procured passage on board of her. On the 25th of June they arrived at Portsmouth, and on the next day at London.

We will not describe the reception they got from the Royal Geographical Society, nor the intense curiosity and consideration of which they became the objects. Kennedy set off, at once, for Edinburgh, with his famous rifle, for he was in haste to relieve the anxiety of his faithful old housekeeper.

The doctor and his devoted Joe remained the same men that we have known them, excepting that one change took place at their own suggestion.

They ceased to be master and servant, in order to become bosom friends.

The journals of all Europe were untiring in their praises of the bold explorers, and the Daily Telegraph struck off an edition of three hundred and seventy-seven thousand copies on the day when it published a sketch of the trip.

Doctor Ferguson, at a public meeting of the Royal Geographical Society, gave a recital of his journey through the air, and obtained for himself and his companions the golden medal set apart to reward the most remarkable exploring expedition of the year 1862.

THE FIRST RESULT OF DR. FERGUSON's expedition was to establish, in the most precise manner, the facts and geographical surveys reported by Messrs. Barth, Burton, Speke, and others. Thanks to the still more recent expeditions of Messrs. Speke and Grant, De Heuglin and Muntzinger, who have been ascending to the sources of the Nile, and penetrating to the centre of Africa, we shall be enabled ere long to verify, in turn, the discoveries of Dr. Ferguson in that vast region comprised between the fourteenth and thirty-third degrees of east longitude.

A Note About the Author

Jules Verne (1828–1905) was a French novelist, poet, and playwright who is credited as being one of the originators of literary science fiction. His *Voyages Extraordinaires* series of novels include such classics as *Journey to the Center of the Earth* (1864), *Twenty Thousand Leagues Under the Sea* (1870), and *Around the World in Eighty Days* (1872). Although he was often regarded derisively as a writer of genre fiction or children's literature, his influence extended to French avant-garde and surrealist circles, and to this day he is considered one of the finest writers of his generation and a key figure in world literature.

A Note from the Publisher

Spanning many genres, from non-fiction essays to literature classics to children's books and lyric poetry, Mint Edition books showcase the master works of our time in a modern new package. The text is freshly typeset, is clean and easy to read, and features a new note about the author in each volume. Many books also include exclusive new introductory material. Every book boasts a striking new cover, which makes it as appropriate for collecting as it is for gift giving. Mint Edition books are only printed when a reader orders them, so natural resources are not wasted. We're proud that our books are never manufactured in excess and exist only in the exact quantity they need to be read and enjoyed.

Discover more of your favorite classics with Bookfinity™.

- Track your reading with custom book lists.
- Get great book recommendations for your personalized Reader Type.
- Add reviews for your favorite books.
- AND MUCH MORE!

Visit **bookfinity.com** and take the fun Reader Type quiz to get started.

Enjoy our classic and modern companion pairings!